PESTILENCE

PESTILENCE
TRAVELING MERCHANT BOOK TWO

William J. Seymour

PESTILENCE: TRAVELING MERCHANT BOOK TWO is a work of fiction. Names, places, and incidents either are a product of the author's imagination or are used fictitiously.

A Book Furnace Publications Book

ISBN 978-1-943266-10-4

Cover Design: Book Furnace Publications

Cover Image: ©Grandfailure | Dreamstime.com

Skull Header: © Ss1001 | Dreamstime.com

Without the Darkness there can be no Light

Prologue

Welcoming fires point defiantly to the night, dancing beneath the moonlit sky. A gentle breeze sways the flickering flames and the smell here is fresh and dry. Giant ominous shadows, darkened cages of unbreakable walls and unclimbable roofs. A patchwork of quiet and emptiness.

But they are here. Their smell is too strong and sweet.

Moisture wets the tongue. A warm stream burns the skin and tastes of salt. Weak, bleeding feet drag across the cutting gravel. Heels are torn open. Toes are missing and stone cuts deep into flesh. Blood trails over thorns and dirt, soaking into the earth as quickly as it can leak from infected wounds.

A dog barks in the distance. Quick and short, the abrupt call echoes across the silent plains.

The cages do not stir. Small prickles of fire create eyes of bright pupils and dark irises in windows that watch as the stranger draws closer.

Food!

Hunger eats away at an empty stomach. Cravings that never go away. A mouth full of putrid acid. A tongue that is shriveled into a hollow husk. Flies buzz everywhere. Swatting at them does nothing. Eating one or a dozen does even less for the hunger that burns all the way to the crusty pants that scratch with every step.

Why do these irritate me so? Where did they come from?

Torn denim pulls at scaled flesh. Strings of fiber pierce as deep as needles against skin pulled tight against bone and muscle twisted into a thick cord and frayed tendons. Each step brings excruciating pain that wracks the body through brittle bones and clenching teeth.

Saliva drips from chapped lips.

Food!

The smell of fresh, untainted meat grows stronger.

No shadow moves, and no one hinders their progress. Anticipation grows. A small hiss escapes a scorched throat. The blocks of shadows and danger remain silent and yet the aroma of a meal is so close. A weak heart beats faster. Knuckles pop as bleeding fingers flex and tighten at the sight of fresh blood and warm meat dancing before blurry eyes.

There are so many of them!

A small voice nags at the back of the darkness, fighting the urges filled with the need to eat.

CAUTION!

But there are so many! I will never be hungry again.

The dog barks again and this time it does not stop. Vile beasts. A symphony of calls and howls. An even less human growl escapes between chipped teeth and bleeding gums.

Little beasts taste of gristle and greasy fur. The whole meal cannot touch the starving pinch that only real food can quench.

More lights begin to push away the night.

Quickly now! Back into the darkness where the light cannot find us.

Voices carry easily in the night. Deep, strong voices. Filled with muscle and warm blood. No coughing or infection.

More saliva burns at dried sockets. So… much… food.

The light sways back and forth as the voices draw closer. First left, then right. Up and down. A hypnotizing yet burning thing. Fire that does not hurt but tears out the eyes. Must be avoided.

One of them speaks, and the other agrees. One so deep and strong, the other softer and full of youth.

Food!

Shadows retreat as the yellow glow of fire is almost upon us.

Inch back! Around the next corner!

There is no turning away. Food is so close. The voice falls on deaf ears as the sweet, salty smell of meat is almost within grasp. Little trembles shake the dirt beneath calloused feet.

The pain is gone. Glorious warmth runs through veins and muscles tense. Teeth itch nervously and the light is as bright as the sun. Eyes squint as the pain sears them. Dry skin cracks and bleeds.

More words come from the strong voices. No possible way to understand what they say.

FOOD! WE MUST HAVE FOOD!

The light explodes as broken, dirty hands stretch around the corner of the building. A high, shrill voice pierces the night. The shadows are so tall, and broad!

FOOD!

A vice like grip wraps around a starving mouth, jamming broken teeth into bloody gums. Hands cannot reach their prize. Scratching at the air, the shadows are too far away. Fear takes over. Mind runs in circles.

FOOD!

The ground cracks ribs and air hisses between tight fingers. The dark shadows behind the blinding sun do not run. A new monster sits atop as hard dirt grinds into the brittle bones between the shoulders.

"Shh, my child," a soft voice whispers.

Words mean nothing. Gnawing with teeth and gums, the taste of salt is so sweet! The tongue hurts as it laps against the hand that squeezes tight. So…. gloriously… sweet!

The stranger sits upon the chest that wheezes and struggles. So much weight. Too much pressure. Flowers and sugar engulf and overpower the smell and taste of blood that fills this world. Breath is hard to take as bones crack beneath the weight of shadow and death.

"Calm. Take deep breaths, my long-lost child. This will take no more than a moment," the voice continues.

White streams of light begin to break away from the swaying sun that blinds away the shadows that watch. Above the tiny lights of the sky fade into darkness as the world glows and brightens. Tiny ribbons swirl and dance in the calm night, carried by a will of their own as they take their time coming to the grip that pinches dried lips shut.

The light does not diminish. It grows brighter and the heat from the fire within begins to burn at the skin. At first it is comforting. Like a touch that cannot be remembered or the exhilarating sensation of that first bite into warm flesh, the heat works its way into cold muscles and bones. But it does not stop there.

Fire catches within the flesh and the smell of rot and decay sours the air. Bubbles pop and the rending of flesh sends geysers of blood into the light where it wraps around the streams of golden magic. Screams are muffled beneath the iron grip and nails break as they dig into the broken earth.

"That is it, my son. Let it take you away," the voice soothes.

Searing hot embers erupt as eyes explode and bones turn to shrapnel. Every muscle cramps and the taste of blood chokes as lungs fill. The darkness is a comfort, a respite from the pain and the hunger but beneath the molten rays of light there is no solace to be found. Yellow fire consumes them all until the world itself has burnt itself out.

Chapter One
Nebraska: Somewhere Dead in the Center of Hell

The dead are not the quietest of companions. "I'm fucking starving, here," Cherry Red says. The living are hardly any better.

A sharp wind, cool and edged like a knife cuts through the early evening air. The smell of burning pine, sweet and sticky, fills the small gap beneath the broken underpass. Water drips its sad, slow song in the distance. Shadows grow long from where buckets of rust and jagged metal reach for the sky.

Empty, forgotten husks of old cars. Scavenged for parts and torn by time and rabid animals of both the four and two-legged kind have begun their slow decline as the stretch between civilization and the wilderness of the damned grows longer.

Green grass springs from soil that is filled with muck and run-off. Hardpan cracks and the thick clay turns the world into a never ending red between tufts of desperate vegetation and slowly burning brush. Spring is in the air, or what is left of the two weeks between the frozen tundra of nuclear winter and the arid death that summer brings at the edge of a sun-scorched spear.

Drip.

Drip.

"I offered you something an hour ago," Merchant responds.

He pokes at the fire with a stick and watches as tiny embers lift into the air. The puddle next to him ripples with every drop. The newest wave never able to catch those that came before them, but as soon as it tries, another is right behind, ready for the race. He takes a deep breath and lets the smell of wet rot settle into his chest.

"You know those lights remind me of something, bugs or something. Wasn't there once a bug that lit its butt up or something?" Red asks.

With a wave of her own hand, dismissing her comment, she turns away. Scrounging through a small nap sack she's been carrying for two weeks, her eyes narrow in frustration. He is barely listening, but he lets her ramble on.

There is nothing inside of the bag and she knows it. Merchant turns his gaze away from the small flickers of light and watches the gray smoke as it climbs into the coming darkness and disappears.

"Fireflies," he answers.

"What was that?" she asks.

A small glance her way shows her hands shaking themselves into a nervous twitch. Merchant does not say anything or spare her a second look.

"They called them fireflies. My sons would chase them on nights like these."

Red stuffs one of her hands into the bag and slips the cover over her shaking wrist.

"Oh, yeah, the bugs with the asses that light up," she says. "Why do you bring those up and since when do you have kids?"

A smile creases her scarred face and a few drops of pus leak from the cut that extends between the peak of her cheek up to where her ear has crumpled onto itself.

"You know she is better off dead," Snake-Eyes whispers.

The ghost materializes beside Merchant and he can feel the cold touch of the afterlife brush the back of his burning shoulder.

Merchant ignores him and throws the stick into the fire. More sparks of red and orange glide gently into the air.

"Never mind, forget I said anything," Merchant mumbles.

"Look, I know she helped you out back when she was worth looking at, but the freak inside her is taking over. Just glance at the poor monster why don't you? She wants you to call her Red but there is hardly anything red left to her," Snake-Eyes continues.

Merchant takes a deep breath and scoots himself backward until he is seated against the cold stone of the overpass.

The fucking ghost isn't too far off. Even with his missing eyes and body that is more linen curtain than substance, the asshole doesn't miss much. Large chunks of hair are missing across Red's bleeding scalp and her left eye is milky and most likely blind where the other is jaundice yellow with rivers of red running through it.

"What are the chances we are going to find an open store out here somewhere?" Red asks.

She resorts to tossing away what little belongings she has already removed from the bag.

A small knife. A few shiny stones. When she gets to the pistol, she lifts it from the ground, looks it one time over before turning back to the distance they have traveled and drops it back in.

"I've got enough for both of us," Merchant says.

He pulls out a few sticks of jerky from the inner pocket of his coat. Drier than the dirt beneath their feet, but at least it's something. Squeezing the pieces in his hand, he holds them out to the light.

Saliva drips from her lips as she licks across the broken skin.

"Are you sure?"

She rolls onto her knees and crawls the short distance between them. Merchant turns his hand over and drops them.

"We don't have any idea how much further it is until we find civilization again," Red's words are wet and slurry between the chewy bites. Her teeth slash into the dried meat like chipped razors. "And you are one big motherfucker. You sure you have enough stuffed into that jacket of yours?"

A wave of his hand sends her back to her seat on the other side of the fire.

"I have more than enough of what I need," Merchant says and rests his head back against the stone.

Cool waves run through his skin and he lets them wash over his body. The fire inside screams in horror as the two sensations fight. There is a storm brewing inside of him. He can feel it. Every day the churning deep within him grows like an animal trying to claw its way right out of his gut.

He rubs a heavy hand over the smooth skin of his abdomen.

As if something was spilling its way out.

He grabs his duffle bag and pulls it closer. The only possession he can have.

His alone to carry.

A burden worth a thousand souls.

Snake-Eyes drops down next to him, his smile as wide as his ears and he digs at dirt beneath his nails.

The pull to go west is as strong as it has ever been. That is where he must go, but something follows. He can feel it in the earth, a trembling that quakes the stones beneath his boots. Like a shadow that hides in the darkness of the night.

"Tell me about him again," Merchant says.

"Who?" Red asks.

"Here come the lies again," Snake-Eyes chuckles.

He bites at his nails and spits into the air. Nothing hits the ground. Red licks every bit of skin between her fingers, the three sticks of jerky long gone, and the edges of her knuckles are raw where she chewed them until they bled. A small drop of blood is smeared beneath her lower lip. It trembles as she turns back to her bag.

"Don't play games with me, Red. I told you anymore of this forgetting bullshit and I'll leave you out here with the rest of your kind," Merchant answers.

Her jaundice colored eye goes wide, and she looks out into the coming night. Not west, nor south or north. She watches back east.

"I'm not sure I remember," she stumbles.

"Stupid bitch is losing her mind. The infection is taking over," Snake-Eyes says as he materializes and paces behind her. The ghost flicks a knife end over end in his hand with each step. "Kill her now. Maybe if you are lucky, you can find a few pieces worth saving to eat later. Because if you don't kill her, she won't stop lying, and she'll soon no longer be able to tell the difference."

Merchant grumbles.

"OK… ok," Red says and pulls her knees to her chest and rocks on the balls of her feet.

Large welts of infection crack open along the pale skin of her arms and small streams of blood drip out. The muscle and bone beneath the denim of her jeans is pale where holes pull further apart and the little substance left of her frame barely fills out the attire. Snake-eyes squats behind her and pokes at them with his knife. She does not feel a thing.

"They called him, The Collector."

"Who?"

She takes a deep breath.

"Those of us who still had the brains to talk, that is who, you damn asshole," she says before picking up a stick and tossing it into the fire. Embers and sparks fly into the air and the smoke swirls as the ashes scatter. "He lived down in that pit. At first, he just wanted odds and ends. Small things easily taken from abandoned towns and cities. Then it changed."

Merchant sits forward. He can't feel the heat of the fire but the fire within his blood is enough to boil water.

"What changed?"

She never mentioned anything about changes the last two dozen times he asked her.

"I'm not sure but he started muttering about not being alone and how he was always right. How he would always be right because he was always the smart one." Red bites down on a knuckle and draws blood. Then wiping it on the side of her crusty jeans, she tucks it under her folded arm and begins to rock back and forth even more. "Anyway, his tastes changed. Bastard started asking for people. Anyone and anything we could get our hands on. Children, men, women. Anything he could get those dirty, little, boney fingers on he'd drag down into that pit."

"Did he tell you why?" Merchant asks.

Both her and the ghost look up with eyes that scream, FUCKING MORON.

With a sigh Merchant puts his head back against the cement of the overpass.

"Then you found me," Merchant says.

Red spits into the fire and her phlegm sizzles and pops.

"Yeah, by some shear stroke of fucking luck, old Hectar was always good at smelling out the fresh ones. Followed you and that bitch's trail even through that damn storm. Damn near killed half of us. Hooked up with that monster and his lackeys… and well," she trails off.

"Well, what?" Merchant asks.

He can feel the night pulling closer around his shoulders. A blanket of darkness that hugs him tight and suffocates him with its warmth. They will not be alone this evening. Their hunger is as strong as their odor. Some are too close for his liking. He opens his eyes and Red is back to digging into her bag. Snake-Eyes is nowhere to be seen.

"You know the rest. Your stupid heavy as shit bag,

the pit… that stupid dead bitch back in old crazy town. You having a hard time remembering too?"

No, he isn't having a hard time remembering anything. With a squeeze of his arm, he pulls his bag closer.

"There wasn't anything you could have done to save me," a new ghost says.

The veil between their world and hers wavers and melts like white foam as she materializes. She looks just like the last time he saw her. Brown hair growing gangly from a rough shaving. Face gaunt from a hard life and too much pent-up anger. There is a difference though. Her eyes are softer, less dagger and more pillow as they watch the fire.

Merchant takes a deep breath full of smoke and shadow. The taste is sweet on his tongue and he feels the darkness sink deep within his soul; where it belongs.

"I realized what I wanted before the end," Elizabeth says. Her chest is a bright red against the white blouse were the bullets from the rifle tore through her. "You gave that to me. All that time I had wanted to be alone. Needed to be alone, but it wasn't right."

He can feel the cold touch crackle over his skin as the ghost presses right against him, shoulder to shoulder as if for warmth as she sits on the dirt with her knees pulled over the gaping wounds in her chest. At least this time she doesn't have a shotgun pointed at him.

"I had found my freedom, and, in the end, I found my peace. Can you do that, Merchant?" Elizabeth asks.

Can he?

A howl cries into the night and the last remnants of a red sun dip beyond the horizon. The hunting has started.

Merchant pushes away from the wall and finds his way to his feet. Red looks up from where she digs deeper into her empty bag, searching for what isn't there. Like a small pet her eyes are curious and her mind excited at the slightest movement.

"I'm going for a walk," he says.

She tilts her head to the side but doesn't say anything.

With a grunt he hefts his bag over his shoulder.

"When I get back, you are going to finish that damn story and tell me more about this 'Collector'."

Red's eyes widen and then narrow.

"What Collector?"

He growls back at her.

"Just stay where you are."

Grinding his heels into the ground with each pounding step, Merchant heads into the darkness of the night.

Chapter Two
When Evil Comes to Town

A clean white sheet. A blanket of soft cotton pulled tight over chest and shoulders. There is no movement, yet the day has left the morning behind and the sun is high and warm.

"Do you think they are still alive?" Kelly asks.

The door on the other side of the darkened room begins to open, and she drops down off her toes and lands hard on the ground. A small pinch of pain rattles her butt and she can taste the dirt around her dress as it puffs up into the air.

"Brother George wouldn't be keeping them in the sick room if they were dead," Albert answers.

Fat Albert as they call him sits beside her. Denim overalls and thick wool shirt even though the summer heat is quickly approaching. He wipes the wet locks of his dark hair away from his eyes and watches both directions of the small alley between the Sick House and its neighboring tool shed.

The other teenagers can be so mean to him because he's a little round and always smells of the pigs they raise at the edge of town, but he's the nicest of them all. He makes her smile and though the others don't know it, he's really good at keeping a secret.

"I know that stupid, but didn't you see it? They weren't moving at all, not even breathing," she says.

Pushing off the wall, her knees scratch over the dry dirt and she grimaces at the feel of the fabric pulling against tiny stones. The thought of spending another night mending clothes pulls a dread on an evening that is still hours away. Patting away the coating of dust and debris, she checks the damage as she stands up. Not too much. A few streaks of stretched thread. Quick work that maybe no one will notice.

Taking a deep, hushed breath, Kelly turns back to the window and pulls Albert up with her by his shirt's collar. It is sweaty like the rest of him.

"Look, they are going to try and feed them," she whispers.

The windowsill smells like dust and tickles her nose. Small flakes of paint poke at the skin of her chin but she can see enough to look inside. One of the town nurses, in her scrubbed white dress and dark hair pulled into a tight bun, is taking a seat by the bed with the stranger. They don't move. The sheets remain still even as a towel is pulled out from a water basin and placed gently over pale skin wrapped in dark hair.

"See, would they be doing that for a dead person?" Albert asks.

"But they aren't moving at all. How would you react if I threw a bucket of water on your head while you were sleeping? Huh, Bert. Or maybe I should throw you in with the hogs next time I stop by your house," she says.

A quick punch to his shoulder and his eyes narrow as a smile spreads across his round cheeks. She takes a swipe at the locks of damp curls dangling over his eyes. He ducks below the swing and she lazily misses by inches.

"I won't be the one who's the pig's dinner tonight, little missy," he chides.

She giggles.

"You'll have to catch me first!"

Kelly spins on her heels, and though her thin shoes of worn leather give no comfort from the hard ground and pointy stones, she leaves her best friend in the dust.

She races around the corner. The thunder of his heavy boots, as loud as a bear's paw clawing its way out of the forest, already begins to fade. He isn't exactly the fastest runner, but what he lacks in speed, he makes up in tenacity. He'll never give up, no matter how far she runs.

The chase is short and sweet as her face meets with an unexpected chest and her feet slip over tiny pebbles. The bright sky opens up, and the ground hurts as rock and tuffs of grass poke like needles through fabric and into skin not so welcoming to harsh treatment.

Kelly hits the ground with a thump.

Not exactly how she wanted this race to end.

"Hold on there, child, where do you think you are going?" a deep voice, soft and warm like milk and honey asks.

Kelly swipes at the cloud of dust like an annoying fly and the sweat in her face stings at her eyes. She can taste the sharp and gritty grains of dirt as they crunch between her teeth.

Albert slides in beside her, kicking up a wagon worth of more dust with his boots. Kelly coughs and chokes with the cloud.

"Oh, hi, Brother George. We didn't know you were there," Albert says between gasps of breath.

"I can be kind of sneaky like that," George says. He reaches out and extends an open hand to Kelly. "Like God above, there is always someone looking out for the people in his flock."

Taking a grip of his long fingers, Kelly lets him pull her off the ground. She isn't a very large woman, now having seen sixteen summers, but Brother George barely seems to notice her weight. A good bet he'd notice George though.

Her lips curl at the small joke in her mind as she eyes the burning cheeks and rivers of sweat on the young man's face before turning back to the priest. She bites at her tongue to keep the chide to herself.

"So sorry for running into you like that," she says instead. She tries to pat at the dust that now covers his flannel shirt and flat pants, but he quickly swats her effort away with gentle hands. "We were just trying to have some fun before the weather gets too warm."

George puts a warm hand onto her shoulder. There is so much strength there, the weight both comforting and solid at the same time. She can feel it make its way down her body and even the slightest worry of what will happen as the harshness of the coming months hangs in the distance washes away.

"Youth playing beneath the warm, open sky is one of God's greatest gifts. Of course, one of man's greatest follies is enjoying the plight of others and telling false truths. There are many open grounds around our little town here, is there a reason you are playing around the Sick House?"

Kelly looks over at Albert for support, but the pudgy brained one is all wide-eyed and sweating bullets. Under his arms the large dark spots grow wider with each heaving breath. She would think they had stolen something of significance and been caught already.

"No reason. Just having some fun. Isn't that right, Bert?"

She turns so that the priest can't see her face as she glares at her best friend. If he notices her there is no way to tell. His lips are already moving, and she doesn't want to hear the words.

"Oh, forgive us, brother!" Albert blurts the words which could not come out faster if they were rolling downhill. "We were curious that is all. We didn't mean anything by it. The rumors… they talk of a new one who has come to town. We… we wanted to see for ourselves before God had worked his miracles."

Like stones falling off the back of a cart, Bert's knees hit the ground and she can feel it beneath her feet. An earthquake shattering any hope of this day ending well. Oh, what she would do to be able to slap him across the back of his big, sweaty head.

"Get up my child," Brother George says with a chuckle. "There is nothing wrong with being curious and yes, the rumors are true. A new member of the family came home last night though in his poor condition there is still so much to be done beneath the watchful eye of our lord to see them back to health. We will pray for his speedy recovery today at church, but the other matter at hand is what do we say about liars?"

His gentle eyes turn hard and firm as he looks to her, and she fights with everything she has not to drop onto her own knees and start blabbing on about every little thing she has done. Her knees shake, and it doesn't help that Albert is already reciting several 'Our Fathers'.

"I'm sorry about that," she says with her eyes at her feet. She kicks at a pebble and watches as it rolls through the dirt. Anything to avoid looking back up at his disapproving glare. "We know that it's not right to spy and we shouldn't be here, but the other people can be so mean to Bert. I wanted us to have some fun, so we came over just to sneak a peek. Only for a minute though and just through the window. We weren't going to bother anyone."

"And what else, Ms. Rodgers?" Brother George asks.

"Ugh, alright. I'm sorry for lying. I just didn't think it really mattered and if I could keep the conversation from going where it has, I could stop…"

Kelly waves at Albert who is now bobbing his head with his twelfth prayer in twenty seconds.

Brother George chuckles and taps the top of Albert's head. Somehow the words speed up and Kelly can't help but roll her eyes.

She looks at him again and somehow the worry washes away like a nice cold shower. His deep brown eyes sparkle in the sun and the dark skin of his face is smooth as he smiles. He looks at both her and her newly pious friend who is now on his elbows and knees reciting his fifth Hail Mary.

A firm hand wipes through short cut hair of ink black before reaching down to pull her friend off the ground like a puppy.

"I think that will be for God to decide. Besides, I have service to prepare for and it just so happens to be that I'm looking for two helpers with today's sermon. How would you two like to volunteer?"

Kelly looks over at Albert who is already shaking his head yes.

"That would be great, Brother George," Kelly says, each word pulling the child's soul trapped deep inside of her.

She can already feel the heat of the sun go a thousand degrees warmer. There goes an afternoon of games and fun. She takes a deep breath and lets it out slowly.

The priest smiles at her before turning and leading them away from the Sick House.

***

The church is empty. Dark and silent it sits and waits as she counts the pews.

Thirteen to a side. Ten deep if everyone pushes in shoulder to shoulder. Bright streams of light shine down along the aisle ways from arched windows cut high into the rafters. The glass isn't painted like she's heard from those who remember the days before the world ended. She remembers some pictures in books that Brother George has shown her, but these aren't the same. They are bright and unbroken, but clear and practically invisible. Dust filters through the air of the empty room, dancing in the light, and giving everything a warm feeling though it is empty save her and her loosed lipped friend. She really needs to teach him how to keep secrets when it comes to Brother George. The other people in the village? He's a safe with a lost key, but here in this church, she's seen cheese with fewer holes in it.

With a sigh, Kelly leans against the altar, her chin in her hands and both elbows holding the weight of the world against the table.

"You ever thought about what's outside this town, Bert?" she asks.

Her friend doesn't answer. Dishes clang together and the empty room is a horrible echo chamber. Breaking an entire box of dishes wouldn't have sounded any louder.

"Could you possibly be anymore clumsy?" she chides her friend with a roll of her eyes.

Cheeks red and sweat pouring down his face from hair now knotted with curls, Bert tries to shuffle the instruments of afternoon mass across the clean linen from the vestibule.

"I… I want to get it perfect. You saw the look on Brother George's face. He saw what we were doing. We have to get things perfect," Bert says.

Kelly rolls her eyes again.

"And what? He'll tell your parents we were chasing each other next to the Sick House? Mass is in less than twenty minutes. I'm pretty sure he's already forgotten all about that," she says.

With hands of a doctor compared to his shaking digits of scrubbed red sausage, she takes the crystal glass of farmer Yarial's wine and the empty serving saucer and puts it in the middle of the small tv tray table. A Bible sits in the corner, already opened to where Bert pulled the silk ribbon to today's sermon.

"You sure he won't tell my parents?"

She sighs and puts her arm around his shoulders and rests her head against his. Cold and clammy. He relaxes as she pulls him against her.

"Trust me on this one, Bert. The man isn't going to tell your parents anything unless we give him reason to, and if I'm correct, you've already said enough penance prayers for the both of us. Now where are you going to be sitting?"

Letting him go Kelly turns and heads to the front of the altar as the double doors at the end unlock with an earth shattering click.

"Are my two apprentices ready to serve the lord this wonderful afternoon?" Brother George's voice bellows out across the empty hall.

Kelly nods yes as dark shadows piling in from the bright light of the town square materialize into people she would recognize in the blink of an eye. Townsfolk she has known for the only years she can remember slowly make their way in from a procession that lines up as far as she can see through the doors.

The older families come in first. Some with walking canes and others with arms wrapped around one another. Bert and herself are quick to take shaking hands within their own and lead the way to the front pews where they can see and hear the best.

Those young enough to still have children her age and younger fill in last. Babies and toddlers cry and chatter as the silent chamber quickly fills with the sound of life and contentment. The air warms to an uncomfortable level and smells of salt and work.

This is home. Kelly smiles and takes it all in as people slide together and individual voices meld together into a song with words that make a melody to comfort the heart.

Bert slips in beside her as she stands against the frame of the open double doors. To her back is the whole world, the heat of the coming summer already drying the air and before her is all that she has ever known. The last few members of the congregation trickle in and fill the final seats.

"Where are your parents?" she asks.

"Ninth row, tenth in. No one likes to see my father or brothers in the front. Someone once accused us of secretly bringing baby pigs in with us. Stuffed into our pockets."

"Well, then maybe you shouldn't," she chuckles and punches him gently on the shoulder.

"Come on," he answers with a few rubs of his shoulder.

"It's never bothered me," Kelly adds and before he knows it she plants a small kiss on his cheek. "Why don't you go and sit with your family. There is enough room for you. I can look after old Brother George today."

"But… but he said he needed two volunteers," Bert says though his face is so red it may as well be on fire and his eyes dart across every face in the entire building.

He goes back to rubbing his shoulders, and she nibbles on her lower lip to stop from chuckling.

"Two volunteers to help him set up. You did enough and now get yourself moving. I've got this covered," she says and spins away before he can say another word.

A strong gust of wind brings in a rustle of old, dry leaves and helps stir the dust into the air as Brother George makes his way up to the altar from the vestibule in the back. Silently, she tip-toes to the nearest wall and slides along like a shadow to get closer for when he needs her help.

"Good afternoon my beloved family and friends," the priest starts.

Kelly, as silent and as slow as she can be, slips around the edge of the altar and makes her way to the far side where the serving wine and plate wait with today's Bible reading. No one pays any attention to her. Even Brother George gives no notice as his arms raise to the heavens and the words of everyone around them merge into one voice.

"Good afternoon to you, Brother George," they all say.

"Today is a great day beneath the ever-watchful eye of our great lord and father," George continues.

Several 'Amen' answer in agreement.

"Some of you would know, because I know that you track the calendars with eyes like hawks, that today marks four years since the founding of our blessed home here in the great plains of Nebraska."

"Here, here!" several voices call out from the back of the room.

Brother George gives a small nod and smiles.

"Four long years we have worked together, lived together, loved together, and prayed together for our salvation from the perils that were stricken upon this earth. Disease, war, famine, and death stalk the weary and the weak among us who still suffer across this land. Those of us sitting next to you are proof of what our father has given us as we remain here, together in peace and harmony. Through all that has befallen we still sit here today. Because of his belief in the good in every man and woman we have been saved from the ravages that have torn lesser believers from his very grace. Today, marks another year as we give thanks to the one up high who has shown us the true path."

The room fills with cheers and words of praise. People clap, and Brother George opens his arms wider as the congregation lifts its arms in tribute and homage. Kelly keeps herself in the shadows. She doesn't want to fall into the trap of hysteria that befalls them all every time. The words comfort her, the feeling of being as one, but she knows deep inside things feel different. There is more to her life, and though they are all family, she has always been alone. Even in the eyes of the lord above, she is special. In more ways than what Brother George likes to tell all the children and teenagers during his sermons.

Quietly she begins to mouth her own words of gratitude. Eyes closed, she lets the whispered words slip from her lips.

"Thank you, God, for all you have given us in our time of…"

Glass shatters and the sound of explosions rock the church. Kelly is slammed from her trance so hard she stumbles and tips the tv tray. Fingers fumble and hands go numb. The purple wine inside the glass is no better than milk in an open bucket as it twists and turns from her grip.

She drops to her knees. The pitcher just out of her reach as she falls forward.

A finger catches on the small handle and lifts as she lands on her side, the bottom dangles perilously an inch over the wooden slabs of the floor.

Then all the world comes rushing at her like a tidal wave of a summer sandstorm. Screams echo around the room like a tornado of sound. People are on their feet. Two more explosions erupt, and a second window shatters out and rains on the people below.

"Outside now, priest!" a man's voice demands.

The men of the congregation begin to bark back, and Brother George tries to calm everyone with words that no one can hear. Kelly puts down the wine and crawls until she can lift herself back to her feet. She stays behind George as he makes his way down the center aisle of the church. Bodies push together. Huddling closer to the aisle and quickly falling in step behind their pastor they follow as he makes his way to the rear of the church.

"I'm giving you until the count of ten or I'm burning that whole damn building down with you in it," the man outside screams again.

Holes rip through the boards nearest the front door sending shards of wood flying into the first rows of pews. Rays of light chase the bullets in.

Babies and children cry. Men and women scream and try to talk over one another. All have questions, but no one offers answers. Silently, the soft hands of Brother George beckon everyone to calm and obediently everyone does.

"Please, everyone, stay calm. This must be some kind of misunderstanding," their priest pleads.

Showing the same steadiness as he would standing in front of hundreds of people, the leader of their small town makes his way out the door. Kelly is a few steps behind, the first of the men following directly behind her.

The light of the afternoon sun is blinding even where it reddens the western horizon. Shielding her eyes, Kelly blinks away the tears as she is pushed to the side.

Car and truck engines rev and headlights blind everyone as if the high sun wasn't enough. Pushing shoulder to shoulder, the community files out of the church. More people ask questions, but none loud enough to be spoken over the sight of two dozen armed men with rifles circling the front of the building.

"There you are, in the flesh and blood," the voice who had called them out says.

Brother George steps forward as the congregation stays huddled in front of the open doorway. Kelly keeps herself to the outside. Everyone has their eyes on George and the one who steps forward.

A tall man. Almost a head taller than George who isn't small himself. Red burned skin shines where he smiles with a piece of straw dangling from between stained teeth. He wears one of those stupid cowboy hats and two pistols hang from his belt.

She's heard stories like this before. If this was the old west, he'd be some kind of rich cattle baron coming to claim what isn't his. The men behind him are not riding horses and the weapons they carry are not like the movies of old. Some wear uniforms. Browns and tans beneath vests and straps covered in bullets. These men have a tough look to them, their faces flat, emotionless, and made of edges that could cut. She can feel her heart race as Brother George draws closer to the one demanding their attention.

Running away, turning the corner and getting lost behind the church passes through her mind a dozen times in a split second. No one would notice. There are too many of them standing huddled together and they would easily miss one simple girl in the heat of the moment.

"Can I help you with something this afternoon?" Brother George asks.

The large man chuckles as he starts a small pace, turning his attention to the village awaiting his every word.

"Yes, I think you can. Do you know who I am?" the man asks.

George shakes his head no, his dark hair shinning in the light and the afternoon heat not touching him where it burns their assaulter across face and bare hands.

"I believe this is the first time we have ever met, sir."

Another chuckle.

"Sir? At least we are starting on the right foot. Well, my name is Logan Barnett. Me and my boys here are from a city just north of here called New Frontier. You ever heard of it?"

There is a pause as Logan continues his three-step pace.

"I have never heard of such a city," Brother George answers.

"No… I would guess you haven't being so tied up in such a small community. The thing here is… Father…?"

"Brother George. My people here call me Brother George."

"Ah, your people," Logan says and stops to take a long hard look at all of them. Kelly can feel his eyes go over her, his vision seeing right through her. "And I would assume you would do anything for 'your people'. Would I be correct?"

"We take care of each other in this town. What I would do for them, they would do for me," George answers.

Logan nods again and begins to dig a tiny trench in the dirt as his pacing resumes.

"As I was saying, my boys, and I have heard of your small town here. Even with what remains in this disastrous world we call the grand old U.S. of A. the reputation of your town and its 'miracles' precede what should be even possible."

"What miracles are these, Mr. Barnett? For whatever it is you may have heard about us, I can assure you we are nothing more than a small community of farmers and workers who struggle like anyone else trying to make something of themselves in what is left of this world."

Logan turns back to the semi-circle of his men and vehicles and sits on the hood of a dark painted Jeep. Tires rock as he lets his weight settle and the men standing on the front seats let their rifles drop forward as they keep their balance, the barrels pointing dangerously toward the center of the crowd.

"Yet, nothing of what this world has become seems to be anywhere near this place," Logan says.

He opens his arms wide to sweep in the village and all of its people.

"By the grace of the lord above, we have been spared most of the trials that afflict so many," Brother George says.

Long fingers tap horrible notes on the hood of the Jeep.

"See, that is where I think you are lying, Brother George. See, my city is a fortress compared to this collection of buildings and shacks you have here, and on all sides, we are besieged by plague and famine. The infected as you know do not care about your god or your prayers. They only want one thing and that is to eat. Looking at your nice, healthy group here with what appears to be absolutely no protection, I'd say they'd have a feast worth killing for, wouldn't you?"

Brother George doesn't flinch or show any sign as his face stays as cold as ice. Kelly can feel the sweat drip down her neck and arms, yet he looks cool and undaunted. The tension mounting within the people next to her is enough for them all. She can feel the need to bolt build, not just from her, but everyone who isn't holding a rifle or a man of God. Mouth as dry as cotton, she tries not to cough between large gulps of held breath.

"The infected suffer just as much as we all have. Their actions are a result of a curse brought upon this world and they have little control of what drives their deteriorated minds. We do not fear them for they are only fighting for survival like we do. Yes, you are correct Mr. Barnett, we do not have defenses as you would describe them. But do not for a moment think we are helpless."

The clicking of metal echoes through the empty streets as several of the men prepare their rifles. The man with his stupid hat holds up a hand and the men behind him do not move.

"Is that a threat, Brother George?"

A small shake of the head.

"There is no threat. We are nothing more than simple folk, but the will of God with the strength of our devotion is what keeps us safe. As you can see we have very little here, Mr. Barnett. At this time, the sun will soon begin to fall beyond the horizon and I do not yet understand your reasoning for coming here and putting holes into our beloved church. Is there an explanation for why we are standing here, and a purpose for your men to be scaring the good people behind me?"

Logan pushes himself off the hood of the Jeep and steps forward until he is less than a finger's width away from Brother George.

"Is there a reason why we are here?"

"Let me go!" a woman yells out.

Several of the townsfolk shuffle as dust kicks up in the air. Kelly steps forward to come around so she can see and some men huddled together with their families begin to yell.

A rifle barks into the early evening sky and kids scream as people trip to cover themselves.

"We found this one hiding out in a building across town," one of Logan's goons says as he pushes the nurse forward.

Her feet stumble over the stones of the road but Brother George quickly steps forward and catches her before she tips too far. With a huff of breath, she rights herself and wipes away at the dust and grime clinging to her long dress and white apron.

"Hiding something from us, Brother George?" Logan asks.

He reaches forward and tries to put a hand on the nurse's shoulder but is slapped away with a resounding crack. A smile creases the sunburned face, and he wags a thick sausage of a finger in her face.

"A nurse taking care of those who are sick is hardly something to hide. Nurse Porter here is just one of my assistants and she takes care of those who I cannot see while I give sermon."

Brother George wraps his arm further around the

nurse's shoulder and pulls her closer. Chin up, the woman has eyes of daggers as she watches the man with the big hat's smile grow wider.

"What of the sick did you find? Any of them infected?" Logan demands.

The man who dragged Mrs. Porter shakes his head and shrugs.

"Not from what I could tell. Looked like the poor guy had nothing more than a fever. Definitely wasn't infected."

Logan turns back to Brother George.

"Are they hiding any medicines?"

His voice takes in a low growl and he uses his bulk to tower over the priest and his nurse.

"Nothing that you wouldn't find abandoned. Some pain meds, a few of those fake herbal supplements. There is nothing here, boss," the goon says.

Kelly can feel her face redden as the silence falls like a knife between the two groups. She wants to run, but like ice her feet are frozen in place.

"I don't know what you are hiding here, George. But I'll tell you what. If any of my men begin to feel sick, we might just be willing to send them here to partake in this healing of faith you preach about. If though we hear another word, even on the wind that more of these infected are coming here and being cured, you can bet your life I will know what is going on. You cannot hide these things from me, Brother George. I will know your secrets even if I have to kill every one of you to find them."

The nurse slumps in Brother George's arms as Logan turns back to his men. With a wave of his hand he climbs into the Jeep and several of the trucks rev their engines as they turn to leave.

"Remember what I said, priest. I will know your secrets. One way or the other I will know."

In a storm of dust and fumes, Logan and his men speed off into the coming night.

Watching them fade into the distance, no one leaves the front of the church. People whisper, and others cry openly. Kelly doesn't know what to think. They have no weapons that she knows of. Nothing that would count against men like that. Bert's father has an old rifle he uses to hunt deer or scare off wild dogs. There is a rumor of a few other guns between the homes but that is it. What are they going to do?

"That is enough for today," Brother George starts. Words of protest and fear begin to call out, but he silences them with a lift of his hand. Kelly even tries to say something but the moment that palm is risen she can feel the fear wash away with the breeze. "Do not fear these men or the other afflictions of this world. We have survived so many other trials and we can survive this. Go home. Tuck your family in for the night and rest your weary heads. Our lord above will provide as he always has."

"But those men!" voices fighting the reassuring words call out.

She can feel the will of the people teetering.

Brother George helps the nurse who still leans heavily against him make her way to the crowd and he opens his arms to them all. Even Kelly can now feel the warmth and trust as it blankets them with an invisible touch.

"Those men are as lost as we were four years ago. They will come, and they will go, but if we keep our faith true, we will remain within the sight of our lord father above. Trust in him as you trust in me. We will see each other through all of this and whatever is to come."

The thoughts of denial and disbelief are gone with a tidal wave of hope.

"Yes, Brother," people call.

Slowly families begin to peel away and become lost in the lengthening shadows. Kelly pushes her way through the thinning crowd and finds Bert being squeezed to death by his mother, his face smashed tightly against her wide hips that somehow reach the bottom of her breasts.

"There you are, big man," Kelly says.

Cheeks red as cherries and eyes just as swollen, her friend pries himself from the woman's arms. Kelly can't tell if it's from crying or the death grip of his mother.

"So, you are OK?" Bert asks.

Looking at herself as if realizing it for the first time, Kelly shakes her head.

"Yep, no bullet holes. How are you—" she begins.

"We are fine and going home right now," Bert's mother cuts in.

A pinch of pain crosses her friend's face as he's spun around and Kelly watches as they begin their march away from the church. With a sigh she turns back to see Brother George talking with a few of the older men of the village. She can't hear their words but each of them is staring out where the dust of spinning tires is finally setting.

She wonders what they are thinking. Probably exactly what she is thinking because to her there is little else that she wants to know.

Prayer or no prayer, what are they going to do if those men come back?

Chapter Three
Just Passing Through

The talking does not stop.

Neither does the heat as the night gives way to the day. The dark shadows of the west disappear beneath the endless flatness. A haze of radiation lifting off the dirt horizon like a frying pan cooking over the fire. There is hardly a cloud in the sky and dark-winged creatures float in slow methodical circles.

Circling.

Waiting.

Hungry.

"So where were you last night?" Red asks.

Merchant grunts and doesn't answer.

"I know where you were, demon," Snake-Eyes says as he appears from dust in the wind.

Both of them will not stop. In the middle of the open plains, surrounded by empty space and the hollow graves of lives lost to death and misery, these two and the hundreds that follow him refuse to be quiet.

Red continues her chatter, but he does his best to push it out and the words are hardly more than the cracking of stone and dirt beneath his threadbare boots. She leads the way for all of them now. Hardly an accomplishment since they haven't turned off the highway in weeks. Kicking at stones, spitting on the ground, and rambling on about anything and everything that passes through her deteriorating mind, mile after mile breaks beneath the weight he carries on his shoulders.

"Got anymore of that jerky? I'm dying of hunger over here and as you can see, it is going to be a long damn time before we find anyone out in this wasteland," she says.

Without turning her head, they continue forward. Merchant shifts his bag over his shoulder and reaches into his pocket. A few more sticks won't hurt her, but he begins to wonder how much more she can fight the disease. She hasn't said anything, but the limp of her left leg is so pronounced that she's leaving a widening trail in the dust behind them.

Strong girl. Should have died months ago, but she keeps moving along. He takes a hard look at the shoulder bag held tight against her hip. Empty of everything but that damn pistol, she clings to it for what little life she has left.

"You keep telling me about this 'Collector' and I'll give you a few more pieces," he says.

She turns to him as if he had just insulted her mother and then looks back in the direction from which they came.

"How about you start with where you were last night," she responds.

Putting her good foot down on the ground she watches as he continues to walk without her. His hand drops the dried meat back into the pocket of his open coat and he doesn't slow a step.

"Wait!" Red scrambles to catch back up. "You said

you had a few pieces I could borrow."

Merchant doesn't bother. Sweat beads on her face and what little hair she has left is plastered to her cracked scalp. The bright sun, high enough now to turn the sky the brightest blue it has been since the bombs dropped, burns and peels her skin away like dried paper. To his dark scalp and dry skin, the heat is a touch of home.

"And you have something you are hiding from me," he answers.

"Fine, you asshole. When he finds us, you didn't hear any of this from me," she says.

The sway of his shoulders and gait open his jacket across his bare chest and she licks at her lips as the tips of the jerky stick out.

"We called him the Collector because that is what he does. At first it was just random things we stole from people who were too dead to care. Pictures, dolls, mostly children's toys for some demented reason. Then one day it all changed," she says before trailing off with her eyes locked on the never-ending flat land before them.

"You stopped there every time. What changed?" Merchant growls.

"His mind. He was a reasonable person to talk to before he cracked. Muttering about always being correct and how family was meant to be together."

"Family?" Merchant asks.

He stops walking, and she stumbles into him. Her bad leg goes crooked, and she tumbles to the ground.

"Fucking prick!" she screams.

His hand envelopes hers like a small child's as he pulls her to her feet.

"You said family," he ignores her screams.

"Didn't hear me the first time? Yeah, he started running on and on about family. Like he was this entirely different person. That's when he started demanding we bring families to him. Like he wanted them all to be his own little cult. Or he was searching for them. We never could figure it out. His mind was so far gone that ramblings of his brothers and them finding him trailed off into languages we couldn't understand."

Merchant grabs her by the arm and he can feel the bones beneath crack under his grip.

"You brought him entire families?"

She takes a swipe at the jerky in his jacket and misses badly, the end result nothing more than a light slap on his chest. With a squeeze her knees begin to buckle but he holds her steady.

"Of course not, you fucking idiot. We brought him whoever we could find. Men, women, and children. Whatever we could get our hands on. It was all the same to him. Have you seen a complete family in this place since the war started? What wasn't killed by you and your fucking bombs and poisons, the infected quickly took out. Anyway, with each new person he grew wilder and screamed that Daddy's favorite was coming to town. If it wasn't for fear of the monster he'd become, I would have left him to rot in that pit like I did those loonies and their camp."

He lets go of her arm and blood and pus leaks from new cracks and tears in her skin.

"Afraid of him, why?"

Red licks her lips and an unsteady hand reaches slowly for his jacket. Quickly, he takes out a piece and lets her take it. She hardly has the wrapping off before tearing it between her teeth. A small chip of a tooth flakes off over her bottom lip as she devours it in seconds.

"Those people down there weren't like me. Real infected. That monster in that camp with all his devoted followers was just some crazed doctor with too much time on his hands. Down in that pit. That is where the real demons were."

"You were feeding those people to them?"

Merchant can feel the fires in his chest flaring to life. An inferno searing at his skin and the bones growing red hot as he thought of the women and children screaming as they were led down into that hellhole.

"Really having a hard time keeping up, aren't you, demon?" Snake-Eyes asks.

The ghost is sitting on a lawn chair with a drink in his hand. One of those fruity red ones with an umbrella on the top. Large drops of condensation run from the rim down until they drop and disappear before hitting the dry dirt.

"Of course not, you bastard," Red answers, her shoulders pull back and she stands as straight as her bum leg will allow. "Those infected who tried to eat you down there, WERE the people we brought to him. He was changing them all. But it wasn't like me and the others. We were experiments gone wrong. These were the real infected. Their minds gone. Eating each other and anyone else they could get their teeth into."

Merchant turns back to the west. He's had enough and continues down the road. She struggles to keep up but her dragging foot is a constant against the sound of silence that follows them.

"Wait, you said I could have several pieces," she says.

Two more chunks of dry meat fly over Merchant's shoulder and land in the dust covering Interstate 80. A little dirt doesn't stop her, and she is munching away like a child in a candy store.

"Looks like your 'Collector' is going to have a little time to catch up," Merchant grumbles.

"Oh, come on, do us all a favor and throw yourself down there. You know you want to," Snake-Eyes mocks.

Red is too busy licking at her fingers and chewing at what little nails she has.

"Huh, why?" she asks as she stumbles passed him.

With a grip that pops the joint of her shoulder beneath his fingers, he stops her before she can walk too far. Tiny rocks tumble over the edge and if she wasn't as light as dry paper, she would have followed them down.

A giant chasm cuts through the highway. Forty feet at least separates them from the other side. The sound of water rushing over rapids carries up the crevice like thunder.

"That can't be," Red says.

"Come on big guy, throw yourself in. I want to see if you float," Snake-Eyes says and then walks off the rock.

The ghost falls into the darkness leaving a puff of smoke in his wake. A small smile pulls at the corner of Merchant's lips.

"The wind is really nice on the way down," Snake-Eyes says from behind Merchant's shoulders.

A cold chill runs down his skin as the ghost reappears.

"Is it the same river from the pit?" Merchant asks.

Red turns her gaze north and south, chewing on her bottom lip.

"It can't be. We are what? Several weeks to the west? I was certain we left that behind us."

The heavy army bag hits the ground like a boulder.

"Is the water down there poisoned?" Merchant asks.

"How the fuck would I know?" Red responds, but he isn't looking at her.

His gaze creeps over his shoulder and the smile on Snake-Eye's face is wide and full of perfect teeth. One of the serpent irises winks as smoke swirls in the empty sockets of his head.

"Never mind," Merchant grumbles. "We'll find a way around."

Lifting his bag back onto his shoulder, he turns south and begins the trek along the cavern's edge. Red hesitates a moment before shrugging her shoulders and following along. Two travelers making their way around a split in the world with an army of dead following in their wake.

***

"It would have been so much more fun to see what kind of splash your broken body would have made falling from up there," Snake-Eyes says.

The ghost crouches down, sniffs the water, and wrinkles his nose.

Merchant looks back the way they have been traveling. Four hours and they have managed to follow the flow as the ground descends beneath their feet and what once sounded like a raging monster pulling to escape insufferable bonds, is now a wide impediment of small rapids and a few boulders large enough to remain above the surface. The cliff face they followed rises high in the north, clear drops of jagged stone like the ax of God himself gouged a hole directly into the center of Nebraska.

"Is this the same water we left behind us?" Merchant asks again.

Red turns her head, but he isn't looking at her.

"You talking to those ghosts of yours again?" she asks back.

He glares at her for a brief moment and then turns back to Snake-Eyes. The ghost has his shoe off and gingerly puts his foot forward, a look of fear creasing his face as his big toe gets closer to the water.

"Now the question that you should be asking is would you believe me either way?" Snake-Eyes returns before putting his whole foot into the water.

With a gush of mist and steam the ghost vanishes as the water opens and swallows him whole. Merchant doesn't move or even bother. His life would be better if the bastard did actually disappear.

"I saw the look on your face, you didn't even care. asshole," Snake-Eyes complains as he rises from the rolling broth of white foam to float above the surface. "And for that I won't tell you what this is."

"You're as useful dead as you were alive," Merchant grumbles and turns back the way they came.

Dark shadows and a veil of black moves closer as the sun falls for its evening rest. The west is a field of fiery red and the heat of the evening runs away in fear of the coming chill of the night.

"I'm not a big fan of crossing this at night," Red says, "but if it puts some distance between us and everything on this side, I'm all for giving it a try."

Kicking at the ground, dust picks up into the air until her shoe catches the edge of a dry stick, brittle and flaking at the touch. A quick pitch has it floating in the air and making a splash hardly noticeable over the turbulence of the water.

Bobbing and swaying above the current, the stick floats and spins its way downriver.

"Looks like we don't have as much to fear this time, big man," Red says before licking the tips of her fingers.

Merchant hefts his bag higher onto his shoulder, but he doesn't take his attention away from the encroaching darkness.

Yes, it would be better if they were on the other side.

Snake-Eyes dances over rocks, waves, ripples and rapids as Red and Merchant wade into the water. As cold as ice and as strong as a pack of wild dogs, the current pushes and pulls them as they move through. Walking in ankle high mud, each step is heavier than the next and Red's bad limp has her moving more to the south than she does to the west with each step.

"Damn… bitch… is cold, isn't she?" Red calls out.

She is now easily ten feet further downstream. Her teeth rattle and he can hear the bones and joints crack as they slam together.

"Keep pushing. Once we get to the other side, we'll sit and rest," Merchant says.

He can feel the cold seeping into his jacket and pants, but it does little to squash the fire burning through his skin. The river is up to his waist, but it almost has her by the breasts.

"Yeah, and maybe something to eat as well," Red struggles to add.

Anger and fire roars through Merchant's chest as the current changes beneath his feet. Like a hungry bear he can hear the difference in the water before they can see it. Something is trying to stop them from crossing. Planting his feet, he turns to look upriver.

The shadows are moving. At first only the corners inch closer, but there is no hiding it. The red light of the sun, stretching as far as it can go from the edges of the horizon, does nothing with the wall of black steaming along like a freight train.

"Red, get moving!" Merchant shouts.

Heart racing, his legs pump through mud and muck as he drives his large frame with the current as it rushes toward his half-drowned companion. She looks no better than a wet rat as she drags her foot across the bottom. Hands clutching her shoulder bag over her head, her crippled leg anchors her within the river as the rumbling turns into a thunderstorm bearing down on them from every side.

"Get a move on!" Merchant yells.

He is almost to her. Her muscles are pulled taught and her teeth are bared as she fights the restraints that hold her. Blood seeping from her lips is quickly washed away as water splashes against her face leaving red and brown streaks against the pale white skin.

"Red, move!" Merchant gets out before the wall crashes in on them.

The current impacts with the force of a runaway bus and even Merchant feels the ground go out from beneath his feet. Tumbling over, the water is all around him and he feels the sharp edges of stones cut and jab at his arms and body.

He doesn't know which way is up.

Each breath brings a lung full of water and he coughs as the world spins filling his mouth with the taste of sand and oil. White flesh and skeletal limbs reach out for him as he's swept away. Letting go of his bag he tries to catch Red as she spins into the darkness.

His fingertips nip the edge of one of her legs, but he can't get a grip.

The emptiness swallows her.

He tries to swim to the surface, but there is no way to tell which direction it is.

He is drowning. No matter how many times he pushes with his arms and legs, the end of the torment is nowhere to be found. His lungs burn. His limbs are going numb and the fire inside is choking beneath an ocean of water.

The light begins to fade. Ahead, he can see ripples in the shadows.

He reaches out to them. Feint silver strings swimming through his murky existence as chains of debt weigh heavy on his limbs.

He's going to sleep. The world has finally taken him. There will be no reaching the city that touches the sky. His nightmare is over. Pain pulses through his body and a smile cracks the edges of his lips.

Then a grip of iron latches onto his wrist as the world fades into nothing.

Chapter Four
What Doesn't Kill Us

The night is beautiful. A dark blanket filled with a million stars that reach into the heavens. Merchant relishes in the comfort of the pillow that softens the bed beneath his head. The shallow lapping of water in the distance is music as he takes in a deep breath, the clean smell of fresh water and trees reaching the peak of the spring season tastes terrific on his tongue and he can't get enough with each breath he takes.

He closes his eyes. The warmth of his wife, body curled into his and the sound of his boys sleeping within arm's reach comforts and rocks him.

A shooting star streaks across the sky. Bright flashes of yellow and white dot the mosaic peacefulness above and he makes a wish.

"Baby bear, look," she whispers, the caress of his wife's hair tickling the tip of his nose and chin.

Shock.

Confusion.

Anger.

Every emotion he has ever felt rushes through his body in the span of a heartbeat. His wife is not beside him. The smile is wrong. Lush, full, ruby red lips part and teeth as white as snow sparkle. Her eyes swallow him. Bright blue, he feels himself swimming through the universe, lost in their depth.

A soft breeze picks up and the long strands of her dark hair tickle at his face. He wipes them away, his tongue thick and heavy as she grabs his wrist. Her chocolate brown skin a soft hue against the depth of his own.

"Be silent, my general," she purrs.

He tries to answer. The taste of dirt and poison fills his mouth. It is hard to breathe.

A finger touches the edges of his lips and the grueling filth washes away and he is whole.

"You must keep moving," she whispers. Pushing herself off the ground, she sits beside him.

They are at the river. Water moves gently over the flatland, tiny ripples skipping over stones as the quiet rush of water and life sings a song as it passes. The white dress she wears shines like a star against the darkness of the night. Her shoulders roll, and she leans back, the angle and curves of her body the perfect image of everything a man could ever want.

"They are beginning to know of your presence. From here on out the road will grow tougher. They will do everything they can to stop you. Even those who you aid will see you for who you are, but in their ignorance look to prevent your mission."

Merchant forces himself up. In the peace of the night, every limb in his body is old and cracks and pops echo into the evening.

"Who are they? Why would they try to stop me? All I want to do is see…" he begins, and she stops him with a smile and a soft finger to his lips.

"I will tell you no more. You know your mission and

you cannot be deterred. For everyone and everything in this world to survive, you must reach the city. All that you have asked for will be found there," she says.

With a lean forward she is inches from his face. The smell of wild flowers and life fills the gap between them. Merchant's heart races and he looks deep into those eyes. There is no darkness, only life and happiness can be found in the depthless sky of her beauty.

"I will continue," he whispers.

"Good," she purrs.

Before he can stop her, though deep down he is not sure he wants to, she moves closer. Her lips brush his and the fire that ignites burns the sky away, and the world disappears in a flash of pain and exhaustion.

***

To the east the sun creeps its way over the flats and the golden glory of its power stretches and burns the horizon without fear and retribution. White, lazy clouds move like boats struggling to pull anchor as they fail against the tide that sucks them into the burning destruction that awaits them.

Merchant opens his eyes and coughs. Long pulls of water and mud belch from his stomach and lungs and he rolls to his side as it piles against the sharp stones and dirt of the riverbed. Sticky, acidic pools of phlegm turn to mud and small bits of chewed beef float against his cheeks as he struggles to fill his chest. The world spins in his mind.

Up is down.

Down is up.

The mere thought of sitting rolls his stomach and clenches muscles into an agonizing cramp.

He gives up the fight and rests against the muddy soil, letting his arms stretch and the taste of water and waste permeate his mouth.

Birds call out deep angry songs as they circle overhead. Dark silhouettes against the warming sky. Lower now. He can see their curved beaks and the talons of their feet as they open and close in their ritualistic dance.

Fighting every instinct he has to continue to lay down and die, he pushes himself until he is seated. Patches of mud cake his clothes, his jacket weighs a ton, and he smells of rot and decay.

He is alone.

For the first time in an age he cannot remember, he is alone.

Red is nowhere to be seen and his bag is lost in the current.

He takes a deep breath and lets the morning light warm itself against his skin.

She did it again. He should be dead after all of that. Drowned at the bottom of whatever river this is.

With a sigh he moves his legs until they roll beneath him. Pain and bruising swells across his knees and thighs but it does not feel like anything is broken. A shake of the head sends bright lights across his sight, but nothing else.

He is in one piece. At least for now.

"You are one tough son-of-a-bitch, aren't you?" Snake-Eyes says as he materializes beside him.

"Fuck," Merchant groans.

He is no longer alone.

The ghost is wearing a swim suit and his white skin and tattooed body shimmers against the clear water that runs by. The snakes on his neck coil onto a pole that stretches from between his breast down below his navel. A fruity drink rests in his hand.

"Was really hoping that you didn't know how to swim," Snake-Eyes taunts. "Would have been comical to know all that you have survived only to be taken out by a little stream. Ha! I would have lost the bet, but it would have been worth it."

Merchant glares at him though he knows it is useless.

"You made a bet on me?"

The ghost's face sneers and the eye on the left side of his neck blinks.

"It's all we have to do, plus you know I'm on your side. I've got all I have riding on that it takes hell risen to take you down. Now don't go disappointing me."

"Wouldn't dream of it, prick," Merchant says and pushes himself from the ground.

The ghost fades away in the breeze that skips its way over the cool water and materializes again by his side, now wearing his white shirt, white blazer, and white pants brighter than sun-bleached bone. In the glaring mid-day sun, he's a shining star and sadly there is only one person who has to suffer the sight of the asshole.

"Didn't see what happened to Red, did you?" Merchant asks.

He doesn't wait for the answer and starts to follow the riverbed to the south.

"Probably cracked that soft skull of hers on a rock and bled out for all I know. Didn't know I was supposed to keep an eye on the girl. She really isn't much of a looker nowadays."

Merchant waves him off. It was a stupid question from the start and he already has his answers.

Dark shadows that trail his movements from above begin to fade as the ground beneath his boots turns to dust and his clothes cake with drying dirt. He is not their next meal. They wouldn't want his cursed flesh anyway, but he can see they have picked fresher pickings.

A full swarm of wings and unrelenting hunger circle in the distance. Hardly over the ground they are a tornado swooping to touch down. He picks up his pace from a slow walk to a slow jog.

If she is dead, there is nothing he can do to help her. If she is hurt, there is even less he can do. She can hardly be considered on the right side of the infection anymore, and with her bum leg, any injury would make it too much to survive. Her mind will crack if her body does not give out first.

He knows he won't let her suffer more than she has to. Even without his bag he can feel the weight of what follows behind him. A thousand silent footsteps tread the riverbank in his wake. What is another one? Dirt grinds between his teeth as he draws closer.

Several of the large vultures are prancing on the ground. In a giant circle they preen and call at each other, circling their newest claim.

Rocks are not hard to find beneath the surface of the river and where the water ripples along its current he finds a good palm sized one. Hardly any heavier than a baseball, Merchant lifts his weapon, and he throws it into the dancing carcass fuckers.

A bone snaps.

Dozens of cries pierce the air which thunders with the wind of wings racing to reach the sky.

A limp body twitches on the ground.

Blood pools were feathers flutter.

The bird is dead.

A scale covered hand scratches at the ground. Dark rivulets of red leak from open sores and mud as gray as stone forms a paste over body and face, but Red still clings to life.

"Stupid bitch just doesn't know when to die," Snake-Eyes says.

Merchant gives the dead buzzard a kick with his boot and takes a closer look at Red.

Her eyes are not focused. She glares at the open sky, the sun now racing its way to the west and her mouth opens and shuts but no words come out. Drops of blood leak from the corners of her eyes and pool within ear-lobes that do not hear any of the world around her.

Squatting down, he cradles the side of her face in his hand and turns her toward him. If she recognizes him, she gives no sign of it. Her eyes look through him and to the world on the other side. He has seen this before. She is lost to him and everyone else.

"Oh, look there, isn't that helpful," Snake-Eyes says.

Merchant glares up at him, but the ghost couldn't care less and isn't even looking in his direction.

His face with its empty eyes are watching the river behind them. Shifting on his heels, Merchant does the same, careful not to move Red too much.

Floating atop the water, dark and wet, his bag washes up against the shore. The single arm strap that still works hooks itself around a stone and holds it in place. Caught against one of the buttons, the thin leather band which seals it shut stretching with the water that rushes by is Red's shoulder bag.

Gently placing her head back on the ground, Merchant stands. No words of argument pass her lips and her breathing is rattled by the sound of fluid washing through her chest.

"Floats pretty well for all the horrors that thing carries," Snake-Eyes says as he watches Merchant step into the water to retrieve their belongings.

Turning Red's bag over, a full allotment of water spills out in black streams and with an open hand, Merchant catches the pistol that she always keeps by her side.

"Won't be needing that anymore after you use one on her," Snake-Eyes says.

Merchant looks up at the ghost and the urge to put one right between his eyes is overwhelming, but he drops the weapon back into the bag. No reason to waste a shot. Throwing him out a window didn't do the trick, shooting him now would be even more of a waste.

With a grunt, Merchant picks up his bag from the surface of the water. His boots sink deeper into the mud as he makes his way back to Red. She is still unresponsive. Saliva and mud mixes in large bubbles around the corners of her lips and her one good eye is rolling up into her head.

The handbag feels heavier on his hip than the army bag over his shoulder. He knows it has at least a few rounds in it and there is always a chance the bullets aren't too waterlogged to fire. She doesn't deserve to end like this.

He eyes the dead bird where it fell, its neck bent in an awkward angle.

Food for the vultures. Isn't that what they'll all become when this is all over?

The revolver is small compared to the palm of his hand, but this isn't his weapon. She kept it with her this whole time, and in the end, it will be the death of her. Taking a better grip, he runs his thumb over the hammer and pulls it back as the small bag slides away.

Snake-Eyes giggles as he lifts his own hand up, index finger out and thumb cocked back.

Merchant says nothing. There are no words to say.

"On the count of three," Snake-Eyes says.

Merchant ignores the ghost and watches as her mud-caked shirt slowly rises and falls. He aims for the base of her skull.

"Hey, you need any help down there?" a voice calls out in question.

With a swift motion Merchant slides the revolver back into its concealment and shifts his Army bag higher onto his shoulder.

A half-dozen people begin to make their way down from the dune that rises to the west of the river. Sliding and kicking up enough dust for a storm, three men and three women materialize from the growing shadows. They do not carry weapons, and two of them have simple school yard backpacks strapped across their shoulders.

"Could we be of any help?" one of the men's voice calls again.

Merchant looks down at Red who still does nothing and turns back to those approaching. Wearing simple matching shirts and pants of browns and black, they are the cleanest and healthiest people he has seen in the longest of time. Bright eyes, sun tanned skin, all of them with long hair held beneath wide-brimmed hats, and smiles lighting up brighter than the afternoon sun.

"Who the fuck are these bozos?" Snake-Eyes asks.

"Oh my god," one of the women exclaims before running forward.

"Wait, Mary!" the man who had been calling says but is too late as she reaches Red.

The other five slow to stop as their eyes travel from Merchant, his body and bags covered in mud, to Red who is now as pale as Snake-Eyes and his abhorred suit.

"Are you two, OK?" the man asks but does not step any closer.

Merchant looks back down to Red when neither of the five make any sudden movements and watches as Mary cradles Red's head on her lap. Blood smears and water soak into the woman's black blouse and brown pants. She ignores it all even with Red's obvious infection. Her thin hand strokes at the wet strands of hair curled against the torn scalp.

"A storm washed us away when we tried to cross the river," Merchant starts. "I washed up a couple miles upstream, but Red here didn't stop until she reached this place."

"She's alive," Mary says. "We need to get her to Brother George. He'll know what to do."

"Let's get her to the carriage and head back before the sun goes down," the first man says. The other four remain silent.

"Are you sure you want to do that?" Merchant asks.

Mary looks up at him and begins to speak, but Merchant lifts his hand.

"You can see she is infected. Most cities and villages won't have her kind."

A smile crosses Mary's face.

"Doesn't seem to have bothered you," the first man says as he steps forward.

He's a good-sized young man. Broad shouldered, fresh cheeks, and a twinkle still in his eyes. Merchant turns his full attention down to him and though trying to radiate confidence, the man shuffles half a step back.

"I'm special," Merchant says.

"Well, I'm Derek, and Brother George is as special as they come. Help us get your friend to our cart and we can get her back before the good lord above takes her home."

Derek waves the others forward and they begin to move Red into a better position so that she can be carried back up the dune.

Merchant looks at Snake-Eyes whose jaw hangs wide open. He shrugs his shoulders, and the ghost slaps his mouth shut.

"Don't look at me," the ghost says. "You are the one who washed up on the shores of crazy town."

Chapter Five
Life Will Never Be the Same

An empty church.
Silent.
Hollow.
Cold for a late spring evening.

A perfect place to think and listen after failing to sleep beyond a wall of nightmares and cold chills. Kelly sits by herself in the first pew looking up at the pictures of Jesus and God and all the saints they pray to on a daily basis. She can remember the more important ones, but there are just too many. Closing her eyes, she waits for them to speak to her, but the tapping of wood shutters and the creaking of the rafters is all that answers.

With a sigh, she looks at her hands. Dirt beneath her nails and the dancing light of candles highlighting tiny scars. She begins to dig at them. No matter what she does she can never be as clean as the others. No matter how much she tries. At least this will help take her mind away for a few minutes. With the edge of a tooth she pulls on the first tip she can latch onto.

"Is something bothering you, my child?" Brother George asks.

Startled, Kelly jumps from the pew, trips over the kneeling bench and slides over the polished wood before tucking her hand beneath her legs.

"Oh… no, nothing Brother George," she stammers. "I was just praying to God."

His smile warms her from the inside and her mind loses its hold on what was worrying her. Clinging desperately, she tries not to let it go until she has found a solution for the entire town's problems. He seems unfazed. White shirt opened a couple of buttons on the top, eyes at ease and there doesn't seem to be even the remotest sign of tension in him.

"I can see that," he answers.

Looking up at the picture of Jesus, cracked and old with age and weather, the frame is huge as it stairs down at them. She can feel those eyes burning deep into her, knowing and demanding she confess to her weakness and doubt.

"What are you doing here?" Kelly asks, waiting for him to turn and demand she tell him everything he already knows.

The silence between them and the judgment of God himself begins to choke her into submission.

"Do you know some people say that isn't a true representation of him?" Brother George asks.

Now, she is completely confused. Tracing his eyes, she follows until she sees that he is still staring at the portrait over the center of the alter.

"Who? Do you mean, Jesus?" she asks.

He chuckles, and the painting's face breaks its hold of him.

"Of course, who else would I be talking about?"

The smile on his face brightens up the room and she can't help but smile herself.

"I don't know," she answers and looks around the empty church. "There are a lot of people here to pick from."

With a tap on her knee he turns back to the painting.

"Long before the end of the world, back during a time where the world had simpler things to argue about, like the color of Jesus' skin, there was a big argument whether he was white or black."

"People fought over that?" she asks.

Of all the stupid things in this world people are going to fight over, it's the color of a man's skin who died thousands of years ago? She shakes her head as a million other things cross her mind. Like surviving in a world full of infected.

"Throughout history, men have found a way to fight over everything. Why not the color of a single man's skin? This isn't the first time this world has fallen apart though not this bad before. Fighting over the color of the skin of the man you worship isn't exactly out of the realm of possibilities, is it?"

Kelly turns back to the painting and its perfectly olive skin gone gray with dust and its long curls of brown hair falling down to its shoulders. It's hard to imagine that image looking any other way, but even if it did, would she fight about it?

"Which do you believe?" she finally asks when the silence hurts as much she can feel the confession strangling her tongue for its release.

"I believe Jesus would be whatever his people would need him to be. See, belief isn't just about seeing and feeling. It's about letting yourself go to something greater than yourself and knowing that as long as you stay true, then in the end, everything will be OK."

She squints her eyes at the man because she knows that he realizes that was not a real answer.

"So, what you are telling me is you believe that Jesus was a different color depending on the situation, like a chameleon. To some he looked black and others he was white?"

The smile on her face can't hide her chuckle and he gives a little one himself.

"No, my sweet one. I think he is whatever you need him to be. And as long as you believe that he is the son of God and has been given to this world with a purpose that is all you will need to know. That is what I believe."

Kelly turns back to the alter and rests her head against the back of the pew. She isn't sure this is really helping her churning mind, but at least she isn't alone.

"Somebody get Brother George!" a voice startles her from outside the church.

It's Derek, she would recognize him anywhere.

"They must have found…" she starts but Brother George is already around the edge of the pew and heading up the aisle in a quickening walk.

Stumbling after him, she's barely able to clear the first few candles without knocking them over and he is already out the door and into the night.

Warm air, dry and dusty hits her face like a wall as she exits the doorway. Lanterns swing where they hang from the corners of the wagon and the horses on the front breath heavy as they kick at the rocky ground.

"What is going on?" she asks.

Derek is talking in hushed tones with Brother George as they huddle over the back where a lump remains curled under a layer of blankets. She sees Mary giving instructions to Jezabelle and Patricia, both of who are barely two years older than she is. Without turning, both women quickly run off into the darkness.

"Mary, what is going on?" Kelly asks again, this time finding her way off the front steps of the church and over to the wagon.

The wind shifts, and she gets the first smell of rotten filth and wet mud. Inside, her stomach churns and her mouth fills with the taste of acid and vomit. Grabbing onto the wooden edge of the cart, the wheels rock as she doubles over.

"What… what is that smell?" Kelly asks, but no one is answering her.

Taking in deep breaths through her mouth, she tries to calm her heart down and ease the cramping of her stomach.

One breath.

Two breaths.

Finding the strength, she pulls herself up and looks at the blankets that everyone is huddled around. Dirty white feet stick out from beneath the dark canvas and blood trickles out from between the toes. There is no movement, and the stench keeps growing the longer the body sits there.

"Are they dead?" Kelly asks again between coughs.

"Please, honey, let's go back inside," Mary whispers as she wraps her arm around Kelly's shoulder.

When did she get so close? She didn't even see the woman come around the horses.

"Is… are they dead?" Kelly asks again as she follows the leading footsteps back toward the church.

"Not yet, we may have found them in time. Let us both go inside and pray for a miracle. Brother George and the nurses will need all the help they can get if she is going to be saved," Mary says.

"It's a woman?"

Mary nods her head.

"Yes, we found her down by the river."

"Was she alone?"

The smell by the church is less tainted, and it is a lot easier to keep her legs from shaking as the warm dry air helps push back the need to vomit.

"No, she was…" Mary starts but is cut off by the sound of dogs barking in the night.

Going frantic, the howls echo and Kelly turns before entering through the door.

Shadows approach from the road that leads to the river. Slowly, they walk and the closer they draw the wilder the dogs in town begin to grow.

"Who is that?" Kelly asks.

One of them she recognizes by sight. It is Derek's brother, Trevor, but the other is someone she has never seen before. He towers over them even from a distance. As dark as the night, he's easily the biggest man she has ever seen. As wide as Bert's father but as muscled as the horses pulling the wagon. Over his shoulder he carries a bag, but he doesn't seem to be in any kind of hurry.

"Did you find him with her?" she asks when Mary doesn't answer.

"Yes… yes we did. How about we get inside and start those prayers?" Mary says and with a firm hand she pushes Kelly inside.

Once through the door, Kelly spins to get one more glance out the door.

The stranger reaches the church and begins talking with Brother George. Where that Logan Barnett with his men was tall and demanding, this one towers over them and there is something else about him she just can't place. She cannot hear their words. Behind her she can already hear the whispers of prayers as Mary starts without her, but for the first time in the four years she has been here, she sees something she has never seen before.

Brother George's shoulders slump and standing before the dark man, the closest thing she has ever known to a father since her parents died, looks defeated.

***

Metal utensils clang on teeth between unsmiling lips and empty bowls. Drinks are consumed, and time passes. No words are spoken, silence hanging over the room smothering any attempts to communicate even before the words are thought of.

Fires burn on scentless candles, the sizzle of their wicks fighting against the buzz of insects singing into the night.

Kelly bites at the corner edge of dry bread. It scratches the roof of her mouth and tastes like ash. The stuffiness in the air itches her skin and no matter where she scratches, she cannot make it end. She watches a half dozen heads bob as they eat, and no one looks up. Dark mops of hair with a thousand feet of distance between them all, yet they are shoulder to shoulder.

Long shadows stretch across the wooden bench polished to a shine that reflects the light of the candles like a mirror. Time passes at a snail's pace and she can hardly stand it. Her toes curl and her muscles ache with pent-up tension. She kicks at the floor and the impact echoes like thunder though no one looks up or seems to notice.

"I'm told you were traveling along the river," Brother George says.

A breath of relief washes over Kelly and she sighs. Everyone turns their heads her way for the first time this night. Heat washes over her face and she looks back at her empty bowl. The bottom is clean, but she can't let them know that. Scratching with her wooden spoon, she scoops at the air and pretends to enjoy every taste of it.

"We were looking for a way to cross and got caught in a storm. Washed us downriver. You found us climbing out," the tall, dark stranger says.

He sits larger than any other person at the table and he picks at his food with an uninterested glare. As if insulted by the mere presence, he ignores most and instead spins the broth in large, looping circles. A small bite here and there are his only attempts to bother with the passing of the dinner.

She can't seem to pick out what is different with him, but no one seems comfortable. Other than Brother George, everyone fidgets as if the only thought in their mind is to run for the nearest door. Inside, the feeling runs within her as well, though there is a part of her that asks, why?

She needs to know the answer.

"God must have a purpose to keep you alive during such an ordeal," Brother George says.

A few at the table whisper Amen, but Kelly cannot make her lips move. For some reason she cannot fathom why the words will not budge. The shadows swirl around the stranger's shoulders and without knowing the reason, she can feel God will not be a part of this man's story.

The dark man lifts his head as if he could hear the words in her mind and she turns back to her empty bowl.

With the smallest glance she can dare, she can see him reveal the bright whites of his eyes and nothing more. The darkness held within threatens to pull her in, a void sucking them all into a trap they'll never climb out of.

"My purpose is my own, priest, and God has little to do with it," the man answers before going back to his food.

He does not take another bite.

"The Lord our father works in many ways, my son. Even in the darkest of days he watches over us and leads on a path he deems worthy. Even if we do not see it for ourselves."

Spoon rattles on bowl and everyone freezes as the man stops acting like the stew in front of him is worth his time. No one looks up except her. Brother George does not flinch.

Kelly moves from head to head. The big man grips the table and begins to push himself away.

"What do they call you?" she blurts out, anything to change the subject.

She doesn't know why, but the voice in her head will not let him leave without her finding out something about him. A dark enigma with an answer she won't rest without. If Brother George is right and God brought this man here, then they must find out why.

Mary and Derek look up, Brother George turns his head toward her. The man at the end of the table settles his gaze on her and she regrets even being born. The room darkens. She is suddenly the only person in the world.

"People call me, Merchant," he answers.

She can feel his words down to her bones. His voice is as old as time and deeper than the shadows filling in the spaces between her and him. She regrets ever gaining his attention. Her blood runs cold and the thumping in her chest is so loud she knows the others can hear it.

"Just Merchant?" she asks and hopes he cannot hear the chatting of her teeth.

"Please, Kelly. Let the man eat his dinner in peace. We know he didn't come here to be badgered by young women," Brother George cuts in.

A rush of embarrassment punches her in the gut and what she has eaten knocks on the back of her throat. She turns her gaze to the hands resting on her lap. Why do they shake so much? Balling her fingers into fists, she squeezes until her knuckles turn white.

"I'm sorry..." she starts.

"The girl can ask whatever she pleases, priest. Are you her father?" Merchant asks.

Brother George turns back to him with a soft smile.

"All of us here have only one father, Mr. Merchant. But if you are asking if she is my daughter, then no she is not. Though I would think of her in no other way."

Merchant's hard gaze moves back to her and the pressure to melt into her chair and be gone is enough to crack the bones in her lower back.

"Questions have no weight unless you aren't prepared to hold the responsibility of the answers," Merchant says. "The only name that still matters to me is Merchant. A long time and a long road have passed since anything else has mattered."

His reply tightens the feelings churning in her stomach. How long has he been traveling? Where does he come from? Why is he all the way out here? She can still feel Brother George and his judgement weighing heavy on her. She has never disobeyed him like this. What is this stranger doing to her?

"Well, enough with the small chat. I bet you are getting tired, Mr. Merchant. You've suffered a great ordeal and I know you are anxious for some rest and word on your partner," Brother George says.

He pushes away from the table himself and the others follow suit leaving Merchant and Kelly remaining.

"Her life is her own and of no concern of mine," Merchant says.

Breath catches in Kelly's throat burying a thousand questions behind it. What kind of man doesn't care about the woman he travels with? Doesn't he have a heart?

The darkness around him begins to make sense. This is not a good man that sits at their table. Kelly wants to scream out at the others to let him go. Leave them in peace, but her throat is dry, and her tongue swollen as the edges of her eyes begin to burn. She feels twelve years old again and hates it so much.

"Surely if you were traveling with her than you must care something for the woman," Brother George says.

Yes, he must!

The shadows become real and begin to pinch at Kelly's shoulders. They are no longer alone. The room fills with eyes that watch their every move. She cannot see them. No one else can either or they'd all be running for shelter.

A dry sweat runs down her back and she shivers in the warm night. Air is hard to come by as the room is so stuffy she can feel the droplets and tiny rivers tickle the skin on her forehead.

"Infection has taken more of her than she can control. Even if she wakes up from her injuries, she will be less human than a wild animal needing to be put down. I would have done it myself, but your man here stumbled upon us and I didn't want to start trouble where there is no need to. Do what you can for her if you will, priest. I will be gone by the morning," Merchant says.

He rises with a grunt though his movements are cat like and smooth. Muscles bulge as if pulling a heavy weight and he turns to his bag that has rested by his feet the entire meal. Thick calloused fingers lift the lonely strap and the darkness crowds the man's broad shoulders like a jacket.

"You can't mean that!" Kelly blurts out. "Give her a couple of days. She'll be perfectly healthy. Brother George will show you!"

"Kelly!" Mary yells out.

"Shut your mouth, girl!" Derek demands.

Any retort is lost beneath the glares from all at the table. The room is no longer friendly and for the first time since she stumbled upon this town, she feels like a stranger in her own home. Brother George's unmovable calm demeanor is lost behind the sea of bitterness, and one risen eyebrow that Merchant turns her way. Darkness fills in where the dark man stares, and his eyes do not blink.

"Though I know you mean well, there is little to be done for Red. Especially at the hands of a priest or a town full of farmers. I've seen one infected, I've seen a million. Once the disease has taken its grip there is nothing to be done. Even your god himself cannot help her. If he ever existed at all."

Mary gasps behind a hand pressed tight against her lips. Derek mutters a few words of prayer and Kelly can't find a single friend in them.

"Just give us a chance. We can prove you wrong. She'll be good as new," Kelly pleads.

This man is a monster. If only she could make him believe. His friend will be like new. They all know it. God has always provided for them and he can provide for Red as well.

"Even if so, Red can stay with you when she has recovered. My path leads me west and I do not have time to wait for a miracle to save one woman. I thank you for your hospitality and your food, but I will show myself out and be gone in the morning," Merchant says. "It is better for us all. Especially you folks. Trust me on that."

Merchant turns to leave.

"Tell him, Brother George. Show him what you can do. He can't leave her like this," she pleads.

A barely noticeable shake of the man's head is the response.

"You will regret this, Merchant," she calls out.

He is at the door, his head ducking beneath the top of the frame and his shoulders turn to avoid squeezing through.

"I regret more than you'll ever understand," he says, his voice distant and echoing.

"George, tell..."

He reaches out a hand and puts it on top of hers as Merchant walks out the door. A wave of calm and ease washes through her.

"It is OK, my dear child. Your heart is in the right place, but there are things in this world you cannot change. Let the man be. Maybe a good night's rest will change his mind," Brother George says.

Kelly looks back to the door, the burning light of candles flickering through the opening and the darkness outside shifting in the man's wake.

"How could a person be so heartless?" she asks herself and everyone in the room.

Mostly herself though. She doesn't understand. If it was her friend, she'd never leave. The idea of it being Bert sickens her at the slightest image, but her spine stiffens at the thought of staying at his side.

No. She would never abandon her friends like this.

There are no answers to questions that will not be asked. Nothing she could possibly accept will make her accept such a reality.

How can he be so cold?

***

Peaceful and quiet.

The air is warm, dry, and all wrong. Merchant shifts his bag higher onto his shoulder and moves his way between dark buildings with little candle eyes that follow his every step.

There is something here that is not right.

The buildings do not close around him, and the softness of the lines ease the tension in his body. Quiet homes. Simple cottages made of wood cut fresh from trees that could not have grown in this war-torn country. It is as if the end of the world forgot about everything for miles.

Merchant does not feel comfortable.

This feels out of place. He can hear the soft murmur of voices carrying in the night. No one cries. The infected do not scream out and hunt.

It reminds him of a place he left far behind and the burning acid in his gut churns as his eyes flare in the night. Those memories are gone, and his family taken with them. The bag on his shoulder droops and pulls at the skin stretching with the weight.

He takes a firmer grip and shifts his burden forward.

"Bunch of crazies here. Worse than the last time you stumbled upon the savior of God himself, demon," Snake-Eyes says.

The ghost materializes from the darkness beside him, his ethereal form misting as he attempts to pick up a rock, fails, and then skips a disk of blue smoke across the dry path they walk.

"That girl seemed pretty insistent. She's certain they aren't crazy," Merchant says.

He's retracing the path shown to him before meeting for dinner. Ahead waits the structure they called the

'Sick House'. Red lays in there. The infection eating away at her body if it hasn't killed her already.

"They think they can cure the infection. What is crazier than that?" Snake-Eyes asks.

Merchant tilts his head to the silence of the wind.

"Those who think they can control it," he answers.

They are being followed. Something moves through the darkness, keeping pace with them and staying out of the little light that shines along their way. They think to sneak up on him, but a thousand miles by foot and the darkness is his home. He shifts his bag higher onto his shoulder and the weight dissipates to nothing.

"Well, that one was a special kind of crazy, and that crazy bitch we left behind, she was something different as well. Of course, that was before she went and got herself popped trying to save your dumb ass. Biggest mistake of that woman's life. Do you think she'd do it again if she knew who you really are?"

Merchant does not answer him. He knows the answer, but the ghost isn't worth the breath needed for the words.

"But, to tell you the truth I'll probably miss your number one fan when you leave her behind," Snake-Eyes says.

Merchant stops.

"Who?"

The eyes on the ghost's neck blink and stare wide with astonishment.

"Our own local monster and probably the only living thing within a hundred miles who wants to ride you like a freight train going downhill. She isn't much to look at anymore, but she's more conversational than your dumb ass. I'm lucky if I can pry a single word out of that mouth of yours with a crowbar. Do you realize how quiet it is when you are dead? You can't even listen to yourself think because you don't have a brain left to think!"

A small tug pulls up at the corner of Merchant's lips.

"What?" Snake-Eyes asks, the tattoo blinking and the hollow eye sockets swirling with empty air.

"Quiet," Merchant demands before turning away toward the Sick House, his eyes passing by his lodgings for the night.

Their tail follows. A brief glance disguised as a shifting of weight reveals nothing, but he knows they are there. A road of shadows and watchful eyes.

"Paranoid tonight, are we?" Snake-Eyes mocks before lighting up a cigarette and blowing large circles of bright smoke into the night air.

"Something is not right with this place. I don't think I'll be waiting for the morning," Merchant says.

Snake-Eyes coughs.

Merchant turns to the ghost and the formless body bursts into nothing. Inches from his face is Brother George. A stout man himself, the priest does not flinch.

"You bring with you a heavy burden, Mr. Merchant," the man says.

Without thinking, Merchant shifts his bag higher onto his shoulder again. He does not like this man though he does peak his curiosity. There is no threatening manner within his movements or frame. The priest smiles, and others calm around him.

Merchant tilts his head.

"Been carrying this thing a long time. Gets pretty tiresome after a while."

He taps the strap pulled tight against his neck.

A sad smile crosses the other man's face.

"If it was only your bag, I'd believe you, but we both know your burden is a past that follows you with every step that you take. Shadows do not disappear in the night. They grow stronger and reach for you every moment you feel weak. You can feel them, can't you?"

"Not sure what you mean by that, priest. All I own is what you see in front of me and once you take the burden of that woman off of my hands, I'll be free to do as I need to."

Merchant goes to turn and a grip of iron locks to his arm and holds him steady. The man is stronger than one should be at his size.

"We both know that is not true, but we all have our own lies we hide behind," Brother George says, his eyes moving past Merchant and off into the distance. "Where are you headed, Mr. Merchant? What drags you back to the road so quickly that you can't wait a single day for your friend to recover from her ordeal?"

This brings a chuckle to Merchant, and he bares his teeth.

"A single day will do nothing for the woman. Even a miracle like that young girl asked for won't be enough."

"God can do many things, Merchant. You do not give him the credit he deserves. Especially for someone as touched by him as you are."

Ever ache, scar, break, and trauma in Merchant's body flares to life. His skin is on fire and every urge he has tells him to strangle this man where he stands, yet he cannot make his hands move. The priest smiles and with a slow breath the anger and torment spills away, but the smoldering fire within his soul will not be diminished so easily.

"If there ever was a god, he does not know who I am, priest. There are things in this world you would not believe, and I have seen them with my own eyes. I have felt their blood run between my fingers as much as I have bled out my own. Tell your stories to these people if it makes them feel better. Tuck them in at night and do whatever it is that you do that keeps the monsters at bay but remember one thing. Not all the evil in this world comes with scars and open wounds. Those are the easy ones to see."

Merchant steps close enough that they are almost touching.

"Some look like you and I do. Men are capable of many horrible things, priest. Sins as deep as mine cannot be washed away or forgiven with prayer. I will leave at first light. It is better for you and your people if I do so."

Brother George steps back and nods his head.

"If that is what you desire then I will not stop you, Merchant. All I ask is that you keep an open mind about your friend, Red, and never forget no matter what you think, God will not abandon you. Everything you have been through may make you think you are alone, but you never will be, my son. There is always someone walking by your side."

Merchant turns around.

"For once, priest. You are more correct than you can ever imagine."

The priest does not move as the shadows swallow him whole and Merchant draws closer to his lodging for the night. Like ice on a cold night, Snake-Eyes' form materializes from the darkness and the touch is like death warmed over.

Yes, priest. There is always someone walking by my side.

In silence, Merchant hefts his burden higher onto his shoulder.

Chapter Six

Disturbing the Peace With Miracles

The morning arrives too soon. Light fights with the haze of the ceiling overhead.

So many shadows. Too much darkness.

Limbs are heavy and numb. Breath is hard to take in and eyelids are slow and anchored with rock.

"I'm… so… hungry," Red tries to say.

The sound tears tissues in the back of her throat and the small opening fills with blood. She coughs, and the darkness closes in. She tries to turn but restraints hold her down. Shackles tear at skin as she wrenches her body back and forth.

Let me go!

The words echo in her mind, but she does not hear them. Her mouth is dry cotton mixed with sharp stone. The sharpness of her teeth cut gouges into her tongue. A single word echoes in the room. It is not her voice. The shriek cannot be from her!

FOOD!

Wails scare the darkness away as the room becomes a red ball of fury. More thrashing cuts deeper into her skin and the bonds that hold her down soak in a sticky warmth.

"Strap her down," a man's voice instructs.

Soft and calm, the words bounce off the rage like pebbles against the walls of a metal fortress.

"Food!" the words echo through the room.

Red bites the empty air with chipped teeth as figures pass before her eyes. She can already taste the blood and the meat between her teeth. She needs to eat. Without anything the hunger will drive her mad.

Yet, she is so tired.

The exhaustion gnaws at her slowing mind.

Why won't anyone give her any food?

Where is Merchant? He always has something in that jacket of his. It's dry, stale, and as hard as the dirt on the ground but it keeps the demons at bay.

Where is Merchant?

Who is…?

Food!

Just a bite or two. Her mouth stings as it fills with the warm sultry taste of blood. She licks her lips. Cracks burn, and the salty taste sends shocks of excitement through her veins.

"Food!" she hears her voice scream again and her lungs are on fire.

Rough hands grab her shoulders and pull her down. Vision blurs with rage. She sees these monsters looking down at her. White and brown faces, blotted out with a bright sun in between them all, stare at her with disgust. She tries to spit at them, but nothing touches that pure burning nothingness that remains under their judgmental eyes.

The stench of something strange tears at the inside of her nose, her lungs fill, her head cracks with pain, and the world spins. Iron and alcohol choke out all tastes within her mouth as pressure fills her stomach. Rolling her head, she sees a man sitting beside her.

A dark figure. Head lowered, and eyes closed, his single touch holds her down.

Demon! It must be a demon!

Red tries to scream a name. The memory is right at the tip of her bloody tongue.

"Food!"

The sound bloodies the inside of her ears.

"Stay calm, my daughter," the man's voice soothes.

A warmth begins to spread through Red's body. Fire and anger fight against the intrusion and her muscles cramp into balls of agony and defeat. Screams cough out of her lungs, but everything is wet and thick with blood and salt.

"Let the light in, my daughter. Your father will see you home," the man's voice beckons, but he is too far away.

The words are lost beyond an ocean of fear and hatred. Red is alone as the world around her fades. Searing fire rips through her veins and her bones crack as her body falls apart.

Darkness recedes into the corners of the universe as light scorches the sensitive parts of her eyes. Bubbles pop and her vision bursts in bright rays of pain. Warmth and needles tear their way through her flesh down to the toes she has not felt in weeks.

Skin opens across her palms as she squeezes her hands and her knuckles break. Nails pierce flesh and pus and disease leak out in waves as the world is washed clean by fire and light.

Red cannot breathe. Her lungs ache. Her throat opens, but the world is silent behind a wall of pain and brightness. Years flash before her eyes.

Before the infection. A time prior to the bombs lighting the horizon up in a fire that would last forever. Inside her chest the pain explodes and there is no more air. Her mind spins and she remembers her parents.

She reaches for them. Her brother by their side, but she cannot speak. Choking sobs push out what little air she has trapped in her tiny body.

Her eyelids grow heavy. Sleep calls for her as the pain begins to fade into the distance of the darkness. Little fingers stretch and wiggle.

Just one touch. They are so close, she can almost feel them.

The darkness closes in around her. Warmth fades and the comfort of nothingness eases the fall. In the distance her parents and family become one with the horizon. They are no longer there, and her world shrinks to a pin prick. She is blind. The pain is gone. Suffering and agony is washing away over a slow trickling brook leaving a single word hanging in the nothingness.

Her mind locks on this word. Holds it tight for dear life. She will not let it go. Like a puppy she has never had, this is her salvation.

Rest...

Yes... She will do just that.

***

Birds chirp and the empty smell of dry air mixes with the soft touch of honey. A gentle breeze tickles the tiny hairs of bare arms.

Such comfort, such softness.

Red jolts awake and sits up with enough force to send her pillow skidding across the wooden floor.

Warm light filters into the room through open windows and thin cotton curtains dance with the golden rays. Empty beds sit undisturbed throughout the room. Tucked in sheets are pulled tight, the crisp white brightening up the darkness of the shadows.

"Hello?" Red says.

"Rather surprised, aren't you?" a man's voice answers.

She spins and throws her feet off the mattress.

Cold shivers run through her legs as the chilled floor kisses the soles of her feet. Goosebumps prickle their way up her bare legs and into regions of her body she hasn't felt in a long time. A stiff breeze catches her backside and for the first moment she realizes that whatever outfit she is wearing it is open where her bare ass hangs out.

"Who are you? What the fuck is going on around here?" Red demands.

A figure materializes out of the shadows behind her bed. Slow, cautious movements rock back and forth as the figure holds itself steady with a hand on the mattress closest to her bed.

It is a man. Narrow shoulders, long neck, and a face starved into sharp edges looks back at her. Knees shake and muscles strain to keep him upright, but his eyes do not hold the same illusion. They are strong and wild. Like a child running outside for the first time after a storm, he looks amazed with wonder.

"I could ask you the same thing, but if you are

anything like me, you probably don't remember either," he answers.

With a groan he throws himself onto the bed next to her, his body collapsing onto the sheets. Large breaths come quickly, and his chest expands and contracts with the effort. A shaky hand lifts into the light above him, his fingers stretching and playing with the dust dancing in the warm air before falling down onto his stomach.

Red looks all around and this time is certain they are the only two inside.

"My name is Cherry Red," she says. "My friends call me, Red."

"Is that because of your hair?" the man asks and tries to point toward her head, but his index finger barely extends before his arm drops again.

"Yeah," she starts. "Something like that."

Self-consciously, she reaches up to run her fingers through the few strands she has on her scalp and her breath catches in her throat and lungs as she begins to cough. Thick strands of silk run through her fingers all across the top of her head and the skin beneath is warm and smooth. Rivulets of cherry cascade over her eyes and tickle the tip of her nose with the smell of jasmine and lavender.

"Hell of a surprise isn't it?" the man asks.

Red looks at him. He is struggling to sit himself up and every joint of his body shakes with the effort.

"Who did this to me? What is going on here?" she demands.

The smile on his face is crooked and his eyes tear.

"God himself did this to us. I don't know about you, but I can't remember anything beyond the fall of Chicago. The bombs. The lights. Then the sickness. Everyone who wasn't dead was starving and going mad. Half my team were charred husks before the sun ever rose. The others… those like me tried to flee, but we were so hungry. Where were we to go? The city was crumbling on itself. Buildings falling. The air was so thick with smoke and dust we could hardly breathe, but God-damn we were hungry. Then one day I got separated and woke up here."

Red pushes herself further up onto her bed, curling her legs under her ass. He doesn't move toward her, nor even try to move away from the pile he has collapsed into, but a little distance between them doesn't hurt.

"You… you were infected," she says.

He turns his face to her, his hollow cheeks peppered with the first signs of hair darkening the edges.

"Infected? Infected with what?" he asks.

With a grunt the man gives up and lets himself fall back onto the bed, the mattress rippling with his weight.

"Everyone in Chicago died almost five years ago. Half this country died when the thousand bombs dropped. Those of us who survived took shelter in the less populated areas. No one bombs towns with one stoplight, but then they came," Red says.

His eyes grow wider, and his lips move, but no words come out. She lifts her hand to silence him and begins again.

"The infected. Men and women ravaged by some disease that made them nothing more than monsters. Hunger drives them to eat and kill anything that moves and breathes. They are animals. Better to be put down than to suffer having them around."

He takes a deep breath.

"I was one of them?" he asks.

Red takes a good look at the man. He is dressed in a white cloth of very thin material. She can see his limbs move beneath them, but there is something missing.

The scars. The infection.

He looks normal. Lifting her hand in front of her, she sees her own skin for the first time. White, tan, red, and in some areas pink as if newly healed scabs had just fallen away. Running her hand over her face, she feels the soft touch of the pads of her fingers.

The skin is smooth. There are no scars and the tingles in her fingers and cheeks send shivers down her body. Ripping away the gown over her legs, the heart in her chest jumps as a lump forms in her throat.

Smooth white skin, so bright she begins to squint; but it's her legs. There are no signs of disease.

This can't be real. Pushing away from the bed she goes to scream at the man across from her, the feeling of joy pulsing through her body like it never has before, but he's fallen asleep. His eyes are closed, and his breathing is slow and shallow. A foot dangles from the edge of the bed.

Red takes a step and the strength in her legs gives.

The world spins and she crumbles to the floor. Pain surges through her body, but for once it dissipates quickly. Cold floorboards sooth her skin. She smiles beyond the embarrassment and lifts herself onto her knees.

Joints do not pop. Her muscles scream, but not from decay and infection. They strain with the weight of her body. Healthy, she takes a long hard look at the blue veins on her hands. Blood pulses through them, but she does not hate it. Something has given her life back to her.

Hair tickles the edges of her cheeks and she blows at the strands like a child in the summer. Her hair dances in the stream and falls back against her face.

She is 'RED' again. A giggle erupts from her chest and she nibbles at her lips. Hugging herself, she can't help but feel the tears as they trickle down her cheeks one by one. Whoever did this is a miracle worker. Maybe even a god.

Carefully, one foot and hand at a time, she lifts herself off the floor. The material of her clothes opens in the back and a stiff chill runs up her spin when she finally balances herself and none of it matters. A dream has finally come true. In a world made of shit and misery, all this surviving and fighting has finally paid off.

There is a door across the room. A way out. Back into the world and to find the man who has saved her. Straightening the front of her gown, Red prepares herself to see what other miracles have been wrought upon the world. Whatever it is, she has a new lease on life. She has to be presentable. Rolling her shoulders back, she is ready to go.

A new hope arises inside of her. The light shining through the windows is brighter and the birds sing louder than she has ever heard. Red takes a deep breath and tests the muscles of her legs. Shaky and weak, but they will hold.

One foot in front of the other. Balance is difficult. The world spins, but a deep breath clears the way. The distance between her and the new beginnings shortens. Her heart races. The palms of her hands begin to wet.

What is out there for me? Can this be real?

Metal creaks as the door handle turns before she ever reaches the end of the room. Silently the wooden portal slides slowly open and the light from the outside spills in with a cascade of new smells. Fresh air. Dry dust and a wall of heat wash over her.

Standing before her, bathed in darkness, is the man who saved her.

Tall.

Dark.

Formidable.

It is not Merchant.

Chapter Seven
Miracles Do Happen

A heavy, dreamless night.

Unwanted rest and a morning long passed.

Merchant turns from his bed where it sits, tucked in and undisturbed. He shifts his bag where it rests below the window. He shouldn't be here. The road calls to him, pulls at his soul as the western horizon stretches to the end of the world.

Heat lifts off in waves where the shadows burn away. Men, women, and children keep to the shriveling areas of shade as they pass between buildings and the unexplainable trees this town seems to possess. All varieties. Healthy and beginning to bear flowers and new leaves that should be no more than distant memories. Pinks and reds. Whites and oranges. Untouched and thriving in the middle of a country gone to shit. A countless collection of homes and storefronts, long porches wrapping around, and a quiet civility belonging to another time. A mirage of safety and comfort. Reality has come to a standstill here. There is no other way to explain it.

Though not everything can remain untouched.

Wood panels crack and peel from the intense sun and dust kicks up beneath scurrying feet. Long hats shield eyes and a few dogs, pigs, a single goat, and at least a half-dozen cats meander their way across the dirt road. Noses to the ground, ears held at the ready and twitchiness in their limbs, the animals know the truth. All but the careless goat. The beast munches on peeled bark as it stands in front of the building across the street. Door hanging wide open, Merchant watches as men and women make their way in and out, wool sacks of goods held in their hands or over their shoulders as they leave.

They all pet the goat

He stands there and munches away. Chin high, he regards them with little more than passing interest. Servants to his whims which at the moment consist of little more than the hard pieces between its teeth.

No one forgets to pet the goat.

Floorboards creak above Merchant's head and he regrets how high the sun is already. He should have woken up before the day broke the cover of night. Taken his stuff and disappeared into the darkness before they could drag him to stay and become part of their family.

Hadn't he heard enough of that already? Come back to God. He'll save this world.

Merchant holds onto his bag with a grip that could choke the air out of a tree. God has given up on this world. Moved on to better pastures. There is no Heaven when Hell is all that is left.

"Almost high-noon, cowpoke," Snake-Eyes jokes.

The ghost materializes in the bed behind Merchant, cowboy hat tipped forward on his eyeless skull and a long piece of straw dangling between his perfect teeth. A large brass colored belt buckle shines beside two holsters empty of pistols and the eyes on his neck remain half closed and leery.

"What the fuck are you supposed to be?" Merchant asks.

The bed doesn't make a noise and the floorboards are silent as Snake-Eyes climbs to his feet and walks over. He pulls out the straw and blows out a long drag of smoke and now there is a cigarette burning with a mile of ash hanging between his fingers.

"Need to fit in with the crowd before you kill them," Snake-Eyes says with a wink. "Nice people if you ask me. Naïve as fuck, but nice people. Too bad they don't understand what they let in through the front door."

Merchant turns away before hefting his bag onto his shoulder. The wood beneath his feet groans with protest as the weight shifts.

"I'm hitting the road no matter what any of them say. We'll put miles between us and them before nightfall."

A smile opens a wide mouth of teeth and a small tear drips from empty sockets.

"You said we," Snake-Eyes fakes fainting on the floor.

"Don't press your luck. I'd kill you a second time if I had the chance," Merchant grumbles and turns to the door.

Pulling on the nob and cracking the seal is like sticking one's head into an oven. The air blasts everything his lungs empty, his skin pulls tight and sweat glands erupt as the heated vacuum dries everything out. Merchant's eyes water and he shifts the bag over his shoulder as he shuts the door behind him.

Just great. Now I don't just live in Hell, I have to walk right through it.

No one pays any mind to him as he leaves his shelter behind. Dust kicks up around his boots as he turns west along the road and keeps his head down. People talk, dogs bark, and everyone moves along as another day passes.

"Wouldn't think of skipping town without saying goodbye, would you?" Brother George asks.

Merchant stops but does not turn around. Snake-eyes spins on his spurs and puts both hands over empty holsters as he backs away three paces.

"Give me the word and I'll take him out now," the ghost says.

"I told you that I'd be gone by sunrise," Merchant says.

"Looks like you overslept," Brother George adds.

Merchant shifts his face toward the sun scorching the blue sky.

"Appears I have. If it means no difference to you, I'll be on my way, priest. There are plenty of hours left in this day and I need to keep myself moving. I have a long road ahead of me."

Brother George steps up beside him and places a firm hand on his shoulder.

"We all have a long, hard road ahead of us, my son. How we choose to walk it and with whom by our side is the real question we must answer."

Slowly, but with little gentleness, Merchant drops the man's hand off his shoulder.

"What I do and what lays ahead of me is of my concern. Keep your flock with you. Protect them any way you can, but there are things in this world you don't understand, priest, and I am one of them."

"I understand more than you'll ever know, Merchant. There is a plan at work between you and me. My father above has put into motion events that neither of us can change, but it is up to us to find a way to overcome these obstacles if we are to see the other side."

The bag shifts again and the objects inside settle with a weight that pulls on the skin of Merchant's shoulder.

"Whoever your father is has clearly underestimated how truly fucked you all really are. There is nothing left of this world and the path for me is west. I didn't come to your village by some divine intervention. I nearly drowned trying to keep a stupid woman from drowning herself before the disease killing her had a chance to do the job for me."

"Your friend, Red," Brother George cuts in.

"Call he what you will. She'll be dead in a few days and I'll be long on my way. Trust me on this, priest. It is better for you all that I keep moving."

Not waiting for another word, Merchant steps away.

"You can see her if you would like," Brother George says.

Merchant shakes his head and continues to walk away. A strong sniff of baked bread clings to the air as dirt grits between his teeth. He pats the inner pocket of his jacket and feels the jerky inside. There is enough to carry him the rest of his trip.

"Your problem now," Merchant says to the wind.

Brother George does not follow him.

"She's been asking for you," the priest calls. "Says she needs to talk to you. It's about a collector."

Merchant stops. Anger flares up, hot and wild. The goat walks up to him and taps his leg with the top of his head. Teeth opening wide, the beast grabs a hold of his pant leg and begins to pull.

"Her mind is gone. The infection has driven her crazy. That is all," Merchant tries to convince himself.

"Not from what my nurses say. Woman has been nothing but chatty and insists she needs to see you. Says you'll understand."

A buzzard calls into the air as it circles the town. Wings wide in its slow glide, the shadow is a jet plane making a long surveillance run of its target below.

"Tell her I already left," Merchant says.

He doesn't move. There is no reason to. He already knows the answer.

"She says she'll follow you and I will not lie to her. I am a man of the church after all," Brother George answers.

The small chuckle at his own joke is evident from a mile away.

"Can she follow me? Does she have the strength to do that?" Merchant asks.

"Why don't you see for yourself?" Brother George is behind him without the slightest of sounds. "She waits for you in the Sick House right beside where you slept. It will take nothing more than a few moments for you to see her."

No other choices, no other options. Merchant sighs.

"Tick Tock," Snake-Eyes says and points to a gold watch on his wrist. "High-noon is coming, and you have these people in your cross hairs."

"Make this quick, priest," Merchant says and follows Brother George back the way they had come.

***

This house does not match what it should be. Clean air, fresh soap, and the gentle touch of warm milk carried between four walls and a short roof.

Merchant follows behind Brother George as the man takes his time leading the way. The Sick House is not unlike the home where he spent the night. Two floors, with the lowest level split into a half dozen rooms with a cast-iron stove at the center of the hallway warming everything within reach when the weather finally reaches that time of year to need it.

"How much further do we have to go, priest?" Merchant asks.

Snake-Eyes does not follow. The ghost disappeared before they ever stepped foot through the door.

"Not much. Be patient, my son, you are as anxious as she is."

Merchant looks through a couple of cracked open doors as they pass by. All of them empty. Beds are made and small tables with pitchers of water sit ready and waiting.

"I do not have time to delay. Every minute we waste here is another I lose finding my way back to the interstate."

"The road you travel will be there when the sun rises again, I can assure you of that. Patience is a virtue. You would take heed to remember that."

A growl grows in Merchant's chest, but he suppresses it by shifting his bag over his shoulder. Surprising even him, the burden he carries does not pull so tightly on his body. Prying his thumb under the thick strap, the weight shifts onto his hand with little resistance.

"Ah, here we are," Brother George says when they reach the end of the hall.

Before them sits a closed door. Solid oak stained dark with a polished knob waiting to be turned.

"Don't make her wait any longer," Brother George whispers. "She's already expecting you."

Merchant eyes the man who now has the smile of a father happy to give his daughter away.

With a silent twist, the door opens easily and Merchant steps in.

The room is no different from what he saw earlier. A single bed rests by a window looking into the afternoon light outside. A thin curtain flickers from the wind making its way through the opening and on the edge of the bed sits a young woman. She does not turn to look at him. Dark waves of red hair lay across her shoulders and she sits straight as she gazes toward the outside.

"There must be some mistake," Merchant says as he turns back to the door.

The priest puts a single finger up to his pressed lips and pulls the door shut before him.

"No mistake here, Merchant," Red's voice says.

The bed creaks as the girl at the window turns. Merchant's eyes go wide and then narrow.

"Red, is that you?" he asks.

Her smile is alive with youth and the fire in her eyes glows brighter than the sun of a warm summer after-noon. Her cheeks are as red as her hair and the skin of her face and arms is pale but shines with the beauty of a woman hardly past twenty.

"It's me, Merchant. Look what they did to me."

She holds out her arms and there isn't a single mark on them. No scars, no wounds leaking pus all over the clean sheets. He was never able to take notice before, but the woman would be heart stopping if his heart didn't burn with the hatred that drives him down the highway.

"How did they?" he begins.

Red giggles and shakes her head.

"God did this for me," Red says and bounces onto her knees on the mattress like a child. "The nurses told me how the work of God comes through the hands of Brother George. With a single touch he can cure the infection."

"That isn't possible. I've seen thousands of infected. This isn't some cold, Red. You don't wake up one day and the disease is gone. It's fatal."

Merchant turns back to the closed door.

"You haven't been infected," she calls out to him.

He drops his bag onto the floor and the contents rattle, but the sound is hollow and empty.

"I'm different."

She crosses her arms.

"How different?"

Walking around her, he puts an arm across the top of the window frame and watches children at play and men and women finishing up their work as the sun continues to dip toward the west.

"It's a long story," he answers.

"Tell me it then."

Merchant shakes his head no.

"Too long and I don't have enough time. I need to get back on the road."

"Still going west are you?" she asks.

Red swings her legs off the edge and her feet tap onto the wooden floor. The skin is smooth enough to shine the light from the window like a mirror and she wiggles her toes back and forth.

"There is no stopping where I'm going."

He turns back to the window. Dark clouds blot the horizon and the wind rattles the rod holding the curtain.

"Why can't you stay, Merchant? This place is like heaven on earth. The people are nice, and they have enough for everyone. Even if the infected find their way here, Brother George will just cure them," Red says.

A small laugh and he turns back to her.

"He's going to cure a thousand infected if they charge the limits of this village? Even if I believed he had the hand of God himself, there is only one of him and a million hungry monsters out there. They'll eat him alive and anyone stupid enough to stay here."

Red plants her feet on the ground and stands up to him. Her eyes flash with anger and she presses herself against him and she barely reaches his shoulders.

"We'll protect them," she says.

"Protect them?" he laughs again. "You and what army?"

A finger pokes the center of his chest twice.

"Me and this walking monster who dragged my infected ass here. I've seen what you can do. Those things may be monsters, but you are something else, Merchant. There is enough blood on your hands to drown that river that washed us here."

Anger flashes through his eyes and he pushes her aside with his shoulder. Losing her balance, she falls onto the bed.

"I've had enough of this place, Red. I'm leaving, and you can stay if you're smart or follow me if you want to die. I have no understanding of what has been done here, but part of me is glad you get a second chance. Don't waste it. I'm leaving and there is no coming back. Make your choice quickly," Merchant says.

He hefts the bag over his shoulder and makes his way to the door.

"Asshole. We finally find a place that has everything we need and you're going to leave it in the dust behind you. What the fuck could possibly be out there, Merchant? What is so fucking demanding that you'd give up your life to claw your way half way across this damn country? Tell me, Merchant. None of this, someone stole something from me bullshit. We have something here, Merchant."

He does not answer her. Grabbing the doorknob, he turns and pulls it open.

"Goodbye, Red."

"Fuck you, asshole! Just tell me! What is so God-damn important you will leave me for it?" Red screams.

Merchant shakes his head and walks out the door.

Chapter Eight
Let's Make This a Home?

The storm rolls in quickly. Earth shaking thunder. Lightning flashing across the sky. A bolt hits a tree and splits the trunk through the center and sends embers of burning wood and pitch high into the darkened sky.

Shutters rattle and crack as the wind howls and screams its fury. Candle flames flicker and the demons of the night dance in the corners as dinner is put on the table and everyone waits for the storm to pass.

"He left you behind like you were nothing," Kelly grumbles.

There are so many questions and not enough words to get them out as everyone eats in silence. The woman who calls herself Red looks up at her, a small bit of potato hanging from the corner of her ruby red lips. She eats like it is the last time she will ever see food. Shoveling it in faster than it can be served.

"An asshole, through and through. More monster than man if you ask me," she says and turns back to her plate.

Roasted chicken, potatoes from last year's harvest and the remainder of the spring peas before they all bolted and became bitter. Biting down on her own serving, Kelly can tell the two days they had to harvest was still too long as the taste of iron from the dirt mixes with the starchy fiber between her teeth.

What would it be like to think this was the best food left on the planet? Putting her spoon down on the plate, she pushes it away.

"Very quiet for a monster. All he talked about was going west. Why were you traveling with him if he treated you so badly?"

Derek slaps the edge of his plate with his fork. There is a darkness to his eyes this evening. A brooding beneath the deep ravines stretching across his forehead.

"Hush now, girl. Let the poor woman eat in peace and recover some of her strength. There is no reason to go on interrogating her like she isn't welcome at our table," he says.

He turns back to his plate and takes another bite, the same uninterested look on his face that she knows all of them feel. Mary taps him on the leg. He spares her a quick look before hunching over his cooling food.

"I never said that she wasn't welcome with us. I'd never say that. All I want to know is why this Merchant would leave her behind like he did. Would you leave Mary behind? Could you make her wait here while you went off across the country?" Kelly asks, her own words too harsh for her liking.

Derek drops his fork and grips the table for support. Knuckles turn white as he starts to rise from his chair.

"It's OK. The girl can ask anything she would like," Red interjects, a piece of bread slurring her tongue.

"My name is Kelly."

Red nods her head yes and rolls the end of her fork in the air. A signal to go on as her lips continue to smack.

"Why were you with him?" Kelly starts again.

"That is the easy one. I don't know when the last time anyone of you left the boundaries of this town of yours, though I can't see why you would, but the world out there has gone to Hell in a hand basket. If the poisons and dangers of a world with no technology doesn't kill you, then a million infected and beasts you can't even name anymore will surely do the job."

"Merchant protected you?" Kelly asks and now everyone is looking toward Red.

Though she sits opposite of Derek and Mary, they all no longer care for eating. Only Brother George is paying more attention to the food on his plate though she is certain he is still listening. Nothing gets by him if he doesn't want it to.

"Protection isn't exactly what I would call it."

"What then? Did he own you?"

Red looks up at her, eyes narrow and lips turn into a straight line.

"Kelly! Now that is enough," Mary jumps in.

The features on Red's face soften as a few strands of red hair drop down over her eyes and she wipes them away, the half-smile returning with the passing of her hand. She waves the heal of the bread in the air like a baton instructing them to wait. Her eyes turn to the back of her hand and she examines it like she hasn't seen it in the longest of time.

"No, he did not own me, but it's hard to say I didn't owe him something," Red says.

"He did something for you then?"

Kelly can't stop herself.

"Again, with another one of those 'hard' words. I wasn't exactly in any danger of dying, but I wasn't exactly with the greatest of crowds. We kind of took something that belonged to Merchant before we knew who he was and when he came looking for it," Red slides the dull edge of her knife across her neck.

"He killed everyone?"

Red chuckles and takes the whole heel of the bread into her mouth, the bulge stretching the skin of her face before her eyes roll into the back of her head.

"You know this is the best tasting bread ever? So fucking good," Red says as small bits fly from between her teeth. Mary gasps and puts a hand over her mouth.

"What did he do, Red?" Kelly insists.

"A lot worse than you can probably imagine. Honestly, we also didn't give him a choice. Like I said, the people I was with weren't exactly the nicest, you know? A girl has gotta do what she has gotta do to stay alive. When I told him he could take back whatever he wanted, he left me alone. Then after a few other misadventures, I figured it was safer staying with him then out there on my own."

"But he's killed people?" Kelly says as a matter of fact.

The idea sickens her stomach and she can see the look on Mary's face, pale white and her tongue holds back something that doesn't want to stay in her mouth.

"We all have, but in his case, he seems to only kill those who he needs to. At the moment it didn't seem to be me, so I figured if he could keep the monsters at bay, I'd be willing to follow behind for a while."

"That means you've killed people," Derek cuts in.

He puts his hand on Mary's shoulder and pulls her and the chair she sits on closer to him. Red shrugs her shoulders.

"Isn't that what I just said? Anyway, you do what you have to if you want to survive out there. I don't regret doing anything that I've done. I'm still alive and that is more than a lot of people can say."

Words fail as the room goes silent. Kelly watches as everyone turns back to their plates, some empty and others barely touched.

"Do… do you think he'll come back?" Kelly asks.

As if the wind itself tries to answer, the howl outside the wall rattles the roof and the shutters of the parsonage.

"Merchant?" Red looks her way. "Not if the fucker is smart. I'll kill the bastard if he comes back this way."

Kelly doesn't know what to say to that.

"Find a way to forgive the man, my daughter," Brother George cuts in. "He carries a weight and burden on his shoulders that no other man can carry."

Red smiles and points her fork in Brother George's direction.

"That is one true statement, my good man. That bag of his. God-damn thing weights a ton and if you try and carry it yourself, you might as well cut your own throat. It will kill you as sure as if you injected the infection directly into your arm."

"Please don't use our father's name in vain," Brother George says, his voice calm yet final.

Red looks at all of them and shrugs. Kelly can feel her cheeks redden with embarrassment enough for the both of them.

"Have it your way, but I know that weight he carries. It's a real bastard and if I see him again, I'll drop it on that silly cue ball head of his."

A chuckle breaks from Kelly's lips and Red winks her way.

"Plus, he made his choice and I've made mine. Of course, if the offer is still good," Red says and goes back to eating.

Brother George puts his fork and knife down and turns to look her in the eye.

"Never once did I think of rescinding my offer. Our town is home to anyone who chooses to stay here and live in peace. We ask only that you take comfort in our hospitality and treat your new brothers and sisters with the same care that they have shown you."

Caught with a mouthful of potato and chicken, Red's eyes sweep across them all. Kelly can feel the smile of her own shining bright at the idea of Red staying. It is always a cause for celebration anytime someone comes and joins their community.

"Have yourself a deal then, George. I can't say no to the man who made me back into what I am, now can I?"

"Brother George."

"Huh? Oh… yeah. Brother George. I'm glad to be a new part of the family," Red says and turns back to her plate once again.

***

The butterflies have not gone away.

Eyes burn. Muscles ache, stomach tosses and turns, but Kelly does not care. Long beams of light shine low into the window of her room as the sun breaks over the horizon in the east. Robins and mourning doves sing into the air and the heat of the day has yet to settle in.

She stretches and the nerves running through her body twinge with excitement. She cannot believe that Brother George has given her the duty of showing Red around. Usually one of the older women, no longer able to tend the fields or work in the community shops, work with any newcomers.

Not today.

Throwing on a new set of clothes, one of her best Sunday dresses of reds and yellows, Kelly pulls back her hair with a comb and does her best to straighten out any knots. Today will be so much fun she can already picture all the things she will show her. For once the room around her feels empty. Brother George isn't for keeping much and its rubbed onto her as well. She tries to imagine what it would have been to live in one of those great cities, full of people and things from all over the world.

The feeling of emptiness hits her quickly, heavy and cold, but the light coming in from the window quickly warms her feet and helps push it away with the blood running through her body.

Taking a deep breath, she forces her mind back to what lays ahead.

First it will be the farms up on the hills. The heat of the day will scorch the ground dry and there is very little shade there. Then through town there will be all the shops and other community buildings. There is no way she won't be impressed with all the crafts they have collected in their community. Or the way they all work together to keep things going and to provide for anyone who lives here. Anything she wants is within reach. She'll introduce her to everyone she knows and maybe even Red will share a few things with her.

What is it like outside in the wild? Is it really as dangerous as she has been told and dreamed in her nightmares?

Kelly's heart races as she finishes tightening her shoes and runs to the door.

"Remember Kelly," Brother George calls from the back of the parsonage. His voice is as clear as if he was right beside her. "Take it slow with Ms. Red. She's been on her feet barely a day or two. Let her lead the way and give her anything she needs. Remember, we want to treat her as we want to be treated ourselves."

"Of course!" Kelly answers and is outside the door in the blink of an eye.

Dirt kicks up into the air beneath her feet as she turns up the road. The Sick House is around the nearest corner and three buildings down. No hesitation will slow her as she speeds along the path. Breakfast can come later. She doesn't have time to stop and eat.

"Watch out!" Bert's voice calls out.

Elbows and knees hit soft flesh as Kelly collides with a body much rounder than her. The shadows of the side street spin and the hardpan of the road loses its grip on the soles of her shoes as she spins and tumbles into the ground.

Oink! Oink!

A piglet squeals.

Waving at the dust, Kelly opens her mouth to scream, but quickly bites her tongue. Bert looks down at her, a look of pure dread on his face and the soft pink flesh of a tiny pig trying to claw itself free beneath the arm held tight against his chest.

"Are… are you OK?" Bert asks.

Her friend looks her over as if she has fallen from the sky and splattered on the ground.

"Of course, I'm alright you, knucklehead. Help me back to my feet," Kelly says and reaches up for his empty hand.

Wiping it dry on his overalls, Bert reaches out and helps pull her back to her feet.

"Where are you going in such a hurry?" he asks.

She wipes the dirt off her dress, the material clinging to every last grain. The pig in his arms squeals in fury as it tries desperately to fight its way to freedom.

"Didn't you hear we have a new member in town? She came in three nights ago and Brother George asked me to show her around."

Pulling the pig higher into his armpit, Bert looks up and down the road, his eyes scanning for something that isn't there.

"Isn't that someone else's job?" he asks.

She punches him in the shoulder. He goes to rub it but stops as the little pig almost slips free.

"Today it's my job, and that is all that matters. Plus, I thought you told me it was only a rumor that you and your family carried around little piglets in your pockets."

Bert's cheeks turn red. His smile returns when she reaches out and scratches the little squealer behind the ear.

"My dad told me I needed to carry this one into town to see if Mr. Yerlan wants to take him in."

Now it's Kelly's turn to look confused.

"What would Mr. Yerlan want with a pig?"

Bert shrugs his shoulders and puts his open hand gently on the pig's head. The little monster tries to bite his fingers and gets a tap on the nose.

"Dad didn't tell me, but my brother says it's because we don't have any dogs for his little girl. I guess he figures a pig will have to do."

Kelly chuckles.

"I can see it already. Mr. Yerlan's daughter walking this little guy around on a leash. Maybe they can teach it to sit and roll over?"

Bert joins in on the chuckling.

"They'd be lucky if it doesn't eat their couch first. Darn thing won't stop nibbling on anything it gets its little snout near."

Kelly pets the little guy again and it tries to bite her as well. She frowns and shrugs her shoulders.

"You wanna come with me and meet her before we go exploring?"

"Show her around, Kelly. You know better than anyone, Brother George will be angry with you if you try and go exploring outside the village limits again."

Bert looks up and down the street. A few people are out and about, but no one looks their way.

"I know how to take care of myself," Kelly responds.

"I'm not sure it would be such a good idea to join you. My dad said to go right to Mr. Yerlan's place and then straight home."

Shoulders stiffen, and his breathing stops as Kelly wraps her arm around his wide shoulders. She gets a strong whiff of dirt, mud, and pig. Everything she always recognizes about her best friend.

"Today is making to be a heatwave. You know your brothers will be in the shade before it ever approaches noon. I bet they will never even notice you are gone. Live life, Bert. You're a grown man now. Come with me and meet our new friend."

Bert's face is as red as a tomato.

"If you say so… Maybe until mid-day. Then I should be home by lunch."

"That's the spirit."

She hits him again before spinning him the way they need to go.

Arm in arm, Kelly leads Bert through the streets. Dust kicking into the air behind their heels, they duck in and out between the early risers warming up for the day of work and play.

"Come on, we don't want to be late," she says.

Red cheeks puff and Bert loses his breath quickly. The pig squeals angrily and bites at his arm, but tucking it tighter, he does his best to keep up.

"What is the rush? It's not like she is going to go anywhere," he coughs out.

She doesn't look back at him. Sick House coming into view, she can already see the plans for the day playing out in her mind; fresh, fun, and right at the end of her fingertips.

Gaping open and empty, the front door to the house is silent. Kelly slows to a halt and lets Bert catch up, his big boots crushing the dirt like thunder. His breathing is short and shallow, and he rubs the back of his sweaty head with a dirty hand.

"Can we at least take a moment's break before we

start," he says.

With a cry of victory, the pig breaks free of his arm and hits the dirt road running.

"Get... back... here!" Bert yells.

Kelly chuckles and shakes her head as her friend goes off chasing the little beast. He might end up spending the entire morning catching him now. The pig gives another squeal of joy.

Wiping the damp hair away from her eyes, she pats away the dust from her dress again and approaches the opening with her shoulders back and chin held high. Red doesn't seem like the person who likes weakness.

Why would she? She's killed people. She said so herself. Kelly's hands tremble at the idea of such a world. Death isn't uncommon but finding your path to God while you sleep is different than being shot or possibly eaten by these infected.

What are they like anyway? Are they really monsters? Too many questions to ask, but today she really has the time to ask them.

Boards creak beneath her feet as she steps up to the door.

"You're the one they sent for me today?" Red's voice echoes from the quiet hallway inside.

Moving with a confident sway to her hips and shoulders, the woman steps out and leans against the frame, a slender hand shielding her eyes from the brightening morning. She is everything Kelly imagines being a woman should be. Confident, strong, and fearless. The borrowed white work shirt and brown canvas pants cling tight to her recovering body.

A ball as thick as her neck lodges in her throat.

"Um… Brother George said I have the opportunity to show you around your new home," Kelly starts.

Red looks over at her and smiles. Flames work their way across the startling red hair that cascades down over her shoulder and the depth of the dark beneath the light is endless against the softness of her skin. Even her ruby red lips are brighter than the sun.

"My new home," Red says and looks up and around at all this quiet town has to offer this early in the morning. "Those aren't words I ever thought I'd hear again. Well, what are we waiting for? Lead the way my new friend."

Pride and excitement fights for control as Kelly can feel her chest stretch inches wider. Something about Red is different than anyone she has ever met. For the last four years everyone in this town has been her family, but something about this woman feels so much more, exciting.

Kelly notices that Red is looking down at her, her lips cocked to the side and her arms crossed over her chest.

"Yes… we better be on our way. A lot to cover and the sun will be too high and too warm soon enough," Kelly stammers before turning back to the path that led her here.

"Hey, there you two are," Bert calls out.

Dust covers his legs up past the knee and his white t-shirt is wet with sweat and dark with mud smeared by the angry hooves of the pig still kicking at his chest.

"Who are you and why the fuck do you have a pig?" Red asks with a chuckle in her voice.

Kelly can feel the fire searing the skin on her face. Bringing Bert with her was a big mistake. Maybe the biggest mistake of her life as his eyes dart between them and he licks his lips, smearing small streaks of mud in thin layers beneath his tongue.

"His name is Bert," Kelly says. "He's a friend and said he'd walk with me to pick you up on his way to sell the little beast on the other side of town."

"Little beast?" he asks. "Walk you here?"

Kelly turns the way they need to go and leaves him behind her. She can feel his eyes cutting through her back, but maybe he'll get the hint and let them go without too much of a fight.

"You can't imagine what we would have done to find something like that when we were starving last winter," Red says before making a slurping sound with her lips. "Out there you would kill someone even for something that small."

Kelly turns back toward them. Red reaches out and softly pets the animal's pink head.

"We really should get moving," Kelly says.

Red lifts her hand and taps Bert on the cheek with the tips of her fingers. If they thought his face was red from running to catch the pig, he's absolutely on fire now.

"Yea... yeah, I really should get moving now. Maybe I can catch up with you guys later," Bert stammers, his eyes locked on Red.

With a sigh, Kelly looks down at the ground and refuses to look at either one of them.

"Fine. You will probably find us near the town square by the time you're done. We won't wait for you though."

Bert wipes his hand through his dripping wet hair and then back at Red.

"Don't look at me, handsome. She's the boss today," Red says with her thumb hooked over at Kelly.

The smile on Bert's face beams and Kelly can feel the pride swell up enough to push back the annoyance of having him take away her moment.

"We'll head down this way, Red. Follow me and I'll show you the best places that no one knows about."

Red nods her head and steps up behind her. Before them awaits their whole world and Kelly is going to show her everything.

***

Buzzards swirl in endless circles high over the town. The heat crackles with its own song and the water in the air sizzles beneath the high-noon sun. Dry tongues lap at sweaty skin and those forced to move beneath the hellish slaughter of heat and invisible burning rays walk with drooping shoulders and hats pulled tight against sweaty heads.

Kelly rests beneath the shade of the Central Market store. Her skin burns though she tries to keep it from the sunlight as much as possible, but her back feels cool as it presses against the shaded boards.

A dog barks in the distance and a dry wind scatters a ball of dead grass across the street. Boots clap against the dry boards and she looks back to the open doorway.

Red bites down on a carrot and it crunches with loud snaps beneath her teeth.

"You have a wonderful town here," she says between bites. "And such wonderful food."

Small bits of orange flake away from the small

wrinkles at the corner of her lips and fall to the dust at her feet.

"This is your home now too," Kelly says.

Red winks at her and the butterflies in her stomach jump.

"Of course. It's going to take a lot of getting used to though," Red adds. "This world has been pretty fucked up for a long time and it won't go back to being normal again so easily."

Kelly turns back to the road and its glaring yellow haze.

"Brother George does his best to make sure everyone has what they need," she says.

Red takes another bite and slides in next to her, the heat of her skin an inferno against Kelly's shoulder.

"He means a lot to you all, doesn't he?"

Kelly looks over at her.

"To the people he is their leader and their savior. Next to God, his word is the law around here."

With a final bite, Red flicks the green leaf of the carrot into the road.

"A single man with power over others is a dangerous thing."

"He's different. All he wants to do is save everyone he loves and show us that this world has not become so... fucked up... as people think."

An eyebrow wrinkles over Red's eye.

"Fucked up?"

Kelly blushes and turns away.

"Sorry. I mean that he believes this world can be a better place. Maybe one day return to the way it was before all the fighting and death. If people would treat each other with kindness and follow the word of God, maybe we wouldn't be in the middle of all of this."

"Good luck with that. This whole fucking place went into the deep-end long before the bombs dropped. I can hardly remember a time when the world wasn't fighting itself. There is no returning to a better time, Kelly. A better time doesn't exist."

Red pushes away from the wall and leans against one of the long-carved poles holding the roof over their head.

"That isn't true. Brother George talks about it all the time. He shows us with his miracles what this world could really be. If people only believed and cared…"

"Cared about what? People care about one thing and that is themselves. You seem to think rather fondly of this, Brother George. Is he your daddy or something?"

Kelly wraps her arms around her chest regardless of the heat and leans away slightly at the memories trying to break free.

"He's the same thing with me as he is with everyone else. Our leader, spiritual and in life."

"You live with him though and you're easily a woman grown now. Men, even as pious as he seems to be, have urges."

Biting her lip, Kelly turns her back to her.

"He is nothing like that. My parents died before I ever found this town. I would have been on the streets, not much unlike you, but this older couple took me in. Spent most of their time screaming about God and the damnation of man, but they were good at hiding. We traveled south from the Black Hills of South Dakota and ended up here."

Red picks at a piece of carrot in her teeth.

"Where are they now?"

"Dead and buried up on the hill," Kelly answers and points at the rise in the land to their west. Grave-markers made of wood are hard to see but there are enough to form a small forest about the height of Red's knees. "Died in their sleep holding each other's hand. Brother George took me in after when there weren't enough families in town to help."

More dogs barking cuts through the dry air and the wind whips by with a harsh squeal.

"He couldn't cure them like he does the others?"

A small chuckle breaks the tension in Kelly's chest.

"Can't stop death itself, Red. Brother George can cure what makes you sick, make you better if a better person is what you are on the inside, but if it's your time, there is no stopping it."

Red sighs.

"A better person? I'm not sure about that, but it's good knowing it's not my time."

The sound of dogs grows frantic off to the east where the road exits the town to a hill that climbs up the horizon. Red steps out from beneath the porch and shades her eyes from the sun.

"What's going on over there?" she asks.

Kelly can't think of anything special that would be happening this late in the day, so she steps out beside her.

Dust clouds kick high into the air and the wind roars as the storm grows closer. Light reflects off sur-faces within the building cloud and the roar takes a deafening tone.

Kelly looks around and several other people find their way onto the street and stare off into the distance. Everyone seems mesmerized and no one moves.

"I... I think I know who that is," Kelly stammers.

The cloud of dust rushes into the first buildings that make their home and the screaming thunder that is engines revving over the hard-packed dirt is unmistakable.

"Come... come with me, Red. We have to get Brother George."

Red looks at her and then turns back to the approaching vehicles.

"Who the fuck are these assholes and where did they get trucks?"

"Please, Red. Follow me, now. These are not good men. We need Brother George. He'll know what to do."

She pulls at the sleeve on Red's arm. The woman resists the tug at first, but then turns and follows behind her.

"What is he going to do? Pray them to death?" Red says as she runs behind her.

"I'm not sure, but he'll figure something out. Hurry, Red."

Sweat and dry air slaps her face like an angry fist, but Kelly cannot slow down. Brother George will know what to do. He always does. What will they do if he doesn't?

Chapter Nine
A Monster by No Other Name

Loud engines. Angry faces. Guns ready to bark and a haze of hanging dust and drying tears. Everyone stands together in front of the church, huddled in a big circle like mother hens holding onto their dear little chicks.

Kelly clings onto Red's arm, the muscles beneath tense and unforgiving. Red's heart beats a mile a minute but not in fear. She does not shake like those around her. She has seen men like these before. Killers, rapists, thieves the whole lot of them. The silence of the world is painful as everyone watches the two men stare at one another and none know what she would do to have that revolver in her hand again.

What the hell caused her to forget it back in her room? This place really is getting to her.

The two leaders sit jockeying for who has the bigger set of balls, yet no one is willing to whip it out and end this senseless waste of time. One a fat cowboy and the other a useless priest.

"What is happening?" Kelly whispers.

Red shrugs her shoulders.

A pig oinks and yelps and nobody moves. Bert, the boy who sweats too much and smells as bad as his pet is huddled behind them. He keeps looking into the mass of bodies, but the crying and the frozen fear wouldn't let him push through if he tried.

"I see we meet again, Father Charles," the big bellied asshole starts.

"Brother George."

"What? Oh yes, Brother George. It looks like we meet again here at your lovely place of worship."

The cowboy opens his arms to the people gathered. A shiver runs through the group and Red grits her teeth. Everyone but her takes a collective step back and Red watches them. Like sheep they wait to be told what to do. A dozen men sit ready in their vehicles, all of them armed.

Where did they get those working trucks?

She eyes each one individually. These are definitely men used to getting their way. Their eyes are tired, but their jaws are set, and they are ready for whatever this man in the stupid cowboy hat tells them to do. She almost chuckles. Two very similar groups of people, yet each is the other side of the coin.

Hunters and killers on one side, peaceful victims on the other.

The world never changes does it?

"You gathered us here for a second time by gunpoint, Mr. Barnett. There is no reason to frighten all these nice people. Tell us what you want, and we will gladly be of help if we are able. There is no reason for violence," Brother George says.

He does not move. He does not show any signs of flinching. The man is stronger than he should be with hundreds of pounds of lead aimed at his chest and nothing to stop it.

"Miracles, my brother. I am looking for miracles."

Logan walks right up to the front row of people and tears flow freely behind sobs. Parents push the children into the middle.

"Then I believe you have come to the wrong place as I told you before," Brother George adds as he moves to separate the people from the man with the tipped cowboy hat.

Red reaches behind her back but disappointment is quick as she remembers there is nothing there.

Damn it.

This place is already making her soft.

"I know what you told me, priest. I don't think I'm inclined to believe you. See, I have this little birdie who keeps talking in my ear. Says it flies over this town and watches what you do in the cover of darkness, Brother George. Do you know what this little birdie tells me?"

Logan turns on his heels and stands nose to nose with Brother George.

"I do not."

A devilish grin inches over Logan's face.

"You are hiding things from us, priest. I've been told more infected have come to your town and yet here you all stand as fit as a fiddle. I even had my men check your little hospital and the man who was there isn't anywhere to be found. How do you explain that?"

"The gentleman had a fever, and that was all. After a couple of days, he was good to return home. There is no miracle in a little chicken soup and prayer, is there Mr. Barnett?"

A couple of chuckles escape the men with the guns

and Logan is quick to silence them with a look.

"I want to see him, priest."

"Who?"

Logan pulls a fist full of shirt and forces Brother George up against him.

"Show me this man with a fever. If you don't, I think I might start filling your hospital with people who need a lot more help than chicken soup and prayer. You've got until the count of ten."

Women and children scream as the people in mass begin to panic and struggle to hold themselves upright. Red steps to the side and with a hand pushes the young girl, Kelly, behind her. That is a lot of guns pointed their way, but if she can just make it to the closest while they concentrate on everyone else, she might have a chance.

She wouldn't be able to save them all, but there is nothing to help that.

Cold sweat runs down her spine and the adrenaline stiffens her fingers as she readies herself to run as fast as her legs will carry her.

"There is no need," Brother George starts.

"One… two…" Logan begins.

"Please, Mr. Barnett. There is nothing but good people here," Brother George tries to plead.

"Three… four…" Logan continues.

A warm body presses against Red's back. She can feel the soft shudders of sobbing. Reaching back without turning, she puts her hand on the girl's shoulder and feels the shakes slowly subside.

"Mr. Barnett, will you…"

"Five… six."

Logan backs away and several rifles are chambered. Brother George steps to follow but Logan puts up a finger and wags it back and forth.

"Seven… eight."

"I'm right here," a man's voice cracks over the crying crowd.

Men, women, and children part reluctantly as a figure steps forward. Red lets go of Kelly's shoulder as the man comes into view. It's the same one from the Sick House. His strength is back, but he still has a limp. A few red blotches scar pieces of his neck, but at least his face continues to fill in. If they weren't surrounded by armed thugs, the man may even be cute in the right light.

"I'm the one you are looking for," the man says.

Brother George pats him on the shoulder as he steps up beside him.

"So, I hear you had a fever, my man. Is this true?" Logan asks.

He walks around the two and looks them over like a new car or woman he's about to purchase.

"Yes, it is true."

"What is your name? Where are you from?"

The man looks at Brother George.

"What is the point in this, Mr. Barnett?" Brother George asks.

Logan stops his circling and pulls the revolver from his belt.

"The point is, priest, I asked this man a question and I want it answered. If I was asking you, I wouldn't have to be pointing this at your fucking head, now would I?"

The dangerous end of the barrel taps Brother George on the forehead.

"My name is Martin. Martin Edelwood. I'm from Chicago," Martin answers.

He didn't remember his name the other day. Probably made up, but better than nothing. Red clenches her fists. There is no way this is going to end well. She can already taste the blood.

"Martin. You look pretty strong for a man who was suffering from such a bad fever the other day. How did you get here from Chicago? By train?"

Logan goes back to his circling, this time tapping his thigh with the revolver with every step.

"When the fighting got bad, I ran with friends and family. We… we headed west where the fighting and the sickness wasn't so bad. I ended up here. Stumbled upon it one day."

"And the others?" Logan asks.

Martin looks back at Brother George.

"The others?" he asks.

Pistol crunches as it connects with the soft spot of Martin's gut. Air and wet coughs escape faster than anything can come in as the man topples over. Dust and dirt kick up into a cloud and screams crack into the afternoon light.

"Your family, you fucking moron. You said you ran with your family and friends. Did we forget that little detail?" Logan demands.

He spits on Martin's curled body. Brother George kneels beside him and helps roll him over to steady his breathing.

"They died before they ever reached us," Brother

George says. "Most people never make it this far into the country. Everyone knows that. Surely you do Mr. Barnett. The dangers out there are too great and even when you travel in groups, people are bound to be lost."

Logan waves off the answer and heads to the semi-circle of vehicles.

"I still don't trust you, priest. But seeing as I'm a forgiving man, I'm ready to give you a chance to make it up to us."

With a nod of his head, the back door of the center Jeep opens. Two men shoulder rifles and reach in with grunts.

"I have need of your services. One of my men, a good man I may add, has fallen sick while guarding our city. I want you to cure him."

Brother George turns from treating Martin.

"Whoever told you these lies is playing a dangerous game, Mr. Barnett. There are no miracles here. If your friend is sick, try to give him some medicine. We have little enough for the people here and even that only helps with the common cold and simple injuries. Surely you have better stored with everything you control."

Logan waves the men forward and between them they are carrying another who is practically lifeless. Even from the side of the group, Red can see the infection making its way up his leg. Cheeks sunk in, his skin is pale and dark blue veins map out the muscles in his neck and hands. Beads of sweat cover his brow and he mumbles though he lays semi-conscious between the men's arms.

"Please, Mr. Barnett. There is nothing we can do for him," Brother George pleads.

"Come over here and help this poor man," Logan demands.

With a wave of his revolver, a couple of the younger men from the village step forward and lift the infected from the arms of the thugs and hold him steady as they back away.

"You have a week, Brother George. When I come back, our friend here better be as healthy as these people you care for so much. If I see even a cracked piece of skin on his body, you'll pay, priest. Miracles and prayer may protect you from the disease ravaging this great country, but as our Second Amendment always proclaimed was our God given right, does your prayers protect you from bullets?"

The smile on the man's face as he climbs into his Jeep is the most sinister thing Red has ever seen. His men keep their rifles trained on everyone as they climb into their own vehicles and with the roar of engines, they turn and leave.

"What are we going to do?" everyone asks in a collection of a dozen voices.

No one can answer.

No one can move.

Brother George struggles to help Martin back to his feet and those carrying the infected step beside him. Red moves in to help as well.

"Here, let me help," she says reaching for the fallen man's arms.

The priest shakes his head and pulls Martin upright by himself.

"No, my daughter. I'm not sure you can help here," he says with a voice as defeated as the tears of the people who fill this town.

"What are we going to do, Red?" Kelly asks.

The girl curls up beside her and rests her body against hers. Her soft arms wrap around her waist. She can feel the young woman's strength fade as she uses her for support.

"What would you normally do?" Red asks.

"Pray, I guess," Kelly says between silent sobs.

The words have no conviction. Kelly doesn't believe any more than she does.

"You go ahead and do that," Red says.

Kelly pulls away and looks up at her.

"What are you going to do?"

Red doesn't look at her. The horizon to the west is blood red and closing with darkness. A perfect color for a solution she isn't sure they are ready for.

"Go, Kelly. Be with your friends. I've got to go see a man," Red says and with gentleness steps away.

"See who?"

Red doesn't turn to answer. Instead, she continues to walk away. They cannot know where she is going. She doesn't know where she is going. But she does know where to start.

West.

Chapter Ten
The Offer is Made

Warm thick blood drains out, pooling on the hard ground. The stick slathered in pus and grime drips from Merchant's hands. The bodies are scattered. A dozen at least, all of them lifeless now that they are bled out and broken across the landscape in a circle of death and devastation.

He pants to gather his breath.

The fire in his blood boils and he looks for more challenging them to try again. Their hunger seeks his life and flesh, but the eyes in the darkness retreat. Yellow and red points of light reflecting the moon as they watch and wait.

Merchant drops the broken stick, the hollowness of the wood echoing the emptiness that burns within him. Already it begins to fade. They will not come after him again tonight. The smell of death is in the air and it will drive them to easier meals. Muscles ache and joints stiffen as his body calms down. He picks up his bag, his fingers slippery with blood and torn tissue and he throws the weight over his shoulder. With a grunt he continues to the west.

"A real mess tonight," Snake-Eyes says as he materializes next to Merchant. "Didn't even see them coming, did you?"

Merchant growls and spits out the taste of iron and dirt from the back of his throat.

"Real pity. If you would have listened and talked Red out of her craziness, she'd be here with you. She'd have seen them coming. Young girl in the prime of her life. Not an old demon like you, slowing with age. She'd have seen them coming."

"Go fuck yourself," Merchant mumbles.

He needs to rest. The night is still young and there is always the chance something else will find him. The infected aren't the only thing that prowls these lands in the darkness, and some of them aren't afraid of the stench of death.

Walking beneath the bright light of the crescent moon his boots drag over the dirt. He stumbles, the weight of the dead heavy on his shoulders and the endless chatter of their calls ringing in his ears.

A wolf howls in the distance.

A stiff breeze follows in quick pursuit, and the air is scratchy and dry. He can taste the change in the land. Out west, somewhere he can't see, the land will begin to rise. At first a slow climb until all at once the earth itself will burst from its cage and reach for the sky, but not here.

The shadows and endless nothing are absolute. Figures and ghosts dance behind the veil that blinds his way forward. He does not fear them. He does not fear death. More times than he can count the cold icy touch has frozen his veins, yet he still walks. One of these days he'll find something that will stop him. Either the city he searches for everyday or a monster that is even worse than he is.

His boot hits something hard. Maybe a rock, or a root so desperate for water it broke the surface of the ground in a desperate search for life, but it doesn't matter.

Foot twisting, Merchant goes down hard.

Knees crack. His bag rolls off and his palms and elbows cut divots from the concrete dirt and he tastes dust all the way down his throat. Coughing, he rolls onto his back.

Stars stare back at him. More than a billion as he watches them pepper the sky with twinkles for as far as he can see. From the west a burst of light races across the sky. Bright and white it arcs through the darkness and fades to nothing before reaching the horizon to the east.

Merchant closes his eyes. Relaxation. Something impossible to find outside of old memories. He remembers those times. They weren't that long ago. A few years and a whole lifetime ago.

***

"Take cover!" Merchant shouts.

The ground shakes with the fury of the gods spilling dirt and rocks from the air like rain. Men fall to their knees covering their heads and the world rings with the endless sound of a thousand bells. A jet engine roars overhead, the buzz of fuel and rocket turns everything into ozone as another missile speeds by faster than sound and buries itself tip into the concrete wall with the fist of a giant.

Gray chips and dust settle to the ground. Grinding under boots and digging at skin beneath collars and underneath jackets.

Merchant coughs through lungs that burn. The men around him scream but he can barely hear them. Some point in the direction of the enemy. Most look back the way they had come from. Everyone is as white as ghosts with dark circles under their eyes. They smell like three-week-old dirty underwear and the taste of MREs is permanently caked to the inside of their mouths.

He spits on the ground, an action of instinct more than pleasure. His hands shake as he grips his rifle tighter and turns to look across the field.

Smoke lifts from the ground in a mushroom of gray and horrific black. Concrete bones and solid rock is scattered over three hundred yards of open field, the grass and dirt scorched with fire and chemicals. Radios chirp as the sound of jets buzz and the ground tremors with the aftershocks of bombs dropped on someone else's head.

"We have orders to hold, sir," a man yells.

Merchant ignores him.

The captain is on the far side of the trench. Go tell him.

Merchant doesn't know if he says the words or only thinks it.

He eyes the distance from here to the enemy. Shadows move through the smoke and disappear as fast as they form.

Movement.

Soldiers survived.

He smiles.

The fire inside his gut ignites and the palms of his hands sweat through the thick layer of dirt. His finger twitches and he sights his rifle across the field.

"Sir! We have orders from the LZ," the man's voice drowns beneath the crackle of cover-fire deeper in the city.

Merchant does not recognize the commands. A half dozen shapes dart through the confusion.

Targets.

Unmistakable enemies that must be eliminated.

His finger flicks at the safety as the fade of the shot locks into his mind. One dot left, two up.

Merchant takes a deep breath and his pulse slows its beat within his head.

He lets the breath out and feels the cold steel beneath the pad of his finger.

"Sir!"

A hand grips onto his shoulder like a vice and pulls him back. Elbow out, he feels the crunch of bone beneath the blow and a body drops at his feet.

"What the fuck is going on?" Merchant demands.

The world goes silent. Men stop what they are doing. The world continues to fight around them, a rain of dirt and death falling all throughout the trench, but within their small confines all time ceases to exist. At his feet a soldier lays crumpled with hands holding together a jaw bent awkwardly inward an inch before the ear.

"Hold the hell on, Sergeant!" Travis yells.

Merchant watches Corporal Travis turn the screaming soldier onto his back. Jaw shattered, his eyes are red and pinched tight with tears and Travis is yelling something.

"There is no time for this shit," Merchant barks and pulls Travis to his feet. "What the fuck is going on and why did this piece of shit try to get himself shot?"

Travis looks down at the man splayed out in the dirt. One of the medics is trying to hold his mouth shut as he eases him to a seated position and blood drains freely along with a line of spit down his neck and chin.

"That is Major Ortiz's runner," Travis answers, his eyes hard as he looks Merchant in the face.

"Then what the fuck is he doing over here and not with the brass waiting for us to do our job?"

Merchant spits on the ground and the medic is quick with a glare made of daggers and as useful as a butter knife at a gun fight.

"Ortiz and the others are dead, Merchant," Travis answers.

What?

A quick glance to their north and the world is no different than the muck and blood they are standing in. Merchant grabs Travis by the shirt and the man doesn't flinch.

"Then find someone who cares. First Sergeant Emery has to be around here somewhere if he hasn't locked himself in some shitter clicking his knees together."

Travis shakes his head no.

"Dead. They are all dead. Truck bomb followed by a missile strike."

Merchant releases Travis from his grip.

"All of them?"

Shaking his head yes, Travis turns and points the medic and the half-dazed messenger away. He spins on his heels and looks at Merchant eye-to-eye.

"To the man, they are dead and that leaves you in charge up here. Word from the radio says we are to withdraw until further orders. Brass wants us to regroup for another push when they can restructure the chain of command."

Another jet and another bomb rock the ground like a cradle from a parent who hates their child. Dust from broken cement fills the air between them. Everyone coughs. Merchant bites down on his tongue and lets the blood fill the gaps between his teeth.

"Fuck them!" Merchant says and turns back to the three hundred yards separating them from their enemy.

Lifting his rifle, he readies for the shot he did not get to take. Travis rips him around like the other idiot who should have known better. This time Merchant doesn't swing though every fiber of his body says to do so.

"You're in command now and they expect you to get us back."

Fire lances through veins and muscles twinge with fury.

"And fight all fucking week to get back to where we are now? Hell no! We didn't bleed and die to get here and turn around."

"Our orders, Merchant!"

With a grip of iron, Merchant shoves Travis against the wall of the trench, sand and dirt cascade down in waves breaking over his shoulders and arms.

"Fuck our orders and the men who gave them. We are going across that field and pushing those fucking separatist bastards back into the cesspools they climbed out of. Either you are with us, Corporal, or I'm going to field judge you right where you stand."

The sound of a rifle barrel tapping on the wooden frame of the trench sends the lump in Travis' throat bobbing and his eyes looking for support. A manic smile stretches over Merchant's face and he glares at the other drawn faces around him. Tired and worn the whole lot of them, but none show resistance.

A shoulder shrug and push, Travis steps back between Merchant and the others.

"You're in charge here, Captain. What are your commands?"

Merchant pulls back the bolt on his rifle and it is ready.

"Load up boys, we have a lot of ground to cover and nothing stopping us from getting our asses shot but God himself."

He gives them all a smile, and no one returns the favor. Looking back over the edge of the trench the smoke is still clearing over the field. The wind is dead and so are the lives of the men on the other side. Their souls are his to take and he can feel their dreams slipping through his fingers. His heart races and the adrenaline courses through him like gasoline on a fire.

Men all along the trench climb the bottom steps and ready for the command. Turning, he lifts his arm to signal the mortars at the rear. Thirty seconds and the field will be peppered again with enough smoke and debris to clear their way.

They'll lose some. He knows that, but it won't be enough to stop him. Once his boots are on the ground everyone is dead to this world. One last check and he has everything he needs.

Rifle.

Pistol.

Field knife. He'd never go anywhere without it.

Like clockwork the world in front of them lights up

in a glorious show of the red and yellow damnation of Hell. Rocks and the vibration of violence shakes their world, and he yells the command. Words of fury and wild abandon drown the concussion of blasts as the men charge over the top of the trench and across the field.

Bullets pepper the ground and wiz by like angry hornets. His men return fire as muzzles light the way through smoke and fog as more jet engines rip through the sky. Merchant can barely breathe, but he doesn't need it. The thrill of the hunt. The joy of the kill. This is all he needs to survive. Their blood will fill his lungs and he will revel in the gore their bodies will spill upon the ground.

Shadows move in the distance. He fires his own weapon and two explode into nothing. The joy is overpowering, and tears burn his eyes. The distance disappears beneath his pounding boots and he pushes even harder. The smoke will choke them as he clears the distance and then he'll be on top of them like a wild cat.

The sound of his men is deafening around him. A hundred men. Maybe a thousand all scream at the tops of their lungs on every side. He can't drown them out. Three more missiles streak through the darkness over-head, yellow lines of angry fire arc across the sky and toward his enemy.

He begins to slow as the sound around him fades into a distant murmur. He's still jogging, but the smoke and fog is not clearing. Gunshots rattle but further away and from all directions. The buzz of bullets missing by inches or less fills the air. He is untouchable.

More shadows dance and he screams as he answers with barks from his own rifle. Black figures explode and more fill in. Anger fills him and he runs harder. Throwing his rifle over his shoulder, he unholsters his sidearm and fires until it locks back. Shadows explode like confetti.

He keeps running. The end is a mile away and his isn't getting any closer. The sound of his men is a distant memory. A single flash here and there is all he can see.

The world goes silent.

Merchant slows.

The taste of blood is on his lips and in his mouth. He reaches to touch his face. He does not hurt. The smell of spent gunpowder burns his nose, but fresh blood still drips from between his teeth.

His boots stop. Gray smoke and shadows swirl around him. With a look, they explode. In all directions anything he sees dies and rises once again.

Merchant is lost. Everything is silent. The world at war has moved on and left him behind. He takes another cautious step forward. Dirt crunches beneath his boots. Firecrackers whirl through the sky and the explosion in the distance is muted. He reloads his weapon.

Keep your eyes ahead. The end is near.

Steadying himself, Merchant picks up his pace from slow steadying steps to a muscle warming jog. The world spins in his eyes, but he cannot stop. The pounding of boots is just ahead. More shadows run across and dance before exploding into a substance free gore.

Grey smoke clears. As thin as a veil he can see the trench in front of him. Men scurry back and forth. None of them have seen him. His smile is rabid as he readies his grip. Site locked on, his finger twitches with the expectation of the shot.

A deep breath.

A steady hand.

The trigger is warm to his touch. Knuckle flexes and finger squeezes. The pistol does not fire. Merchant squeezes again.

Nothing.

The enemy turns his way. Their eyes are wide with horror. They do not turn their weapons his way. Frozen, they stare at him as he stares at them. A shadow eases behind them.

Quiet and unnoticed.

A predator.

He watches the stranger. It does not stab, shoot, or order any of them. With a delicately cloaked hand, it touches them one by one as it passes by. White faces, drawn and tired as his own, curl inward with agony as black veins spread from neck and shoulder through their faces as skin splits and their eyes go milky.

Bodies twitch. Hair falls out and blood pours from open cuts as teeth gnaw at lips. Twelve monsters turn their attention to him. Merchant turns and looks around. The sea of smoke and dust is endless behind him and he hears nothing of the men he leads. Turning back, the devils begin to climb from the base of the trench. Dark nails claw at the hard earth and rip apart smearing patches of fresh blood into the soil.

Their calls are moans from the pits of Hell. They crawl forward, their joints cracking as drool and bile leaks from their mouths. He tries to backpedal. His feet are locked into place.

The stranger.

It watches as its new beasts close in around him

from where it waits within the trench.

Merchant throws his pistol, and it cracks one across the left temple. Dark streams of blood and infection leak down an ear that folds into itself. White bone sticks out where flesh is ripped. The monsters do not slow.

Unstrapping his rifle, he fires the rounds he has left. Bullets tear through bodies, organs and bile spewing on the ground, but they continue to approach, and he is frozen in place.

They are almost within reach. Death surrounds him, and the stench of decay burns his lungs. Merchant tries to scream but the poison leaks into his lungs and kills the pleas before they can start. The first tries to reach for his legs and gets a rifle to the nose, shattering half its skull. A second grabs the weapon and rips it free. Turning back, the monster is rewarded with eight inches of steel through throat and spine.

Moans and the pains of hunger fill his ears until they bleed. Merchant keeps them at bay with the only weapon he has left. They circle him, and he cannot run. Those that have fallen begin to rise regardless of their injuries.

He looks back to the stranger. Shadows swirl and cloak him in a shroud of death and mystery. A crooked hand lifts Merchant's way. The first monster catches his arm and the touch burns down to the bone. Nails cut through flesh and muscle. Blood fountains and the knife falls. Merchant will not follow. Another grabs and he wraps his good hand around throat and rips until blood and tissue fly away.

Another glance to the stranger. This is the end. His days are finally over. A wash of relief floods Merchant's body. He always swore he'd die on his feet. Throwing the two monsters separating him from the unknown away, Merchant stares in defiance at the shadow aiming to claim him.

Light flashes from the end of a pointed finger. Pain slams into Merchant's chest with the force of a tornado and blood balloons out with the little breath he has left in his lungs. He topples to the ground as his mouth fills with the salty taste of iron and each breath chokes him. A third burst rips his chest across the sternum and he watches another streak of light flare its life across the sky.

Shadows look down on him. Yellow eyes stare hungrily into his torn flesh. He is done. He is dead.

The darkness takes what it wants.

Chapter Eleven
You Cannot Refuse

Dead bodies do not move.

They tend not to breathe either.

Red squats on her haunches and pokes Merchant in the chest with a long finger. He grumbles and stirs but does not open his eyes. The smell of death is everywhere, and she does not blame him. Bodies rot in the morning sun and the darkness filling in from the west tells a story of the pain and misery to come.

She pokes him again, and he grumbles words in a language she doesn't understand. With a sigh, she stands back up, stretches her back and feels a few pops relieve the stress. It has been a long three days on the road and she is too tired to deal with his lazy ass sleeping in the middle of a cow field where the cows were smart enough to have left a long time ago.

"I hope you aren't too mad about this," she says.

Spinning on her heel, she lets a kick fly and hits him square in his ribs.

Air jets out followed by coughs that rack his huge body and Merchant curls onto a shoulder and spits on the ground.

"What… what the fuck is going on?" he demands.

Red stands there with her fists buried into her hips.

He doesn't notice her at first. His eyes move over the dead bodies and he shakes his head.

"Don't even think I was willing to give you CPR or anything like that," she says.

He turns his head, a small look of confusion that quickly fades to anger and then his normal pained look of hatred.

"Can't get rid of you, can I?" he asks.

"Many men far better than you have tried, but none of it ever lasted," she answers

Stepping away, she distances herself from him and the corpses littering a circle around him. The smell of the infection and decay is bitter sweet like rotting apples and sour milk. Her stomach churns. A buzzard swoops down a dozen feet away and bites down on an arm and tries to pull it away.

"Where did they all go?"

Red chuckles.

"In the grave most likely. Probably where you would be if I didn't find you out here passed out drunk in the middle of… where the fuck are we?" she asks.

Merchant looks up at the sky and then in all directions.

"How the fuck would I know?"

He grunts as he struggles to get himself off the ground. Knees wobble and his center of balance sways above his feet.

Is he really drunk?

"Well, I'm the one who found you here. I figured you knew where you were going you were in such a hurry to leave."

Rubbing the top of his bald head, Merchant pulls

his bag closer to him and stretches out. The popping of his bones crunches louder than the birds gnawing on the bodies in the distance.

"This is west," he says.

"West? You led us all the way out here to end up in a deserted field?"

Merchant, with the grace of a man sixteen drinks past liver cancer, swings the duffel bag over his shoulder and begins to stagger forward. A crack of thunder in the distance roars like a cannon.

"I'm headed west. This is more west than I was a day ago. Tomorrow, I'll be farther west than I am right now. What part of that doesn't your infected brain understand?"

She watches him go, his confident walk of anger and destiny gone beneath the labored stumble of pain and exhaustion.

"There are a lot of places west of here, Merchant. Wherever it is, you are going is a long way off and at this rate you aren't going to make it."

A wave of the back of his hand is accompanied by a streak of lightning and a boom loud enough to rattle the buzzards back into the air.

"I'll make it. No matter how hard I want to stop, the road won't let me go, Red. Go back to town and those who cured you. You're better off there than with me."

Anger flares in her gut. Stomping the ground dead beneath her feet, she runs up behind him.

"Don't you think I'd be there right now if I wanted to be?"

"What's stopping you? Sure as hell isn't me."

Red punches him in the shoulder and he doesn't

flinch. He hardly cocks his head to the side. Just one foot in front of the other.

"The town needs you," Red says.

Merchant chuckles and shifts the weight on his shoulder across his back.

"I'm fairly certain I'm the last thing that place needs. Go back, Red. A storm is coming, and no one is going to be left out dry when this is all done. Live your life. Enjoy it while you can."

With the strength returning to his legs, Merchant picks up the pace.

"It's not them who needs you, Merchant."

He doesn't slow.

"The town is in danger. Some guys. Real bad ones. Ex-soldiers if I'm guessing right are ready to shoot up the town if someone doesn't stop them."

Merchant keeps walking.

Droplets of water splash in tiny explosions across the dry dirt of the ground leaving craters over the dark soil. A few here and there at first but with each passing moment it begins to turn into a minefield as red splotches lift into the air before falling to the ground to as mud. Red watches the distance between them grow. She doesn't know what to do if she can't convince him to come back with her. The memory of this Logan Barnett creeps into her mind. His wicked smile. That stupid hat of his and the thousand-gun army at his back.

Her palms sweat, and she wants to run back and shoot the man dead herself. But she can't. She isn't Merchant. He's an army himself and without him, the people, her new family, are as good as dead.

Warm streams of rain run down her cheek and she lifts a wet strand of hair away from her eyes. The soft silky feeling on her fingers tickles as she holds it out enough to see it.

Look what they gave her. Asking for nothing in return, she is back to who she was meant to be. The wind howls and lightning flashes across the darkening sky. Empty husks of trees long dead sway beneath the coming storm.

Merchant is already a hazy figure in the distance. His broad shoulders sway as his swagger returns and he quickly becomes a memory. Growling at herself, she cannot give up. If he won't listen to reason, then she'll do whatever it takes to change his mind. Even if she has to threaten to kill him herself, he will come back with her and save the only family she has left in this world.

Because if she doesn't, life itself won't be worth living.

***

The fury of God unleashes across the plains. Red is fairly certain it is barely mid-day and the small fire Merchant is able to start is the only light for miles. Huddling beneath the half-fallen roof of a bomb gutted house, they sit and wait out the storm.

Sheets of water rake across the barren ground, mud splashing in giant waves. The wind howls and the clouds above roll by, angry and determined to destroy everything in their path. Red pulls her knees to her chest and gnaws on the end of a jerky stick.

"Now, I know it's been awhile, but I can't tell you how much I've missed these," she says, her back pressing against chipped drywall and pealing wallpaper.

The dry as death meat cuts at the roof of her mouth and it takes what feels like several minutes of chewing to soften the meal up enough to swallow.

Merchant bites down hard on his own piece and crunches it like dried bone between his teeth.

"You didn't complain when you had to beg for it earlier," he says.

Drawn off into the distance, she watches his eyes as they gaze with an unblinking stare.

"Like I said. I'm not complaining. Though, I always wanted to ask why you never seem to be out of them. It wasn't like we raided a jerky factory every couple of days."

He doesn't turn to her, but he shrugs his shoulders.

"I have enough for what I need."

Red pulls her knees tighter against her chest. A bomb of thunder rattles the floor over their head and dust and debris falls. More drywall and broken plaster. All of it bleached white from the sun. Lightning brightens the sky, and an explosion rips a mushroom cloud from the ground and sends it up into the air.

"Gods are angry today," she mutters.

The jerky turns stale in her mouth. This isn't going to get her anywhere. The more time they waste here, the less time those depending on her will have.

"There are no gods," Merchant says, less to her and what seems more to himself.

"Brother George seems to think differently."

He shifts his weight and lays back against the wall, hands behind his head he closes his eyes.

"They'll all learn soon enough. Eventually this shithole of a world will catch up to them."

Red takes a deep breath.

"See, that's why I'm here, Merchant," she says and turns to face him on her knees. "They are in big trouble. None of them understand what is coming for them. They think God will come down and save them from everything that is out there. Only we can help straighten this before it's too late."

Merchant shifts himself until he's seated upright, back straight against the cold wall.

"What is this we?"

Anger flares in her gut. Insolent asshole doesn't even want to bother.

"I came all the way out to the middle of bumble-fuck nowhere to find you Merchant, and it sure as well wasn't for your great company. We need to help them before it's too late. He said they have a week, and it took me three days to find you."

"We?"

"For Christ's sake, Merchant. I can't help them on my own."

Red is on her feet pacing along the edge of their shelter. Stopping, she plants her fists on her hips.

"And what makes you think I can do anything about it?" Merchant asks.

She doesn't turn to look at him.

"I know what you can do, Merchant. I've seen the blood on your hands. These people can't fight. For fuck's sake they carry around pigs as pets. They'll be slaughtered to the child if no one helps."

Red spins on her heels and he's looking off into the distance.

"Not my problem. I'm no hero if that's what you

think I am."

She growls.

"I don't need a fucking hero you asshole!"

With the side of her boot she kicks a wad of mud and dirt onto him.

"What is it then, Red? Why the fuck did you track me down out here? You had everything you wanted back there. Your health, your life returned. What else could you want? I'm heading west and that is final. You can tag along if you want. It will end your life sooner than you hope, but I'm going where I need to go. They've survived this long without my help, they can keep going on their own."

"Uh! Do I need to spell it out until it sinks into your thick head? I don't want some knight in shining armor. This world would spit and swallow that shit up like it does the poor souls of people like Brother George. We need a killer, Merchant. A cold-hearted bastard who knows how to spill blood and put an end to people who shouldn't still be walking this God-fucked world."

Merchant waves her off.

"If it isn't this person, it'll be the next. What then, Red? Are we going to stay and babysit them until we are old and gone? When the storm clears, I head west. Enough talking."

Pulling his bag closer to his side, Merchant tilts his head back and closes his eyes.

"Uh!" Red storms around their dry island.

Fuck this shit and fuck him!

She stomps out into the storm. Warm water rushes over her body and soaks her to the skin and bone in seconds. Tasting salt on her lips, Red looks to the sky.

Water droplets fall in waves and she closes her eyes as the tears flow freely.

Her hands shake, and she just wants to scream, but it won't do any good. The asshole has made up his mind. She thought she knew him better than this. He fought his way through all those men and that monster of an asshole to save that woman who couldn't have given two shits about him.

Why is this different?

Lightning flashes across the sky in a jagged bolt. Thunder rumbles like angry boots crushing the clouds and she can see more fire in the distance. Not small campfires like theirs, but the harsh glow of something burning that spreads over the horizon. The thought of that little village becoming a smoking ruin spreads its way through her brain.

She can see Brother George and the others burning inside of buildings or being shot down by bloodthirsty men with rifles and no sympathy. Then there is Kelly. A young girl. Not too much unlike she was at that age. So much to learn, maybe with enough teaching she'd become strong enough to make it out here in the wilds. But the image of her body, riddled with bullets lies on the ground at her feet. The mud swirls a dark red and those eyes of hers are blank and staring directly into her soul.

They cry for an answer. Why? Why wasn't she there to save them?

Fury burns through Red's veins and her muscles twitch. She will not have this. He is coming back with her whether he likes it or not. Reaching into the pouch that hangs off her belt, her fingers wrap around the revolver like a glove. Her finger caresses the trigger, and she pulls it free from its cage.

Stomping through the mud like an angry bear, she marches back into the alcove.

"Hey asshole!" she yells.

A shot echoes into the afternoon storm. Thunder answers in giant booms from drums a thousand miles away.

Merchant opens his eyes. He doesn't flinch as the flakes of fading wall settles on his shoulder.

"You're coming with me whether you like it or not."

One eyebrow lifts, but Merchant doesn't answer.

"Next one, I don't miss, asshole. Grab your shit and let's get moving. We don't have any more time to waste."

He doesn't move. A big arm settles on his bag and the fabric crinkles under the weight as it rests against his ribs.

Blood splatters against the wall where the bullet tears through fabric and tissue. Merchant doesn't move. A knot ties itself into her throat as the gunpowder smoke settles in the growing darkness and then unravels as she confirms she isn't that bad of a shot. Only a flesh wound as the bullet barely nicked his coat and only enough to graze him.

"You done yet?" he asks, turning his shoulder to see the thick stream of blood leaking from the open wound.

"What kind of monster are you?" she demands.

Huffing, Red turns back to the storm.

"I'm not sure I even know," he answers.

Tears run down her face again, mixing with the water dripping from her hair.

"I can't leave them behind, Merchant. I don't know how you can. Isn't there any humanity left inside of you?"

Looking back, the man is tending to the cut in his skin and shows no sign he is listening.

"What am I to do, Merchant?"

Red throws herself against the wall and ground beside him. Deep sobs shake her body and her fists rub her eyes so hard they hurt.

"Everybody can't be saved, Red. This is your choice to make. They made theirs and I made mine a lifetime ago. You are the one who has to decide what you are going to do with your life."

She looks at him as he pulls a piece of cloth, torn from the bottom of his canvas jacket, tight around his lower shoulder. He doesn't flinch as the material squeezes into the open flesh and quickly soaks itself red.

"I… I can't do this anymore, Merchant. All I see is their dead faces. If I go back, I'll end up like them. I can't fight off an entire army myself, but…"

Tears cut her words off.

"But what?"

Merchant settles himself against the wall again and closes his eyes.

"There is nothing out there for me either. If I go west with you, what will I find? More death and heartache. They are still alive and all I can see is their deaths following me everywhere. Once we leave, they'll have no chance and I'll never forgive myself."

Her hands are weak and the revolver tips into her lap.

"The pain fades over time. Ghosts can follow you, but the pain and the memory will fade."

Red runs her finger over the curved edge of the weapon's grip.

"I don't think I can live with that, Merchant. Until we met them, I thought my life was nothing but a ticking clock until the infection took me for good. Then they showed me I could have everything back. For once I saw a light in this world I had forgotten ever existed. They gave that to me, Merchant. I can't leave them to die on their own."

"Then don't. Go back. Fight alongside them," he says.

His voice is deep and distant, and it unnerves her.

"They won't fight, Merchant, and I can't just kill myself fighting a battle I know I can't win."

Red turns her head to him and lifts the revolver into her hand. She does not put her finger on the trigger, instead turning it so that she holds it by the barrel. The tears on her face a warm stream that tickles as it makes its way down her neck.

"What is that for?" he asks.

She chuckles. It is a sad and long sound.

"Take it. It's all I have left. Only has three rounds in it, but I figure if you use one to put me out of my misery, then there will be enough to end a couple more infected before you are done. At least with that I can say I helped do something in this God forsaken shit hole."

"Put it away, Red. I'm not going to kill you," Merchant answers and closes his eyes again.

"Do it you stubborn son-of-a-bitch! I can't do it myself and I know you have an ocean of blood on those big hands of yours. What is one last little whore's life going to do to you?"

"I said—"

"I know what you said you piece of shit. Take this gun and kill me as surely as you are all those people back in that village. Because if you won't kill me, then at least take it and help me kill that bastard who is going to murder Kelly and the rest who don't deserve to die!"

Merchant opens his eyes and shifts his body until he is looking at her. His gaze travels from her to the pistol shaking in her hand.

"Your choice, Merchant. It's all I have left in this whole world. Kill me and put me out of my misery or fight alongside me one more time. That is all I ask."

With a sigh, Merchant slides back against the wall.

"Get some rest, Red. We'll move once the storm stops."

"We don't—

Merchant's arm snatches the revolver out of her hand and its on his lap before she can blink.

"If there are as many as you say there are, you're going to need all the rest you can get. Close your eyes and shut your mouth. I have some thinking to do."

Red goes to say something, but the words lock in her throat. He isn't looking at her, but deep down she knows he will not let her speak again. She settles back and closes her eyes. The images of the soon to be dead rush into her mind. But this time they do not hurt as much. If they hurry, maybe they will still have a chance. If only they can get there in time.

Chapter Twelve
A Choice and a Supper

The stink of rot is heavy. Like nothing Kelly has ever smelled before. People scatter in all directions, aimless and going in circles. The rain continues, and small rivers run through the streets.

Her feet are cold as the water sloshes around the insides of her shoes. Pulling her coat tighter across her shoulders, she moves across the street toward the Sick House. Two of Mr. Tarlem's boys stand out front. Big arms bulge beneath wide shoulders, but both are young and keep their eyes locked on the roads leading out of town. They don't even turn to her as she approaches.

She knows it is all for show. Brother George told them to go home, but some of the other men in town, much older than she is, demanded they watch over their newest guest. A wind blows hard against her skin and it bites her down to the bone. The stench does not follow it. She can taste the rot and mold on her tongue. Like week old bread, it sours in her mouth and she spits on the ground.

One of the men, no, boys, looks at her. Too much is on her mind. She should know his name but can't remember and he's hardly a year or two younger than she is. Returning his glare, he turns away and eases to the side of the entrance to the house.

A cough forces its way out of her lungs. Each step and the smell of poison and death chokes out everything. She can practically swim in it. A single candle burns in the room for the sick. A soft golden light flickering its way through an open door and into the empty hallway.

Kelly hears two sets of breathing. One is labored and full of liquid. Bubbles and coughs are wet enough that she can feel it in her own chest. Death is in this room. Its presence looms over the door as darkness pushes down on the single candle burning inside.

Then there is Brother George. He sits beside the dying man. Shoulders hunching forward, he looks years older than she has ever seen him. Deep furrows cut through the dark skin of his forehead and he rocks as he watches over the infected man. A wash cloth twists between his hands as he rolls it back and forth, a wet spot smeared across his lap.

"Brother… Brother George?" she asks.

He doesn't look at her. His eyes do not leave the patient in front of him, but he releases one hand from the towel and waves her in. Slowly, she steps into the room. There are eyes watching her from the corners. She can feel them.

How many times has she come here? A hundred times? Maybe even a thousand?

Now it is foreign to her. A stranger waiting to take her from all those she loves. A small voice in the back of her mind screams for her to forget it all and run back outside, throw herself into the mud and drink up the dirty water. Anything that could possibly cleanse her from the mistake of ever entering this place.

"Are… y… you… O… K?" she stutters as she speaks.

A crooked smile bends the crease of his lips.

"Did you come all this way to check on me, child?" he asks.

Kelly rings out the bottom of her shirt onto the floor. A crack of thunder explodes like a canon and she jumps beside herself. The light of the candle bounces as the little table it sits on rocks.

"I…," she is ashamed to admit it. "Yes, Brother. I did come to check on you."

He sighs and for once turns away from the sick man in front of him. A new and this time soft and gentle smile glows on his face.

"You are also worried about us all, aren't you?"

"They have so many guns, Brother George. What are we going to do if they come back? Can't you heal him?"

She doesn't think, her feet move without any direction and she is by his side kneeling on the floor. His bright eyes look down at her and inside she begs for something to hold on to. Even if it is only enough to get her back out of this room where the darkness of the outside is better than the death that this room has surely become.

"God will provide for us, my daughter," he says and then chuckles. "My daughter. You really have been one for me all these years, haven't you?"

Kelly nods and his smile grows a fraction of an inch.

"Heal him then, Brother. Take away the infection and let him go back with those monsters. Maybe they'll leave us alone."

She takes a firm grip onto the sleeve of his arm. A warm hand pats the top of hers softly.

"If it was only that easy, my love. See, the miracles do not come from me. They are a work of God and his alone. What is the one thing God always asks of us when we have sinned? The only thing that he ever needs from us before we can stand before him."

Rolling back onto the balls of her feet, Kelly looks at the man lying on the table. Infection peels away at over half his body. Flakes of dead skin melt away as black blood seeps from open wounds and some pus filled green liquid crusts across his eyes and at the edges of his mouth. A deep yellow stain weaves its way through his nails like snakes scratching to come out.

"We must ask for forgiveness," she says.

Brother George nods and turns back to his patient.

"And above just asking for forgiveness, Kelly. We must want to be forgiven."

Taking his hand away from hers, he reaches out and places it on the infected's chest. A soft moan comes out as dry lips crack open and small droplets of blood dribble down pale white cheeks.

"Whatever he has done, I'm sure he regrets. Doesn't God know that?"

Lightning flashes in a show of strength and the thunder that follows rattles the roof and floorboards. Gripping the back of the chair, Kelly does everything she can to stop herself from crying.

"God knows everything, my daughter. Even the dark hearts of men cannot be hidden from him. That is why inside, I do not think he wants to be saved."

In shock, Kelly takes a step back.

"What do you mean he doesn't want to be saved? Who would ever want to be a monster like this? He's dying. Are you saying he asked to die?"

Pulling his hand back, Brother George goes back to ringing the wet cloth between his hands.

"No, I don't think he wants to die. Something isn't correct. I don't feel as if the infection is such a burden on his soul. Deep within, there is something else there. A…," Brother George says and then stops with a shake of his head. "Forgive me, Kelly. I'm only rambling because I'm tired."

She tries to smile and feels how fake it must look.

"I understand," she says and puts her hand on his shoulder.

It is so tiny compared to the muscles that sit ridged with tension on the man she has come to call her father. He pats her hand again as he turns back to her.

"Have you had dinner yet?" he asks.

Kelly tries to feel if she is even hungry, but the smallest thought of food turns everything upside down as her nose burns at the mere mention of food. She cannot tell him that.

"No, I haven't," she answers.

"Good. Go round up the others. I'd like us all to sit down tonight and eat together as we discuss the future and how things will be," he says and then with a big sweep of his arm pulls her in against him and the chair for a hug.

"How things will be?" she asks as she pulls away.

"Yes, how things will be, my child. I think no matter what happens with this man, things will not be the same. Let us all come together and talk about what the future holds for us all."

She goes to say some more, but with a shift of his seat he is back to tending to his patient. Kelly turns and watches another flash of lightning cross the sky. The two boys outside cast large shadows that have now found their way inside the door and beneath the dry roof.

Round up the others? She hopes they are hungrier than she is. Because after tonight, they have less than two days left before those men return.

***

Silent dinners are horrible. Especially after an argument or when you're trying to hide something. Sitting in a room with a dozen people with less than a handful of words between them all, the emptiness can be suffocating. Kelly knows this all too well as forks and spoons clack off wooden bowls and grinding teeth. Nothing is said as the soup passes across the single table capable of holding twice as many using both sides. The bread is split amongst all the guests as it moves from one end to the other.

The urge to stand up and demand to know what everyone is going to do is overwhelming. The twelve longest standing members of the church and community are here. A mix of men and women from some of the largest families are gathered and Brother George sits at the center of them all. Head down, gives no notice to those around him. As if he is in another world, he keeps entirely to himself, his eyes locked to a spot some place off in the distance. Very unlike him and it unsettles Kelly to her core.

Even Bert has found his way here. Sitting to the left of his father, Kelly tries not to spare too many glances his way. It is nice knowing she has a friend here. For as much as this whole town is her one big family, nobody is as close to her as he or Brother George are, and at this moment, the latter is as silent as a mouse.

Tink.

Tink.

The tapping of a spoon on a bowl turns them all to the center of the table. Brother George suddenly waits for them all to settle in with their eyes locked on him and he smiles. He sighs loud enough to draw all the air from the room. A sense of relief washes over Kelly and she can see the others shift and relax into their chairs. They do not turn away, but stiff shoulders and arrow straight spines grow soft as they settle in.

"My sons and daughters," he starts, his arms open in warm greeting. "I am thankful that you all have come here tonight. I could not think of a better group of friends and family to share this dinner with."

Everyone voices their agreement as several pick up glasses of beer or water and toast to his good health. With a lifting of his hand, everyone falls back into waiting for him to start over.

"We all know that a danger approaches from the outside, and it is one that without the help of God himself, we are unequipped to handle by ourselves. A man currently lays within the confines of our Sick House and with him he carries the infection that has plagued this world for years. He has been with us now for almost six full days and he has made no progress since joining our community."

He speaks the words that they already know. Kelly looks back and forth between them all. They all know what is happening, why don't we just get to the point?

"You mean being dropped at our feet," Bert's father Harold cuts in. "God tells us, Brother, that we should take in the sick and the weak. Tend to our flock and protect those with the gifts that he gives us, but what of those forced on us as judgement? Is there anything in the good book about what to do when healing a man is done as a test to see who lives and who dies?"

Kelly turns to Brother George who at first does not answer. Heads nod in agreement and some sit with eyes too wide or bloodshot with tears to answer themselves. Meals that are barely touched sit in front of all of them, the steam cooling in the tension filled air. She knows she has barely let a sip pass her lips because this is the only reason she is here.

"The story of our father and his love for us speaks of many trials and judgements, my son. Who are we to speak badly of the newest placed at our feet? How do we know that God has not put this man here himself to show us that the gifts he has given us are not for us to decide who shall be healed and who shouldn't be? Would you have us turn out this man and those who brought him here though God has given us so much by accepting everyone who has come here seeking aid?"

Harold looks back at his plate and spins his spoon around the bowl.

"As you said, Brother. The man is dying. Talking with the nurses, even you yourself haven't been able to do much for the man. We all heard what Mr. Barnett said. If this man is not cured by the time he returns in the next twenty-four hours or so, he will take out his punishment in flesh and blood. What do we do then?"

Kelly remembers the looks on those men's faces. So many guns. An army against the men and women of this town. She thinks of Red, probably the only person there that day that didn't look scared and helpless. But she left. Within an hour of those men riding off back the way they had come, she vanished as quickly as she had arrived. A small bit of anger ignites within her and she doesn't know to be angry or jealous. Pushing it all away, she realizes she wishes Red was here to help them figure out what to do.

"That is why we are here tonight, my son. To discuss what must be done," Brother George adds before he turns back to everyone. "Many things will happen over the next two days and I want us all to be prepared for what will be coming."

"What is coming is death to those who fight and pain for those who remain and wait," Derek adds. He pushes his seat back and pivots to lift himself up, but a soft hand from Mary keeps him in his chair. "I for one do not want to see the consequences of either choice. I say we all pack everything we can and head down river. Mary, I, and the others have traveled out more than a hundred times and the paths are dangerous, but there isn't anything we couldn't get through. We pack and leave by the morning. Those who want to fight can stay and do their best, but those of us strong enough help those who can't will head out at the rising of the sun."

A few more murmurs come from lips unwilling to give full support. Brother George smiles and nods

Derek's way before the man slides his chair back to the table.

"A fine suggestion, my son. Though your heart is in the correct place, I do not see that as an answer for our dilemma. God, our father, put us here on this earth for a purpose. By that I am sure we did not find this village and build it from a pile of dust and weeds for any other purpose than it has served up to this point. If we are to abandon it at the first sign of trouble, then what are we to answer when we question the gifts he has given us?"

Questioning eyes, wide but soft sweep across the room and everyone shies away from his glare. Kelly has no answer. This has been her home for as far as she wants to remember. The thought of abandoning it makes her as sick as the idea of those men and their guns coming for them all.

"Then what, Brother? Do we all sit here and wait for our demise to arrive at sunset? Like sheep waiting to be culled by the wolves?" Harold adds in.

"Wolves and sheep were both put on this world by our father, Harold. Both have survived for centuries and the pain of thinking this will be the end of it all is hard to fathom. Though it may seem so, and I do appreciate your sentiments and ideas, I truly do, this is not why I have gathered you here tonight."

Like an audience stunned into silence, even the sound of breathing stops as they all await his next words. The back of Kelly's throat is dry, and her tongue goes limp as her heart beats against her chest. If they aren't here to discuss what they are going to do about Mr. Barnett and his men, then why are they here?

"I have brought you all here tonight to share this dinner with those that have meant the most to me and shared my secret for the longest of time. We have lived, loved, grown, and died on this land and in the end, this village is who we are. When those men come tomorrow, our visitor will be just as he arrived. We will not fight Mr. Barnett for our father would not have willed it to be so."

"But, Brother…" Kelly blurts out.

His hand raises, and her words are cut short by the look in his eyes. Sad and distant. He knows what is coming, they all know what is coming, and they aren't going to do anything about it.

"I know several of you will have your doubts about God and even more so myself after this night. I ask of you only one thing and that is to trust in me and for the sake of all our people, trust in God our father for one more day. I know and feel the same fear that you all feel at this very moment, but I know there will be a light at the end of the tunnel. What feels like the end will only bring a new beginning for us all. After we end this dinner tonight, I want you all to go home and share with your family these words. God has a purpose for us in this world. Through me, we have seen life and love in a world driven mad by the sins of our people and in the hour of our greatest need, we cannot forget that. Hug your children close. Talk to your neighbor who sits at home right now shaking within the darkness of their own minds. Comfort them with the knowledge that we are not forgotten, and when the sun rises on the second day. This village and its people will still stand."

No one says anything. Kelly can feel the tears running down her cheeks. How could she have ever doubted? The fear and pain of everything is lost behind the sadness that she ever doubted the love of God and Brother George. The others are no different. Every pair of eyes in the room glistens with moisture and shoulders shrug to ward off the sobs that cannot be stopped.

"Now everyone, please take my hand and one more time, let us pray together."

Kelly is glad to feel the warmth of another in her hand. The strength of them all pulses through the connection of flesh and blood. She closes her eyes, and the darkness does not scare her. A comfort passes through and she can feel it flow through her fingertips as the prayer is recited.

Tomorrow will be another day, and no matter what happens, the sun will still rise in the east the following morning. No matter what, she cannot forget that.

Chapter Thirteen
A Cowboy with a Debt

Those eyes stare back at him. Emerald green swirling behind the darkness in dead sockets locked within the hooded confines of hatred. Merchant can still feel the three holes in his chest. He rubs at the spots with his hand as the miles of gravel and dirt pass beneath his boots. The skin of his body is marred by the scars of countless battles, but there is nothing but smooth flesh where he feels the emptiness of that touch.

"You OK over there?" Red asks.

Merchant shakes his head to clear the cobwebs and looks ahead where the storm is a distant memory and the angry revelation of humidity and death swats at them like a vengeful lover. What remains of the mud on the ground sucks at his boots and the bugs feast upon his flesh before falling dead.

"Thinking," he answers.

"Not suddenly regretting what you've agreed to do are you, demon?" Snake-Eyes asks as he materializes between them.

The mud and bugs never seem to notice his ghostly form as he shimmers in his bright white suit and empty skull. Winking, the eyes of the tattoo on his neck leer at him as he chews on a long piece of straw between his teeth and he tips an oversized cowboy hat toward Red who does not see him.

"Thinking of what?" Red asks as she shuffles a few steps forward.

Her walk has improved and so has the demeanor of her attitude. Like a weight has been lifted off her shoulders and found his instead, she walks with the strength of her youth.

"What lays ahead," Merchant says.

"Murder, mayhem, and a whole lot of dead people. Who else are you going to force to follow in your footsteps? Though I gotta say it's getting a little crowded in there," Snake-Eyes says and taps on the bag over Merchant's shoulder.

Unable to stop himself, Merchant spares a quick glance behind and the vision of an army of faceless men and women filling the empty plane shimmers and disappears with the mid-day heat. He shakes his head to clear it once more.

"You said this cowboy had an army with him?"

Red plops her hand on his shoulder.

"OK, not really an army I would say, but at least a dozen or two men. All of them well armed and definitely killers. I haven't seen faces that hardened since the blockades of St. Louis," Red says.

"You were in St. Louis?"

Merchant stops walking and forces Red to look at him.

A mischievous look crosses her face.

"Would it matter to you?"

Merchant doesn't answer or turn. He waits and the look on her face turns worried as she looks back to the east.

"Alright, not really. I saw a lot of the leftovers as people fled in all directions. Everyone talked of the destruction there. Some even spoke of the devil himself rising up beneath the arch and destroying the entire city with a single swipe of his arm."

Spitting on the ground, Merchant turns back toward the path that Red used to find him.

"There is no devil," he grumbles.

"Yeah," she says, her voice less convinced.

"If you count the devil as a single man with a bad attitude and a bag of tricks at his disposal, then yes, I would say it was the devil," Snake-Eyes says.

The ghost taps on the watch shining on his wrist. The arms no longer move, but the clicking of his tongue does enough.

"What was it? On the count of three… Three, two, one… boom. No more St. Louis? And I used to love the sights from the top of that monument back before… well you know. Good place to fuck if you ask me. Screams echo like crazy in that thing and boy, having a woman spread out in front of you as you watch the world bend at your feet. Oh well. At least I still have the memory."

"Shut-up, you weren't even there," Merchant barks.

Red stumbles away, mud splashing up to her knees as she almost falls to the ground.

"Look, I said I wasn't there already. Hector was one of the survivors I found. Told me many stories I didn't believe. Haha, the fucker was deranged as it was, but you don't need to be all pissy about it," Red says.

Merchant waves her off. She wouldn't understand anyway.

"Ghosts talk, Merchant. I wasn't there, but those who were told me everything. They don't forget and I'm pretty sure they want you dead as much if not more than I do. They screamed your name when they died, did you know that? Your name was the last words on their lips and I bet you can hear it at night. You'll never make the city that reaches the sky. We won't let you. You're gonna die out here, Merchant," the ghost taunts.

Shifting the bag on his shoulder doesn't shut the man up, but it does relieve some of the stress on his body.

"You certain that we had until the end of today, correct Red?" Merchant asks and stops walking.

Red moves up beside him.

"Yeah, I'm pretty sure, why?"

From this distance it is pretty hard to tell for someone with even good sight, but for him there is something else in the air. A rotten taste as death passes over the land. Mixed with the sweet and bitter twang of burning wood, he can feel the spilt blood and expended lives. They call to him as much as the crying of those he is forced to drag along on this endless trek across the world.

"What is it, Merchant? I know we've got some distance left, but the day has just started, and we'll easily reach it before sundown."

Red's voice is filled with worry and it should be.

"I think we are too late," Merchant says and hefts the bag as high as it will go across his back.

Beginning to jog, Red bolts ahead of him. He wants to yell at her to stop, they can't just go running into the devil's playground without a plan, but he doesn't need to. Evil pillars of smoke rise slowly over the horizon, dark splatters of burned life against the bright yellow of the sun making its way across the sky.

Red slows her running, and he catches her. Tears are falling faster than rain down her cheeks and her shoulders curl with the pain.

"What happened, Merchant? We still had one more day," Red sobs.

He stands beside her looking at the testaments to destruction and his knuckles crack as he squeezes the strap of the weight upon his shoulders.

"I'm not sure, but we are going to find out," he says.

"Then what?" she says between wet sniffs of tears and emotions.

"I'll be checking in with a cowboy on a debt that needs to be paid."

Merchant begins his slow walk to the village.

***

She approaches in the waning hours of the afternoon. Her hips sway with every step. The type of walk you can't take your eyes off of as her ass dips:

Left.

Right.

Left

A breeze stinking of fire and ash kicks around her bright red hair, but she doesn't seem to notice. Her eyes twinkle and her smile hides a naughty streak just waiting to be let out. The guards shift on their feet. Rifles adjusted across their folded arms, they try to keep their eyes peered to the horizon, but they fail miserably.

Red keeps getting closer.

The one on the left now smiles and taps the other on the shoulder. Forcing a frown, the more disciplined one grunts and steps forward to stop the young woman in her tracks. Red continues until she is all but pressed up against them, her shirt pulled as tight as she can get it. Pointy breasts screaming LOOK AT ME! and working just as planned.

Merchant slips closer from the south. Slowly, his boots tread over gravel and packed dirt with less than the sound of death. His bag hugs him between the shoulders and he draws closer as the two do not see the darkness falling behind them.

"So, what does a girl gotta do to find some fun out in this shit hole?" Red asks.

Both men chuckle as even the one with the smallest amount of brains is trying to get his feel of Red's hips. She returns the favor. A simple touch of her finger runs across each of their arms and they begin to step around her. Like animals circling for the kill, they move to cage her in.

Too late as Merchant slides in behind them.

Death falls quickly on the friendlier of the two. A rock caves his skull in with a wet crack and his body crumples to the ground. Semi-alert, the other turns his head but his jaw cracks as an elbow bloodies his lower lip and sends teeth through flesh. Dust kicks into the air as he tumbles backward and spills to the ground.

Rifle hitting the ground like a toy, Red jumps forward and crushes the bones of his wrist with the back of her boot. Screams come out in a wet gurgle. A second boot to the throat ends the noise and the cracking of bones is all that remains.

"So, what now, big man?" Red asks.

Lifting the unused rifle to her shoulder, she checks the magazine for ammo and slides it back into place. Merchant grabs the first body and pulls it to the nearest scrub brush large enough to hide it for a short time. A long streak of dark black mud trails behind the limp boots, but it doesn't matter. They'll be done before anyone even notices.

"Where do you think they'll keep the survivors?" Merchant asks.

Red turns to the village, the road leading in remaining empty as the buildings trail into the growing darkness.

"Are we sure there are any left?" Red asks, a strange crack in the voice of a woman who has recently killed a man with the back of her boot.

"They wouldn't be guarding an empty village," Merchant says and secures his bag across his back.

He does not pick up a rifle. There is no need to, yet. She nods and steps ahead to lead him in.

"Last time they corralled everyone to the church in the center of the town. It's the biggest building they have so anyone still alive is probably huddling there."

"I remember where it is. You make your way there as quietly as you can," Merchant orders and slips toward the shadows that lead outside of town.

She stops and turns to him.

"What are you going to do?" she asks.

Flowing in a seductive glow only moments before, the freckles on her cheeks and the dark circles forming under her worried eyes reminds him just how young she really is.

"Don't worry. I have a cowboy to find and it's better I do this alone."

Red nods and moves the shadows of the first building.

Merchant does not follow. Turning his pace from a slow walk to a jog, he follows the town south and then east with the sun behind him. Pillars of smoke still climb high into the air and he can hear a wailing in the distance.

At first it sounds like an animal calling for its lost mate. Mixed with the hungry calls of the night's hunters, the sound is disturbing in its familiarity. Whole cities were reduced to rubble and broken camps during the war and this one is no different. Fewer people, no bombs, but in the end a shattered existence for anyone lucky enough to survive.

Gripping the strap pulling tight against the skin of his shoulder, he knows the bitter taste of that word, survive. No one really survives these outcomes. Their bodies still breathe, their hearts still beat, but parts of them die when their world is shattered by the realities of this sick world. People weren't meant to survive this. Death should have claimed them all.

Merchant feels the weight grow heavier as movement catches his eye.

Death is coming to claim them all.

In a crouch he darts in between an outhouse and the home that once used it. Voices carry into the lengthening evening. Harsh words mixed with the calmness of a trained killer. Sinking further into the shadows, Merchant waits. The heavy cloth of his bag slides from his body and he places it on the ground. The weight of the world off of him, he flexes the muscles of his legs and prepares to jump.

Two men again. Shoulder to shoulder, one holds his weapon loosely and the other straps his across his chest. They do not see what hits them. A freight train with no breaks, Merchant cracks the first in the temple with a fist that shuts the lights off in an instant.

Surprisingly, the second reacts better than the rest. With a spin, the barrel of his rifle turns and gets a round off before Merchant barrels into him. The shot tears through cloth and air but hits no flesh. Big arms wrapped around, Merchant squeezes as hard as he can. Joints pop along the smaller man's back, but he is undeterred. Teeth snapping, he cracks his forehead into Merchant's nose.

A flash of light and stars everywhere, Merchant's knees go weak and he stumbles as the man slips from his grasp. Rifle comes back up. Fire erupts and the loud crack echoes into the night.

Smoke rises from the empty barrel and the burning metal sears dark flesh, but the angry lead does not hit its target. Regaining his footing, Merchant keeps his arm extended and lifts the front of the rifle up as he extends himself to his full height.

The guard tries to pull away, but it is no use. Cemented in place, the weapon will not budge, and the man's eyes go wide. He stumbles backward. Rifle forgotten, he turns to run but his boots catch on scrub grass and his ankle twists. With a yelp he hits the ground with a clap against the hardening soil.

Merchant flips the weapon around.

Rolling to his back, the man looks up with a plea

of mercy. Fingers and palms dig into the ground as his lips go dry and he licks them.

"P… P… Pl," he starts.

A bullet liquifies his brains and shatters the back of his skull as it exits and sends a dark puff of mud and gravel into the air.

More gunshots echo into the night. Further into the village, there is more return fire than there is attacking. Merchant eyes his bag and the dark sky overhead. A red fire burns in the west, long orange flames flickering across the empty plains as the sun falls for the night and the white purifying light of the moon clears its way for the ghosts and the demons.

Screams and more gunfire. The village is turning into a war zone before they know it. Finding a knife and ending the man who grumbles as his mind clears, Merchant takes what he can carry. His bag and his burden will have to wait where they are.

He doesn't have far to go, and no one will find it while he is away. Men will die tonight and if he finds him, this Mr. Barnett will be the last of them.

Chapter Fourteen
All is Lost and Nothing Changes

The shadows are long and the pain is deep. Orange fire spits and hisses as a couple of houses burn filling the air with the stench of smoke and death. Sobs and wails call into the night and the pain of loss and uselessness are chains holding hands where they are and rooting feet in the place.

Red looks down at the congregation huddled before the church. Shadows and dirt, soot from smoke and wet blood creates ghosts of them all as they pull each other close in fear and desperation. The smell of spent gunpowder tickles its way across her nose before the silent steps of the large man stepping beside her.

"You get them all, Merchant?" she asks.

She doesn't look at him. His presence presses down on her easier than his massive frame towering over her.

"If any remain, they will be dead by morning. A few tracks lead out into the darkness. The infected will pick them off," he answers.

Red fights back a sob looking down at the uncontrolled crying and pleas for help as the two of them stand before the group, their words lost to anguish and hostility.

"There isn't an infected for miles. Doesn't matter. That cowboy, Barnett. Did you find him?"

A rifle settles on Merchant's shoulder and the smell of fresh blood coats him like a cologne.

"Fat man, big hat, impressive belt buckle?"

She nods.

"Wasn't here. These were soldiers and hardened men. Ex-cons most likely. Nothing like you described."

"Bastard never even showed up."

Merchant nods his head. She doesn't need him to answer.

A board snaps from a broken roof and crashes to the ground with a crack like thunder. Women and children scream as they pull each other tighter.

"Look what they did to us!" some of the survivors scream.

It is hard to distinguish any of them from each other. Their minds are hardly working and Red fights back the urge to yell at them to shut the fuck up and think for a God-damn second. A wail echoes into the night as another succumbs to his injuries. The pain of the loss unbearable as an older woman covers the corpse like a shroud with her body. More reach over to comfort her but she swats them away.

Red has had enough.

"All right. Who is going to tell us what the hell happened here?" she barks.

Eyes swollen with fear and pain stare at her. At least those who still care enough to not want to die right where they sit. She hardly recognizes any of them. Too many inside too little of a space.

"Look, we got rid of them. You are all safe now. Can anyone tell us what happened?"

The middle of the pile begins to pull away. A dark

figure steps forward and for a moment Merchant steps between her and the newcomer, but quickly, he steps back.

Brother George.

Eyes swollen barely above being closed. Fresh blood drips from his lips and his walk carries a heavy limp. He is no longer the imposing man he was.

Defeated.

Worn.

Aged.

He is almost as dead as those laying on the ground. With a slow turn he regards his congregation with a mournful look and then comes back.

"Mr. Barnett sent his men to collect their charge. He was no better than he had been when they left." A sob shakes the man's body, and he almost falls with the buckling of his knee. A man goes to step forward and help him, but he is waved off with the back of a hand. "Truthfully, I believe they would have done this even if the man had been cured of the disease."

Red looks around at the surrounding eyes all bleeding red with pain and misery.

"What did they do? Why didn't you fight back?" she asks.

Brother George snorts and winces as a few bubbles of blood burst from the corner of his lips.

"Fight them with what? They have guns and we have prayer. We are not like you, Red, or Mr. Merchant here. Our best defense is our faith in the lord above. When these men were told we could not cure their friend, they dragged his sorry soul in front of us all. The infection was taking over his mind, and they gave us one more chance to cure him. We… I could not do it. They slit his throat right where you stand and then said their orders were to take the cost of this man's life in flesh if we did not pay up. I offered myself in sacrifice," a true smile lifts the man's face temporarily. "But our family here would not have that. These lost souls opened fire as some tried to defend me. In the end it was a futile effort as those with the courage to fight lost their lives and they still took their payment in my blood mixed with those of these good men and women."

Red turns to Merchant who looks at them all with a face of stone. The anger boiling her blood spills over as she chambers another round into her newly acquired rifle.

"This is what you get, Brother, for trusting the safety of your people to your god! Prayer and faith do not stop bullets," she screams and pounds her feet into the ground as she pulls up short of the huddled mass of shaken people. "The only thing that stops them is making sure they are dead before they can hurt you."

Looking over them all, Red finally catches a glimpse of someone she truly recognizes. Kelly, her long hair matted with blood and her face shiny in the moonlight where tears soak her from eyes well past her collar. Blood spots darken her shirt as she cradles the head of a young man across her legs. Skin gone pale she recognizes the chubby friend of hers with the stubborn pig.

He looks peaceful. A streak of brown stretches from neck to ear, but if not for the pooling wound of darkness stretching over the hole in his chest, she could almost guess he was sleeping.

Kelly's eyes look up to her. A fire burns silently behind that look. Hidden and consumed with grief there is a fight there, but it's being smothered.

Fear.

Torment.

Loss.

All of it is crushing the life of this young girl.

"We could do nothing else," Brother George says and steps toward her. A dark hand clamps down on his shoulder and holds him tight.

Good thing, because if he had gotten any closer, she was going to ram the working end of her rifle into his gut and show him his god once and for all.

"Nothing? You mean stand here like a bunch of fucking paper targets for men who are already trained to kill? You could have fought. You could have run. Something other than just waiting here to fucking die!"

Red wheels around and kicks at the dirt. A puff lifts into the air and coyotes call into the middle of the night. Without a moment to think she lifts her rifle and fires a half dozen rounds into the darkness. The howls of the roaming beasts stop, but the crying behind her takes on a new cadence. This one wilder as those closest to her scramble back toward the broken doorway of the church.

"Red," Merchant says.

She spins back on him. Finger on the trigger she's ready to kill anything that moves.

This was her family. The closest thing she has ever had to one in years and now it's been cut down like a wounded dog. A dozen or more of them are dead. Their lives spent for nothing and what of those that remain? Lives are broken just as easy as their hearts stop beating. They will never be the same. This village will never be the same.

No, this is not her home. With a heavy breath she looks up at Merchant. Part of her hates the thought, but there is a hidden voice that says otherwise. Nothing out in this empty wasteland will ever be home. Everything changes in a world lost to chaos. Only one thing in her short life has stayed the same so far and he stands right in front of her. A monster with a death wish, and a bag that one day she will take from him. She tries not to smile.

"Merchant," she whispers. Her shoulders are too tired, and she lets them drop as the fire in her blood cools fast and drains her of everything. Brother George nods and goes back to those that need him the most. "What are we going to do?"

The big man steps up to her. In the darkness he is a featureless monster of bulk and height. Within those shadows the whites of his eyes glow brighter than the moon itself.

"You wanted Mr. Barnett to pay for what he has done. He is not here," Merchant says.

"It's too late, Merchant. What can we do? He's already destroyed everything these people have."

Strength gone, Red sinks down into a crouch and tries not to watch the sobbing Kelly wipe away the soft hair from her friends closed eyes.

"He is still out there. Regardless of how they feel, these people are still alive, and he will return. You know that. They know that."

With a deep breath she looks up at him. His face is

expressionless, and he turns to the east and the shadows that cover the distance beyond.

"You're going to go after him, aren't you?"

He turns back to her and shifts the rifle he holds over his shoulder.

"I don't have any other choice."

Red takes one last look at Kelly and then a quick glance at the others. So much blood spilled and so much pain that will not go away for a long time. Dark mounds fill the shadows where the men they have already killed wait lifeless on the ground.

"No reason to stay here and do nothing," she says. Pushing herself back to standing, she puts her hand on Merchant's chest. The warmth there is enough to melt away even the deepest of cold. "We have a date with Mr. Barnett and I feel it would be most kind of us to show up on time."

Merchant nods.

Red shoulders her rifle and leads Merchant away from the collection. Eventually they'll find the strength to get up and rise above the loss. Tonight, will not be the night. There is nothing she can do for them. Patience and forgiveness are not in her nature and neither is grieving. The heavy boots of Merchant follow right behind her as she leads them to the empty rooms outside the Sick House.

No, she cannot forgive nor forget. And in the morning, they will make their way to this Mr. Barnett. He may be a rich man in this world, but he has a debt to pay, and she is going to be the one collecting.

***

The ghosts of the night do not fade quickly. A blood red sun rises in the east and the smell of smoldering lumber and gunpowder hangs in the air. The wind is too weak, nor does it care enough to try to carry it away. The smell of warming bread and cooking sausages is rancid with the stench of death coating everything from one corner of town to the other.

A world broken must move on. Lives do not stop where the hearts of loved ones fall silent. Tears dry. Nightmares persist. The pain fades but is never forgotten.

Red steps out onto the porch across from the Sick House and takes a deep breath. Even the wood beneath her boots creaks and groans with agony. Her body is sore. A throb aches between her shoulders and her neck and no matter of rubbing will ease it. The joints of her fingers are stiff and painful. The rifle on her shoulder is heavier than Merchant's bag and she regrets how long it has been since she used one of these.

She spits on the ground. A lingering taste of metal and bile burning her tongue. The killing comes easy. Bodies drop, and she stays on her feet. If there is a God upstairs with a plan, she wonders if this is what she was meant for. Dried dirt and blood cake beneath her fingernails. The fight from last night took more out of her than she expected, and her hands shake, but a fist hides it all away.

Empty streets whistle in the early morning and they go on forever in all directions. No dogs. No people. The only living souls visible are the dark shadows of the birds that circle overhead.

Where is Merchant?

She considers going in and knocking on the door to his room. Maybe he could still be asleep? She doubts it. The man can fight for an entire day and still be up before the break of dawn. No, she won't have him beat.

A quick thought sends a cold shiver down her spine and sickens her stomach. The doorframe struggles to hold her up, but it succeeds none-the-less.

What happens if he left without her? Would he do that? The acidic taste of vomit fills the back of her throat. Of course he would.

He has one thing on his mind and that is going west. Dumb fucking bastard. Him and that need to reach the city that touches the sky. What kind of fucking shit hole place is that, anyway?

Red hacks back the phlegm from her throat and sends it splashing into the dirt of the road. He went west didn't he? Anger spikes within her and she grips her rifle like it's the only thing holding her to humanity itself.

"Fuck him," she grumbles.

If the bastard left her behind, he can go fuck himself. She'll do this the hard way. Shoulders back, stiffness and sore muscles forgotten, Red heads into the center of town and toward the church.

Everyone will be there. They haven't buried their dead yet and Brother George talked all night about having a full day service for each of the fallen. What was the point? Dead corpses can't hear your words and if there really is a Heaven, they sure as well don't give two shits about what you say once they are worm food.

She spits on the ground again as the anger turns into a sour mess between her teeth. The church stands like an ugly pillar beneath the darkened shadows of the town. The bell does not ring, and the holes ripped open across its face are as sorry looking as they are dreadful. Black soot stains the blue paint where the bastards tried to burn the place down and the scars will not leave this place as they won't leave those who survived.

"Red!" Kelly shouts as she steps outside the open doors.

Young and naïve. Wet streaks from her eyes have turned into swollen cheeks and hair that resembles the mess of dried, brittle grass that piles beneath porches. The half smile on her face is the happiest thing Red has seen in what feels like ages.

"Everyone here already?" Red asks.

An adjustment of her rifle brings the teen up short as her eyes widen and stare at the weapon like it's about to go off in her face.

"Um… no," she says without her eyes moving.

A hesitant step keeps a small distance between them. Red reaches over and puts her hand on the girl's shoulder. Turning her around she starts them heading back to the church.

"Who's missing?"

The tension melts away from Kelly's shoulders and she counts a few numbers beneath her breath.

"Some of the surviving men and women refuse to come. They say they are packing their bags and heading to the river. They are going to follow it south and see where it leads them."

Reaching the front of the church, Red can hear voices whispering inside and the air hangs heavy with the smell of incense.

"Anyone else?"

Kelly shakes her head before peeking into the gloom inside.

"Those who are staying are arguing what we need to do next. Some want to collect what guns we have and get ready to fight should Mr. Barnett and his men return," Kelly whispers.

"And the others?" Red asks.

She knows the answer. Against all hopes she has to ask, but the regret of wasting her breath isn't lost at all. Kelly kicks at pebbles sending them rolling across the road.

"Most trust in Brother George. He says the Lord will take care of us all. They will follow him to the end of the world, Red," Kelly whimpers.

Red squeezes her shoulder and sits. The young girl turns to look down at her, dark storm clouds circling the poor child's head and tears heavier than rain falling from her bloodshot eyes.

"What do you believe, Kelly?"

With a snort, the girl's eyes flicker into the church and then back.

"I… I don't know. He's been like a father to me. Ever since I arrived here, he has kept me… us all safe."

"Until now," Red finishes the sentence.

She pats the spot on the porch beside her and waits for Kelly to sit down. It feels like forever, but slowly, Kelly finds her spot.

"Until now. I'm… I'm not sure I can do it anymore, Red."

With a soft but firm embrace, Red pulls the girl closer.

"I understand," she says. "There aren't many people

left in this world anyone can trust. It's pretty fucked up out there. Look where it got me."

Kelly shifts away and returns a look of wide eyes and confusion.

"Where it got you? You are here with us after all you have been through. If it wasn't for you and Mr. Merchant, we'd all be dead right now, or worse."

Red scoffs before spitting on the ground in disgust.

"Yeah, me and that bastard. Damn idiot left the first moment he got. Like I said, Kelly. Don't trust anyone in this world. They may help you out when it suits them the most, but everyone will look for a way to stab you in the back when they get the chance."

Kelly's lips move but nothing comes out. Looking off into the distance she slides back against Red and leans in for comfort and strength.

"I'm guessing you are right. You've seen a lot more than I have of this world. Please promise me you'll come back when you are finished, will you?"

Now it's time for Red to be confused. Turning and pulling away from the Kelly, Red is lost for words.

"What are you talking about?" she asks.

Kelly's eyes trace the road away from the church and leading out of town.

"Mr. Merchant. When I saw him this morning, he told me to let you sleep. Said you'd catch up to him soon enough. I begged him to stay, but he said there was no time to waste and that it was better he finds out what lays ahead of you two before you came in and messed everything up."

"Wait, what? Where did he go?"

Red is on her feet and looking both directions. Inside

she knows there isn't a chance she'll actually see him, but for some reason she can't stop herself from looking for the dust cloud behind the monster of a man's boots.

"He left town and headed east toward where Mr. Barnett and his men went. Brother George and a few of the others tried to talk him out of it, but Mr. Merchant stopped them cold without saying a word. I begged him not to go, but he said he had to. Said something about a debt that had to be paid and that once you were rested, I was to tell you where he went."

Heart beating faster than ever, Red can't hide the smile forming across her face. Palms sweaty and muscles aching to run, her mind spins with the possibilities.

"That crazy bastard didn't leave me behind after all," Red whispers to herself.

"About two hours ago," Kelly says.

Red turns and looks back down at her naïve friend.

"He did leave you behind. About two hours ago to be exact," she says again and points to the road leading east.

A chuckle breaks itself loose and Red feels all the tension in her body leave a moment before the fire inside her belly ignites once more.

"I'll catch up to him," she says with a wicked looking sneer on her face. "Merchant and I have some unfinished business with Mr. Barnett."

Running her fingers through Kelly's hair, Red smiles one more time and turns to walk away. She's ready to run. Merchant is big and will cover a lot of ground, but he won't get there before she finds him.

"Will you come back?" Kelly asks, rising to her feet as shadows begin to move within the darkness of the church.

"Soon enough, my friend," Red calls back.

Rocks kick up beneath her feet as she begins to jog. She has a monster to kill and an even bigger one to unleash. The fire behind her eyes is unmistakable as she leaves the town behind her.

Chapter Fifteen
A Home Without a Welcome Mat

They described it as a fortress. A haven for those willing to live under the boot and law of a crazed man.

It definitely is a fortress, but one built in the middle of a crater. Scorched land stretches for hundreds of yards in all directions. Blackened by fire and expended powder, bones stick out in gestures of defiance in their sun-bleached glory.

All around, the world is ablaze and angry. The smell of war and death sits heavy in the air. Acidic and painful with each breath, the dark clouds hanging over the city roll across the sky but do not leave.

Thunder rolls in the distance. A drumming that falls across the land in heavy waves that wash the sound of life away. A bolt of lightning streaks across the afternoon and ignites the ozone with a pop.

Death is not a visitor here. It is a welcome sight among the other secrets this place holds. Merchant can feel it where he watches from a safe distance. Bodies begin not far down the single road leading to New Frontier. Desiccated from heat and disease, the corpses are almost comical. Torn to pieces by weapons and madness. He leans against the cold husk of an Oak; the life drained away when this land gave up years ago and looks down where his prey waits for him.

"It's a god-damn battlefield down there," Red says.

She steps up beside him and wipes away the thick dust streaked across her forehead. Her hair is matted against her head and the cheeks beneath her intense glare are brighter than the blazing fire pushing its way through the deep clouds.

"A killing field," Merchant says. "Look at the path of the stones. Narrowing as they get closer. Draws them to a single point and crossed lanes of fire kills them before they ever get a chance."

Smart tactic. Someone there knows what they are doing. Red scratches at her head and looks to consider the idea.

She shrugs.

"Fucking dumb infected. Would run into a wall of bullets if it meant they had a chance at a single bite," she says.

Pulling her rifle off her shoulder, she checks the ammunition for the thousandth time since they took up residence here some half mile from the walled-in city. Merchant shifts his own burden across his shoulder and watches as a few buzzards circle in the air high above. Slow deliberate movements. They wait for the coming night when there will be more to eat. Fresh kill. Not this rotting mess left to petrify across the empty plains of Nebraska.

"Something drives them here," he adds and Red turns his way as if she had forgotten he was even there. "They may be crazed but look how many of them there are."

He points, and she follows his line of sight. There must be hundreds upon hundreds of bodies in some state of burial or decay between them and the metal barrier. Flesh pulled from bone and bones broken into points from bullets and bombs.

"What would that matter? Once they know there is food nothing will stop them except a bullet to the brain."

Merchant shakes his head. She should already know this, but something has her crazed. Is she turning again?

"The smell is too thick and the distance too far. Even if led here, the stench of their own dead would drive them away. I can't believe the people there can stand it themselves."

Red nods and wipes at her own nose.

"You have that right. Bastards are going to pay for all of this," she says before throwing herself against the nearest tree trunk, the bark braking away into dust, and slipping to the ground. "Do we really need to wait till sundown?"

He takes another look at the sky. The shadows are lengthening and the land just beyond New Frontier is slipping behind a curtain of haze and darkness.

"We have a better chance at dusk. My guess is they are preparing for another onslaught this evening when the sun falls. If we approach just before the fight starts, they'll be too busy and startled to bother with us. If we are lucky, they'll just let us in without too much of a fuss."

She spits on the ground and he watches her knuckles go white as she grinds her palm into the grip of the rifle. A loose cannon. He'd have been better off leaving her behind, but this isn't a fight he can do alone. She knows who they search for. He'd have to kill everyone to be certain, and best to avoid that if he can.

"You better be correct. That bastard Barnett is in there and I don't want to lose our shot out in the middle of a desert full of infected."

Merchant shakes his head. Too anxious, too dangerous. But she is correct. The time is near.

A cold chill rustles the brittle branches around them, an old sound, sharp and piercing.

"Really going to walk right into the open maw, aren't you?" Snake-Eyes asks.

His voice appears moments before the blue smoke molds itself from dry leaves and the ghost pulls itself together next to him. Merchant doesn't turn to look. He's seen enough of those never sleeping eyes and hollow brained skull.

"It's not too late to stop and keep going that way," Snake-Eyes says and points in the opposite direction.

That is different. Merchant turns and eyes the ghost who greets him with a smile and a wink of those damn snakes tattooed into his neck.

"Taking to caring?" Merchant whispers.

Snake-Eyes grasps at his chest and stumbles backward.

"Disrespect! To think you believe that I do not care about your well-being, Merchant. And after all we have been through?"

A wicked smile creases his translucent face.

"Who are you talking to?" Red asks.

Merchant ignores her and steps toward the ghost. Leaves crack beneath his boots and thunder explodes overhead.

"You know something, don't you?" he asks louder than he intended.

Something is amiss here, and he is having none of it.

"With you? Everything is amiss, but I'm just saying. Give the stupid bitch back her pistol and let's be on our way. If we hurry, we could be back on the highway by sunrise and this place would be nothing but a bad memory."

"Merchant... everything, OK?" Red asks again and moves to lift herself from the ground.

"Speak now or I'll find a way to end you like Barnett when I find him," Merchant growls.

The hollow gaps in Snake-Eye's head look for support but there is nothing but them in this desolate world. Skin bobs between the eyes of the tattoo and if he wasn't so angry, Merchant would swear the fucking thing just blinked away fear.

"I'm... I'm just not certain going in there is a good idea," Snake-Eyes says.

"You can't be certain of anything. You're dead and if you don't stop wasting my time, I don't care what I have to do, but I'll make sure you end up deader than you already are."

Red grabs his shoulder and tries to pull him around. She would have a better chance ripping the trees from the ground than moving him. With a shrug he pushes her off.

"Hey, you bastard. Are you fucking losing it?"

A single finger lifts in front of her face and she falls silent. The hand before her does not waver.

"You are out of time," Merchant threatens.

Snake-Eyes pulls at the collar of his perfectly white shirt and licks at his perfectly white teeth.

"There is more down there than this Barnett," Snake-Eyes starts. Merchant stiffens and turns toward the fortress. The sky quickly turning to a velvet smothering the receding red flames. "I can feel it and every part of me says we can't be down there."

"We?"

The ghost moves up beside him. "It's waiting. Whatever is down there wants us there. I... I can't explain it, but I can feel it. If this was just a city full of infected, I'd revel in the idea of watching you torn bit by bit. The escape would be orgasmic, and you know how much I love a good orgasm."

"You're not going all shady on me, are you?" Red asks and steps beside him. Her rifle is in her hand and she keeps a measured distance between them.

Merchant gives her a quick glance but then turns back to the walled enemy.

"We are going," he growls and shifts his bag on his shoulder.

"Last chance, Merchant," Snake-Eyes pleads. "If you go down there, neither of us are leaving, you bastard. I wasn't meant to live trapped in such a place!"

"You're dead, you asshole," Merchant groans.

"He sure will be," Red adds and readies her rifle.

Merchant doesn't correct her. His eyes scan the distance before them. A killing field. A death trap. Exactly where he is meant to be.

***

The doors are barred from the inside. At least twenty feet tall, it's a castle built in the middle of a crater and they are little more than ants beside a thousand tons of steel and rock. Heads stand at attention from corner tower to corner. A dozen or more rifles all trained on them.

A calmness settles over Merchant. His heart slows where anyone else's would speed up. His hands loosen, and the weight of his burden lessens as the shadow of the fortress settles over him.

Death to his rear. Pain and suffering before him. Red and her nervousness more explosive than a bomb ready to explode beside him. He can feel her anger. Disarmed before they reached the door, she is pissed, and he may be lucky he had her drop the rifle.

There are plenty inside to be had. He knows this. She knows this. In the end, she still said he can go fuck himself.

Good, she's finally thinking straight. Snake-Eyes is gone. Like the weight of his burden, he can no longer feel the hatred from the vile man. This is worrisome, but it's too late for that.

Merchant waits.

The darkness closes in as the last of the sunlight ignites the horizon behind the fortress with an explosive burst and then is gone. They will soon be here.

"State your name and your purpose," a voice calls down from the top of the wall.

No emotion, all business. Almost as if it was an everyday occurrence.

"This is Red. My name is Merchant," he answers. There is no reason to give what is not given. Not if these are soldiers like those they left to rot back at the village.

Boots shuffle and he can still feel the barrels of enough weapons to fight a war aimed at his chest.

"Your purpose, and don't make me ask again or we'll open you up where you stand," the man command with more bravado than is necessary when speaking a dozen to two.

Hefting his bag higher onto his shoulder, Merchant looks at Red and then back to the nameless heads above.

"Traveling west, we are looking for shelter. We need the rest and if we are lucky maybe even trade for some supplies. We've put a lot of distance behind us and could really use a roof over our heads for the evening."

Nothing in response.

"Infected aren't too far behind. We are unarmed and if you don't let us in, we'll die out here no matter what."

Lightening streaks across the blackness of the sky and the dead forest behind them is a mass hovering and waiting to attack. The shadows move, and he knows they are running out of time.

"You're out of luck partner. Night is here, and we do not open the doors once the sun is down. If you are lucky you can stay out ahead of them. Keep away from the forest edge and do not look back. By the grace of God, they'll be too busy fighting us and you might have a chance," the voice calls down to them.

Merchant growls but not enough for them to hear. These bastards don't let anyone in. He glances back the way they had come and the white bones of the dead spread from the ground like a graveyard.

How many of these were people looking for shelter?

There is no way to tell. The dead are the dead, infected or not. Once the bullets and bombs take you, everything is the same. A sense of vile hatred warms in his belly. He will find a way in. One way or the other he will find a way in and this Mr. Barnett will not be the only one he has a word with.

"If there is going to be a fight, let us be a part of it. But at least give us a chance. Let us in and we'll gladly stand by your side and fight these monsters."

He tries another tactic. The emptiness that fills up between them reveals he hit a nerve. Maybe one sensitive enough to work.

"You a soldier?" the man above asks.

Merchant looks at Red. Her eyes are trained on the mops of hair and hats poking out from above the protection of the top.

"Nope," Merchant lies. "Was raised on a farm back in Pennsylvania. Was pretty good with a rifle though. Have had to kill plenty of these beasts since then, but never out in the open like this."

Another grip of hesitation and Red begins to grind her heels into the ground. A bull ready to charge. He puts a hand on her shoulder and she shrugs it away. They better answer quick. Her leash is growing shorter by the moment.

"Still can't do it, son. Orders are orders. It's how we stay alive back here. Get a move on. Your time is running out."

That's it. There will be no more pleading. He can feel any further argument will not be answered unless it's with a hot piece of lead.

"Come on, Red. We need to get moving," Merchant says and puts a hand on her shoulder again. This time with a firmer grip.

With a small tug he works to move her toward the far corner of the fortress wall, so they can put some distance between them and the incoming army. He can already hear their wails of anguish and hunger. The sound of rustling branches and snapping limbs are not far behind.

"No! I will not leave!" Red loses the fight against her anger.

Eyes radiating a fury not seen in a millennium, she yanks away her arm and stomps her feet back to the front gates.

"Open these god-damn doors, now!" she demands.

There is movement above them, but no one answers.

"Did you not hear me, you pencil dicked assholes? Open these fucking doors!"

A shot rings out and a hand sized crater fractures the caked dirt beside Red's boots.

"We'll find another way," Merchant says.

He's just as mad as she is and has no intention of leaving but waiting out front until they kindly change their minds is no answer for either one of them. His hand covers her shoulder, and he pulls her back toward him. With the swat of her hand she shoves him away.

"Listen you bastards, I have a message for Logan Barnett," Red yells and this time gets a wall of silence.

They are listening. That is good if not too late. Merchant turns to look at the forest behind him, but it is nothing but an impenetrable shadow.

Nope, this is not good.

"Ah, you know who I'm talking about," she mocks. "Tell that bastard that I know the secret of Morninglight. If he doesn't let us in, the secret dies with us."

Defiantly, Red crosses her arms and waits. The commotion above takes on a frantic murmur and the heads become a blur across the top of the wall. Merchant lets his eyes move from the wall to the shadows of the forest behind them. They are closer. Much too close and he clenches the muscles in his arms.

The ground vibrates at his feet and their time is up. Anger flairs and he drops his bag. Fuck these men and fuck the infected. He doesn't have time for this. Wheeling around, the first of the monsters breaks through the darkness, eyes glaring a feline yellow of jaundice and disease.

"Red!" he yells.

An inhuman call echoes as more break through the void. It's a mad rush of every sight and sound ever seen. Some are sickly and stumble to keep their footing as they crash through the grave yard. Others are injured and hobbled as bones protrude from joints at weird angles but not enough to stop them. Blood and pus drips from open wounds and nails and teeth slash for their first taste of blood.

The majority though are fresh and fast. They overtake the front rows as Merchant and Red come into view. A few of them glance at the walls above. Most do not bother. There is fresh meat ahead and they want the first bite.

A symphony of shots rings out. First the song of war starts with the tiniest of pitter-patters. Pops that drop the charging wave followed by wails and screams of anguish. Then the chorus kicks in and the storm is a tidal wave of destruction. Bright lights flash from the cover of the walls and bodies drop in quick succession.

Skin is torn from bone and muscle is ripped as metal penetrates and liquifies tissue as it cuts its murderous path. Heads explode. Guts spill and the dry caked pan of earth they stand on quickly turns into a churning bog of blood and guts. The bullets and training of the defenders are not enough. Many get through. The first unlucky bastard runs directly into the waiting arms of Merchant and ends with a crushed spine and an unnatural posture after hitting the ground.

A sickly one leaves the large shadow of death behind and goes for the glowing pale white of his companion. Knife in hand, a throat is cut, and guts open before a finger even touches Red's body. Two more stumble on as bullets pass through but hit nothing vital as they spring on their prey.

Merchant grabs both like dolls and drives their skulls together. Teeth and blood splatter on impact and the sound of cracking bone is brittle and short. The dead weight falls at his feet and the orchestra above takes on a fervent pitch. Weapons he hasn't seen or heard in years open up as the sea of monsters before them push further ahead.

There isn't enough to keep them all at bay. Merchant and Red give ground as more bodies drop before them. Red drips with blood, a little of hers and more of theirs. Merchant is covered in gore and droppings. He does not waver as his strength and anger build. Another gets through and its throat is out and sent flying back into the mass of hysteria and hunger.

The wall looms behind them.

Massive.

Imposing.

Impenetrable.

They cannot get inside and running is impossible. Even if they try, they would just be caught. Merchant spares a glance at Red and she waits like a cat pushed into a corner. Knees bent, feet dug into the ground. The knife in her hand is as dark as the bits of entrails glistening their way up to her elbow. The other has its claws out. She sways from foot to foot, but she is not as quick to attack. The next infected that comes within reach, she does not jump on. She waits and lets it run into her and die before it can catch her. Stepping over its prone form, he can see where her leg buckles slightly on the left side.

Red is hurt.

Another breaks through, ignoring Merchant the monster veers towards the girl. Merchant grabs its long hair, chunks ripping away but enough still stretching to stop it in its tracks. Wrapping his arm around its neck he squeezes until he hears the bones pop and the last gasp of air escapes its lungs. Twisting, he feels the warm gushes of blood as he rips the head from the creature's shoulders.

The gunfire continues and now a few explosions send bits of unidentifiable pieces high into the air. Tiny suns, bursting and fading in the blink of an eye, rain mud and gore all around.

Merchant turns and hurls his newest prize as high as he can. The head rolls over itself as it arcs over the top of the wall. He can hear the shouts over the gunfire. They are as distinguishable to him as his own heartbeat. Three more explosions rip the word in two and this time they are close enough to force Merchant and Red back to the wall.

They are trapped. Cold rock and welded metal press against them. The nearest monsters try to charge but a minor thought makes them hesitate. Most die in this moment as gunfire chews them apart. Those who have given up the fight with the two meals sitting directly for them make their last valiant attempt with the wall itself. Trying desperately to find a handhold, fingers claw and bleed as they dig into the solid surface.

Cries of hunger and anguish call out as there are more failed attempts than successful. They die by the score. A small countless number near the top only to touch their skin to the hot end of a barrel before the explosion sends their brains spraying out on those below them.

"What are we going to do?" Red screams with little breath.

He doesn't know. Several have already found their way around the corner of the wall and have tried to come in behind them. More cuts are open and actively bleeding across Red's body and even he has been torn in several places. The fire of the injuries ignites his blood, but he knows it is slowing her down.

"Try to get behind me," he orders.

They can't do this all night. He has killed many in his life, but not an entire army by himself. Kicking at his bag, he feels the contents inside rattle but there is nothing that will help. They are on their own. A small chuckle tickles his throat as he feels her push up behind him.

Side by side they fight surrounded by the plague that haunts this world. He always knew this miserable existence would end sooner or later. He just didn't think it would be standing out in front of a locked gate without getting the chance to finish one last job.

Such irony.

He chuckles again as two more bite and tear their way to him. Bones break, and breath chokes out as they die at his feet. A mountain of bodies begins to build in front of the fortress. Blood and shadows swirl all around them and there is no room left to fight. They can feel the hands reaching out for them. Sharp nails and diseased fingers pulling them in.

The doors of the impenetrable walls groan as they slide open and the roar of a bear rips through the night. Bright beams of light burn the eyes of the nearest infected and the charge of a thousand horses comes to life as the nearest are flattened beneath the spinning tires of an armored truck.

"Get your asses inside!" the man from up top yells. "He's making one pass and then these doors shut for good."

Merchant does not hesitate. Scooping up Red wand his bag, he's through the opening as the head of an infected explodes, leaving his back warm and wet. The defenders of New Frontier cover their retreat with marked precision and in moments the truck returns, glorified by the carnage dripping from every panel and the doors are slammed shut behind them.

Chapter Sixteen
Restraint is in Order

The doors slam shut with a resounding, finality. Metal screaming as gears grind and there isn't enough oil left in this world to ever hope they are to open again. Men circle, guns are pointed, and the engine of the vehicle from hell growls with discontent. Bits of gore drop from its armor plating. A scarlet paint of infected meat and rotting innards smear across its outer shell and splatter away as the windshield is wiped clean by wipers dotting everyone standing beside the killing machine. A heavy gun, almost longer than she is tall, turns their direction and the masked man standing behind it fingers the trigger.

Red refuses to back away. Merchant stands beside her, his presence a steadying rock. A need to kill flows through her deeper than the blood in her veins. She can see those tears and the cries of anguish that drove her here. Every man now surrounding her is Logan Barnett. His face belongs to every one of them and she'll rip them off until she is certain she got the correct one.

A feral growl slips from her lips and a heavy weight drops on her shoulder. She turns her head. It's Merchant and the slightest shake of his head tells her this isn't the time. Her hands ball into fists and he can go fuck himself. She feels naked without that rifle he took from her. Ass out and blowing in the wind, she is exposed and surrounded by the enemy. It doesn't matter. All she needs to do is get her fingers on a single one of these bastards and she'll clean this house out of all of its rats.

More men climb down from the wall. All of them look hard and angry. Scars paint faces beneath darkened circles that tell stories of long nights and unforgiving days. Ruffled beards, balding heads, and uniforms tattered with age and use. They are hungry for something. She imagines its rest and a life away from this, but this world is fucked up and where else are they going to go?

The wails and hunger cries from outside die down and the sporadic pops of gun fire fade into memory. She can count at least twenty of them. Numbers was never her strong suit and there are definitely more than she has fingers and toes.

Fuck it. None of it matters. There is only one reason she is here, and that is Logan Barnett. Where is that asshole?

"You two don't know just how lucky you are, do you?" the commanding voice from before asks.

Red and Merchant turn as the men surrounding them part and one individual approaches. He does not carry any weapons in his hands. Why would he? There is so much lead already pointed at them, they'd end up killing half of themselves if they all decided to fire.

"How about you enlighten us, ass…" Red starts before Merchant steps up between them.

"I'm not sure we would have made it much longer if it wasn't for your assistance, Mr.?" Merchant asks.

The stranger stops at the edge of the guarded circle. Grey hair peppers the dark hair that sticks out from beneath his army issued hate and the uniform of fatigues are stretched around his fit frame for a man who looks more than twenty years passed his prime.

"Sergeant Halton. CO of this group of fine men. Been fighting here in New Freedom going on four years now," Sergeant Halton says but does not come closer. Neither do his men lower their weapons. "I've seen many things in my time here. All kinds of nightmares and beasts charging relentlessly at these walls. My men and I have killed more than we would possibly count, but tonight is a first."

The soldier rubs the tip of his chin with a hand and looks around at those circling before returning to Merchant and her.

"Sure was a lot of them out there. More than you expected?" Merchant says.

Red grinds her teeth and wants to spit at the man and demand to talk to Logan now. There is no need to waste any more time chit chatting like a pack of old hens. She is here for one reason only.

"Numbers hardly matter to the infected, though, I will agree that over the last several months there seems to be even more of them than before. Doesn't matter. They could send a million and my boys and I would hold them back. Wouldn't we?"

A cheer of the men rises into the air and several fire a round or two into the night before settling their weapons back with the barrels pointed straight at her chest. Oh, what she wouldn't do for her rifle back.

"See the thing here is, you two," Sergeant Halton

starts again. "I know what it takes to survive out there in the wilds. I've spent enough of my life running and hiding. Killing and hunting. Anything to keep myself alive. Here with our fortifications, training, and probably the last weapons on this very Earth, each man standing beside me is worth a thousand infected. They outnumber us, but their minds are gone. Madness has driven them to the brink of death and they welcome it when it comes. But out there," he waves to the walls of sharp metal and the deadly grounds beyond, "I would say the best of them is worth maybe ten. Fifteen if we aren't caught off guard. Not you two though. That was something special."

The soldier eyes Merchant as he takes a step closer. Not enough to be within arm's length, but still inside the protective circle of his men. She can see his eyes moving up and down the big man's body. She almost wants to laugh. He has no idea just how close he is to his own death.

"People will do what they have to when backed against a wall," Merchant says as if he doesn't notice a single thing.

He shifts that bag of his higher upon his shoulder and she knows he's growing agitated. He does that when he's close to pouncing and someone is close to being a corpse.

"Backed against a wall?" Halton chuckles and pats the nearest soldier on his shoulder, maybe catching the message in Merchant's movements. "You two had nowhere to go and would have died if it wasn't for us, but by the lord above, how many would you have killed in the process? One hundred? Two maybe? I've never seen such work with my own eyes. You're ex-army, aren't you? Maybe even special forces?"

The smile on Halton's face is lit up like a torch and he's animated like a child. Merchant does not answer. Still, the smile grows.

"Come on, you have to be. Maybe even black-ops. Trained killers, those men. I've heard stories of the things they did. Yeah…," Halton trails off and looks at the men surrounding them. "I've heard those stories and if you weren't one of them, you sure should have been."

Merchant is a stone, and she is losing her patience.

"What about her? She doesn't look like black-ops to me," one of the soldiers says.

Red growls and can already see the look on the man's face as she rips his still beating heart from his chest. A smile tugs at the corner of her lips.

"A friend maybe?" Halton asks. He takes a step closer and her palms grow wet. She can already feel his blood between her fingers. "A lover perhaps."

He draws out the final S and Merchant steps up. Several rifles echo with the sound of rounds readying in their chambers.

"She travels with me. I've already told you we are headed west. Where she wants to go when we reach there is up to her. Until then, what happens to her, happens to me," Merchant cuts in, his voice low and the meaning loud.

Halton looks up at Merchant's face towering over his own.

"Yeah, your travel buddy. I read you loud and clear," he says and backs up to put a layer of his men between him and them. "Well, at this point in the night, you will be staying here with us. You can rest and when the sun comes up, we'll see about you getting back on the road."

The soldier turns to leave, but those surrounding them do not move.

"What about Logan?" Red blurts out.

Merchant reaches out to pull her behind him, but she side steps it easily. Several men change position to clear their path to her. She doesn't care. Halton stops moving, and she has what she wants.

"Oh, he'll probably want to see you soon enough, my lady. You wouldn't be here and alive if it wasn't so," Halton says. Without turning he begins his trek toward the middle of the fortress, mumbling to himself. "Black-ops. I never thought I'd live to see the day."

Several of the surrounding soldiers begin to back away, a path clearing in a direction toward the interior, but not where Halton is headed.

"What the fuck are you doing?" Merchant asks, his voice a surprisingly low hiss.

Red does not care. She waves him away and begins the march down the path they are being shown. None of this bullshit matters. They do not need rest. If they are going to be pushed out by morning, she has only tonight to finish the job. Merchant has her gun and the strength, but if he isn't going to finish the job, then she sure as hell will.

***

Night is not as dark here as it is in the rest of the world. Fires burn on torches and candles and even a few light bulbs flicker with the hum of electricity. A chugging clears the night air, a slow sound off in the distance carrying with it the smell of old diesel and the taste of lead.

Red paces in front of the barred window. Light filters in with an off-white hew and she digs her nails into the palms of her hands. There is a guard outside the front door of their confined room. Besides the stench of the air, she can feel the humidity squeezing itself against her skin and Merchant's dark personae sitting quietly in the furthest corner is not helping anything.

"Do you have to sit there like that?" she demands.

Merchant's eyes open, the contours of his face lost to shadow but the whites of his eyes as clear as a midday sun.

"Would you prefer I follow in the steps you are burning into the ground?"

She stops and regards the flat brown carpet beneath her boots. Dulled by age or use, the threadbare covering doesn't move as she scuffs a toe across and there are more than a dozen stains in the small area illuminated by the outdoor lights.

"You could do something! Maybe try and think of something that will get the job done," she demands and goes back to pacing.

Even if she was burning a hole in the carpet, she wouldn't fucking care.

"Believe me or not, I am doing something," he answers.

She cannot hold back the small chuckle.

"What? Collecting dust while that asshole sits out there and makes us wait?"

Frustrated, she slams her fist into the wall beside the window and the glass shakes. The shadow of the men guarding the door shift and she catches the man's face as he looks in. She gives him her best smile and his eyes travel as low as the window will allow.

He finds her middle finger pointed right at him. She doesn't care when he goes back to his seat.

"You don't think there is any way they remember you?" Merchant asks.

Red stops her pacing but doesn't look at him.

"Not a fucking chance. They were too busy playing footsie with the good old Brother George back there and those who didn't give two shits about the holy man were spending too much time looking at the girls a lot younger than myself. Whole fucking crew needs to take a dirt nap."

She spits on the ground and kicks at the wet spot. Fucking dust covered carpet.

"Good because someone is coming," Merchant says.

Red looks his way but then spins as the lock on the door begins to turn.

Halton and two of his goons stand in the doorway, their silhouette darkened by the lights behind them.

"Mr. Barnett will see you now," Halton says.

Stepping out of the way, his men back up leaving the door wide open. Red makes it to the portal first with Merchant on her heels.

"Just the lady, for now," Halton says with his hand up and the barrels of two rifles following the trail of his arm. "Mr. Barnett finds there to be no reason you both need to come since it was the lady who said she carries the secrets he needs. I assure you, Mr. Merchant, that no harm will come to your friend. I implore you to remain and rest. Let my men know if you need anything and they will oblige you where they are capable."

Merchant gives her a look, his frame stretching within the door, and she nods without saying a word. His eyes narrow but he backs into the room and lets the shadows fill in around him before they shut the door.

She turns to Halton and does her best to ignore the four men with rifles surrounding them.

"Where do we go from here?" she asks.

The smile on Halton's face warms his tired features and the guards slide back as they move out onto the road.

"He's waiting for you in his guest house. Was anxious to meet you once he got word that you have what he has been seeking for so long."

Red lets the questions in her mind go on hold as they make their way through tight streets tucked between dark and cold structures. Like the walls that surround them, everything is made of reclaimed and re-purposed metal. Sharp edges cut into the jagged holes of the ground and high above they resemble spikes waiting for heads to be put out for display. A million rusted knives slicing at the cold world giving the whole fortress the feeling of an angry mob.

Dark smoke lifts into the air above fires and the sound of engines grows louder. A soot darkens the edges of her shirt where the blood has dried brown and heavy. She can see the thinnest of layers covering her skin where they let her wash away the blood of the infected as she waited for them.

"Took him long enough to come and get me if he really needed it so badly," she says.

At first, he does not answer. Hands in pants pocket, he's content with walking beside her, his men shadows following their every move.

"He's a busy man. Plus, we needed to make sure you were the real deal. Can't just let anyone in through our front door just because they promise to pay their way, now can we?"

Red can feel more eyes watching as they continue along.

"And he is sure now?" she asks.

"As sure as he will ever be. Can't know anything for certain anymore, but Mr. Barnett is a calculating man. He's been weighing the odds since the moment you neared our gate."

"Let me guess. The odds are not in my favor," Red says.

Halton chuckles.

"On the contrary, my beautiful friend. They could not be any better," he replies with the sweep of his arm and a twinkle in his somber eyes. "If we felt you were lying, you and your big friend would already be dead. Black-ops or not, your friend looks like he's one hardened man, but flesh is flesh and, in the end, we all will die."

Red basks in the revelation that he doesn't know he may have never spoken more true words in his life.

"And you are ready to die defending this man?" Red asks.

The softer look on Halton's face hardens into a rock. He stares straight ahead.

"I will die defending my men and my home. Do not get me wrong. Mr. Barnett is a generous employer, when the need arises, but he, like everyone else, is just a man. These soldiers you see with us, they are the real deal. Fighters every one of them. Their blood runs so those that live here may rise to see another day. I do not take their sacrifice lightly, and neither should you."

Red nods her head in agreement. The buildings with their murderous points and unwelcoming glare continue as they turn this way and that. Any attempt to keep track of where they are was forgotten roads ago. She can do nothing but hope that Merchant will find his own way in the end. A small smile creeps its way to the corner of her lips. The vision of Barnett's death already plays behind her eyes.

"How many people live here, Halton?" she asks, trying to soften the mood once again.

A relaxed look returns to his face and his stride lengthens into a confident and relaxed walk.

"Exactly two thousand, six hundred, and forty-three. Women and children make up a large portion of our population as any man capable of bearing arms is conscripted into the defense of the city. Sadly, it keeps the population of the young soldiers at a declining rate, but we do our best to mitigate the losses where we can."

She stares hard into his face and a chuckle echoes as he drops his head back into a laugh.

"Don't look at me like that. This world isn't going to repopulate itself and no one is forced to do anything they don't want to. We have strict laws and punishment here. Murder, rape, abuse, or anything not within the culture we aim to cultivate here will find a swift end outside those gates. This is a harsh world here, Red. People must do what they can to survive. You and your big friend should know that first hand by the way you two handle yourselves. I doubt the blood soaking into your shirt is the first you've ever spilt."

Red pulls at the cloth clinging to the skin of her chest. She smells like iron and filth, but it won't be the last time. She'll deal with it a little longer as long as it's Barnett's in the end.

"Does terrorizing a small village not count as going against your culture?" she asks.

Halton stops and turns to her. His men without hesitation work their way around and she is surrounded.

"There are those in this world who would work to keep things from the greater good. Who has the right to keep things from others who would see that knowledge used for the good of everyone? No Red, terrorizing small villages are not what we do here. Seeking truth in a world lost beneath a blanket of death and despair is all any one of us can hope for. As for those you speak of, we tried our best to be reasonable. Am I finding myself believing that you think otherwise?"

Turning on his heels like a good soldier, Red is forced to catch up.

"Curious that is all. I was there one of the times you stopped into town."

"And after that?"

She looks at the soldiers hemming her in and none of them spare her a glance. Fingers itch near triggers and she turns back to Halton.

"Merchant and I left. As we said, we are headed west. Easiest way to do that is follow the interstate."

"You were a bit south of that, weren't you," Halton adds without emotion.

"Washed down the river by accident. All we care about is getting back on our path and I figured that maybe a little help wouldn't hurt along the way."

Halton stops again.

"A little help?"

It is time for her to smile.

"Now, you wouldn't expect me to come all the way here with the one thing your Mr. Barnett has been looking for without expecting some kind of payment? What kind of woman do you take me for, Halton?"

A wicked smile crosses his face.

"Smart. I thought from the moment I watched you cut down those infected that there was something special about you."

Following the older soldier, they turn down a wider corridor made of piled metal and hollow sounding containers. The road opens into a path capable of allowing the vehicles she had seen them use. The ground at her feet rises slowly at first and then faster. Up ahead the jagged lines of the city and its hidden denizens gives way to an elaborate structure that fits in with this place as much as snow in August.

Metal shingles sit in neat rows over a high-pitched roof that stretches for at least a thousand feet. Walls of mortared stone sit squat with high pressed windows of real glass and three chimneys slowly churn a white smoke into the dark night. Beneath the poisonous stench of the fortress hangs the sweet smell of pine.

Red turns to Halton, who is now all business as he climbs the wide steps toward the front of the 'guest house.'

"Barnett lives here?" she asks.

A nod is all she gets in return.

Climbing the shallow steps two at a time, they stop at the front where two guards, body armor and helmets making them look more like machines than human, converse with Halton before opening the double doors and letting them in.

Where the outside is all torture and pain, the inside is something she has not seen in a very long time. Soft carpet cushions her steps and the warm air of a burning fire tickles her chest. The heat is not stifling, and the walls are plastered with paper a comforting shade of blue. High above, the roof sits pitched into darkness, yet the shadows remain at bay with the presence of burning candles, a crackling fire in the front room, and the one thing she has not seen in almost as far as she can remember.

Electricity.

Lightbulbs are bright beneath dark red canvas shades filling everything with a soft glow. Cushioned chairs are arranged lazily and always within reach. This is a home of a king. Without noticing, Red realizes her mouth is watering.

She licks her lips.

Is that the smell of cooking meat? The pains of hunger bite at her stomach. All she has had since she left to search for Merchant is dried meat stored in Merchant's jacket pocket. Two strangers exit the nearest door, dressed in the cleanest whites she has seen outside of Brother George's Sick House, and without a single glance they enter another room where the aroma of food is overpowering.

The sweet taste of vegetables hits her like a hammer to the gut. Another grumble escapes, and she covers her abdomen with her hand.

Keep your wits about you!

She bites down on her tongue. This is not how she can act. These are not her friends, and this is for certain not her home. They took her home from her and that is why she is here. A fire tries to flare deep in her belly but is quickly extinguished with the thought of warm soup and a cold drink. She balls her hands into fists.

Can… not… forget.

"Follow me this way," Halton says.

Red's eyes snap open. She never even realized they were closed. She nods and steps up behind him. They move deeper into the building, the hallways long and decorated with paintings beginning to show their signs of age. Fading corners and colors washing into one another. She isn't one for art because there really isn't any reason for it anymore, but the slow approach of decay is inevitable. No matter how men try, this world will catch up to them all.

"He's right inside," Halton says as he steps to the side of a closed door.

Painted white and large enough to dwarf even Merchant, the entrance to whatever lays beyond is as magnificent as it is gaudy. Red rolls her shoulders back. Her palms are wet, and the strength of her fingers has fled with the hopes and dreams of everyone outside this city. This is her shot. For Kelly. For everyone back in Morninglight.

She'll have to get Merchant after. If she survives. With a quick glance at Halton waiting beside her, the quick thought of what happens after enters her mind. Just as quickly, she shoves it away. No time for that.

The hinges give a gentle creak as the portal pushes inward. A cool air sweeps out and trusses the hair in front of her eyes and on her neck. The darkness inside is thick and majestic where it isn't broken by soft candle light stretched along the back wall.

A single chair sits in the very center of the room. High backed and elegant in its resemblance of a king's throne, there is no movement that she can see. Red takes a deep breath to settle herself. She steps in and the door swings shut behind her, a finality in the crack of wood on frame. A shiver runs down her spine and she flexes her fingers to stop the shaking.

Another deep breath.

Her heart pounds and a pain pierces her head.

"You're not exactly what I expected," Barnett's voice says.

Red grinds her teeth.

"And what were you expecting? Groveling at your feet?"

The anger that brought her here flairs, hot and wild. An urge to charge the back of the chair, fists flying, and nails clawing is overwhelming, but she fights it back.

"Ha! Ha. No, I always wondered what a person willing to turn over the lives of others would look like. They come in so many different sizes and shapes, yet most are not as pretty as you."

A shadow shifts from the front of the chair.

"I think you've done enough with those people already," Red says and starts to circle around from behind.

Only one chance at this. Take it now or she'll never get another one.

"I heard my men did a good job showing those in that pitiful little town that I meant business. Why does it take so much for people to learn? Do I look like a liar?"

Barnett pushes his way away from where he is seated, and he is much larger than she remembers. His neck like a tree trunk and his shoulders darkening half the candles. Red hesitates.

"An asshole is more like it," she says. "Those men and women did not deserve what you did, and it is time someone taught you a lesson."

He chuckles again, a short and uncaring sound.

"I bet you think you are the one to do it?"

Red growls.

"What about your big friend? Think he's ready for what we have in store for him?"

She is locked where she stands.

"Yeah, we know who you are. Don't think we didn't before we let you in. Did Brother George, isn't that what he calls himself, send you?"

Red steps forward, fists coming up. Barnett puts his hand up in a placating gesture, but with no other movements.

"No, I'm guessing he didn't. A man of the cloth like him wouldn't send a couple of killers, now would he? That is what you are, aren't you? A pair of killers with a lot of blood on those pretty hands of yours."

She has had enough. Too much talking, too much time wasted.

"Time for you to find out, you fucking piece of..." Red begins to shout, but the rest comes out in a wet slur.

Lightning shoots through her body and tears at muscles and joints before she crashes to the ground. Her body convulses out of her control as the light of the candles and torches dance in her blurring vision. Pain like nothing she has ever felt pulses through her body and spreads like cold ice from her shoulder.

Two shadows lean down above her, blackened behind shadow and the water that runs freely from her eyes. The taste of salt and bile foams in her mouth. Her tongue is swollen, and she can barely breathe.

"We have so much planned for you two," Barnett says. She cannot make out the other. The pain intensifies, and her left arm goes numb and dead. "Not nearly as much as we have for those stupid simple people back in Morninglight. They'll pay dearly for this, but not before you and your friend do, my dear. Not before you do."

A hand the size of the world comes slowly down to her face, and for a moment she can smell the stench of decay and rot. Strong and pungent, Red chokes as the world flashes in a blinding green light and her thoughts flee to the back of her mind.

Chapter Seventeen
Should Have Come Alone

Little changes in the darkness. Merchant sits and waits. The air around remains cold and the bench seat digs deep into the back of his legs. Uncomfortable and annoying.

He lets the discomfort settle into his mood and keep it churning. Pulling at his bag as it sits next to him, it's light and practically empty. The sound of pieces of plastic tapping against each other rattles and he doesn't bother looking. Whatever this is cannot be good.

Taking a deep breath, he looks to the light outside. Hours have passed. No way to tell how many, but Red has been gone too long. He can feel the darkness fading. Soon a new day will rise and any chance they have of completing this and moving on will have passed.

With a grunt, Merchant gets up and moves to the door. There are at least two men still out there. He's listened to their useless conversations and banter about the roundness of Red's ass to no end except that they have a week's rations of honey biscuits riding on that the one named Luther would last longer than Alex once they got Red back to their rooms.

No better time than now.

He knocks on the door. Three quick hollow thuds and the door rattles in its frame.

"What you need, big man?" Luther asks, his voice carrying a small chuckle.

"I could take a piss if you two could show me where an outhouse is," Merchant says.

Both men chuckle again at some unseen joke.

"Why don't you just go in the corner?" Alex asks.

Merchant sighs.

"Your boss said to ask you two for anything I might need. Well, I need to piss."

A little shuffling on the other side of the barrier.

"Maybe he did, maybe he didn't. Whose word is he going to take, yours or ours?" Luther asks, his voice louder and closer to the door.

The flap on top of Merchant's bag opens with a click and he reaches for the bottom. Hesitation staggers him for a moment, but not enough to stop as his hand finds what he is looking for.

"Look, I just need to piss. Real quick. Around the corner and back. I'm not sure how long it will take Red to work out a deal with your boss, but I'd rather not be sitting here wasting time in my own piss," Merchant says.

Another small chuckle.

"Guess you're out of luck, partner," Luther adds, his voice right up against the door.

Merchant kicks his heavy boot behind the handle and wood splinters into the air as it swings open. He hears a wet thump of a sound and a body hits the ground hard.

"What the..." Alex starts to say and silences as he rounds the edge of the door frame.

A bullet explodes through the back of his skull and he drops hard and fast.

Luther crawls backward. His jaw works through soundless words and his hands claw at the ground, his rifle more than an arm's length away and forgotten.

"But... but...," he is finally able to get out.

Merchant towers over him and drives his foot into the man's groin. Another gust of breath and the soldier rolls up with the pain and pressure. Hands on ear and chin, Merchant spins and the man's neck snaps like a dry twig.

Voices begin to call across this end of the fortress. No alarms, yet. Hopefully they thought it was another infected coming too close to the wall. Pulling both bodies, Merchant places them inside his cell and works quickly to reset the door. It won't shut but it doesn't need to. The men inside won't be looking for a way out anytime soon.

Stepping out onto the road, there is still no one around looking for the source of the gunfire.

Strange.

Merchant shrugs and keeps to the shadows. Red and that bastard Halton went toward the center of the fortress. From the description, this Mr. Barnett is not a simple man. He won't live in one of these small salvaged structures. He's too important for that.

Bag bouncing lightly over his shoulder, Merchant begins to jog and lets the warming of his muscles flow through his body. All he has to do is find the largest building in this place. That shouldn't be hard.

If it is, there is more than one way to smoke out a tyrant and fingering the trigger of his newly found rifle, he knows exactly how to do it.

***

Wide, flat, and guarded like a palace. Six guards, three going north and the other two going south, march in trained paths. Two more remain stationed near an entrance.

Yep, he's found Mr. Barnett and Red if she's still alive. He hasn't seen any sign of movement going in or out of the building since stumbling upon it and the horizon to the east is shifting from a cobalt blue to a light pink.

The sun will be up, and this will be a lot harder than it should be.

Sounds of engines revving and voices carry farther in the late evening air. Patrols are more frequent this close to Barnett and the shadows are much thinner.

Merchant checks his rifle. Seventeen rounds and that is it. Not much to storm in with, but he's had less and done more with it. Securing his load across his back, he shoulders the weapon and steps out. Maybe they won't even notice him until it is too late.

The roar of an engine like a dozen angry bears flairs up behind him and he's forced against the sharp cold wall of a storage hut. Metal creaks as it struggles to hold him and the vehicle blasts past with the soldier manning the mounted rifle on the back hanging on for dear life.

Dust kicks up into the air leaving an easy trail to follow. Merchant steps out behind. He watches as the driver makes for a direct path to the target. Men shuffle and brace as the big tires skid to a stop in front of the porch and door.

Scanning the road behind, he watches as the driver jumps from his seat and races inside.

He's been discovered, or at least they found those two dead men taking his place. Merchant's heart steadies. Edging forward, keeping his shoulder against the sturdy wall and his presence in the darkness, he waits for the alarms that are sure to come.

A lifeless silence hangs in the air, a blanket over the hum of engines and fires in the distance that have become their entire world. Less than two hundred yards separate him and the guards out front, yet they have shown no sign that they have spotted him.

Good luck for once.

With a crash, the front entrance slams open and men spill out like rats fleeing a sinking ship. The driver heads back and jumps into the driver seat followed by the one person who refuses to run. Shoulders back and everyone else scattering around him, it's Halton, and Merchant can see that from here.

The engine roars a cry for battle and dust spits as the tires spin. Those stationed at guard remain as those who come pouring out head around the corner and are lost to the darkness. More engines fire up and come alive.

A mechanical thunder rumbles the ground and lights flicker to life on both sides. Bursting from the shadows, Merchant watches as armored cars and trucks spill out and circle the front before turning down the path that leads directly to him.

Stepping back, he moves until he slides around the nearest corner. It's a tight fit. His chest rubs against the sharp corners of a wall and his shoulders pinch against rusted edges as the weathered metal bends. He can taste the aged oil as it fills his nose and chokes in the back of his throat.

The vehicles close the distance in a few heartbeats and without slowing they are gone. Eyes of hard men glare as weapons remain held at the ready and they all look like they are going to war.

A look he is familiar with, he hasn't seen it in a long time. One he recognizes from another life.

Merchant waits for the sound of the army to fade. The vibration at his boots is gone and what little time he has left will soon be closing if he does not move quickly.

Shouldering his rifle, he steps out and turns toward the front of the place he seeks. There will be no sneaking this night. There is no other choice.

Both guards stiffen as he approaches. His boots clacking on the gravel road, but neither give warning. Who would approach at this hour? Locked behind their protective walls, there is nothing they cannot control. Merchant smiles, a curling of his lips that is barely noticeable.

"Who are you? State your orders, soldier," the guard to the right of the door asks.

Merchant does not answer. He shakes his head, rubbing at his ear, he again shakes his head and then taps twice with the palm of his hand.

"I said state your purpose, soldier. You have a problem hearing?"

Impatient, the guard steps away from the door and the other slides directly in front to protect against any intrusion. Professional. Well trained. Merchant is impressed even if it is not enough.

Tapping at his ear again, Merchant waits until the man is within arm's reach.

"Stop right where you are," the soldier commands.

Merchant looks up and whatever his face says, the man is a half second too late. A fist crushes the man's throat, his breath coughing out in wet chunks. The man's knees begin to buckle but Merchant grabs him under the shoulder and steadies him.

The one behind doesn't move. His partner wavers regardless of Merchant's grip. Ripping the man's side-arm from its holster, he presses it deep into the man's belly. Not much of a suppressor, but it will do.

Two shots rip through the man's midsection. One hits the target in the left hip and the other explodes against the doorframe, wood chips flying everywhere.

"What the f—" the guard starts to scream.

Merchant drops the dead one on the ground and clears the short distance between them in the blink of an eye. One hand squeezes around the man's cursing lips and the other drives a fist into his gut.

Air explodes, and tears run down his eyes. Merchant takes a hold of throat and soft flesh and starts to squeeze. Tongue flaps and lips call out, but there is no room for escape. His eyes race and he beats at Merchant's shoulders and arms.

The light behind his eyes begins to fade. The bone deep in his neck begins to crack under tightening fingers. A small pop sends the man into convulsions. His life is over.

Looking around, there is no one in sight. Testing the door, it is not locked. Cracking it open, the inside is quiet and dark.

Good.

Merchant eases the entry open enough to fit himself and the two corpses in with him.

Still silent. His luck is holding out.

Bunching both men into the nearest corner, he moves slowly down the hall. Everything feels empty here. The shadows are heavy and in no race to leave. Candles burn in distant corners and the air is thick and old.

He puts his rifle down against a darkened doorway and crouches as he moves as silent as a ghost. A shadow swimming within the sea of his own kind. Merchant fingers the trigger of the stolen pistol, and he lets the warmth of Red's revolver press against his back.

The further he moves into the building, the colder and more humid it gets. Windows are darkened by heavy curtains, keeping the quickly approaching morning at bay. Thick carpet muffles any noise his steps may make, and the building is far deeper than he would have expected.

Where is everyone?

That could not have been them all racing out like they did. Even if it was, they will be back soon enough. Those two lying dead in his cell won't be hard to find.

A whimper brings him up short. Was that Red?

Another calls from the end of the hall. Now it is a few sobs. This has to be her. They must have caught her. Merchant lets the fire in his blood cool his nerves.

This is his job to finish. She set him on this course. She should have let him do it himself.

Silently, he makes it down to the end of the hall. All shadows and empty paintings. Memories of a world lost to the past. All doors up to this one are locked with not a single sign of life behind them. For a big man, hungry on power, this Mr. Barnett does not display it except for here.

Merchant pulls up short before the giant double doors. High arches of white with gold plated hinges and matching handles. Twin candle sconces flicker in the shadows as he waits on the wrong side.

Another set of whimpers calls from the other side. Even if this Barnett is not in there, Red has to be. He'll get her free and then finish this job before it gets them both.

Slowly, he tests the handle, and it turns easily beneath his grip. The gears click and there is little noise.

The whimpering turns into a gasp that is suddenly cut off. Merchant slips in through the door and slides it shut behind him.

Shadows fill in around and he edges toward the nearest corner. A dozen candles burn in the far corners, their flames tiny as it nears the bottom of their holders.

A figure moves in the dimming light. Not towards him, but also not enough for him to make it out.

Merchant places his bag on the ground behind him. He grips the pistol tighter and moves out from the darkness. He cannot see who it is, and with his vision if he doesn't see them, they cannot make him out either.

Another sob.

Merchant's heart quickens.

"Red, is that you?" he asks.

A short, soft sob. Merchant edges closer. A body lies on the floor. Curled up into the fetal position, the figure is slender and long, but there is strength there even though it cradles its head like a child.

"Red, it's going to be OK. I'm going to get you out of here," Merchant whispers.

Nothing stops him as he approaches. It is definitely Red. Her bright hair still shines even in the orange glow of the candles as it sits chaotically over her cradling hands and shoulders.

"Red, speak to me," Merchant says and reaches out to her.

Her skin is on fire as he gently takes a hold of her shoulder and pulls her toward her back. With a start he pulls away as the light reveals what has been done.

Infection peels at her skin where it swells with blood and green pus. Her left eye is swollen shut and the lower lip is split in two. Wide blotches of infected scales ooze openly across her upper chest and the stench that he could not smell from the other side of the room is heavy with poison and sickness.

"Red, how did this happen?" he asks.

She squeezes her eyes shut and a thick liquid drips out. She turns her head away.

"Why don't you stay around for a little bit, brother. We'll fill you in on our little secret with your friend Red here," a voice whispers from so close behind Merchant's ear he can feel the warm breath on his skin and taste the vile and putrid stench on his tongue.

Giving no warning, Merchant explodes into a spin and roll, his hand bringing the pistol around. He never gets the chance to finish as lightning flares to life before his eyes and thunder rips apart the inside of his head.

Darkness takes hold, and he knows nothing more.

***

Pain and darkness. A splitting headache like nothing he has ever felt before.

Merchant coughs when he tries to breathe. The taste of blood fills his mouth and the skin at his wrists tears with a weight that pinches to the bone. His arms are pulled to their full length above his head. Shoulders stretched and stiff, he tries to move but the popping of the joints stop him.

His legs are weak. Terribly cramped, the soles of his feet barely touch the ground.

Merchant opens his eyes. A painful endeavor, but the struggle is real enough. Vision blurry, all he can see is small fuzzy lights flickering in the corner. Candles, wax piled in heaping globs, burn and hiss in the wet stagnant air. Spitting out the fluids in his mouth, he takes a deep breath.

Damp, moldy. Metal grinds and grates against itself as he sways back and forth. A few drops of water tap on his skull. The sorry reminder that he is still alive.

"Took you long enough to come back, brother," a man's voice says.

The tone is wet and gritty. Like the words are spoken through drowned lungs slowly decaying over a thousand years. Boots clap across wet stone and Merchant fails to lift his head. He tries to turn and see but the pinch on his neck is a vice grip cracking at the bones. A raging fire ignites the pain cramped muscles and stretched nerves. He stops the effort.

"So, this is what those little pissants in Morninglight send us in retaliation for finding their little secret," a fat man says.

Logan Barnett.

If Red's descriptions are correct.

Merchant's chin is pinched between calloused fingers and lifted. A warm liquid drips off of his forehead, a contrast to the shivers fighting to shake through his body. The cold chill of death runs down his spine as the big man circles to the front of him. Even with blurry vision, he can still see a face he grows to hate sneering back at him.

"Morninglight didn't...," Merchant tries to croak the words out of his throat.

A searing pain fills his mouth with the taste of blood.

"Don't even bother to try to lie to me, boy. I've already gotten word from my men to confirm what I suspected. Somehow those little fucks found a way to take out some of my best. They are going to pay for that in more ways than they can even imagine."

Barnett steps closer, his eyes narrowing as he looks up. Merchant does not turn away. Vision growing clearer, he glares back at the man with his perfectly white hat.

"What have you done?" Merchant gets out and Barnett steps away to avoid spittle and blood.

For good measure the man turns and wipes the front of his pressed coat with a cloth from beneath his hat and puts it back on his head.

"It's not what I've done. All I did was ask them for some simple help. You don't have to walk more than ten feet out of our god-damned walls to see how fucked up this world has gotten. Can't you see that with your own two eyes?"

Merchant turns away the best way he can and with clearer vision sees a lump of blankets laying in the far corner, wet and dark. Balled into a giant heap. A dark stain runs through the center and there is nothing else down here but them, the dirty pile and wet stone. He spits a wet wad of blood and phlegm onto the ground.

"Those people had nothing to do with what has fucked up this world. People did this to themselves. What do they have to do with it?"

Barnett notices his glance and turns to the pile as well. A sinister sneer creases his face.

"Worried about your friend, are you? She is a feisty little one, isn't she? Too bad she had to find out the hard way what happens when you lie to me," Barnett says with a chuckle.

Merchant growls and pulls at his bindings. Fire rips through his muscles and boils the blood running down his arms from torn skin.

"If you've done anything to her you will regret the day you first walked this earth, you steaming pile of shit!"

Barnett places a hand over his heart and tips with an arm extending back, a look of mock horror and shock whitening his face.

"Be still my heart. Such strong words from a man who has no right to say them or ability to do anything about it." Barnett closes the distance between them in the blink of an eye and though he has to reach up, he pinches his hand around Merchant's bloody chin. "Now you listen to me, boy. You are the two who lied their way into my home. You two are the ones who killed my men and then broke into my house looking to do me harm.

And why, if not for what happened in that shit hole of a town? Tell me Merchant, why should I care what happens to you after all you have done to me already?"

Taking his hand away, he lets Merchant hang there. The fire of anger diminishes but does not fade away entirely.

Merchant looks over at the pile of blankets and rags. What have they done to Red? He knows why he is here. There is nothing he can do to fight it. Turning his head back to the cowboy, this asshole Barnett is correct.

Why should he care?

The man did nothing to him. What is a few dead villagers in a world where billions have been rotting in their graves or worse for years?

Merchant takes a deep breath and lets it out in a long sigh. NO, there really isn't a reason for her to be here. She grew too attached to those people back in town. Fell in love with the false hope that life could return to the way it was before all this shit happened. Things will never change back. Everything is too irreversibly broken.

Another shot of pain rips through his arm. But can it? The thought of that smile on her face when she was cured of the infection. Bright cheeks and glowing hair. She was young again and for once he could see the beauty she must have been before everything went to shit.

A smile now creeps its way across Merchant's face. He looks up at the cowboy whose expression turns from confidence to something of curiosity.

No, there was no reason for Red to be here. She should have stayed back at the village with the others. He could have done this alone. The weight of the revolver is no longer at his waistband, but he can still feel it somewhere close by.

Looking at the dead man walking, the fire in Merchant's belly burns wildly as the gasoline of hatred fuels the flames. Yes, there is definitely a reason for him to be here and no matter what this Barnett thinks, there is nothing here that can stop him.

"Enough of our little games, Mr. Merchant. I have far more important things to do. I think I will leave you to ponder on what you have done and maybe when I return, you'll have come up with a reason I should spare your pathetic life."

Merchant spits at him and the red splatter covers a good amount of real-estate across the man's chest.

"Not a good start," Barnett snaps. "Oh, by the way. There is someone who has been dying to meet you since you came to our great city. He had some fun talking sense into that pretty little friend of yours before you joined us. I promised him he'd get his chance with you before I departed. And being a man of my word as I am, I think I will send him down. Enjoy your little chat, Merchant, because I know he will."

Barnett laughs as he walks away. His voice echoes throughout the room, a harrowing sound as it multiplies and strengthens the rage building and pulling at Merchant's bindings.

No one comes for a long time.

Time slips away into one endless silence as Merchant stares down at the broken heap in the corner. Several times he is certain that it has moved, even groaned with the passing of time, but calling out her name does nothing.

"Red, is that you?" Merchant asks again.

Nothing. Silence only broken by an endless drip of pooling water somewhere in the darkness behind him. Antagonizing with its repetitiveness, it scratches at the nerves and roars like a bolder crushing the ground beneath it every time it drops.

At least it is something new. Within the last hour maybe. Merchant works at his bindings again. The chains are soaked with his blood and each new tug tears at the skin trying to mend itself.

Gritting his teeth, Merchant has had enough and pulls. Metal groans. Tiny bits of paint or rock fall onto his head and face. The taste of iron mixes with the putrid phlegm that coats the inside of his mouth.

"Come... on… you.. mother.. fuc—," Merchant starts as he pulls.

"Oh, come now, brother. Father would not think kindly of you if he heard such language coming from your mouth," a voice like air pushing through wet paper says behind him.

Merchant stops mid-pull and stiffens as the air behind him goes cold and wet. The putrid stench in the room is now so thick it gives him the sensation that he is taking a shower in the remains of a morgue. Something he has not felt in years.

Reluctantly, Merchant shivers.

"Why don't you come around where I can see you, whoever the fuck you are," Merchant demands.

"Tsk, tsk. You don't recognize your own flesh and blood? And to think you were always Father's prized child," the raspy voice says.

A figure steps around Merchant and for the first

time in a long time he fights the urge to pull back in disgust. Stooped and covered in dark cloth, the thing in front of him is not much to look at. Hardly taller than a broken man of eighty, the creature radiates cold and damp like the sewer it crawled out of. An over powering stench of decay and disease fills the space around them.

Merchant wrinkles his nose without even thinking about it.

What is this thing?

"I have no idea who the fuck you are," Merchant says. "But if you are any smarter than that Barnett, you'll let me free and I'll forget I ever saw you."

A wet chocking sound rattles out of the thing, something resembling a laugh that is more cough and ache than anything else.

"Set you free? If father didn't think it was a good idea to set you free, then why in all the heavens would I do that now?" the thing mocks.

Stepping away from him, Merchant watches it shuffle its way over to the pile sitting in the corner. The mound of wet and damp that makes up whatever this creature is moves in shifty uneven spasms as it reaches down to begin pulling away the blankets and spent clothes. A brief glimpse of the palest of skin flashes in the torchlight, the flesh wrinkled with moisture and something else.

"What do you want?" Merchant asks. "He said you wanted to see me before you two went on your honeymoon out there with the fucking infected."

The thing ignores him and continues to pull away the rags. Discarding them as simple trash, the heap grows shorter and now there is ample evidence that something rests beneath that heavy pile of filth. Merchant can see the smallest rhythmic movements of breathing beneath it all.

"She really was something to behold when I first found her. So full of life. A real drive deep down in her heart, especially for everything around her. Willing to take whatever was needed, even this world if she had the chance. Of course, whatever that fool had done to her was amateurish at best. Copying a masters work. That is the problem with the people of this world. No real creative thought. Imitation at best. Especially with the gods. Always trying to be one of them. Why? Underachieving bastards, the whole lot, and honestly not that creative. Now, us. We were always so much better, you and I. Real masters of our craft. Never a dull moment when it came to our jobs. Always looking for a way to one up the other. Do you remember, brother?"

The thing turns and looks at Merchant. Where the hump of its back ends, a head tilts, but the face is lost in shadows even he cannot penetrate.

"I am not your fucking brother. Tell me what you want and then begone. Go pull at the coat tails of that prick and beg for his left behind scraps. Just don't expect any mercy from me when I find you again."

The creature shuffles up to Merchant. The stench of disease and pus burns his nose and has its own heat. Reluctantly, Merchant tries to step away again.

"Oh, mercy was never your style brother. Never your style. You know, if I recall correctly, you did have a pungent love for the heroics though. Men of honor and all that what do they call? Bullshit? Not I, though, brother. My work is slow. All true art comes with the pain of time and perfection. Where your masterpieces were grand. Oh, they were magnificent when you were in your glory, but to be honest, I thought they lacked the… How do you say it? Je ne sais quoi? Of course, the other two never had it in them for anything but the direct approach. No imagination, no creativity. It's why you and I were always so close. Don't you remember?"

The thing moves in even closer. Merchant can feel its breath on his face and there is no air left around him to breathe.

"I'm not your fucking brother," Merchant coughs out.

It steps back and tilts its head. Then a rolling laugh echoes in a horrendous gritty sound travels through the corridor beyond.

"You really don't realize, do you? Did father take that away when he let you free?"

Ignoring the look of protest and hatred on Merchant's face, an arm or whatever it has that is closest to an arm reaches up and the sharp edge of a nail runs down Merchant's cheek.

Fire ignites through dull nerves and yellow and red floods Merchant's vision. His muscles cramp and the warm sticky feeling of blood runs down his neck.

The stench of decay floods beyond the thing that stands before him. Merchant can feel the tear in his flesh rotting and putrefying over his bones. A taste of bile fills his mouth before spewing a foot in front of him. His stomach turns. Knees grow weak.

"Ah, there. Now everything is better."

Merchant struggles to stay on his feet. The pain in his wrists is nothing compared to the agony that rips at his face. His vision doubles and the light of the torches dance across the walls. The entire world spins and begins to take him with it.

"What have… you done?" he stammers.

Reaching up, a pale white hand of gnarled knuckles pulls away the heavy coat and filthy rags that cover its body. A man stands there. Skin shriveled and wet with water running in streams from his hair. Disease marks flow across the sharp features of his cheekbones and yellowish pools of green make up where his eyebrows should be. A green tongue licks at blue lips and eyes as white as milk stare at him.

The smile he gives Merchant is so malformed that another rush of bile fills his throat.

"Don't you recognize me now, brother?" the man asks.

Merchant spits in his direction, the fire in his belly pushing away the pain and sickness. Stiffening his legs, he stands taller and towers over the bent monster in front of him.

"I've told you already. I'm not your brother, you sickly little piece of shit. Now let me out of this and I'll do you a favor and end your pathetic existence right here, right now."

The smell of rot and pain fades to the background as his so-called brother grips his own chin with twisted fingers.

"Never were one for small talk," he says and then waves all of it away before turning back to the pile on the floor. "Whatever has been done, I can see it in your eyes that you aren't ready to learn the truth yet. It will come, with time I suppose. Never thought you were part of the plan. Our brothers thought you were too much of a loose cannon. I argued of course, but you know how they can be. Stubborn bastards. In the end, it works out doesn't it? They always say daddy is right."

Merchant growls and pulls at his chains. The anger now fueling the need to tear the man limb from limb.

"I will track you down and kill you, slowly, I promise you that. You and your master," Merchant threatens.

The man stiffens and stands up straight. He does not turn away from the pile and then goes back to removing the last few blankets.

"I'm sure you will, brother. But understand one thing. That puppet you met upstairs is no master of mine. A tool to an end is all. Too many rumors and secrets floating around this world. Someone or something has found a way to undo one of my greatest creations. He thinks that we are looking for a cure to help protect him and his people. Ha! What the fuck does he even know? Once we find the source of this cure, we can squash it before it spreads like a disease. Then there will be nothing left to stop me. Not our brothers, not even yourself. Though I will enjoy coming back here and seeing how long it will take to jar that memory of yours back to life. How does that sound, brother?"

The man turns as he pulls the last of the pile away. Laying at his feet is Red. Curled up into a ball, her eyes are glazed as she shivers and her cracked lips drool blood and spit on the floor. All across her exposed skin are lesions and scales deeper than ever before and the rawest skin he has seen on anything still living leaks with open wounds.

"Red? Can you hear me?" Merchant asks.

She does not reply. Her mind is lost to the world.

"Your friend here has been fun to work with. So young, and yet I can still feel my touch on her though her skin is as smooth as a baby's bottom. I wanted to show you something, brother. Maybe help clear some of those murky waters you have swimming in your head."

Slowly the man lowers himself to the ground and sits beside the prone Red. Like a friend, he lifts her up enough to slide under and cradles her across his legs. Her senseless naked body slumps as if boneless across him.

"If you hurt her," Merchant starts.

"Give up the threats, brother. We both know you aren't getting out of here, and even if you did, would you kill your own family?"

Merchant smiles.

"If I have to."

The smile on the man's face flattens and an air of seriousness washes over him.

"Now that sounds more like you," he says. "Just to make my point and help you along your journey before I return. How about a small display of my creation for you to think about?"

One of his gnarled fingers extends from his fisted hand and the nail grows in seconds to a sharp point. Carefully, he touches the smooth skin above Red's collar bone and the moment the tip touches it begins to flake and peel. Blood and pus ooze from fissures that open holes across the pale surface and Red screams.

Dark liquid begins to bubble out and her wails grow louder. Merchant joins in with his own. Hers of pure pain and his of unrelenting fury. The man does not stop. His nail continues to trace lines across her body, turning what remains healthy into a diseased mess and there is nothing Merchant can do but watch.

In horror and frustration, he watches as the woman who has been at his side for weeks slowly succumbs to the disease of the infected.

Chapter Eighteen
Our World Ends

This no longer feels like home.

Fences built of charred wood and stones hauled from the river build makeshift walls and knives. Any sharp piece of usable metal is tied to sticks and held with shaking hands. Dark clouds hang overhead, ominous and slow moving.

God himself has moved on and the Devil sits in his wake.

Kelly hugs herself in the growing light of the morning. The shadows shrivel beside her but the one that covers her heart is too fresh. Like the mound of dirt by her feet, the pain and misery hold on to her with chains and locks.

"Oh, Bert, why did you have to fight?" she pleads to the silent sky.

Tears streak down her cheeks and the strength of her legs is gone. Falling to the ground, the newly turned dirt is soft beneath her. The smallest thought that her best friend is still looking out for her from his new home in heaven fights the pain deep inside, but it washes away with the cold dread that floods her with the haunting memories.

Kelly sniffs away the snot rolling from her nose.

"You were always the one trying to prove to me how much you cared."

She chuckles and picking up a small handful of dirt she throws it at the base of the cross made of dry sticks.

"I already knew, Bert. I already knew," she sobs and the tears flow down her cheeks.

Not fast enough to wash away the memory.

The screaming, the guns, and the fear that gripped them and held them all still. Men circling with cars and rifles. Angry words demanding to see the infected one they had left.

He steps forward. Wobbly legs and shaky hands, he presses through the crowded village. Woman sob and men growl while children cry and cling to skirts and pants. Kelly can feel her heart race. The anger in her belly is barely controllable. She doesn't know what she can do, but she wants to lash out. Be a real woman like Red is. If she was here, she would know what to do.

"You really can perform miracles, can't you?" one of the men asks.

The one who calls himself, Logan, is not here. This man is much leaner, wiry, and the hard look to his eyes is scarier than Logan's. His jaw is tight, and his hand keeps flickering to the pistol on his belt.

"The lord works in such mysterious ways, my son," Brother George says from the front of the group.

Unlike when Barnett came last time, their pastor does not approach. She does not see fear in his face, but he stays back with the others. Bert's father and oldest brother stand behind each of his shoulders.

"The lord, huh? God said fuck you to this place years ago, preacher. Something you have hidden in this little village of yours is the answer to a lot of our problems here, and you're going to start with what you did to our man here."

This time the men approach, leaving their vehicles behind. Guns make clicking noises and the circle draws tighter like a noose. Kelly can feel the space in her throat constricting. Her palms are sweaty, and she crouches as she pushes back into the nearest person.

If they get any closer, she is going to jump one of them. Claw at their eyes. They can't shoot what they can't see. It doesn't matter what Brother George says. These men are here for no good and letting them stay will not end well for any of them.

"As I see it, our man here has been cured," their new leader says.

He puts a hand on the survivor's chin and turns his head from side to side. Anyone here can see there isn't a scar on the man's skin.

"Just leave these people be," the man says.

His voice is a gurgle of exhaustion and anger.

"You don't sound so happy to see us. And after what we did for you? Brought your sorry ass all the way out here after you fell sick? What kind of thanks is that?"

The leader turns back and steps away enough to be with the men he brought.

"These people have done nothing but show me kindness and compassion. I'm not sure what god they pray to, but whoever or whatever it is, it worked."

Pistol out, the leader of the soldiers grinds the heel of his palm into his eyes. The barrel of his weapon waves dangerously at them all. Kelly doesn't think about it, but she begins to slide behind the others. This is growing more out of hand by the minute.

"You see?" Brother George cuts in. "Our father above is the one that cured your friend here. Through love and prayer, he has been saved. Why don't you join us and—" Brother George does not finish his words.

Blood splatters as the back of the survivor's head erupts and people try to scatter. Screams and gunfire explode, and Kelly is pushed to the ground.

Legs and feet kick as she tries to claw her way back up. More gunfire and her ears ring. The ground shakes beneath her hands as something heavy hits the dirt beside her.

Mr. Jervis!

A dark pool begins to build beneath him. He is staring at her. His eyes already milky.

Why is he staring at her?

She screams and tries to get back onto her feet but pain bursts through her side and all the air is forced from her lungs.

Dust fills her mouth. More screams. Gunfire erupts like a thunderstorm and the world tastes of burned sulfur.

A warm rain falls across her face as shadows race through the nightmare. Salty, she tastes the liquid as it coats her lips. Wiping the rain away, her hands come back red.

Blood!

Kelly crawls on her butt until she hits the first thing that stops her. Someone's feet. Rolling over, she looks.

Mrs. Mary!

The flowers on her white dress are darkening across her chest. Chin drooping, she leans to the side and then hits the ground with a soundless thud after Kelly shakes her sandaled feet.

Kelly tries to scream. Maybe she does, but most likely she does not. She cannot tell. Shadows and strangers run around. Flashes of yellow lightning and thunder tears at her ears from all around her.

She doesn't know a soul. Everyone is a stranger and a monster. Crawling away, she goes toward the first path where there are no monsters.

The corner of the church is within reach. There is a door in the back. If she can get there and find a way in, she'll be safe. Too many places to hide and they'll have no idea they need to look for her.

One painful crawl at a time, she moves forward. Dirt, stones, and blood coat and cut at her skin. More warm liquid runs down her face. She fights back the tears that want to break loose with those already falling to the ground.

Only a dozen feet left to go.

The thunder is quieting. Even the screams are far away. Freedom is less than a few minutes...

"No you don't, you little bitch," a man barks and pain bursts through the side of Kelly's ribs.

Muscles spasm across her stomach as she collapses to the ground. Blood and dirt fill her mouth as she struggles for air.

A dark shadow stands above her. Rifle points at her face. She tries to turn and crawl away. A hard boot cracks her hip as it crushes the skin beneath its sole.

Kelly screams out.

"What did I tell you?" the man demands.

She tries to respond. The words are lost, her hope

missing, and desperation a memory of the past.

"Ah!" a familiar voice screams.

Shadows collide and the monster above her is driven away. Air floods into her lungs and Kelly starts to cough. Dust kicks up into the air.

More gunfire erupts, and she watches as the bodies roll in a tangle of arms and threats. The tumbling stops. The monster grows large as it hits the other with a fist and the body doubles in pain.

Kelly tries to crawl forward.

"You're going to pay for this you fucking, little, piece of shit," the soldier yells.

Digging into the dirt with her nails, Kelly draws closer. A pale face glares at the man with the rifle. Mud and blood smear against a visage of defiance and rage.

"No," the words gurgle out of her mouth.

A sweat drenched head of hair. Round cheeks and soft face are hard and unlike anything she has ever seen from him.

Bert!

Her Bert. Her best friend. Staring at the end of a rifle. The man continues to scream but she can no longer hear the words.

Only a last few feet separate them. Pain is gone. Lost to the need to protect her best friend.

"No," she mutters again.

Bert screams in defiance and the shot that rings out stops all of time. A thunder loud enough to crack her world in half. The echoes bleed her ears and all the strength in her body drains through fingers and into the muddy earth choked full of blood and dreams.

The next two shots mean nothing to her. All she

can see is the look of shock on his face. Eyes wide, his lips move but nothing comes out other than the blood that wells across his chest.

She reaches him and pulls him to her. The soldier tries to rip her away, and she bites at his hand. A slap rips across her face, but she refuses to let go.

Bert is shaking. Dark pools fill beneath him, and his mouth drips a red river that will carry her away.

"Please, Bert, stay with me," she whispers.

His hands squeeze her arms tight and it hurts. The worst and best pain she has ever felt. He looks into her eyes. Tears burn in hers, and there are no more words.

His lips move, but she can barely hear him. Weight pulling on her body, she leans forward. The secret is short. Spoken softly, the last message of her only friend.

She can hear those words replaying in her mind. Sitting here on his fresh grave, the soil barely settled as repairs and construction continue within the village below.

This is no longer her home. Not after all of this. Where will she go? Who will she run to?

The image of Red and Mr. Merchant pass through her thoughts, but that doesn't help. They could be dead, or so far away from here they are as lost as Bert is.

No, she'll have to do this on her own.

"Remembering the dead is a wonderful thing, my daughter, but do not mourn for those who now sit by the side of our father," Brother George's voice cuts in.

Shock and frayed nerves force Kelly to roll forward and she grabs a rock as she turns around, the weapon of chance held above her head.

The priest holds out his hands and the anger and fight fall away with the wind. He smiles, the same one that has comforted her for years, yet today it means little more than the defenses will if Logan and his men return.

"I'm sorry, Brother George. I just miss him so much," Kelly says and crawls back to the grave where she'll probably lay down and let her own life pass away.

"We all do, Kelly," he says before sitting beside her. The strength she once felt as she slouches against him is gone, the thick cords of muscle and bone beneath his shirt brittle and hollow like their chances in this world. "But Bert and the others died doing what God put them on this world to do. He would not have called them home if it wasn't so."

Kelly thinks on those words as she watches more pikes of sharpened wood driven into the hard earth.

"Do you really think so? God wanted Bert to be shot while trying to protect me? Fighting a man he should have never even tried to in the first place? What small hopes were there to get me away?"

Brother George shrugs.

"What other purpose was there? You are still here, and he is not. I think God has a plan for us all and in this case, maybe he means something special for you, Kelly. Have you ever thought about that?"

She does as the wind brushing against the sweaty skin of her neck tingles her spine with the tiny touches of ice. A death's touch. Sitting in a graveyard, her entire world buried beneath its clay filled soil, yeah, she has thought about that.

"If he does have a plan for me, then I want nothing

to do with it," she says and pulls her knees tight against her chest.

"You do not mean that," Brother George says.

"Oh yeah I do," she answers. Something deep inside ignites and rolling away she gets up and steps away. "If it cost the life of my best friend, God can take his plan and fuck off. I don't want any part of it."

New tears welling in her eyes and wetting her cheeks, she begins to storm way. The pain and memories still chained to her legs, the relief does not come the further away she gets.

"You do not mean that, Kelly," Brother George calls. "In God and his gifts, you will find what you truly need, my child."

Kelly does not turn around. Gritting her teeth, she stares directly ahead.

"No priest, God will not help me. I already know what I want, and it will not be him who helps me," Kelly whispers and does not stop until the blood-soaked soil of the village burns beneath her feet.

***

The night brings everything they did not want. Thick clouds, no light, a howling wind full of hatred and anger.

Men and women huddle behind closed doors. The world lost beneath a blanket of darkness thicker than soup. Metal hinges creak as they sway in the call of the storm. A reminder that regardless of the preparations they have made, they are totally lost beneath the awesomeness of the world that toys with them like children.

"Can you see anything?" Kelly asks.

Shoulder pressed against a boarded window, plank boards hastily nailed to shut off access to the Sick House, she grips the walking stick with a knife tied to the end of it until her knuckles are pale white.

"Child, I couldn't see the Virgin Mary if she descended from Heaven itself on our door step," old man Nicholi says.

Patch over his left eye, the old man holds the only rifle assigned to this house. Thick gnarly fingers grip tight and the guard has been cut away from the trigger so he can fire a shot if he has to.

"What are we going to do if they get here and we can't see them?" she asks.

The thought sends a shiver down her spine.

Wood on the floor above creaks with the wind and she darn near pisses herself at the idea of someone already inside and coming down to get them.

"Please child. If we can't see them, what in tarnation do you think they are going to see out there in all of this? It's not like they are monsters or gods."

Kelly spits on the ground at her feet. They are monsters alright, but at least not the ones with night vision or something like that.

A door opens from the back, the hinges crying before the entrance is closed and footsteps approach from the darkness. Kelly readies her weapon, the tip shaking badly in her hand, but she refuses to think she won't use it.

"This is nothing but folly," Brother George says as he enters the room.

His large frame somehow silhouetted in the darkness. Kelly does not know what to think with him so close. For the longest time he was like a father to her.

Now?

It does not matter. For close to a week now they have prepared the defenses of the village and he has done nothing but given words of encouragement from God where it isn't needed. Sermons on how Jesus turned the other cheek when assaulted and afternoon preaches about how the man who betrayed him to his own death was not to be blamed.

All bullshit to her. Bert and the others are all dead and that is because of one person. One single asshole on this entire fucking planet and now her best friend is gone. Along with others whose memories already begin to fade.

"Only a precaution, preacher," Nicholi says. "God doesn't speak out against those who prepare themselves."

Brother George buries his hands into the pockets of his pants and nods his head.

"You are correct, though preparation for war is prudent to the sins already cast by those you seek to fight."

"They started this fight, George," Kelly cuts in. " Not us. They brought their guns and killed our families. How is it fair that we suffer greatly while they take what they want, whenever they want? How is that?"

Brother George sighs and then steps away to lean against a side wall. She refuses to look at him with those judgmental eyes. Like God itself, she is not ready to see her maker until she puts those who deserve worse in front of their own.

"God is the one and only judge, my child. Nothing these men do, or you do to them, will compare to what will happen when they reach the life beyond. Take solace in that and know that those who have gone before us are in a better place."

Kelly spins on her heels and looks him dead in the eye.

"Better place? How is six feet—" she begins but is cut off when Nicholi grabs her shoulder and spins her back to the small opening between the boards.

"Keep your mouth shut, the both of you. These devils may not be able to see any better at night than the rest of us, but those damn vehicles of theirs make things a whole lot better," he says as he readies his rifle.

Her heart drops to her knees as she sees what he is talking about.

Dozens of lights, the hellish rays cutting through the darkness with the precision of a knife, bounce as they race toward the town. There is no hiding their approach. Engines roar, a guttural sound that shakes the floor beneath her shoes.

A few gunshots ring out into the night. More engines roar to life and the sound of wood splintering pierces the night as more gunshots burst into the darkness.

Now the voices of men come with the sounds of war. Rifles bark, single explosions of thunder answered with unending pops and a ball of fire that rips the front of the market store right off and sends pieces of burning wood dozens of feet into the air.

Kelly falls to her knees. She isn't sure when she started but the tears on her cheeks burn as they run down her neck. Nicholi waits beside her. His face more ashen than it has ever been and somehow the caverns across his face are dark with shadows and fear.

Nothing stops the oncoming enemy. A single vehicle

swerves and topples into the ditch cut behind the new fences, but the others pass without slowing. Yellow flashes come from windows that cave into pieces as walls and glass spill out like guts torn from the hearts of their loved ones.

Kelly settles on the ground as the thunder of engines and gun fire draws closer. She screams but it will not drown out the sound. Nicholi raises his rifle.

The war is right on top of them. The boards of the wall. Rafters on the roof. Everything shakes and dust and grime falls all around them as searching lights cut through holes in their protection. She wants to crawl away. They are going to find her. Kill her like they did everyone else.

Her muscles will not move. Knees to chest, she can barely breath. Smoke and dust fill the air. Like bile, it sickens her mouth and tears burn her cheeks.

The gunfire dies down to a few lonely shots. Light burns through new and old holes and the engines are so close.

"You cock sucking sons-of-bitches," Nicholi growls and presses the stock of the rifle tighter against his shoulder.

Brother George puts a hand on his arm and the shot is not fired. Kelly watches as the old man turns back and the anger in his face washes away. There is sorrow there, loss told in the stories of the shadows that drown his hollow cheeks, but no anger.

Sobbing, she cradles herself. Brother George turns to her.

"You must trust me, there is no other way," he comforts.

In anger and fear, she slides around until she is not looking at him. His eyes burning holes right through the center of her back.

"Get out here now, priest!" Logan's voice hollers from outside.

Two shots ring out and the roof cracks and pieces fall around them.

"We know you are in there. Don't make this tough on those who haven't been smart enough to die already. Get that god-fearing sorry ass out here or we'll show you how we get if you really make me mad!"

"It's alright," Brother George whispers as Nicholi's face grows hard and he steps in front of the priest.

Placing his hand on the man's shoulder, the emotion washes away as water once again and they both turn back to Kelly.

"Watch over her, will you? I'm the one they want. Maybe when this is all done, they'll leave you alone long enough to find somewhere safe to start anew," Brother George adds.

"Don't go out there," Kelly pleads.

The words come from nowhere she can control. Rolling off of her lips, she cannot stop them, and she grabs at his pants. Wet fingers pinch tight and the man does not try to pull away.

"It is time for me to leave, my child. It was only a matter of time before this happened. We all knew this. Even my father, for he would never have put me here if it had not mattered."

A soft hand, as large as the side of her face, cups Kelly's cheek and the raw emotions of hate and fear fade away with the passing of the clouds. Tears still burn her eyes and her throat is dry, but there is nothing left.

She looks into his eyes and there is the caring she so desperately misses. Reflected in two shiny orbs of white, he smiles and the cold touch of darkness warms beneath his touch.

"Please, please don't go," she pleads.

Her hands grab at the ends of his sleeve, but they find no purchase. Taking a hold of her palms, he places them together gently and presses them to her chest.

"Pray as I have taught you, my child. That is all you will need in a time like this," Brother George says.

"Get out here now, priest! My patience is weighting thin," Mr. Barnett demands.

Brother George runs his big hands through her hair one last time and with a nod to Nicholi, reaches for the door.

"Do as I have always taught you and do not follow me out into the darkness," he says before pulling the boarded door open with little effort.

The nails and wood give way as if they were never there, and he slowly shuts the door behind him. Engines roar and gunshots ring into the night.

Kelly cups her ears and tries desperately to cut off the noise, pull herself away from this world, but she cannot. The screaming starts again. Deep from within her lungs the pain erupts as the soldiers outside celebrate and her world falls apart around her.

Chapter Nineteen
Unknown Friends

She would be better off dead. Groans and whimpers echo in a scratching chorus that will not end. Tears of yellow and green trickle over swollen skin and her breathing is an empty can rolling down a deserted road.

"Red?" Merchant asks.

Probably for the thousandth time she does not answer. Her body convulses, and new fissures break across skin that bleeds and pops. His own energy is drained. There is nothing left of him to pull at the chains. The muscles in his legs are balls of slicing torture ripping themselves from his knees and the joints of his hands crack beneath his weight.

"You need to get up, Red. Find something that can get me free. We'll punish those who have done this to you."

No response. The rattling in her chest does not change and the pooling of death and disease beneath her grows where it once it had been dry.

In a rage of fury Merchant rips at the bonds that hold him. New tears in his flesh peel open and a warm splattering of blood catches him across the side of his face.

One drip.

Two drips.

Then a small spray.

Struggling to lift his head, he looks at the darkness the skin peeling from his arms. A spray of dark liquid greets him right between the eyes.

Arterial spray.

He's ripped too deep. Now he has finally done it. There is nothing that can save them.

A small chuckle escapes his lips. Bleeding out in the middle of a basement in some bum-fucked place unknown to anyone else in this whole fucking world. His chuckle becomes full-blown laughter as more of the warm liquid drips down the side of his face. He can taste it on his lips. The thought of dying gives him solace, a reason to stand and wait for it to come. Finding the strength, Merchant pushes through the cramps and pains of his legs to stand straight.

One thing is for certain. He'll die on his feet.

***

The color of the world is a wash of grays and blacks. Even the sky behind the clouds rolling by looks of coming storms and the breeze washing over him is stale and heavy.

Merchant takes a deep breath, the feeling of his lungs expanding in his chest is welcome and the taste a bitter reminder of the fucked-up nature of the world. He lets out the feeling in one long sigh. The exhaustion and fatigue washes over him as the gray puffy balls of water roll themselves across the open expanse above.

What are they going to make of themselves? He is only one man with a lot to forget and a burden he cannot get rid of. Closing his eyes, he tries to forget for a single moment everything that he has done. The world is silent. Gravely quiet other than the small whistle of the wind as it pushes its way over his body.

Small needle points jab at his skin, but the softness of their touch is cool and tickles with the breeze. Laying his hand by his side, the gentle touch of grass between his fingers is delicate and unlike anything this fucked planet should have left on its barren landscape. Rolling his fingers into a fist he lets the blades slide like silk over his fingers, the tips scratching at the soil beneath.

Another breeze washes over and this time it carries with it a smell he will never forget. Sweet and tangy with a burn that ignites from the inside. The smell of ash and smoke fills his nose. Burning the soft flesh within, the sight of fire inflames his hidden memories and jumpstarts his heart.

With a gasp, Merchant sits up. Dark trees of gray and shadow surround him in all directions. A single path cuts into the emptiness of the beyond where it winds its way to the unknown and returns to pass by where he sits no more than a dozen feet away.

Giant shadows dance across the open field and the harshest of memories begins to take seed in his mind.

"This can't be," he whispers to himself.

Rolling onto his knees, his eyes follow the gravel road as the stench of burning wood and bubbling plaster engulfs him like a blanket. A house burns atop the nearest hill.

Not any house.

His house!

Men circle around its furthest reaches. A gun shot echoes within the trees and Merchant is on his feet and running. He screams words but there is no sound other than the rapid succession of gunfire and the crackling of wood.

He watches as two soldiers separate and head to opposite corners of the porch facing the road he runs on. They do not see him coming. His boots pound over the hard dirt but to them he couldn't be more than a ghost.

More gunfire erupts and large pieces of roofing shingles and the structure beneath crash down over the awning of the front porch. Merchant reels to a stop as sparks and ash kick high into the air. Screams, high pitched and filled with terror pierce the horror in front of him.

Without hesitation, Merchant spins and heads for the rear of the house. Another figure beats him around the corner, this one dark and less substance than a shadow. Fists balled and heart beating out of his chest, Merchant rounds the corner to throw himself at the man he knows will be there. He is unarmed, but there is no time to care. This is his family. He can save them.

At least he must try.

If he fails again, this time he'll die with them. Then this whole thing will be over. No infected. No quest to reach the city that touches the sky. Only his beautiful wife and the boys he never got to save.

Wood chunks explode through the back door and the dark figure he followed disappears. Replacing the fading smoke, one of the original soldiers tumbles backward into the yard. Blood fountains from the gaping hole in his chest and the rifle in his hand falls useless to the ground.

The dark smoke reappears and slips through the opening created in the back door. Merchant does not stop. He reaches the doorway and kicks with all the strength he has. The hinges splinter and a crack from the top of frame to the floor wrinkles its way through the wood before another kick caves the entire barrier in.

Clouds of heaving smoke roll in a tidal wave that takes the breath right out of him. He coughs and is forced backward. Covering his nose and mouth with his arm, he cannot breathe. Ripping his shirt off, he ties it around his face. Tears stream down his cheeks, his eyes burn with acid, and his vision blurs as his lungs fill with poison.

Ahead the dark vision swirls through the house.

Growling, Merchant cannot wait and drives forward. Tracing the steps through his home, the memory of every piece of furniture and corner clears the way through the smoke and fire. Flames feed themselves over every wall and the boards beneath his feet groan with dangerous words, but he cannot be deterred.

A soldier pushes his way in through the front window. Nothing stands between him and Merchant. Roaring, Merchant rolls his shoulders forward to charge, and the man makes no move to deter him. Before the first step, the oily ghost of darkness and shadow passes between them a moment before a wooden beam snaps and using the sheetrock above as a hinge, slices its way through the man's torso in a wet puncturing sound before pinning him to the far wall.

Merchant hesitates as the man tries to choke out a few words, the bottom of his mask becoming a wet mess of blood and ash as fire races down the broken beam to engorge itself on his flesh. The dark figure flashes its way through the hall once again and this time slips around the door making its way to the basement.

The screams take on a new pitch and Merchant runs for the entrance. Fire races up and cuts off his path, but in a leap, he is over the flames. His shoulder slams into the wall beside the opening to the level down below and the sizzling of skin and meat is strong as burns open welts from his elbow to his shoulder.

Gritting the pain away, Merchant grabs the handle and a white fire of torturous ruin rockets its way through his hand. Pulling away, large chunks of skin melt from the handle and blood and muscle shrivel in burns across his palm.

Another scream accompanies more beams snapping, and a pile builds in front of the doorway that lead back out to safety. Balling everything he has up, Merchant grabs the handle again, biting down on his tongue to lock away the pain, he yanks on the door and the lock and wood splinter beneath his grip.

Darkness and shadow spew out, but the air is cold and without smoke. Tears blur Merchant's vision and flames quickly turn their attention to the opening and race to block his way.

Face pressed into the crook of his elbow, he races through the opening and down the stairs. He can hear the crying of his family. His boys' pleas for help are muffled and the soothing words of his wife are soft amongst the horror that surrounds them all.

"I'm here, Tracy," Merchant calls.

She does not turn his way. Pulling their boys closer, she hugs them to her chest. Shotgun resting over her legs, their two sons are curled beneath her protective arms and tears cover all three of their faces.

"I'm here," Merchant whispers. He kneels in front of them. "I know I almost failed you, but I'm here. We can get out of the house. You just need to follow me."

His words fall on deaf ears as she kisses each of the two boys on the top of their heads. Gray ash mixes with their dark hair and rivers of black soot streaks from his beautiful wife's face. Lifting one hand away, she reaches into the top of her white blouse, unrecognizable beneath the blood and ashes and pulls at the chain hanging around the slenderness of her neck. Light from the fire makes its way down the stairs and reflects from the metal and jewels of the piece.

"Please, baby. Listen to me. Grab the boys and make a run for it. The men outside have scattered. Go out the back and get to the shed. The ATV is gassed, just like you always made me promise it would be," he pleads.

Her eyes watch the light flicker over the medallion before lifting. Warm blue medallions consider him for the smallest of moments. Red with tears but still the crowning jewels of the world her eyes regard him with the tenderness of pity he has not felt in all his memory.

Merchant reaches forward. His bloody, fire torn hand shaking as his fingers draw closer to her cheek.

Eyes widening, her mouth begins to move but no words come out. Something grabs the back of Merchant's shirt and tugs him with such force it sends him sprawling through the air until he hits the wall on the far end of the basement. Boxes of stored Christmas decorations, dust, and pieces of wooden shelving crash all around him in a jingling mass of trinkets and waste. The bones in his back crack with the pain of the impact and it is a struggle to move.

Lifting his head, he rests it against the stone wall of the basement. The feeling of cold fear ripples its way through his body. He tries to call out. There are no words. Before him the darkness he has been chasing materializes. Pulling into substance from nothing, the figure approaches.

His wife's screams turn from fear into defiance. His boys plead, and he cannot move. The thing has no description. It is not a person, or an animal. It is something, yet not really there, and it locks him to the wall.

He watches as it approaches his family. The fire and chaos above are lost. Silent and dead, the world around them is no more and everything within existence is locked into this room.

The screams and cries die out as the darkness of the horror between them engulfs his family. Merchant struggles to pull free. Tears burn the skin of his face as the unknown chains pinch against the skin of his arms and legs.

He yanks and tugs, screams and curses, but he cannot move. Enveloping everything, the shadows move in around him. He can no longer see anything that he isn't touching.

"Tracy!" he screams.

Everything his tries is useless. He's a prisoner left to be forgotten in the confines of his burned-out home. Given nothing more than a life of misery and loneliness down within the depths of hell. With one more tug the chains and restraints that bind him fall apart.

Merchant stumbles to the floor with the force of his exertion. Dust and ash choke out the air and his tears taste of acid over his lips. Digging his fingers and bloody nails into the ground, he drags himself across the floor.

Light filters in the through holes in the floor above and the opening to the stairs that led him down. The darkness recedes from where his family still rests.

"Tracy!" he cries again.

They are gone. Their burned husks lay quiet and undisturbed. Sobs rack his body and tear at the injuries bleeding across his body. Stretching his hand, he lets his touch rest onto the wilted shoes of his wife's foot. Bones crack and turn to ash beneath his embrace. The bodies dissolve into one another.

A pile spills onto the floor enveloping his misery. His wife gone. The children laid waste within reach of his grasp. The wind swirls and lifts their remains into the air. A tornado takes them up and out through a gap in the charred floor above.

Merchant watches them go. All that he has ever loved and cared for is gone, leaving a bitter taste in his mouth and a hatred that will never be quenched.

He rolls onto his back. The cries of a dead man will never hear the words spilling from his mouth. The disgust for life and anything bright within this world dies as the cracking of his world splits the home around him. He does not care. Pieces of his world crash around him. First a beam that splits the stairs back up to the safety that is the outside. Then the cracked and unrecognizable remains of the television in the living room slips through the floor and shatters on the cement of the basement.

Inch by inch the remnants of his soul crumble around him. Merchant does not care. He welcomes it. Revels in the certainty of it all as the last beams above split and sing the song of death as they plummet through the air.

He does not move, does not try. Death takes him, and he is its willing partner.

***

Gasping for breath, the world spins in Merchant's eyes. A searing fire races through his arm and the taste and smell of blood is everywhere. He cannot move. The feeling in his hands is gone and his shoulders feel pulled beyond the extremes of his joints.

There is no strength left in his legs.

He tries to lift himself up.

Needles cut through his feet and bone scrapes against bone within his knees. The candle light swirls in his eyes and his stomach heaves. Vomit chokes his throat and spews from his mouth. The body of Red begins to move. He tries to speak but only spittle comes out.

"F… foo… food," her voice croaks.

Merchant dangles from his restraints. The vision of her body struggling for the strength to move splits his brain through the center. He tries to vomit again but his insides are empty. A cold chill sends shivers through him.

His eyes struggle to stay open.

Why won't the end just take him?

The shadows begin to close around. There is enough strength left in him to smile. This time there is no escape. No angel to comfort him in his passing. The vision of his wife smiling and his boys playing football in the backyard warms him from the inside.

Yes.

He'll see them again.

Merchant lets the cold hands caress his body. If there is a god in this world, it will all end here. Then the vision of his family turns to dust. Their bodies burst into flames and the ash is picked up and scattered across the world. He screams, and it does not stop.

The world burns around him. Shadows close in and materialize in front of his eyes. That same thing. Whatever that benevolence was in his vision stands before him. He spits blood and whatever is still in his mouth in defiance.

Horror and death do not care. A cold certainty takes hold of him. He does not know what it is, but there is no stopping it.

Maybe this is death.

"Foooood," Red calls out again.

The cold chill wraps him like a blanket and the pain in his body erupts and vanishes with a thought. His arms drop, and he tumbles to the floor. The cold stone cuts into him like a knife and it is everything he has to roll onto his back. Above the shadows hold form before slipping back into nothingness.

Inside he feels the hatred and warmth of his disgust for everything return. Filling his limbs, the pain returns but slowly the emptiness subsides.

"Fooood," Red groans again, closer this time.

Too close.

Her movements are jagged and uncoordinated. Her hand swipes at his torn face but the grasp never reaches. His fingers wrap around the fragile wrist and squeeze until she screams. Merchant can feel the bones beneath begin to shift and crack.

The shrieks from her voice are not human. Rabid eyes filled with hunger and hatred stare back at him as he keeps her at bay through pain as he pivots enough to regain his knees. The bleeding on his arms and legs begin to slow. Fire fills its way through his body and the world stops spinning.

"Hungry!" she shouts and trying to spin away from the pain of her twisted wrist, she tries for his throat.

Merchant swats away the attempt like a lazy fly. With a shove he sends Red sprawling back into the pile of dirty towels and clothes. Laying naked and sprawled on the floor, her body is more shriveled than he has ever seen it.

Feral eyes glare and broken teeth are bared. Like an animal she coils into a spring and he pushes his way to his feet. There is no fear. His bag rests in the far corner. Sight returning, he can see where they left it, disregarded it as nothing more than the useless possessions of a dead man.

Red springs before he can turn to get his things. Hands and nails extended, her grip digs into the flesh of his shoulders but he bites away the pain. Taking a step, he wraps his large fingers around the front of her throat. She tries to bite down, but he feels the pulse of her heart beneath his fingertips. Rapid and wild, her nails continue to dig, and he squeezes harder. The breath from her lungs slow as he closes her throat.

Slapping, she tries frantically to beat him into submission. Drool and blood drip from her lips as the last bits of her body begin to slow. Feet kicking, she does not touch the floor. Pity has no room as he squeezes until her eyes begin to flutter. She stops kicking and slapping. Her arms fall limp against her body and he holds on for a few more seconds.

Darkness has taken her. With a gentleness, Merchant puts her back on the ground. Limp, she sprawls across the floor and he turns away. Lifting his bag off the floor, the strength of his body is still a bit of time away, but inside the familiar jingles of the burden he carries puts his mind at ease. There is a debt to pay, and there will be enough when he gets there. That he is certain of.

Chapter Twenty
Enough is Too Much

The end of the world is a loud thing. Full of screams and cries. Blood spilling everywhere and the pleas of the fallen before death takes them all. This is the torturous nightmare promised to everyone in the holy book.

Kelly cannot stop crying. She has tried, but the sobbing runs through her body with unrelenting force and the pain holding it in is worse than the bruises and cuts over her body. Everything is as it was described. The horror. The death. Hell on earth with no way to survive. She wishes she would have died back before they brought her to this place. At least then the pain would be over.

Smoke rolls through her world casting a haze that filters the rising sun into a hellish red. The remains of every building she can see are nothing but empty husks, dark shadows proudly displaying the reminder of their failure high into the air. Men with guns gather survivors and kill those who even look to have an idea of resisting. Looking at faces is too much for she cannot withstand the gut-wrenching fear of watching them die over and over in her mind.

Women cry in the distance. She is too fragile to do the same. Hers are silent and painful. Their wails rip at her soul as she can only imagine what is happening to them.

Clinging to the thinning arms of Nicholi, she can practically feel his skin go slack beneath her grip as his breaths continue to slow. The dark pool covering his stomach grows darker. The men who did this do not bother her as the dying man sits and rests against her.

She smells of shit and she can feel death touching her body. A cough rocks Nicholi and blood bubbles between his lips.

"Lay still, Nich," she whispers. "You'll be OK."

He coughs again, and the left side of his lips begin to curl up.

"Stupid girl, I'm a dead man and you're using me as a shield," he answers, his voice now like rocks in an empty tin can. Another cough forces his head back against her chest. His eyes stare off into the distant sky and he takes a deep breath. "Good thinking, but what are you going to do when I'm gone? Can't sit here forever. This whole world is gone to shit. Too bad I won't be here to see that bastard pay for this."

Nicholi struggles as more air comes out than he can get in. He spits more blood, and it is brighter than the sky. His eyes close but he continues to breathe. Kelly pulls him closer and watches as more bodies are dragged and lined up in a double-sided path to the church.

She stopped counting at forty-seven. Shoulder to shoulder, their feet make an aisle to the front doors where the entrance has been nailed shut and the building untouched by the fire.

"This is all your fault, priest!" Logan Barnett taunts while waving one of his two pistols around like an empty fork. "All you had to do is tell us the secret of what cures the infection and none of this would have happened. Then, in your righteous stupidity you sent those two idiots into my home to kill me?"

Brother George stands with his shoulders back and head held high. Gray ash covers his burgundy sweater and his pants are soaked in dark blood that is not his own. Deep gashes slice through the upper thigh of his pants, but she cannot tell if he is truly hurt. He does not glance at the bodies at his feet nor the men who begin to make their way toward the spectacle. Guns held lazily across their shoulders and chests, they circle but Kelly can still see them from where she sits against the remnants of the Sick House.

"Everyone's actions are of their own making. We did not send or request any of our people make their way to your home. Nor would we have. As for this secret you are looking for, there is nothing secret about what happens here," Brother George says and then turns to look at everyone, enemy and friend. "We are nothing but a humble community that works with their hands and through the ways provided to us by our father above. Only in his glory have we lived in this world surrounded by such suffering and horrors."

A rifle butt slams into George's stomach and he stumbles before dropping to a single knee.

"Don't give me that shit about God and all those other lies. No amount of praying is going to keep the fucking infected away. They eat, they kill, but they haven't touched a single fucking one of you. It's time to fess up and save who you can. Tell me now and the punishment can end with you."

Brother George looks up at Barnett and his pudgy cheeks bursting at the seams. His large girth blocks the hazy light above and the silence between them sits like a death sentence. Nicholi grunts and Kelly pulls her hand away. White prints puff out where she squeezed her hand too hard on his arm.

"Silly fuck," the dying man whispers. "Really thinks there is some kind of secret to this. Oh, what is going to happen to us when he finally opens that fucking mind of his."

"Shh," Kelly says. "We have to do something."

Coughs rock Nicholi's body. Blood trickles in rivers over his chin and the dark pool grows cold on her legs.

"Do what? I've got a small knife in my back pocket if you want to cut your way through them. Just leave me the fat one. I'm gonna cut his fucking balls off and shove them down his throat. Make him choke on his own cock."

"I have told you all that I can. What do you want me to say?" Brother George says, his voice even and slow. "There is no medicine in a bottle that can do what you ask. We have very few weapons and those we have you already showed that they are hardly adequate to protect our homes and ourselves."

Barnett bends down and lifts Brother George's chin up. Hacking phlegm into his throat, he spits in the downed man's face, the sticky strings dripping from dark cheeks.

"You have doomed your people, priest. No one refuses me. Maybe if I start with this young girl of yours, it'll loosen up those tight lips of yours," Mr. Barnett says and turns to Kelly.

The cold touch of death and fear washes through her veins like a tidal wave and she can barely breath. Her hands shake as the smile on the monster's face grows.

"Leave the poor girl alone," Brother George pleads. "She has nothing to do with this. Your argument is with me."

"Someone bring that girl over here. Time to see just how much this priest cares about his flock."

"Grab the knife and make a fight of it, girl. Don't go down without swinging," Nicholi says, his words broken between drops of blood and hardly louder than a whisper.

Kelly lets her trembling hand slide behind the dying man's back. The cold wetness of blood sticks to her skin as it slides over the heavy shirt, a film sticking to her skin. A bulge sticks out just above the man's belt and she wraps the tips of her fingers around it, her strength barely able to do that.

"Get over here you dumb little bitch," the soldier who reaches her first says.

"Stay away!" Kelly screams.

The man slaps her across the face and she tumbles to the side but not before securing her hold of the knife. Hitting the ground, she leaves the small weapon between her and the dirt as the tears and sobs kick dust into her face.

"On your damn feet," the man barks.

"Leave the girl alone!" Nicholi orders.

He swings his fist out at the soldier and his knuckles crack on the man's vest before being swatted away. A boot stamps down on the hemorrhaging wound in Nicholi's stomach and the curdle that rolls out of his chest is unnatural and short.

"Foolish man," the soldier says.

Kelly lifts herself up slightly and turns at the sound of metal clicking back.

"No!" she belts, but it is too late.

Three gunshots tear apart Nicholi's face and his body transforms into a ragged pile of skin and bones stretched out across the earth.

"If you don't want to end up like your grandpa here, I said get the fuck up," the soldier barks again.

His grip tears into her arm as she's dragged to her feet. Cupping her opposite hand, the small blade slides up into the sleeve of her shirt before she is shoved in front of him and forced to walk toward the kneeling Brother George.

"A caring one we have here, don't we priest?" Barnett chuckles and then squats in front of Brother George. Their faces are barely inches apart. They both watch her approach. "Do you think she'd care enough to take care of some of my men here? Maybe have you watch the skills you have taught her while surrounded by the failure of your people rotting on the ground next to her? She looks like one raised and bred just right for servicing, doesn't she?"

"Please…" Brother George whispers and then lets his head drop.

"I think that will be enough my good man," a new voice calls out, a wet and raspy sound that startles all the soldiers within earshot.

Several check weapons and back away, their attention now drawn to the darkness coming from the dead husks of homes that was their village. Bent and limping, a creature approaches and the look on Barnett's face turns sour. Kelly takes what strength she can from that look to grab the knife with a firmer grip before sliding it out and slipping it into her own pocket.

"What do you think you are doing?" Barnett barks. "We told you we'd come and get you after we found out what this man and his dead flock were hiding. I thought you wanted to spend your time with that 'brother' of yours we left you behind with."

"His time will come, my pet. There is nowhere for him to go and so much more work to be done here," the creature says as he draws closer.

With a clearer look, it is not an it, but a he. Bunched beneath a pile of wet clothes layered haphazardly and looking more like a living stash of dirty laundry than human, a trail of slime and mud trails behind a man freshly dragged from the sea. A snail who not even trained killers approach but Barnett refuses to back away.

"Watch your words. I've spent a lot of time indulging your fantasies and turning the other way with your 'collecting', but I will not be spoken to like this in front of my men."

Snail man waves his comments away with an arm draped by wet clothes and steps to the side to approach Brother George. The look on her father's face turns hard as granite.

"Now this is a surprise, cousin. You are definitely the last person I thought I would find here. I thought maybe ol' Uncle had given up on this little experiment of his. I guess even the best of us get it wrong sometimes. But this definitely makes things more interesting," the stranger says.

"I am not of the same blood as you and you disgrace my father by claiming as such," Brother George answers and begins to draw himself back to his feet.

A long spindly hand with a crooked finger and a nail longer than a tongue presses down on the sweater's shoulder and he stops to settle back on the ground.

"But you were the first to claim that all beings where children of your father. Isn't that how you had it written down, or is that just another lie you had buried beneath all that pretty language? More beautiful lies to keep the sheep in check, are they?"

Brother George turns away.

"Who gives a fuck who this man's father is? All I want to know is what he has to do with the infected," Barnett storms before grabbing and spinning the stranger around. "You have done nothing but feed me rumor after rumor about what these people have been doing and what has it gotten me so far? I've lost good men and nothing to show for it. If you don't give me a reason in the next two seconds why I shouldn't leave you dead here with these pathetic people, you'll be worm food, which honestly smells a lot better than you fucking do at this moment."

"Tsk, tsk," the stranger says.

A white hand of skin wrapped bone shoots out and hits Barnett in the chest sending the fat man tumbling into the dirt and weeds. Men raise their weapons and Kelly edges her way backward. No one is paying any attention to her. She looks at Brother George whose eyes meet hers.

She hesitates, and the slightest curl of his lips precedes his look moving from her to a point away from the violence and the death. The road that leads out of town is silent and empty. Anymore fighting and they'll never see her go.

"You stupid, sadistic, son of a whore!" Barnett storms as he rolls on the ground and finds his feet. His face looks about to pop and his hands shake so much he can barely wrap his fingers around the grips of the pistols laying on the ground beside him. "All that I have given you and this is how you repay me? For this fucking little town?"

The chuckle that leaves the stranger is deep, and it echoes through the depths of the dead village. Dark birds lift high into the air, their cawing a menacing sound as they flee into the shadows of the darkened day.

"Given me?" the stranger asks.

His laugh shakes the entire pile of wet towels. Barnett reaches him in a half dozen heavy steps and the pistol in his hand does not waver.

"I will take more from this world than any that has ever come before me. The remnants of the horror I have wrought will be written in the new histories and my name will be screamed by the tortured upon their dying breath. My brothers will never equal what I have done. My father will see that I have learned all there is to learn, and I will rise by his side. My rightful place, earned and paid for with the blood of all you insignificant fools!"

Barnett goes to squeeze the trigger, but the bony hand is out faster than a blink of an eye and with a single arm the large bastard is lifted from the ground by the throat where his feet dangle like a little child's.

"Do not think to pester me or give demands to those who will squash you like the little bugs that you are. Pawns in a game of chess played by beings who insignificant thought is longer than a single lifetime your species sees on this world. You are nothing but grains of sand passing in the wind. You will bow down to me and worship me with your last breath in hopes that I show mercy where you deserve none," the man says.

A gun shot fires and the impact of the bullet is nothing more than a pebble thrown against a wall. Green pus spews from the opening formed in the layers of wet cloth and everyone freezes, even Barnett who stops kicking.

Kelly begins to back away. A step or two, then more as the sudden urge for distance becomes more than a need but a propulsion forced by a firm hand ushering her away from the violence. She cannot turn away as the distance grows. The green liquid sizzles and spews a white gas as it hits the dirt. The man who fired the shot sits still, his rifle lowering.

"Have it your way," the man says.

Kelly can still hear him even though they have forgotten her entirely, and she has cleared Nicholi's body. Barnett goes flying like a weightless shirt as the stranger begins to laugh and a chanting picks up into the air. The soldiers open fire, their guns a thunder that shakes the ground and burns the air.

Turning and running, Kelly covers her ears, but the storm is too loud. Cracking with pain, her ears pop as louder than the martial thunder of gunfire, the demonic words take on a calling she can almost recognize. The language is foreign, the tongue nothing like she has ever heard before, but the urgency is real.

Inside she can feel its pull for her to turn and come back, but crying and running, she easily breaks free of its hold. Ahead the darkness unfolds and begs for her to enter. Shadows stretch, and she is running into a world she knows nothing about. Legs burning and chest pounding, she pushes on as the monsters and demons of the darkness begin to take shape.

Veering right and then left, she does not know where to go. She can't turn around. Certain death awaits if she goes back, but ahead shapes appear and disappear before her. Even hundreds of feet away from the church she can still feel the words.

The pounding of boots on pavement approaches and she dives to the ground. Crawling, a hedgerow of bushes lines the beaten path leading into the village and she curls into a ball to lose herself in the shadows.

A stampede shakes the ground she lies on as whatever it is draws closer.

There must be hundreds of them. Pulling the knife from her pocket she holds it against her chest for what comfort it can give. Within moments the first of the creatures emerge. A slow twisted jog at first, the infected shambles up within sight of the first building. Nose risen into the air, it sniffs a wet sound as blood and pus leak from open wounds. A broken tooth smile stretches across its face as the words of the call grow louder and the dull eyes of others begin to appear.

Kelly can smell nothing but rot and filth in the air. Like mold baking in the sun, the putrid smell of decay precedes the army that follows. She wants to scream at the sight of them, but her mind is lost in fear and pain. There are hundreds. A monstrous army with the feeling of unrelenting hunger following in their wake.

An explosion rocks the earth as a dark plume of smoke rises from the center of the village. The infected heed their master's call and charge past the first of the buildings. Screams of monsters and people fill the air.

Kelly rolls away from her small shelter and runs in the opposite direction. There is nowhere to go. This world is lost. Everything is dead and soon she will be as well. Cold hand gripping lifeless steel, she runs, and the fire of her tears is no match for the flames licking at her heels. She must put as much distance between her and this place of nightmares.

She will not stop.

She must keep going.

If she doesn't, they will catch her.

If they catch her, then she knows she will die.

Chapter Twenty One
Should Have Left It Behind

The choice is made and the regret sets in all too quickly. Deserted streets. Empty buildings and mangy cats. Rats as big as dogs looking for food and their eyes of fear and suspicion watch as Merchant walks the streets.

It is hard to distinguish the difference between the looks in the eyes of the people who live here, and the animals left to fend for themselves. They are scared. Clothes lines swing in the dry air, empty clips twisting as sheet metal bends and ripples a song of emptiness and regret. The soldiers have left them behind. To fight a war they may not return from. For in this world just stepping outside your door is a risk. Those few who remain to guard hardly look at one man walking the street with a woman held closely before him.

Dark clouds rumble overhead and anyone who isn't beneath a closed roof keeps their head down and the two passing along the empty road do not look their way. Strangers in the evening, their image is hardly a memory that will hold for more than a moment as the minds of those within this world slip further away from sanity.

"I'm so hungry," Red trembles.

"Quiet now," Merchant whispers. "You'll have whatever you want to eat the moment we get outside the city gates."

Red stumbles.

One foot drags over another and she trips forward. With quick hands, Merchant wraps an arm around her body and hauls her back to standing with little effort. The disease has already taken so much of what was returned to her. Back to the depths of her insanity, she is little more than the clothes he wrapped her in to get her out the door. Baggy denim pants. A filthy shirt smelling of week old sweat and mildew. Its gray color is either a trait or a symptom and it's hard to tell which. The thick leather boots, worn thin at the front toe, clap like clown shoes against the hard dirt beneath their feet.

"Slowly, Red. We are almost there," Merchant says.

Teeth snap at his neck and she tries to spin on him, but a squeeze of his hand forces her to remain with her back toward him.

"Watch it now," he adds, his voice growing deeper.

"Sss… sorry," she stutters. "It is harder this time to fight. I'm so hungry. It's like my thoughts aren't my own and there are gaps in my memory. I… I don't even remember where we came from."

"Then stay quiet. Follow my lead and keep your head down. We'll get this fixed and we'll find the one who did this to you."

Red nods her head before wiping away at the drool sliding from her lips.

The large wall looms before them. Huge doors of iron and rust locked shut and the shadow it casts grows darker. Silhouettes of the men who patrol the top move back and forth. They remain unchallenged. Night approaches and with the darkness comes the battle.

Tonight, there will be none. Those who fight and claw their way through waves of bullets and war to feed on the flesh of the people within are not here. They have an easier target this afternoon. Softer flesh with less fight to keep back their hungry appetites.

Merchant does not hesitate as he approaches the locked barrier. There is no way to open it from the outside. Up within the guard tower there must be some control that pulls it open and shut. Letting Red slip behind him, he turns along the wall toward a set of stairs that lead to the top. Metal creaks beneath his boots and he can feel Red's body practically press against the back of his bag as they climb upward. Her presence and weight hardly noticeable against the pull of the burden.

"Any of you looking for some help tonight?" Merchant asks as he reaches the top.

Leaving the last step, the stairs open into a wide square platform with a thatched roof of aged grass pulled tight. Two men look up, their eyes darkened with exhaustion and the cards on the three-legged tray table between them showing the one on the left is having a far luckier night than the other.

"Who the fuck are you?" the one on the right asks.

All facial hair with no cleaning. Knots and snarls curl their way beneath his hat and the skin beneath is pasty and white. He's quick to put down his hand and turn away from the game. Probably ready to lose again.

Neither of them turns their eyes from Merchant. Good.

"I'm the new guy in town. Halton said while everyone is out that any useful hands were to report here to the wall. I figured you'd be expecting the same fight you had the other evening," Merchant says.

"You mean we have every night," the one on the left answers. He drops his cards on the table face up. More kept than the other, this one is clean shaven, though the long brown hair beneath his cap reflects the light of burning candles with a sheen at least a week old. Three Kings hit the table, and he quickly wraps both hands around the small pile of coins sitting between them. "Tonight better be different or we are all in for a hell of a fight. Damn assholes took eighty percent of the regiment and left us with barely a skeleton crew. Who isn't here on the wall is spread thin as it is to patrol the streets and keep the damn looters out. Every fucking time to. Every. God. Damned. Time."

The loser of the two waves the other off with the back of his hand and stands. Both wearing army fatigues stained and worn with age, he extends his hand. Merchant shifts the bag over his shoulder so he can free his own arm and takes the young man's hand. Early twenties, if he's lucky. More like a child than a man as Merchant gives it a good squeeze and keeps the grip.

"Name's Merchant," he says with a small tug that pulls the soldier a step closer. "I was wondering, is this the tower that opens the gate down there?"

Counting the coins he has stacked in front of him, the other flips one into the air and catches it before letting the light of the fading sun catch it with a flash.

"Both sides technically have a switch but ours is the main control. Box panel is over there. One lever opens and the other closes. Just hope the assholes on the other side don't get up to their usual bullshit and try closing everything before whoever is coming or going finishes. Nothing short of a damn tank can stop those doors once they go to being shut."

"Good to know," Merchant says and with a crack of the wrist, drops the one still within his grip to his knees.

"Ow!" the man tries to yell but stumbles as Merchant's elbow finds him square in the throat.

Red's brittle hair waves in the air as she spins around Merchant like a shadow and pounces on the other. Chips and coins fly into the air as cards spill in every direction. The table falls with a cheap plastic sound before quickly being followed with the wet sound of breath pushing through a gaping hole in one's throat.

With a twist of the wrist, Merchant forces the other back to his feet and then to backpedal to the far end of the tower. The young man looks down at the bloody mess Red is leaving behind and his face pales while his eyes bulge at the sight.

"Keep your eyes on me, boy," Merchant growls. "Let's get those doors open and we'll make sure she is full of your friend here before we leave. Fuck with me and she gets a dessert. Do you understand?"

The man's lips begin to move but Merchant is quick to twist his grip harder and the soldier's knees begin to buckle.

"Concentrate! Open the controls and release the door. There are two ways out of this and by the look on your face, you don't want to choose that one."

With a nod, the man pinches his lips shut and shifts until he is looking at the control box. Pulling keys from his pocket, his hands shake and the half dozen keys rattle until he settles on one. The scratching of the surface as he stumbles to finish the job does little to hide the sound of Red feeding. Her growls of hunger and pleasure are feral and inhuman. Merchant doesn't know if he's made a mistake by letting her get it out of her system, but it is not like he has much of a choice. A little food will help keep the sickness at bay. He has more beef sticks, but there isn't a supply in this world that can feed what she has. There is only one way to do that, and he isn't ready for that option.

"Hurry up, boy. She looks like she is about finished," he warns.

Merchant can feel the strength in the young man's arm weaken as he rushes to get the box unlocked. With a final click he throws it open and as promised the inside is little more than two leather wrapped control levers.

"Which one is it?" Merchant asks.

The soldier turns to look as the sound of bone being crunched beneath teeth rattles the air. A bulge grows in the man's throat and his lips pucker as Red pulls a long sinewy tendon from the dead man's shoulder with her teeth and the blood on her chin glistens wet and thick.

"Look, man. Help me get this job finished and we'll leave you alone. She isn't a big girl and your fat friend here looks plenty for her stomach. All we want is to get outside the wall. Close it behind us. Keep the others like her out. Do you really want her to stay within the barrier of this place? Open up and I'll carry her out myself."

A slow dragged out nod of fear and hesitation turns the man back to the control panel.

"Pull this one down and the left door opens. Pull both and the whole thing opens up. Push them back and it closes. Easy as that," he says.

Merchant watches as Red bites and tears into the guts of the corpse. Black bile and brown liquid sloshes between the torn flesh of the opening. She purrs as her face sloshes the gore to the left and right, digging deeper with her teeth.

"Do it. We'll be out once the door is open," Merchant says turning away from the sight.

There is no way this isn't a mistake. Red is lost to the world. He should have killed her back in that basement. She's a monster now. No hiding what she has a become.

"You might have five minutes," the soldier says. "The other side will demand to know what I'm doing. If I don't answer quick enough or give them something they believe, they'll pull their lock and shut the door with you between it."

Merchant nods. He knows the risk. There is nothing else he could do other than fighting his way out and there is no guarantee in that.

"That's my problem. Pull it and keep your mouth shut. If I hear even a single word from this tower, I'll send her up here for desserts."

The man turns and pulls on the right lever. Metal grinds and gears groan as the monster barrier begins to slide. Dirt piles beneath the moving weight and the ache and pains of the city become audible in its torturous path.

"Enough with that, Red," Merchant barks. "Time for us to get out of here."

Bloody gore dripping from her chin and eyes gone wild with rage, Red looks up at him. A pink tongue sticks out and laps up the drips of blood and gristle stuck beneath the folds of her lips. She growls before turning back to her meal.

"I said get the fuck up," Merchant demands and with a handful of the back of her shirt, Merchant lifts her from the ground.

Hands, claws, and boots kick like a wild animal. She hisses and spits, the feral scream of her eyes enough to start a fire and he lets her hang for a few moments.

"Get this shit out of you, Red. We need to keep moving or you are going to die right here within these walls."

She hisses again and swings but catches nothing but air.

"Ah! I will kill you!" she screams.

The sound is sharp and broken with cuts and scratches.

"You... you are... you're going to take her with you, aren't you," the soldier behind him begs.

Merchant spares the man a momentary glance before dropping Red on the ground and with the bottom of his boot pushing her with enough force to roll her to the stairs.

"Yeah, I'm taking her with me. If that door moves even a fucking inch, I'm sending her back up here to finish what she started."

Red growls but shies away as he approaches. Like an animal she crawls to the steps, her eyes and snarl angry but the claws retract. He keeps his eyes on her.

"Move it," he orders.

She looks at the lone soldier and then at the corpse. With another snarl she turns and crawls down the first few steps. Merchant does not turn to look back. There is no time to waste.

Half way down the steps and a half dozen hisses later, their time runs out. Metal steps ping and rock kicks up into the air as bullets slam into the wall, stairs, and ground. Merchant ducks as the wall behind him sparks with the next impact. Red rears and growls before bolting down the stairs.

"Get back here, you stupid bitch," Merchant yells but she does not listen.

Clearing the final steps, she races across the opening of the door where two men step in from the outside. Rifles barking, dirt and dust kick into the air as she drives forward. Bag over his shoulder, Merchant races to keep up. The men's attention lock on the ball of fury clearing the distance faster than death itself.

A yelp escapes as blood jets from Red's shoulder and she stumbles and rolls. Merchant, rolling his bag from his back, heaves it into the air. The sack slams into the first and he tumbles with a grunt. Spinning on heels and palms, Red pounces clear the final distance in a single leap.

The man's screams are muffled and wet as she tears into his throat. Rolling the burden from his chest, the fallen soldier makes it to his knees as Merchant reaches and crunches his knee into chin. Bones crack and dust kicks into the air as the body flips backward with a crash. A boot into the neck silences the man forever.

"We need to move!" Merchant yells and Red growls as blood splatters in all directions from the man beneath her.

Grunting, he picks his bag up and makes his way over to her. Wide eyes of fear stare at him from where she hasn't torn the man's face off. The lower half of his jaw lays slack where she has eaten away the muscle and blood slows as it pumps from the open wounds.

"Get up!" Merchant orders and pulls her from the kill.

This time she swings on him and rakes her nails across his face. Deep cuts burn as blood seeps from torn flesh and he shoves her away. She tumbles across the ground and their world groans with the sound of grinding gears. Beside them the doors begin to pull shut once again. Shadows grow as the shouts of the men above become orders followed by the angry buzzing of bullets before slamming into the dirt.

"I'll kill you!" Red screams before launching herself at Merchant.

With a sidestep and a crack of his elbow to her chin, her body falls limp as she topples to the ground.

"A lot of spunk in that one," Snake-Eyes says.

The ghost materializes beside the torn corpse, his white suit shimmering as he shakes his head in disgust.

"Never thought I'd see the day I preferred the work of that crazy doctor over this mess," the ghost says before a set of bullets tear apart his corporeal presence.

Merchant says nothing. Lifting his bag and Red's limp form, he turns and runs for the entrance. Bullets crack into the metal barrier as the engine of their demise grinds its way shut and shoulders scratching against the sharp edges of iron and steel, Merchant slips through and the darkness of the beyond quickly welcomes him home.

Chapter Twenty Two
Only the Wicked Survive

Pain.

Terror.

Darkness and shadow.

All of them surround her as Kelly crawls through the brush. The sounds of screams and gunfire, war and death, are long in the past. Forgotten behind the need to survive and to continue moving.

Sharp branches and angry leaves reach and tear at her skin. Itchy burns cover her arms and the palms of her hands and the flesh on her knees are torn and raw. Breath comes in large gulps and sweat runs from her face, down her knotted hair, and she pushes on.

When did she stop crying?

She doesn't know. Only silence and the suffocating emptiness of the lonely world surrounds her. Shadows follow her every movement and any number of unknown things track her every movement. But she cannot stop.

Gripping each new piece of ground with as much strength as she can muster, she pulls herself forward. How long has she been running and how far has she gone?

Time and distance mean nothing to her. Only the thought that she can't let anything catch her, not her breath, not fear itself, or the only thing she has left in this world will be lost.

Her life.

"Why me?" she sobs.

The pain is too much, and she tips onto her side against the welcoming roots of an Oak tree. A loving embrace that holds her tight as she curls the smallest ball she can.

"Why did this have to happen?" she asks and looks at the sky.

There is no answer. Darkness broken only by the shine of a distant moon looks down at her with either contempt or disinterest. She is not sure which.

Pulling her knees tighter against her chest, she fights back the shiver that runs down her spine. The weather is too warm to be this cold, but her body does not care. The tiny shakes begin at the tips of her fingers, blood soaked and embedded with mud from crawling so far away.

Is she a coward?

The look on Nicholi's face before they killed him. So much defiance. Determination and anger all to the last moment. Even Brother George did not give up. Those eyes of his telling her to run. She could not have mistaken as she traced his glance to the path that has led her this far.

What was she supposed to do now?

Alone.

Lost.

Helpless if she ever stumbles upon anyone or any THING. She isn't equipped to live out here in the wilds. All it will take is a single infected and this little dream of escape and survival will be over.

The tears begin again and the shakes, tiny but enough to pull a sob out from deep within her throat, take over her entire body. She begins to rock and the sounds of the forest which at one time would have comforted her now close in and terrify her.

Eyes peer out from everywhere. Leaves rustle and branches snap with the unseen approach of her demise. Burying her face into her knees, she waits for the inevitable. There is nothing left for her to give. The peaceful embrace of acceptance sweeps through her body.

More branches break.

Getting closer.

Hugging her legs tight, a sharp point pricks the side of her leg. Reaching down, she feels the object shoved deep into her pocket.

Nicholi's knife.

Jamming her hand in and freeing the weapon, she holds it in front of her with a shaky hand. The blade wavers and isn't very threatening. Maybe three inches and dull, but it is at least something. Gripping the handle with little more than will itself, she lets the strength in its solidity run through her.

Maybe she has a chance. If she heads far enough south, she'll find the river. Then all she has to do is follow it until she finds another town. People need water. Everyone does if they want to survive.

Travel at night. Stay in the shadows. She can do this.

More branches snap, this time closer and with more urgency. The strength and courage fades as quickly as it arrived.

A tree limb falls, and this time is followed by the crashing of something big and heavy against the ground.

Kelly pushes her heels into the dirt and forces herself against the hard strength of the Oak tree. Brandishing the knife like a ward, she watches as the darkness around her shimmers with the movement of the trees.

Light filtering down from above does nothing but leave her world in shades of gray and black.

Her heart pounds in her ears. The pain in her chest cracks at her ribs and the skin of her hands and knees burn as if on fire.

An entire tree begins to shake. A monster has found her. Now the knife feels like nothing more than a twig. Whatever this thing is, it is huge.

Her throat goes dry and fresh tears run down her face. She can't keep her weapon steady. Even seated, the muscles in her legs go limp and she wants to sink into the ground.

"God damn it, you fucking piece of shit," a man barks.

The forest before her explodes in activity and she recognizes him before she can even fully see him.

Logan Barnett.

The fat man trips and crashes down in front of her. Hundreds of pounds of jelly and tailored suit slam onto the dirt floor and dust and leaves kick into the air.

Kelly has no idea what to do. Disbelief. Shock. Confusion. Everything invades her already ravaged body as the man she hates most in this world lays sprawled out in front of her. Face-down, he struggles to climb to his knees as roots and twigs tangle across his arms and legs.

"Fuck this place and its fucking god-forsaken wilderness. Man was destined to live in the fucking city.

We wouldn't have built them if we weren't supposed to. Fuck, I hate all this shit. The infected, these stupid people and their stupid prayers. And most of all I hate these fucking trees. When I get back home, I'm going to…," he rambles on until he finally notices she is sitting right beside him.

He is no longer the powerful figure he once was. Blood runs from welts across his forehead. Mud and debris from his hasty retreat through the forest stick to his suit which is now as brown as the shit he smells like.

A look of confusion mars his face until his brain catches up and the edge of his lips turn sinister. Kelly can do nothing. The knife in her hand, the only shield she has is little more than a paperweight shaped like a pen. She squeezes harder but no matter what it won't become a sword and slay the demon in front of her.

"What do we have here?" Barnett asks.

He rolls himself to his butt with a considerable effort full of grunts and huffs. A lung full of air puffs from his chubby lips and even from a few feet away the man has a horrible stench of shit and sweat. Kelly wants to edge herself away, but the Oak's embrace is now the chains that bind her to her fate.

"Get away from me, you monster," she demands.

His smile grows open and wide as she waves the small knife in front of her. She can see how much of a useless venture it is to him. There is even a bit of joy in his bright eyes, an almost pleasurable sparkle.

"Monster? Did you see those things out there?" he asks, then rolls onto his knees. "Those are the real monsters. I'm little more than a city leader, a mayor if you ask me. Just like your Father George."

"Brother George," she cuts him off.

He wipes away the sweat dripping from the tips of his hair and takes another deep breath with a sigh.

"Yes, Brother George. As I was saying, I am very much like him. I have an entire city to look after. One much bigger than that village of yours and full of people not much different than yourself. Men, women, children, all of them with dreams and hopes of surviving this plague the world has become. Don't they have the right to survive? Do their lives mean so much less than yours? All I wanted was the answer to these demons that have ravaged our world. Is that too much to ask?"

Anger flares in her stomach. Kelly no longer needs this pathetic little knife. She'll kill this man with her bare hands.

"There is no answer! We told you that. Every time you came, we told you it was through God that we cured those people. We had no medicine or machines to fix the sick. You just refused to see it and killed everyone trying to prove us wrong."

"You can stop lying, little girl. There is no God and he sure as hell isn't going to sit there and protect some small, little, insignificant village while the rest of the planet suffers. Your Brother George was a liar, and it looks like he had all of you ensnared with his deceit. Too bad in the end whatever he had wasn't going to be enough to save him."

With all the strength she can muster, Kelly drives her heels into the base of the tree and throws herself at the fat monster. Knife held out before her, she aims straight for his giant belly. Round and wide, she can't possibly miss. However deep this thing can go, she will stab as many times as it takes to tear these hurtful words right out of his guts.

Light flashes across her eyes as Barnett moves faster than she ever could see coming. The back of his hand sends her rolling and leaves her sprawling across the forest floor. Aches and pains pinch at her joints. The side of her face stings and burns where her jaw and cheekbones feel like they are broken. Fresh tears run down her face and she can't stop the whimpering.

"Stupid little bitch. Don't you see. I'm not the bad guy. I want the same thing as you do," Barnett says as he pushes himself to his feet. He turns away from her as the sounds of breaking limbs and rustling leaves cuts him off. Turning back to her, the smile on his face is gone, but it is not replaced with anger. "We want this world to return to what it used to be. Not exactly peaceful, but at least livable. Your Brother George had a secret that died with him back there. It's too bad, because he could have saved a lot more people than the small speck you had collected over the years. I offered him a chance. I really did. Now, if you want to live, get yourself up and let's go. I can forgive these transgressions when we return to the city. More of my men will be waiting, and we'll be safe. Once we are out of the forest, I should be able to get them on the radio and they'll come and pick us up. You ready to play nice and come along quietly?"

Kelly rolls away cupping her hands over her face and curling into a ball.

"Go fuck yourself. I'd rather die here in this forest than ever go back with you," her words are muffled through dirty fingers and sobs.

"Stupid bitch. Don't know what's good for you, do you?"

Tree branches snap in the distance and the sound of footsteps beating on the hard-packed earth of the forest draw closer. Barnett pulls a large knife, twice the length of the silly one Kelly dropped, and easily as wide as her hand. He spins around, his eyes hard and angry.

"They may have found us. Get your ass up and we can get out of here."

Kelly can't find the words. She refuses to go with him. She doesn't want to die, but the thought of following him back to his home is revolting beyond belief. It would be betraying everything she knows. All those who she calls family died back in the village and she lives only to follow and survive with this Logan Barnett?

The strength of her legs and conviction will not return. Even as the sounds grow closer and begin to come from all directions. She cannot possibly pull herself to join him.

"Oh, fuck this shit," Barnett barks. Rough hands with grips of iron squeeze into her arms and yank her from the ground. "Look, I have no problem leaving you here to die. Trust me, you wouldn't be the first person I've left because they didn't have the courtesy to try and save themselves. But while you are here, I may as well keep you as an insurance policy. Now, get your ass moving."

He shoves her, and she stumbles forward, her arm catching the first tree trunk for stability. Another shove scratches the skin on her arm sending fire racing through her body, but it gets her moving.

"Insurance policy?" she asks.

The muscles in her legs cramp and he is a step behind her, his presence baring down on her as the knife wavers between them with every step.

"Yeah, if you don't keep moving and stay ahead of these monsters, I have little to fight with other than this pig sticker I'm carrying. It might keep one or two of them off me, but by the sounds of it there are far more of them quickly closing in behind us. If you don't get that tight ass of yours moving, when they catch us, I'm going to let them feed on you while I make a run for it. Now, it's in YOUR best interest that they don't catch us. Understand?"

Kelly nods and keeps pushing through the undergrowth of the forest. Thick brambles and thorns cut into the denim covering her legs and scratch at the already bleeding skin of her arms. She has nowhere to run. No place to hide. This is the only way she is going to survive.

Logan Barnett.

Her savior.

Her captor.

Her monster.

Chapter Twenty Three
A Tethered Monster and Unleashed Revenge

The trail of blood behind them is thick and easy to follow. There is no time to hide the evidence and looking back, they do not see any signs of pursuit.

Darkness complete overhead, Merchant pushes Red through the moonlight and the forest. Her walk is staggered, and she stops frequently to lean against the trunk of a tree or a rock large enough to rest against.

"We've lost this one again," Snake-Eyes says.

His ghost form weaves in and out between the Oaks and the pines. More shadow than substance, he's little more than a figment caught with the corner of the eye.

"She's stronger than she was," Merchant says.

He watches as she staggers further forward. Blood drips from her, both from the wound opened on her shoulder and the gore left to dry on her shirt and skin where she gutted those men back at the wall.

"Bleeding like a ravaged animal, you may as well put her out of her misery," Snake-Eyes adds.

"You sound like you actually care about her," Merchant says.

The ghost waves away the suggestion with a look and the back of a hand that passes through a bush without disturbing a single leaf.

"We both know what happens if you kill her. That damn bag of yours is going to kill you one day and I'm going to be there laughing when it happens. Every new weight gets you one step closer, and what's the life of a single infected going to do? Go ahead demon, kill her. Add to the memories you already carry."

Merchant grits his teeth and turns away. Red stumbles, falls to one knee, and then picks herself back up.

"You OK up there?" he asks.

She growls but does not turn around.

"I'm fucking hungry again. It's like my stomach can never fill and all my mind can think of is the next thing I'm putting into my mouth. Doesn't help the smell of blood is everywhere," she replies.

"We'll get to the village soon enough. They'll take care of you like they did last time. You'll be home again."

"You mean a fucking monster again. This time it's real, Merchant. You know it. Whoever the fuck you are talking to knows it. May as well take that pistol I gave you and put me out of my misery. All I can do is think of eating. I'm not even sure we are going in the right direction."

"I do," Merchant says.

"What?" Red questions, stops, and turns around.

Merchant doesn't stop and keeps walking. She stares at him as he passes and licks her lips smearing the blood over the white of her skin.

"We are going in the correct direction. We'll be far enough from the city by daybreak and can follow the road from there. You'll make it, Red. Save your strength, you are going to need it."

He tosses her a stick of jerky and she catches it with her good arm. The wounded one is surprisingly still agile, but slow as the blood refuses stop its flow down her arm. The sound of her teeth grinding into the dried meat is louder than the crunch of leaves beneath their boots.

"Whatever you say, demon," Snake-Eyes cuts in. "We both know she doesn't have a chance. You are bringing a lamb to slaughter, and you know it. She'll be lucky if that village is still even in one piece. We all saw the army leaving and with that much firepower, they may even be able to slow you down."

Merchant ignores the ghost's taunts and keeps moving, Red close on his heels. The army isn't the problem. He doubts the men and women of the town have anything to defend themselves against anything resembling an army, but it's what travels in their wake. He can still feel the burn across his face. The damage may have healed, but there is something else there. The look in the man's eyes. He's seen it before.

Evil.

Power.

This isn't the first time they have crossed paths. Trying to think of the last time he saw those eyes, he can only remember one thing. There were a lot more bodies on the ground than that little village and Brother George can supply.

***

Smoke swirls in the air like carrion. Wide, slow circles, meandering and refusing to leave their vigil. The smell of sulfur and death fills the air. The taste of bile from deep within the gut burns the tongue and rots the teeth.

Crackles of gunfire pop in the distance. Little echoes of a world moved on and a war that has forgotten. Movement is pain and pain is remembrance. A memory that the misery isn't over, and the worst is yet to come.

Merchant tries to move but the chains hold him down. Invisible bonds that feel more like an elephant sitting on his chest than bindings refusing to let him move. He squeezes his hands into fists and fills them with blood-soaked dirt. The grains cut at his skin and he watches the smoke above. A tunnel of gray and ash spinning a circle directly down to him.

Lucky for him.

Anyone with twenty miles could follow that to his useless body. Shriveled here like a corpse, all bones and leathery skin.

"You are a unique one," a raspy voice cuts through the air. "Unlike the others, I see great potential in you. Strength, determination, and something else. Deep inside, it waits. Sitting in anticipation of one day being released."

Merchant does not see the speaker, but his chest feels the weight of the words. A needle pushes through uniform and body armor until it breaks skin and his body erupts into a fiery pit. Molten slag fills his gut and he can feel it melt right through his body, out his ass, and pooling where it withers away the muscle and skin of his legs in a charring heap of meat and ash.

He tries to scream but the words are boiled out in bubbles and coughs. Convulsions rampage their way through his limbs, cramping muscles not melted into putrid liquid and bubbles burst with pus and bile.

"Deep inside of you it is. Such a beautiful specimen. They do not make them like they used to, but even then, you would be special," the voice continues. Closer now, the sharp-edged sound cuts through the air and eardrums. "I must have you for my collection. The greatest of my collection. A magnum opus so early in my display. Father would be so proud. I will model them after you, mirror images that will never match the perfection of you, but even minor flaws will create such masterpieces."

A flash of light blinds Merchant as the pain ripples like still water and the skin on his chest heaves as he struggles for air. The stench of burning meat, cooked human flesh after a horrific fire, fills his mouth instead of the life-giving oxygen he needs. His eyes roll back, and parts of his body refuse to move regardless of their commands.

"Do not fight it. I am almost there. I can feel what you hide deep inside you. There is nothing that I cannot see," the voice whispers and the words draw blood that drips hot and sticky. "Yes, I can feel it, almost within my grasp."

The pressure on his chest crushes through bones and Merchant still cannot see anything but the bright blue sky and the gray poison tornado now filled with the cooking smoke of his body.

Why is this happening to me?

The answer does not come. Blood fills his mouth and he can feel the intruder moving through the emptiness within his body the burning has left. Flowing through every cavity within him, the explorer leaves no corner unturned. Every dark spot is examined, his mind an open book.

"I see it now," the voice coos. "Such a secret. Father would be amazed, and to think one of you carried such a gift. We never would have thought it possible, but here I see it with my own two eyes."

A dark shadow draws closer and blocks the light from above. Wraithlike, it sucks the world away in the darkness that competes with life itself. Merchant tries to blink the tears of pain away, but his body is not his own. He coughs and his throat fills.

The figure leans down above his face. Things crawl within that darkness. Insects and the workers of decay. Two eyes open and Merchant chokes out a gasp.

Green flame burns within the shadowed sockets. Pupils made of fire watch with wonder, regarding him as a curiosity and probing his thoughts with a single look.

"It is almost within my grasp. Ooh, father will be so happy," the shadow taunts.

A white flash of flame erupts behind the darkness and the darkness is thrown clear. The pain and pressure rips from Merchant's body with all the air in his lungs. He gasps and the cold sweet taste of dust filled air fills his mouth and a fresh flow of tears clouds his eyes.

"You!" the darkness screams.

White fire, a giant ball of it, blinds Merchant. Walking passed him, the sudden need to roll and look away becomes almost too strong to ignore. Merchant tries to comply, but the muscles in his body cramp and his back arches. A foam fills his mouth and the tongue between his teeth is thick and heavy.

Air refuses to fill his lungs. The bright flame stalks the cowering darkness. Merchant tries to reach toward them, but every movement is excruciating in the tearing of his muscles.

"Your effort here is wasted. He dies and Father will have him," the shadow hisses. "It is too late, and, in the end, we will have him. Look, see for yourself. The light within him fades, the darkness is all that remains."

Merchant's eyes grow heavy. His lungs are thousand-pound weights and he tries desperately to breathe. His entire body burns. The passage in his throat is clogged. His mind swirls in endless circles.

The light stops its approach. Somehow, without being to see any features, Merchant can tell it turns toward him. His dirty, blood crusted hand reaches out. Wanting, needing whatever it is that can scare away the darkness.

The world swirls in his eyes. Confusion and disorientation. He cannot keep his eyes open as his insides burn and scream. He's dying. Chocking on his own tongue and vomit. Hand shaking, he reaches out.

The light draws closer. Almost within grasp. The strength in his arm fails. It hits the ground. Dust kicks into the air. His vision darkens.

This is it.

Merchant wants to scream. Yell that he has so much more to do, but the bubbles between his lips pop and the world is silent once more.

Chapter Twenty Four
Pain Does Not Equal Regret

Whichever is worse, the heartache of loss or the numbing of toes and cracking of aching bones over miles of marching, Kelly does not know.

She has never been this far. Miles, years, an entire world now separates her from home. Whatever remains of it. Her last tears were shed hours ago and now the emptiness inside is an ache that rattles within her, wide and hollow.

Logan remains right behind her. His heavy breathing a constant reminder as it chokes and coughs its way through the empty forest. Whatever had found them is no longer there. No sound of pursuit or attack since they ran into each other and now she isn't so sure she sees it as a good thing.

Leaves crackle beneath her shoes, the splitting pain of her feet driving needles up her legs and the warmth of the coming morning already filling her shirt with sweat. Salt coats her lips and the smell of Barnett is worse than the spring families of skunks that live and make their homes beneath the old hay barn on the west edge of town.

A new sob rattles Kelly's chest and she coughs at the thought. The memory of the flames cutting a mile into the sky as the buildings burned is still fresh and raw in her mind. Probably the brightest light this world has seen in years as the entire remaining supply of feed and supplies burned to ash and fell beneath the wrath of the monster less than two steps behind her.

"We are almost there, sweet thing," Barnett says.

He calls her SWEET THING now and Kelly wants to claw his eyes out and stomp on them until they are mush in the dirt beneath her feet.

"Almost there. Once we reach the road, I'll radio my men and we'll be on our way," he says.

Biting her tongue, she stomps her next several steps into the hardened forest earth and a root gives way beneath her ankle. Pain, a ripping sound, and a shriek sends Kelly sprawling onto her knees and then her face. Tears run from her eyes as fire purifies the inside of her right leg.

"Ah, get the fuck up," Barnett barks.

Rolling away, Kelly grabs for her ankle. The skin is already tender beneath her touch and the pain is half way up her calve.

"Don't touch me!" she shouts and tries to scoot herself up against the base of the nearest tree.

A birch with its narrow trunk and bark of paper crinkles against her body. The leaves above rustle against the lightening sky now a deep purple as it prepares its journey to blue with the coming of the sun.

"I do not have time for this, you stupid little bitch," Barnett barks again and reaches for her arm.

On instinct, she swats away his attempt before pulling her leg closer to her body.

"Get the fuck away from me. I twisted my ankle. I

can't keep walking," she yells back at him.

"You are going to keep walking if I say you are, and I wouldn't give a shit if you broke the damn thing."

He reaches for her and when she swats at him again, he drops his hand before bringing it across her face with a resounding crack.

Tears and sobs erupt from her body as she tumbles onto her side, the roots and sharp twigs of the ground cutting into her face.

"I told you, we are moving, and that is final. Get that pretty, little ass of yours off the ground, and let's get moving."

Kelly claws at the forest floor and tries to pull herself away. Dirt and stone peel away at the nails of her hands and her leg is useless from the knee down. A dead weight that anchors her as the fat man approaches.

"I said get away from me," she screams.

A meaty hand wraps itself around her arm and spins her onto her back. She looks up at him. His face of puffy red cheeks, wild angry eyes, and a matt of wet dark hair plastered to every side of his round piggish head.

"Stupid fucking girl. I'm trying to save your life, and this is how you treat me."

He reaches down again, his giant paw opening to grab the front of her shirt. She doesn't know what she takes a hold of, but it breaks away, and she swings it as hard as she can.

A wet thud cracks the man on the side of the head. His eyes roll back, turning a milky white, and he crashes against the side of the Birch. Leaves and small twigs crash and try to cover him in a natural blanket. His body does a slow slide down the twisted bark and Kelly does not have time to see if she has killed him.

Pain sears through her leg as she rolls onto her knees and begins to crawl away. With every single movement, she drives the torture through her body, but she bites back and lets it fall away with the tears that drip from her cheeks and nose.

Putting one hand in front of the other, she keeps going. Whatever distance she can use to separate them, she'll take. Hide in a bush. Roll down a hill and get lost in the shadows that stay well past sunrise. Once he realizes he can't find her, he'll give up and head back to his hellhole city.

The infected can find him there. Eat out his eyes and burn the world around him like he has done to her. Muscle and joints ache as she moves forward. The thought of the infected sends ice down her spine, but she can't let it stop her.

New cuts open on her arm and the pain is magnified against everything she feels. A darkness opens ahead. Maybe it's a hill. A shallow drop that will help conceal where she is.

It is only a few dozen feet more. Kelly digs her fingers into the ground and pulls with everything she has left. Each step a horrid grind of determination and sheer will.

The end is within her reach. She can feel the ground begin to dip. A smile dares to crease the edges of her lips.

"Got you, you fucking little whore," Barnett's bark is angry and the grip on her shirt as he flips her onto her back is proof he has a bite. "Think you can get rid of me with a simple whack on the head? I'll show you, you little piece of shit. Takes more than a crack on the noggin to stop the likes of Logan Barnett."

Kelly tries to crawl away on her back, kick at his legs with her good ankle and slide down the hill. He moves with her meager attempt at an escape and stomps his boot down on her twisted limb.

"Ah!" she screams.

The fire racing through her leg threatens to black her out. The sky and its lightening blue color swims and tears run freely down her face.

"Don't go calling every fucking monster in this forest, you little bitch. We don't have time for that. I figured I'd get to wait till I got us back, cleaned you up a bit, then taught you how to truly appreciate everything I've done for you. I guess we can start our lessons right here, right now."

Grinding his heel into her leg, Kelly's body convulses, and he laughs as her leg arches but the weight he presses down with refuses to let her move. With practiced hands he begins to work at his belt. The large buckle snapping away with a firm click and springing free of the tension stretching it.

"Now, you are going to be a good girl and stay quiet or this is going to be a lot rougher than you could ever imagine," Barnett says.

The lust and anger in his eyes are clear. Kelly bites down on her lip and tries to let her body relax, but the pressure on her busted ankle rolls through her like a tidal wave. His smile grows as she grips the earth, her fingertips sinking deep.

"Please…" she pleads and tries to pull away.

"Don't give me any of that begging shit," he answers. "We could have played this game later, on better terms, and after you realized everything that I've done for you. But you had to go and make it hard on yourself."

He leans forward, and the pain rolls her eyes into the back of her skull.

"P… pu… please," she chokes and reaches a shaking hand out.

Barnett follows her arm and pulls back the leg that is grinding into the twisted joint and cracked bones.

"Oops, I almost forgot," he chuckles.

The zipper of his pants grinds as the teeth pull loose. Kelly whimpers but does not try to crawl away.

"See, isn't it better to stop all the fighting," Logan says as he begins to lower his bulk down. The large belly pulling the bottom of his ruined shirt free.

"Ah!" Kelly screams as she throws a pile of dirt and leaves into his face.

Barnett is quick enough to turn and let most splatter on the side of his head, but not to prevent her good foot kicking out and catching him in his exposed groin. A heavy gasp and sigh break free of his lips as he rolls backward, tumbling onto the ground.

Kelly doesn't hesitate. Spinning onto her knees, she crawls away. This time not down the hill but alongside of it. No more thoughts of hiding, only distance will save her.

She tries to pick herself up, put one foot under herself, but the grinding of bone sends her back onto her belly. The sound of huffing and cursing quickly follows as she knows Barnett is already after her.

Clawing and pulling, she tries to keep going. The

ground beneath her body hardens and the shadows thin as the morning finally arrives. Trees grow farther apart, and the thunder of Logan's boots is a tidal wave as he chases after her. This is it. He will not forgive her this time.

She must keep fighting. Grabbing onto a rock, she wraps her fingers around it and keeps crawling. Beneath her, the ground slopes down. Quickly, she tumbles and begins to slide. The last of the trees open, a hedgerow of bushes splitting to reveal a clearing to an unkept road.

Empty cars remain scattered like tombstones in the distance. Rusted skeletons, hollow and forgotten in the shadows of the world's passing.

Kelly loses her grip and rolls down the embankment. Rocks, leaves, dirt and debris follow her down.

"Get back here, you stupid cunt!" Barnett barks.

His bulky figure bursts from the trees and crushes the bushes in front of him. Kelly is barely able to glance at his silhouette before the world spins again and she steamrolls toward the broken pavement.

More curses follow the thunder that is his body rolling down after her. Coming to a stop, her head aches and her stomach spins, but Kelly tries to regain ground and pulls herself toward the first broken car. Doors missing, the inside has been gutted by fire and weather, the seats inside a shredded mess of springs and torn cloth.

"You fucking little," Barnett starts.

He grabs her pants, yanks her backward against the hardened pavement and rolls her on her back. Screaming, Kelly swings the rock in her hand, a fist full of stone aimed wide and at his cheek.

Her wrist goes numb as Barnett catches the blow with the back of his arm and the rock spirals out into the air. A fist connects with the side of her jaw. Lights flash and the world goes dark.

"Stupid bitch," he barks. "I don't want to hit a woman, but you are going to drive the monster out of me."

His pants are torn and hanging wide from his groin. Pain explodes through Kelly's face and finding what extra reserves she can she spits at the fat man, a big glob of red phlegm splattering on his shirt.

"Still going to be feisty, are we?"

He backhands her again. A tooth in her mouth breaks loose and blood gushes into the back of her throat. She coughs and the warm droplets spray over her face and neck.

"That's it. Time to think of what you've done," he says.

With a yank he pulls her closer to him, towering over her with his bulk. Searing fire rips through the skin of her back as the pavement tears her shirt and the flesh beneath. More blood fills her mouth and she tries to turn, but he crunches the bottom of his boot onto the inside of her elbow.

"I don't care if I have to kill you out here. Not what I had in mind for you, but you are getting awfully close to forcing my hand, little lady."

Any response she has is cut off by the roar of a mechanical monster. An engine rattles the ground beneath her, the tiny pieces of shale bouncing and chattering as the stampeding metal creation clears the crest of a far hill. Lights, burning in yellow glory, glare as they bounce.

A vehicle approaches. Fast and almost seemingly out of control. The grin on Barnett's face grows wide.

"Looks like I didn't even have to bother radioing my men. They are already on their way," he mocks.

Every hope. Every dream Kelly ever had dies. This is it. Her last chance at freedom and there is nowhere to go. Swallowing hard, she lets the last fires of her soul fade into the darkness that is to come.

***

The hunger is crazy. All-consuming and with a mind of its own. Everything that moves is potential food. Small creatures. Large ones that walk on two feet. She can smell the blood in their hearts, hear the beating even if she can barely see them. Her stomach growls even though she knows it is full. Pus and blood leak from her wounds. They hurt and fester, but that does not stop her.

Red glances back at the man who now follows her. He is big. She can already taste his flesh beneath her teeth.

He looks at her. Those eyes. So clear and with no fear. She wants to rip them out and taste the sweet nectar within them.

He nods at the direction they are going. She hisses and turns away.

She will have him. She has to. The hunger is killing her. The muscles in her body weaken. It is gnawing away at her from the inside.

Red takes another bite of the meat stick the dark man has given her. A cooling sensation runs through her belly. She likes it. Wants more, but he will only give her a couple at a time.

She hisses at him again.

The trees around them do not care. She does not care about them either. They cannot help her hunger. She cannot bite into them. They do not bleed.

"We need to head back to the road," the man named Merchant says.

Yes, that is his name. The cooling of the fire within her begins to clear her mind. She can feel it pull away like a shower curtain. Steam and fog still obscure the finer lines, but figures and thoughts are there for her taking.

"More of them will be that way," she answers. "I can't fight this much longer. If we run into them, I'm not sure what I will do."

He grunts.

She knows he is coming up with a plan. He always does and just as quickly as the curtain was pulled away, she can feel the haze clouding her mind.

A squirrel runs from the bush in front of her and bolts up the tree. Saliva and blood fill her mouth as she spins to watch it scurry with its little claws up the bark and into the shadows.

"Here, eat a little more of this. We need to make for the road," the dark man says.

He thrusts a stick in front of her and she almost bites his hand as her teeth clench down on the stick. The cooling is instant, and the haze recedes like the darkness in the sky.

Morning is almost here. Merchant veers away from their path and begins to follow a small trail between trees that lead downhill. Quickly, she follows in step. On his back, the bag he carries bounces back and forth and she can hear the different objects inside.

Metal on metal. Some even sound like glass and plastic. Is there food in there? Her mouth waters at the idea of that entire sack being filled with those glorious beef sticks.

Shaking, her hand reaches out for the loose buckles that bounce with every step.

"I wouldn't do that if I were you," he warns. "Try to remember what happened last time you did that."

Her mind does not want to go into the past. Memories of darkness and pain. Closing her eyes for a second, she tries to shake away the clouds and remembers snow. Lots of white powder and the cold that hurt her bones. There was blood. Lots of it. Most of it hers and then there was him. Towering over her, darkness and death wrapped into a monster covered in gore and she feels the fear that ruined her body.

Recoiling, she lets a small distance grow between them. The need to eat becomes a distant memory. He is not her prey. He is the hunter. Everything about him tells her to stay away.

"Keep with me, Red," Merchant says. "We don't have a lot of time left. For you or anyone in that village."

Red does not answer. She keeps instep with him but does not get any closer. Ahead the trees begin to open. Voices carry in the distance. Men's voices. Lazy and without any urgency.

Her mouth does not water like has, but her hands begin to shake, and she balls them into fists. Merchant steps to the side and lets the shadows take him in without crossing into the open.

"Not much of a chance you could distract them like you did last time?" he asks.

She looks down to the road at the bottom of the hill. Part gravel and broken asphalt, the path is blocked with tipped barrels, a burned-out car, and several pulled trees rotted enough that the middle sections have already caved in. Behind everything sits another vehicle, its large tires reaching the men's waists and, on the back, sits a large gun, a string of bullets hanging down to boxes at one of the men's feet.

"I could try," she says and smiles back at Merchant. His eyes narrow as she lets her tongue poke out between the missing teeth. "I'm not so sure about this blood though."

He looks her up and down. She's covered all the way down to her waist and it smells of glorious iron and food. Licking her lips, she regards the half-dozen men waiting, watching for anyone to approach.

"What are we going to do, Merchant," she asks.

He does not answer. Birds sing into the morning sky and several take flight over the open space before them. Dark figures in the brightening sky.

Her stomach growls, and she places a hand over the emptiness. Pushing, the flesh beneath her fingers folds with no sustenance.

"I'm going to double back. Wait for my approach. When the fight starts, do what you can to help," he orders her. She nods her head in agreement, but the words are a raft floating aimlessly in a hurricane. "Listen to me, Red. You have to hold on. That truck still works. If we can get it, I'll have you back to the way you were in no time. Just keep it together for a little bit more."

He grabs her chin and turns it to him. His large eyes bore into her. Searching. Demanding. There is nothing else that she can say but a slurry yes.

Without adding anything, she watches him fade into the darkness still finding its home within the forest. Like a ghost, he is gone. His bulk and weight substance less in its passing.

Time passes slow. An endless motion of nothing but light as the sky turns a brighter shade of purple, the peaceful blue a rushing companion frantic to keep up. Then she sees him. A lonesome figure meandering his way down the middle of the road.

Boots kick at stones and weeds broken through the asphalt are crushed in his passing. The men of the barricade take no notice. Their eyes and attention are for that which approaches their home. They are oblivious to what approaches from behind.

The thought waters her mouth. Their blood will be spilt. Her hands are wet and the small breeze carrying its way through the forest tickles the sweat running down her spine.

Merchant is almost to them when one finally turns, hands on belt, he stops as the dark figure does not slow.

"Hold it!" the man yells.

In the clear morning, words carry a long way, but even this far she can feel the uselessness. Merchant pays little to the command. Head tilted to the earth, his bulk quickly dwarfs the soldier and the distance between them closes to a few yards at best.

"I said halt!" the soldier tries again.

Others have turned now, but the chaos consumes

them quickly. Before any reaction can be thought, Merchant is on top of the man, his body lifted clear off the ground.

Crouching, Red leaves the safety of the forest. Heart pounding with anticipation, she fights the urge to run and shout her way down the hill. They still do not know she is there. The men have their weapons drawn and Merchant keeps the man lifted in front of him.

"Put him down," another of the soldiers bark.

A shot rings out and the one giving the orders drops. The others freeze, hesitation marring their reaction and training as Merchant cracks another shot off and the man on the back of the truck screams as he tumbles, grabbing his knee.

Blood fountains into the air from the wound as the man rolls on the ground. Glorious red blood and she cannot wait any longer. Screaming, Red charges down the hill. Feet barely keeping up with gravity carrying her to them, the inside of her throat rips as she yells with everything in her lungs.

They turn her way, rifles leveled. The nearest falls as the side of his head explodes into a spray of mist. The one behind him gets a shot off, a buzzing bee that sizzles as it flies past her ear. Two more shots leave small puffs of dirt before her feet and blood erupts from the man's neck.

She cannot run fast enough. Her stomach pulls her. She must feed to keep the cramping at bay. She is hungry.

More bullets fly but none get near her. The ground below her feet turns to hard rock, and she catapults herself over the first body and into a man rushing with a knife at the dark man. He does not see her coming.

Her head cracks something. Light flashes in her eyes and words are screamed she does not understand. Shaking away the pain, she rolls and pounces back onto her prey. His neck exposed, she rips with her teeth.

Warmth floods her mouth. A euphoric sensation rushes through her body. Muscles tense, the man fights, but she keeps tearing. More fighting continues, but she chomps and chews, even when her teeth hit something hard.

Bone.

Must avoid the bone.

Raw sinewy muscle tears away from the man's neck. He stops moving, and the world clears to her vision. A tooth falls out of her mouth and new wounds leak from her arms. A gob of red hair soaks itself dark within the gaping wound separating the man's chin from his chest.

"Red, get a hold of yourself," Merchant says.

Blood is splattered against his chest. A large gash cuts across his dark flesh, and the fire in his eyes is brighter than the sun breaking the surface in the distance.

"We need to move," he says and grabs her by the shoulder.

Pain and blood ooze where his fingers dig in and he lifts her from the ground. Red claws at him and then turns for one last reach for her newest meal.

"Just one more bite," she pleads.

"Get a hold of yourself. Sit yourself down and keep quiet. This is going to get bumpy," he says.

She is barely settled on her seat as the vehicle surges forward. Wind whistles past, pulling at loose skin and sending stings and twitches through her muscles and wounds. She grins and bares as the truck jumps and skips its way over the road.

Yes, he is correct. Not too much further and this will all be over. They can cure her where they are going. They did it once before, they can do it again. Then she won't be so hungry.

A rumble tickles her gut. Her bleeding hand presses down on the soft flesh and she's sure it can go deeper this time.

Is this her spine she can feel?

Red pulls her hand away. This isn't helping. Watching the lights brighten what the sun isn't clearing, she can barely keep up. The world is a blur and Merchant says nothing. He stares ahead, silent and deadly.

Red grips the side of the seat, her broken nails bending as they press into the worn cloth. Up ahead there is movement. Merchant slows, the engine turning from an open roar to a small purr as the figures ahead become clear.

A young girl lays against the side of a broken car. Blood trails itself across the pavement and a fat man stands over her. Dirty, disheveled. Her stomach growls again and a snarl curls the corner of her lips.

She knows exactly who that is…

Chapter Twenty Five
A Debt is Paid

Luck usually has nothing to do with it. Life can be a series of misadventures and miscalculations all tumbling into a mess that looks like a lot of plans gone wrong. In reality, it is nothing more than a huge pile of bad decisions concentrated into a short existence punctuated by one large fuck-up that sees you six feet under or rotting with your tongue out and a hole in your belly.

All of these seem to be the end of the road at the same time, and as Merchant slows the truck, he lets the engine quiet with the lights shining on the two figures in front of him. A young girl bloodied and looking like she has rolled herself through hell and back. Hair slick with mud and blood, the number of cuts and abrasions on her skin is uncountable even as they get closer.

The fat man over her is easier to recognize. Logan Barnett. His appearance barely any better than hers, the smile on his face puts him at the level of those already living in Hell and Merchant has no problem with the idea of setting him on his way.

Memories of being chained down in that basement. The grinding metal cutting into his wrists and the smell of that thing he let down there with them. Coming to a stop, he puts the truck in park but does not turn it off. Logan steps over the young girl, reaches down and grabs a handful of hair and begins to drag her across the road. She screams with the pain and Merchant hits the high beams, illuminating them with a glare that brings out the thousands of colors now staining Barnett's clothes.

"Will you idiots turn that shit down? Do you want to blind me?" Logan yells over the sound of the engine.

Red makes to open the door and attack, but Merchant puts a hand on her shoulder. The muscles twitch and are barely there beneath his touch. She is deteriorating faster than he could imagine.

"Stay here," he says.

Red snarls at him, but she lets herself rest back on the seat.

"Get your asses out of the truck and help me!" Logan demands.

Merchant lets the truck door slam behind him but makes not move to step out from behind the light. The girl in Logan's grasp screams and he yanks on her more, dragging her across the pavement.

"Stupid bitch. Shut the fuck up!"

Barnett drops his hold on her hair and slaps her across the face. Merchant moves out from beside the truck and lets the light fall onto his back.

"Get your ass off the ground and…," Barnett stops as he turns back to Merchant.

No words pass between them. A moment of silence over the sobs and crying of the young girl, her face pale and stained with blood.

"How?" Logan stammers. He backs away, hands raised open and placating. "You shouldn't be here. That bastard was supposed… That fucking prick. He said you'd be waiting for him."

"I'll deal with him later. Right now, my problem is with you," Merchant says.

He lets his approach match with Barnett's retreat. There is no reason to worry. No place out here could hide him. The fire in Merchant's chest flares to life. A searing heat that fills the empty cavity and flows as quick as the pulse that carries it through his body.

"You like deals? I'll make you one that you can't turn down," Logan pleads. "You saw everything that I have. Together we can have so much more. You and I. Fifty, fifty. We could rebuild the whole USA. What would you say to that?"

Merchant takes another step closer, this one closing a small amount of the distance.

"And what about those back in the village? Did they take your deal?"

The skin of Barnett's cheeks reddens, and he firms his shoulders up.

"Look, I gave them every chance. They held a secret that could save us all. Can you imagine this world without the infected? No more war against these monsters. Just think of it!"

"There will always be war, Mr. Barnett. In the end, all that matters is what side you are on," Merchant says.

He takes another step and Barnett stumbles as he tries to keep them apart. Catching himself, he tumbles slightly into the side of a car.

"How about I try again? Seventy, thirty. You and me. We forget about the village. We leave it alone and move on. We can even leave the girl here. Let her go back."

She's from the village?

Merchant turns back to where she remains seated on the pavement with an ankle swollen past the limits of her boots. A look of recognition crosses her face as her bloodshot eyes widen.

"Merchant, watch out!" Kelly shouts.

Spinning on his heels, Merchant brings his arm up, a flash of steel flicking in the light but the blow never lands. A shadow as fast as a cat blurs between them and Barnett goes stumbling back into the car before falling to his knees.

Red spins and falls herself. Her foot twists to the side and blood flows in a deep river from her forehead. She snarls and struggles back to her feet. Leaning heavily on her good leg, Merchant can hear the bones crack beneath her weight.

"Fucking monster," Logan yells and lifting himself from the ground, he pushes away from the car with his knife in hand.

Red tries to side step the blade, but her knee buckles and she falls. The cutting edge draws a wicked line across the side of her ribcage, but her claws are enough to bring red welts across Logan's face as she stumbles by him. Crashing on the ground, she rolls onto her back to look at him standing over her.

"Fucking little monster. See, Merchant. This is a plague on our world and that village of hers held the secret. They had no right to keep it to themselves, now everything depends on men like you and me. Only we can save those too weak to help themselves. We are the ones destined to lead this world. That is why we are," Logan says as he raises the knife over his head.

The next words fall from a frozen tongue, ears ringing against the sound of the echoing gunfire. Barnett steps backward, knife still raised and chin dropping to his chest.

A red bloom widens inches above his belly. At first the size of a fat finger, but quickly it darkens and fills around where the cloth bulges over his round flesh.

"We could have," Logan starts and another hole rips into his chest.

He falls onto his ass, dust and stones kicking into the air. Wet coughs follow and are chased by the snarls of Red as she tries to crawl her way over to him.

Merchant puts a hand on Red's shoulder and she stops moving as he steps over her. More coughing escapes Logan's body as Merchant stands over the dying man.

"We could have—," he starts to say.

"This is for Red," Merchant cuts him off.

The last bullet of Red's gun exits the back of Logan's head taking half the skull with it. Smoke swirls from the wound and Merchant turns back to the two women sprawled out across the pavement.

"It's over," he says.

Without another word he stops and picks Red up off the ground. Her body barely weighs anything, a bag of bones with a skin leaking from a thousand holes.

"T... th... thank...," Red tries to say.

"Shh," he whispers and carries her to the truck.

Gently, he places her into the passenger seat and lets her rest with her head tilted back, a slow trickle of blood leaking from her lips. Turning back, he goes to Kelly still sprawled on the ground. She shivers in the early morning air. Her face is pale, covered in blood from a thousand shallow cuts and her body has been dragged through a wood chipper.

"You strong enough to get up?" he asks.

She turns her head to him. Her eyes are wide, bright with fear, and red from the terror she has seen these last few days.

"They are all gone," she whispers, not answering his question.

Merchant nods and then turns to the road leading in the direction of the village.

"I figured as much. No hope to make it back in time. You strong enough to walk?"

He extends his hand. She looks at it as if it's there to cut the life right out of her. Kelly glances back at the corpse and then his hand and with a weak grip, she takes it.

"Where are you going?" Kelly asks.

"The same place I've been going for a long time. West."

Kelly looks over at Red. The woman moans as the blood makes roots of red down her neck and a world of gore across her torn and dirty shirt.

"Is she going to make it?" Kelly whispers.

Merchant shrugs his shoulders.

"Probably not. If the old priest is dead with the rest of them, then there isn't much hope for her."

Kelly turns away from the rising sun and lets her sight settle on the path still shaded in darkness.

"Brother George was like a father to me. Saved me when I had nothing left. Raised me like I was his own daughter. Never asked anything of any of us. Just showed us the path to God. He was the real miracle, Mr. Merchant. We believed, and we followed, but it was always him."

Stepping closer, he lets her rest against him. The young woman is nothing compared to the burden still sitting in the back of the truck.

What kind of future does she have?

Her people are gone. Is she any different than anyone else?

Merchant lets the warmth of the coming sun spread the heat already running through his veins.

"He was a good man. Barnett paid for what he did."

Wiping away the tears, snot, and crusted blood from her lips, Kelly slips away.

"What about those monsters who took my village?"

A cold shiver runs through Merchant and the blue ethereal smoke swirls behind the young woman. Snake-Eyes, his white suit, long cigarette and empty eyes lean back against the back bumper of an abandoned Chevy.

"And you thought you were done," the ghost chuckles. "I can already feel the masses growing behind me."

"They are gone, Kelly. The same as this bastard here. There is nothing you can do to save them," Merchant says.

The pale fists of the girl ball up and she rolls her shoulders back. Taking a deep breath, she stands up as straight as she can on her bum ankle, the top of her head hardly reaching his chin.

"We tried it our way. Through prayer and trust I watched as we were overrun and killed for sport and enjoyment. I can still hear the screams of the other women and girls. Their voices echo in my ears, and then there is…"

She trails off.

"Leave it alone," Merchant says. "You are alive. Make the best of what you have left."

Kelly bites down on her lip and the cheeks of her face go red as her eyes narrow.

"Easy for you to say. Traveling west with nothing but the road behind you. They took everything from me. My people, my home, my life! Even your friend, Red, was calling it home. Aren't you going to do something about that?"

Merchant turns back to the truck. Snake-Eyes walks himself gingerly over to the door, making sure to avoid all the blood and muck before leaning against the door. With a wave of a finger he says NO and then flicks away the ashes of his cigarette.

"My work here is done. Barnett is dead and I'm getting back on the highway. If you want to follow, I can drop you off at the first sign of the next town or city. Your choice," Merchant says.

"I'm done doing it everyone else's way, Merchant. This world is fucked, and you know it. You tried to tell us, and we didn't listen. But I'm listening now! Help me, Merchant. Help me like you did your friend, Red."

He stops and doesn't reach for the door. The ball in his chest is an inferno and the sight of Red, bleeding out slowly on the front seat puts a weight in his gut he hasn't felt in a long time.

"What is it you want, Kelly? I can't bring your people back. I'm not your Brother George and even if there is a God, I doubt there is much even he could do."

With what has to be the last of her strength, the girl stomps her feet until she is right up in his face, the anger radiating off of her a heat that he knows all too well.

"Revenge, Merchant. That monster back there took them all. Killed everyone including Barnett's men. I want them dead. Every last stinking one of them. Let them rot on the ground. Leave them as food for the buzzards. Send them back to the hell they came from because they've turned everything I have into hell already."

Merchant towers over her. His dark presence nothing compared to the white rage of her hatred.

"You are free of this, Kelly. There is nothing down this road. I've walked it. I still walk it. Let the monsters lay and I'll get you out of here. This is not a path you want to follow."

She hits him in the chest. Not much of a punch, but it brings the tears pouring from her eyes. He is surprised she has any left to give.

"Fuck you, Merchant. There is nowhere else for me. You can drop me off at any city or village and it still will be a death sentence for me. I don't know what happened to you in the past, but here, I lost everything. Have you ever been in love, Merchant? Have you ever felt the last breaths of the one person in this whole world you were excited to see every day? Even if you couldn't find the courage to tell them. Ever seen the look in their eyes as their soul leaked out of holes ripped into their chest?"

Merchant doesn't say anything, the vision of his wife and children's corpses too quick to flash back.

"I don't care if I die with them, Merchant. All I want is a chance to make things right. They deserve to die. Every last fucking one of them. If you won't do it, I'll walk there and kill that slimy monster myself."

Merchant grabs her arm, a sudden gasp escaping her lips.

"You wouldn't last a moment. It is suicide and you know it."

"Then let me die with my family. You obviously don't care. Drive me as close as you are willing and let me go my own way. This is obviously not worth your time," Kelly says and then snorts back the snot dripping from her nose.

"Who was it?" Merchant asks as he looks to the road ahead.

"What?" she answers.

He does not look at her.

"You said they killed the one you loved. Earlier you called Brother George your father. It wasn't him, who was it they killed?"

Red chuckles in the front seat, a wet gurgling that rolls her head to the side.

"He was my best friend. The others picked on him all the time, but he was always so sweet to me. I thought it was just because we were friends, but when they came that third time," Kelly says through yet more tears. "Those bullets were meant for me. He ripped himself away from his mother to get in front of me. They shot him, Merchant. Like some kind of dog. I never got to tell him how I felt. All I can see is the look in his eyes as I held him. He was scared. But you want to know what he said to me before he died? His last words to me were a simple THANK YOU!"

Kelly falls into Merchant and sobs. He lets an arm rest against her. Whatever fight there was a moment ago is gone.

"You must have been a good friend to him," Merchant says.

"Friend? I let him die for me and I never even told him how I truly felt! How was I a good friend?"

"He gave his life for you. No one does that for someone they don't love," Merchant says as he gently separates her from him.

"I need to give something back. Even the score. That is why I'm going, Merchant. With or without your help. I will kill every single monster in that village. I will die on my best friend's grave if I have to," Kelly answers back.

Merchant sighs.

"That is your choice," he says before climbing into the truck. "I've been down that road, Kelly. There is no return from that dark place. Get in and let the air clear your mind. You'll thank me when we are far from this place."

"I'll thank you if you help me," she says stamping her one good foot into the pavement. "What do you want from me, Merchant? You obviously went a long way killing everyone in your path to save Red. What did she pay you? I'll give you whatever you want."

Kelly looks at Red and then back at Merchant. He helps straighten the dying women in her seat and then glance at the pistol still tucked into the belt of his pants.

"Is that it? That is all you want?" Kelly asks.

Merchant turns her way, a moment of confusion crossing his mind. The young girl reaches up to the last few buttons still holding her shirt together.

"Wow, this definitely got far more interesting," Snake-Eyes adds as he materializes behind the mounted gun on the back, an oversized green Army helmet on his head and a cigar between his teeth.

"I am not as experienced as she probably is, but I've got nothing left, Merchant. If that is what you want to help me, then take what you will. I don't care anymore for this world. Just don't leave me here knowing I didn't try to make amends for what happened to them."

"Keep your damn shirt on," Merchant growls. "I'm not interested in that."

"Then what else? I don't have money. What little I owned was back with everyone else. I'll give you any-thing, Merchant. My body, my life, hell, the shirt off my back. Whatever you want."

Merchant's grip on the wheel of the truck tightens, the skin of his knuckles brightening.

"Where does this end, Kelly? I cannot bring your friend back from the grave."

She redoes the button on the top of her shirt.

"With all of them dead. Every last monster who remains must die. We don't stop until every last one of them no longer breathes and then I am yours, Merchant. Kill me. Take me. Leave me to die in the dust, the choice is yours. I only ask this one thing of you. Kill them all, Merchant."

He turns on the truck and the engine roars to life.

"Get in."

Chapter Twenty Six
Sent Back to Hell

She can't recognize any of it. In the darkness of night, everything had been hollow and empty. Now, the world she had grown knowing was a smoking ruin.

Ash and dark clouds circle high in the air. Bodies lay strewn in all directions along the road leading in. Every house and building is torn and gutted. The bodies of people she knew are lifeless next to soldiers she can't recognize.

Buzzards circle high in the sky and the morning air has turned hot and muggy with the approach of the mid-day hour. The smell of death and decay is as thick as fog. Kelly can see the monsters meandering through the empty ruins of her life. Their broken shambling gaits. Fewer of them than she remembers.

"What are we going to do?" she asks.

Merchant says nothing, his hard eyes set and unwavering.

"Do you think there are any survivors?"

Even she doesn't think there is anyone left. There can't be. She can't see them, but the fear pushing at her from this distance tells her they are waiting in the dark. Hundreds, thousands, even millions of the demons waiting on her to come down so they can claim her like they have everything in her life.

"Doesn't matter what I think. They are down there and that is where I am going," he answers.

The thought of going down there terrifies her. Where was that courage and hatred from a few hours ago? Burning through her like a sickness, the hollowness of her soul is wide and draining. This must be what Brother George always talked about. The emptiness of revenge and hatred.

"There is nothing to gain attacking those who have hurt you," he always said. "It will bring you nothing and take from you everything."

He may have been right, but he never had to look down at the ruin of his whole world. Dark streams of black smoke swirling in the air, the wind carrying away the remnants of everyone she has ever cared for.

"I will go with you," she says, the words tripping their way over her tongue.

A feeling of ice trickling down her spine, the fear overwhelms, yet she will not turn away. If she does, the conviction of finishing this will wash away with the fading of the memories.

"It would be better if you stayed. I'll take care of this, myself," Merchant answers.

"We don't know how many of them are down there. There could be hundreds, even thousands of them."

He does not look at her. Somehow in all of this, his expression does not change, waver, or even seem concerned. A faraway look is chiseled into those hard features.

"Doesn't matter. He is down there," is his answer.

"Then I am going with you and you can't stop me. This is my home or was my home. What do you expect me to do? Stay here and wait?"

The anger rises in her again. Against him and his stubbornness, against the monsters down there and everything they took from her, and the hatred of the fear that will not go away.

"Can you kill, Kelly? Are you willing to pull the trigger and watch someone you once knew die by your hand?"

Merchant looks at her this time, his look unsoftened in the brightening light of the forest edge. Looking at him is almost as tough as it is to watch the death of everything around her.

"Everyone I know is already gone. There is no way they are still alive down there with them."

"Don't be so sure," Merchant says and turns toward Red sitting in the front seat of the truck. Blood trickling from the corner of her lips, scales of red angry skin flaking from the side of her face and scalp. "Remember what you and Brother George did for her. The one who leads those things down there, took all of that away and returned her to this with a single touch. There will be people down there who were not fed upon. They will be one of them. If they come for us, you will be—."

"I'll do what I have to," she cuts him off. "If they are one of those things, they are not the people I remember. I want them dead, Merchant. Whatever it takes. I am with you in this. Until the end, I am with you."

He nods and looks back toward the graveyard that awaits them. The monsters still mill about between the scorching light of the streets and the shortening shadows of the markers decorating everything that once was.

"Do you know how to drive?" Merchant asks.

Red groans and Kelly looks back at the truck. Large muddy tires, the treads slick with dark chunks and broken twigs. The machine scares her. She understands the concept.

Turn the wheel.

Keep it going straight.

How hard can it be?

"I can try. Tell me what to push and I'll do it," she answers.

Merchant does not say another word. Picking his sack off the ground and hefting up on his shoulder, he turns and walks over to where the vehicle rests. Red moans again and her head rocks from one shoulder to the other.

"Ever fire a weapon?" he asks as he drops the green sack on the back, resting it against the pole holding up the largest rifle she has ever seen.

"Nicholi showed me the basics. Pull the trigger, aim the end at those you want to die. Seems easy enough."

He huffs as he picks up a box that jingles like a pile of rocks rattling inside of a crate. Opening the top, a string of bullets follow his hand and he threads it into the side of the rifle. Gently, he puts the box into his bag and lets the strap of copper bullets dangle stiffly between the two.

"Simple enough," he says and steps around to the driver's side and gets behind the wheel. "Climb onto the back. Hold on for dear life and do not start shooting until I tell you to."

"You want me to ride on the back?"

That feeling of ice draining everything from her spine and legs hits her like a wave of the river, cold and with a hand like a rock.

"Can't do any good sitting up here with Red. If you are going to do this, get up there. Once I tell you, kill anything that moves. Do not think, do not stop. Squeeze that trigger and hold on because your life depends on it. Even if they hit the ground, shoot them again. These things are no longer human, Kelly."

She eyes Red and the yellow pus leaking from open wounds festering on her neck. His eyes follow and he turns back to the road ahead.

"Do as I say, Kelly. We only have one shot at this. There is no room for mistakes. We kill them or they kill us. Got that?"

There are concrete weights tied to her shoes as she climbs onto the back. Her ankle throbs, the pulsing pain pounding with every beat of her heart. Grinding her teeth, she forces herself to stand up straight. The metal of the bed cut into the skin of her palms and the cold, dead handles of the weapon are unforgiving as the blood trickles down her wrists.

"I can do this," she says to him as much as she says it to herself.

Taking a deep breath, she squeezes and lets the pain burn into her grip. If she is going to Hell for this, she might as well feel it now. Gritting her teeth until her jaw burns, she does not let the fear build anymore. There is no time for that.

This is it. The end of all things. She is going to die here. She knows this. Barely old enough to call herself an adult and this is the end of the road. A calmness washes over her as Red moans again, slumping to the side and resting against Merchant's large shoulders.

Yes, this is the end. For her, for them, and for the world. She looks up at the canopy over her head and imagines the sky above. If there is a god up there, what would he think?

With a deep breath, she does not care. There are no words of regret. They cannot come from a soul that does not feel. She is already dead and in the next few moments, she will take as many with her as she can.

***

"You know this is insane, don't you, demon?" Snake-Eyes asks, a chuckle in his voice. "A dead infected, a girl suddenly thinking she is Rambo, and one crazy son-of-a-bitch. Of all the ways I thought you would go, running into a fire fight with a child and Frankenstein's bitch was not what I imagined. Though, I do admit it's going to be a show for the ages."

Merchant fires up the engine and the deep-throated growl vibrates through his boots and rattles the closest trees.

"You ready back there?" he asks.

"Whenever you are," Kelly answers, her voice cracking.

Snake-Eyes chuckles.

The asshole ghost is right. What the hell is he doing? A sudden idea of turning the truck around and heading straight for the interstate crosses his mind but his body will not follow those directions. Kelly stirs, her weight shifting from one foot to the other, and he knows there is no ending for this but down there.

Red shifts and he can feel her cold skin against the heat of his arm. Blood now drips from her nose and he can feel the small shaking working its way through her body. A fire flares deep within him.

No, this has to end here. If not for the stupid girl killing herself on the back of the truck, he has to go down there for her. That bastard waits for them. He can feel it. Hidden in the darkness somewhere, the monster waits.

Merchant grips the wheel tighter. He can feel the material and plastic cracking beneath his grip. One way or the other, this all ends in that fucking little village.

Easing off the brake, the truck engine picks up a deeper growl as they push forward. Light swallows them, the shadow of the forest giving way to the quickly approaching high-noon sun.

"Remember," he yells back over the sounds of the engine. The path beneath the tires is broken and just as loud. "Do not fire that weapon until I tell you to. We need to draw as many of them out as possible."

"You can feel her fear, can't you?" Snake-Eyes asks. "She'll squeeze off a round faster than the first boy who ever touched her. You remember those days, don't you? So anxious, so scared. Watch, here they come."

Wild grass bends beneath the tires as the road opens and the ruins of their secluded town opens before them. The monsters have done one hell of a job. Charred skeletons of people and buildings alike are strewn across the road and empty remains.

Merchant revs the engine and does not look back

to make sure she is still holding on. There is no time to worry about one little girl. Any hesitation and they are all dead. He knows this. There is only one way for this fight to end, and if he does not make it quick, they do not have a chance.

Crossing the threshold of the village limits, the open pits dug deep into the earth become visible. Burned remains of cars and trucks remain overturned where they fell to the traps set by the defenders. A decent attempt. Futile, but at least they went out fighting. Too bad the infected do not drive and do not care about holes dug into the ground. Their hunger is insatiable.

"Show them what you are made of, demon," Snake-Eyes yells over the rush of the wind and roar of the engine.

The ghost stands on the back seat, his long hair blowing in the wind as he waves a cowboy hat in circles over his head.

An infected screams in hunger as it throws itself into the middle of the road. Much to Merchant's surprise, Kelly does not fire a shot. A high-pitched howl escapes the monster's throat before the hungry maw of the truck's grill swallows it whole. Bones crunch and the truck lurches as the body tumbles beneath the oversized tires.

"Wait for my word," Merchant orders.

Kelly answers by doing nothing as more of the infected come running from the shadows and from behind broken walls and fallen remains. Merchant turns left and follows the road that runs parallel with the town square. Clawed feet and shambling walks chase as the dust kicks into the air.

More broken bodies fall victim to the crushing weight of 400 horses and Merchant keeps them herding behind them. A growing mob of hunger and disease amasses behind them within the cloud building between the ruins. A collective growl begging for them to stop grows and the need for their death becomes palatable.

"There are too many of them," Kelly shouts.

Merchant looks back through the mirror. The young woman is watching the dozens following them. Another turn and they circle back to where they started. Behind may be dozens, but ahead is what awaited them.

Waves of monsters turn as they catch back up to those who have just emerged. Rows of broken bodies and madness turn their way. A wave of death and disease waiting for them to drive right into their waiting arms.

"Fire!" Merchant orders.

There is a silence in the hesitation. An emptiness as the distance between them and the wall promising their demise closes. Merchant takes a closer look as he punches the gas. If she isn't going to fire, he's going to mow as many of them down with their weight as he can. Drawing closer, he can see the faces of the nearest infected.

Disease barely touches their decaying skin. Blue lines snake down from bloodshot eyes and cracked lips bleed across split chins and torn clothes, but these are the people she remembers. Her family and her friends.

"A mistake, Merchant," Snake-Eyes says. The ghost slipping in beside Red who bounces around the front seat like unsecured luggage.

As if answering the ghost's comment, the rifle over their head barks to life. The force of the concussion slowing the forward momentum as a wall of lead rips into the front lines. Bodies and blood go flying. Parts are ripped off like paper mache and the screams and howls of the dying are no match to the wailing of the woman at the trigger ripping her loved ones apart.

Merchant punches the gas harder and mows down with the grill those who do not fall to the onslaught. Gore splatters across the windshield. The smell of death, putrid disease and scorched metal fills the air through the passing wind.

A hard wrench of the wheel turns them toward the village square. Bones crunch beneath their tires and he presses his boots as hard as he can against the floor and the truck growls as it cuts a line through the dirt road. Casting a long shadow, the church, its front doors barred shut with nailed boards awaits their arrival.

Dark stains of blood stretch down the painted walls, a scar against the only building they have passed that has not been touched by fire. Spinning the wheel, he slows and turns the truck until it backs against the entrance. Waves of infected follow along their trail. Falling like dominoes the monsters continue to come.

The vibration of the gun rattles the truck and Merchant watches the swath of death before them. He can feel the hatred that Kelly feeds off of. He knows where it leads. More bodies fall, their lives ripped through with holes and gaping wounds. Nowhere good is where this will end.

The gun chokes and the bullets stop. A silence cuts the violence like a knife and the dust hangs in the air like a curtain. Moans of hunger and hatred crack the world and time stops. Merchant looks up.

Glowing red, the barrel of the rifle smokes. Kelly keeps squeezing the trigger, but nothing happens. It clicks empty.

"Haha. It fucking jammed, and for a moment there I thought maybe you had them," Snake-Eyes chuckles.

"Kelly, move!" Merchant yells as he begins the climb from the front seat.

"Kk… el… ly," a voice croaks.

The young woman turns. Up above a figure moves. Dark against the glaring sun, bloodied skin sizzles and wounds drip where the man hangs. Wrists nailed to the wall, arms outstretched, and ankles crossed with a spike driven straight through bone and skin, Brother George waits to die.

"Father!" Kelly screams.

Her words are answered with the fury of the dying. Broken from his own minor trance, Merchant jumps onto the back and shoves Kelly away from the rifle, her body hitting the church wall, her attention barely noticing.

Pulling back the bolt, Merchant ejects the jammed round and squeezes down on the trigger. Round after round erupts and tears into the next wave of bodies and monsters. The rifle end glares an angry red, and the heat makes its way to where he grips.

More death. More slaughter. They begin to pile, and he continues to fire, the chain of ammunition an endless string from his burden that pulls at his gut with every ejection. The carnage builds into a wall of gore and tissue. Bodies piled and torn to pieces beneath hot lead and the hunger of the monsters that will not stop until they no longer live.

"Um, demon," Snake-Eyes tries to cut in, his voice hardly a whisper over the thunderous murder of the mounted rifle.

Merchant pays him no mind as the rounds continue to fire, the tearing into the depths of his soul growing into an abyss he can feel swallowing him from the inside. His knees shake, more weakness than concussion. Vision going blurry, he squeezes harder onto the trigger.

"You might want to check your ammunition, demon," Snake-Eyes taps on his arm, the ghostly touch ice against the fire raging beneath Merchant's skin.

There is no time to look.

Click.

Click.

The rifle stops. Merchant yanks back on the ejector and the shell goes flying. The trigger squeezes beneath his finger.

Click.

Click.

Merchant looks down. The chain of bullets hangs empty from the rifle, the box and its contents tipped from inside the burden feeding away at his soul.

"Father!" Kelly screams again, her body curled up against the wall of the church behind the back of the truck.

There is barely time to spare a glance at the dying priest. Infected howl in rage as they climb over the barricade of the dead. A mass of them racing for their first bites, drool filled with blood and pus leaking from their mouths.

Racing around the front of the vehicle, Merchant meets the first with the heel of his palm against a throat that crunches like a bag of chips. The monster's neck bends, then spins as Merchant wrenches its head backward and shoves the creature back into the next three fighting to get into the action.

They tumble and one more agile and less decayed leaps them all, teeth bared and claws ready to rend flesh and muscle. Bones crunch as the front door of the truck dents against its skull. Toppling backward, Merchant crushes its throat and grinds the heel of his boot until nothing but red mud mixes beneath the rubber.

More monsters howl into the boiling sun. Stepping backward, Merchant watches as the attack slows. They do not come wildly. Something holds them back. Either by command or actual thought, they begin to circle, ensnaring Merchant and the others against the church that has become their undoing.

"Not a bad show, demon," Snake-Eyes says. "I would hardly call it impressive, but at least moderately entertaining. Any last words before they tear you to pieces?"

The ghost sets up a lounge chair and crosses one leg over the other as he sips on a clear martini.

"Go fuck yourself. I'll find you even in the afterlife and kill you again. This time I'll make it permanent," Merchant responds.

"Ha, you are going to have to take a number. There are so many here—," Snake-Eyes trails off as he disintegrates into a blue dust that floats in the wind and is gone.

A silence hangs around the world. The soft rustling of the leaves in the nearby trees, the cooling of warm blood, the sobbing of a young girl who death has finally surrounded, and the triumphant murmur of the monsters who wait for their promised meal.

Merchant balls his fists. A caged animal ready for the attack. They will all come at once. He tastes iron on his tongue, the familiar reminder of the blood that he has spilled and that which still drives him forward.

The first row of infected step forward, some shambling, others crouching and ready to pounce.

"Come on you fuckers!" Merchant shouts in defiance.

They do not charge. Taking a step back, they move away and a gap through the greatest concentration of them begins to open.

"Kk.. ell.. y," Brother George moans.

Wales of anguish cuts through the silence and a dark figure emerges from the belly of the army ready to tear them apart.

A walking pile of rags. Shifting, dragging, practically melting beneath the harsh light of the sun, yet Merchant knows there is nothing weak there. It is him. The one who controls them all.

Red begins to choke. Coughing a wet sound, Merchant glances back, blood leaks freely from her open mouth, her eyes open but rolling into the back of her head. Turning back, the figure has cut the distance between them in half. Head shrouded in shadow and damp cloth.

"Hello, brother," the vile, raspy voice croaks.

"I've come to finish this," Merchant says, the anger within his gut growing and pulling at the darkness within him.

The thing before him moves, not threateningly, just a shuffling of rags and darkness that lifts the center of its mass. A cowl reveals itself. A swirling of shadow beneath the thick cloth and from within its depths the eyes open.

Green flames swirl and brighten. Disease and hatred fueling the fire that burns its way deep inside him. Once again, they meet, and this time one of them will not walk away.

Chapter Twenty Seven
The Light is No Place for Secrets

He's still alive. Of all the miracles she has seen, the healing and survival of hundreds in this harsh world, this tops them all.

Blood drips down, a dark stain on the flaking wood of the church. His skin burns beneath the golden light of the sun, a brightness so sharp it hurts her eyes, but she refuses to close them.

He is still alive. Even if they die here, right now, she knows he will be there with them.

"Kk.. ell," he croaks again.

Kelly doesn't know what she can do. He is so high up and those nails. Even from down here on the ground she can see they are thicker than the thumbs on her hand and they stick out of his skin like broken bones.

"Father," she sobs.

The words come out without thought. Yes, that is what he is to her. Feelings of betrayal and hurt swirl beneath the fear that surrounds her. Not at him, but a desperate need to remember and beg forgiveness for what she did the last time they were together. He asked her not to be a part of this.

God expects forgiveness. There is nothing to be gained on the road of revenge and violence. Pulling her knees up to her chest, the smell of burned gunpowder fills in the spaces within her nose that are not already assaulted by the stench of blood and death. Looking out beyond the truck, she sees what she has done.

Bodies are torn apart everywhere. Blood and guts leak across the hard dirt, pooling into swirling mirrors that drives the bile from her belly and into the back of her throat.

What has she done?

What has she become?

Looking at Merchant, the man stands there, arms flexed and ready to fight, a layer of murders so thick it coats him like a skin. She gags as dark drops of blood drips from his fists as the creature approaches.

Kelly has felt fear in her life, the last several days a testament to the limits of her abilities, but the pure depths of her soul are tested as she catches a glimpse of the thing that started this all.

Wet clothes, the smell of decay and waste. The words it spoke that drove the infected mad. She can still hear that voice in her mind.

Pulling her legs even tighter against her body, she fights to hold back the need to flee or lay on the ground and die.

"I see you have not come to your senses, brother," the thing says.

Each syllable is a knife to Kelly's ears. With shaky hands she cups them, but it does not stop, its voice locked permanently to the inside of her head.

"Never thought you'd be able to break your chains a second time, but you were always the creative type. Still a bit slow minded though. Would have done you a lot better to not come here. There is only one way this is going to end."

Merchant shifts his weight from one boot to the other. The monsters waiting in a half circle around them snarl and bite at the air with broken teeth as they wait their turn.

"We are going to finish this here. Let the priest and the young girl go. You have me. Take him down and we can finish this between you and me," Merchant says.

Kelly looks up at Brother George. His eyes are tiny slits beneath swollen lids and buried under the swelling of his cheekbones. A deep gash drains fluid from his shirtless body where a cut has sliced deep into his side.

"You are going to trade yourself for our dying cousin and the simple woman? What would father think of something like that?" the thing says before pulling back its cloak and revealing the man beneath.

White skin, wrinkled with moisture and glaringly bright, flexes beneath the heat and the pinch of his long spindly fingers rubbing his cheek.

"I could just send my pets here after all three of you. You may be able to fend for yourself, but what is she going to do? Cry? Bite them maybe? I even see that you brought your friend with you, thinking maybe ol' cuz up there is going to heal her again? You know, brother, I always did find you entertaining. Because I think we need to spend some quality time figuring out exactly what is going on in that mind of yours, I'll make you a deal. We'll cut him down, and if she can find her way out of here, I'll let them go. But just because it's you. Can't say I never did you a favor. Oh, father would be so proud if he could see me now. Always complained that I would never grow up. What would he think of me now?"

The man turns away from Merchant, flipping his hood back over his head, he snaps his fingers. Several of the closest creatures approach slowly, their eyes never leaving Merchant who doesn't move a muscle. Their teeth bite at the air, but he does not flinch.

Kelly scoots across the ground, pressing her back further against the front of the church as they get closer. She can smell the stale sweat, dried blood, and a sweetness of sickness before they even get within arm's length. Their hungry eyes watch her as they round the back of the truck.

The strength in her body drains as the nearest takes a step away and towards her. Blood stains stretch along the side of the monster's pants, old denim worn thin and more white than blue where mud, blood, and filth covers the material. A tattered shirt reveals melted flesh beneath, a few open gashes peeling away and the organs beneath crusted with yellow flakes.

"Take our cousin down as gently as you can, would you?" the stranger asks.

The closest infected turns away and goes with the others who begin to climb onto the back of the truck to begin reaching for Brother George. Letting out the breath she did not realize she was holding, the stench filled air burns her lungs, and the world spins as tears spill from Kelly's eyes.

Blood shoots out in a long fountain as the first spike is yanked from where the ankles are crossed over one another. The screams tear into her heart and the audience of demons howl with delight as the blood splatters atop the truck like the first drops of the fall rains.

One of the monsters licks its hands where the blood soaks between its fingers. Letting out a howl, the others join in.

Brother George screams in agony.

"Stop!" Kelly screams. "You're killing him!"

Two of the monsters hiss and jump down from the back of the truck. Broken lips bleeding and drooling long lines of saliva, they approach and Kelly scrambles backward. Wet coughs come from where Brother George chokes and Merchant turns.

"Hold it, brother. I made you a promise," the demon man says.

He clears the side of the truck and steps between her and the monsters who open and shut their clawed hands in anticipation of their next meal. A long-crooked finger wags in front of the monsters. Both eye the man and then her.

They watch the finger.

One turns to go back to bringing Brother George down whose wails have turned to choking sobs. The other snaps his teeth at the man and makes a quick grab at the air between it and her.

With speed she can barely understand the man grabs the face of the monster.

"Like children, brother. Sometimes the only way you can teach them is through an example. It's taken me a long time to master what I've created. A family to call my own," he says. The infected trapped between his fingers begins to scream, a high-pitched wail of anguish and pain. Dark red lines crisscross their way through its scalp and flesh as blood pours out from beneath the pale skin of the man's hand. "I can't say they replace what we had with father, such a close dysfunctional group we were, but it's a start. Plus, just think. Now that you are here with me, the possibilities are endless. Our dreams far beyond what even father could fathom. Don't you think?"

The knees of the infected buckle as the skin peels away from the man's fingers and a green ooze bubbles from the exposed bone. Yellow jaundice eyes roll back, the yellowed whites crystallizing and flaking as the skin cracks and falls away. Wet pops crackle within the creature's chest, a bubble of dark liquid pooling in its gut as it settles onto the ground. At last the growth bursts and the liquified innards pour onto the dirt in front of Kelly.

She vomits like nothing she has before. Involuntary spasms that pull deep from within her to hurl her gut across the ground. The smell is beyond anything she can comprehend. A vile sludge of decay and her stomach heaves again. Deep down within her the trauma pulls from the pit of her soul and parts of her she doesn't even know she has wretches through her throat and burns the inside of her mouth.

"Ah!" Brother George screams.

The last of the bolts are pulled and the infected let him drop to the ground without support. Weakened legs buckle and his ankle twists, a dark pool of blood filling beneath him where he crumples to the ground.

"Father!" Kelly screams.

She begins to crawl over to him. The man watching her go, hands shaking, she digs into the ground to pull herself to him. The smell of wet dog, musky and thick yanks at her gut but there is nothing left.

Her eyes stay locked on the man she needs to survive. The last of everything she has ever known. Fingers dip into blackened gore. The warmth and stickiness vile against her skin as she pulls herself through.

"Go to our dear old cousin. Tend to his wounds. He's used to that. Not the first time he's let young women care for him after he's paid for his mistakes. Isn't that true, brother?"

Merchant doesn't answer.

Kelly can see his shadow, a darkness in the glaring sun as he watches her struggle to reach Brother George. The army of monsters behind him nothing more than a distant image. All she can concentrate on is reaching him in time, the pool of blood beneath growing faster than she can cover the ground.

"Kk.. elly," Brother George moans.

"Shh, I'm here," she says back, a whisper meant to comfort, but it's all she can get out. "I'm going to get us out of here."

"Mm.. Merchant," he adds as she pulls herself up against him.

The skin across his body burns, peeling from the exposure to the sun and elements. Dark skin has turned ashy and the wound on his side is red and swollen. The meat beneath bubbles and with each breath more lines of blood trickle down to mix into the dirt and stones coating him where he has fallen.

"Merchant is here. He's going to stay behind while we go find a new home. Some place safe where we can start again. Doesn't that sound nice?" Kelly adds between the tears that run down her face.

"He needs," Brother George begins to say, "to understand."

"Yes, cousin," the demonic man cuts in. "My dear brother here has so much to remember and understand. I am in full agreement that it is time that he hold up his end of the bargain."

Stepping away, the body of rags and disease leaves them where they lay and approaches Merchant.

"They will be set free and allowed safe passage away from this place. They can make whatever is left of this life while you and I stay here and begin to get further acquainted. Still sound like a good deal?"

Kelly looks up and can see Merchant's dark eyes watching her. She pulls Brother George closer to her. It takes all her strength just to move him the few inches until he is settled against her. The idea of lifting him from the ground and leading him out finally sets in.

She sighs.

There really is going to be no way out. The growls and the calls from the monsters beyond begin to settle in again. This is it.

Kelly closes her eyes and lets her chin fall against her chest.

"We had a deal," Merchant says.

No conviction, no hatred in that voice.

The man who has destroyed everything in her life squeals like a young child. The wet rags that cover him from head to toe flap in the air as he scoots from side to side in what she can only imagine is some kind of dance.

"Our brothers are going to be so pissed. You and me. A team at last," he says without settling down. "I can only imagine the look in their—."

All hell breaks loose as a blur of violence and anger sweeps across them all.

***

Merchant has barely any chance to register the attack before it lands.

All nails and teeth, a flash of red hair sweeps across the monster and greenish blood spirts into the sky with a howl and a hiss. Red's grip on the man's back is weak, but the cutting of her teeth across his cheek is deep.

Flesh tears and a vile liquid spews as she rips. Swollen hands grab her arms and shoulders, the long fingers cutting through cloth and skin, sizzling as the disease eats into her. With a sweep of wretched arms, Red goes flying before hitting the ground and tumbling into the monsters who remain frozen in confusion.

Merchant does not wait. There is no time. He jumps for the monster in front of him.

Hands lock down on shoulder and wet cloth. Ripping away, dark liquid splatters across the ground as the man spins from his grip.

A fist hits Merchant square in the chest. Like a battering ram it sends him flying into the side of the truck. Air blasts from his lungs, a ringing in his ears rattles his mind and he slides to the ground.

"Fucking little ingrate," the man barks.

Merchant growls and pivots from his heels and attacks again. This time he wraps his arms around the man's body and spins with all of his weight. Releasing as he falls, he lets the man lift from the ground, the sound of his body and rags hitting the dirt with a wet thump.

The infected go wild. Charging as one, Merchant is barely on his feet as the first swipes at his face. Long claws cut into the flesh of his shoulder, but he grabs it by the jaw and rips as hard as he can. Blood spurts as bone snaps and with a kick he sends it tumbling into the three behind.

Another jumps onto his back. Grabbing clothes and hair, he lifts and tosses the monster into the mass fighting their way to reach him. A blur of commotion knocks several down as they clear their fallen and go to charge him.

Red, soaked in blood and dirt, tears into the back of the one she has fallen onto. Blood and flesh fly into the air, covering her with gore as she doesn't stop until she reaches spine and snaps it between her hands.

One throws itself onto her back, teeth digging deep into her neck. Muscles pull and Red falls. Merchant jams his fingers deep into the infected's eyes, its jaw and teeth releasing as he wrenches the head back, the spine crunching as he folds it like a piece of paper.

Holding the broken body in front of him, Merchant rams himself and the dead infected into the wave that come after them. He does not have time to check on Red. There is only one way that this can end.

Bulldozing his way through, hands and nails cut at his arms. Legs stick out to trip him as they tumble before him, but he crunches the bones beneath his books and he presses through. A stooped figure shambles away in the distance.

Not looking back, his target continues its escape. Merchant roars and gives chase.

Dropping the body, he lets his long legs stretch to cut the distance between the man he must kill and the army chasing him.

"You do not know what you are doing, brother," the man yells as he rounds the corner of a nearby building.

The front walls are burned out, the roof caved in over the remnants of the slabs of wood that made this home. Piles of chopped logs are tumbled ashes mixed with resilient knots that refuse to burn.

"Just think of what we could have together. Father always said you were the unforgiving type. Grow a little. Prove him wrong."

Merchant roars again and jumps the next mountain of ash as he reaches the back of the house's foundation.

A log slams into his chest and sends him spinning. The ground is relentlessly angry as his shoulders and elbows cut deep rivets into the surface and an infected jumps onto his prone body.

Blood leaks from the creature's lips as he tries to bite down. Merchant pushes him off, lifting him into the air and then rolls to drop him to the side like a child. Climbing onto the creature's back, he grabs the thing's face, and twists until the neck breaks.

Another attacks, and he shrugs the assault off. Spinning to turn around, this one catches a log across the side of its head and the skull crushes like a melon and the body drops.

"I cannot let you leave here alive," Merchant says.

"Of course you can. See, we can even leave your friends here. They don't have to move away. This is their home, isn't it? You and me. We'll head south. There are plenty of places I haven't visited yet. Plus, I've heard the bombs did less damage down there. More survivors. Think of what you and I could do."

The man backs away, white hands up and green eyes squinted, flames smoking in the stare of a trapped animal ready to spring. Reaching down, Merchant picks up an ax, the head charred, but the handle still solid beneath his grip.

"I'm not headed south. There is only one place for me and I will make it there even if it takes me a thousand years to reach it."

The man spits on the ground, his phlegm sizzling as the grass wilts on contact.

"Stubborn. Father always said that was one of your worst traits."

An infected throws itself at Merchant. The ax head cuts through neck and chest, guts and cancerous lungs spilling onto the ground.

The man launches himself at Merchant. Long fingers rake across face and chest. The gashes opened spew blood, and the burning pulses deep into the tissue.

Merchant staggers backward. The fire in his belly flares into a boiling inferno.

"Do you think you could actually hurt me?" the man asks. He rips more of his soaking rags away, the skin beneath revealed to the burning sun and the flesh sits untouched. "Those scratches your friend gave me were little more than tickles from an insignificant child. I've seen kittens do worse."

Charging like lightening, Merchant has no time to bring the ax to bear. All he can do is put it between them.

All skin and bones, the man hits like an out-of-control train. Bones crunch against bones, the world spins and they tumble to the ground. Merchant does all he can to roll the man to the side.

Nails cut deep into his shoulders and arms. Blood oozes out and the fire in his belly is burning through his skin. Eyesight narrowing, he flexes through the pain and lifts the monster off him. With a thrust he sends him rolling as he makes for the opposite direction.

"You'll never escape me, brother," the man taunts. "This is where your little escapade ends. Join me or I'll send you back hogtied and crying for daddy. Oh, won't he be so proud?

Lifting himself from the ground, Merchant squeezes his grip on the ax and the worn handle feels natural between his fingers. Blood drips from the well-used edge, chips and cracks working their way through the hardened stone edge.

"I'll be leaving when you're dead," Merchant answers.

Another infected throws itself at Merchant. The body hits him square between the shoulder and claws its way onto his back. Bowing at the waist, he lets the creature fall, a chunk of his ear coming away with broken nails. The head of the ax splits skull and wilted brains leaves the monster dead on the ground.

"This is growing tiresome, brother. I think you need to make a choice."

Merchant looks up. Kelly, body shaking with fear stands beside the man. Blood covers her from head to toe, her hair plastered to her pale face, bottom lip quivering as an infected pushes her until she is close enough for the man to put his arm around her shoulders.

"I made you all a promise. You, for this young one and our cousin who I hope is still alive. Is he, darling? Is sweet old cousin still breathing or has he decided on his three-day rest again?"

"You fucking monster," Kelly answers.

The man shrugs, the muscles bunching beneath his thin skin and the fires consuming his eyes brightening as his smile grows.

"Your choice, Merchant. That's what she called you, isn't it? You were always so fond of the names. I honestly can't keep them straight. I think we are going to have to have a small talk about that after this sad business is over."

Merchant eyes Kelly standing next to the man. There is no time for him to reach them. She will be dead if he tries to get any closer. The anger and hatred in his stomach is relentless as he looks deep into those green flames.

There is no getting out of this. Even if he lets the girl and the priest go, this will not end here. He takes a firmer grip on the ax, the polished wood melding to the knuckles of his grip.

"Oh, come on, brother. Ok, little girl. Let's give him a little show of what will happen should he choose the wrong path," the man says as he turns Kelly toward him and stoops lower to look her eye to eye. "This will hurt for only a moment. I promise it won't be as permanent as the others."

He lifts a hand toward her cheek, a single finger extended, the hooked nail reaching for the stained skin of her face.

A howl rattles the buildings and trees around them as fingers punch through green flames. Kelly screams as the evil burns skin and the smell of charred flesh smokes from the man's face. Shoving her away, the demon rears back and stands, swollen hands covering his face and black smoke streaking its way between fingers and bones.

Merchant does not wait. In a fluid motion he throws the ax. Inside he feels the fire within his gut explode and a tidal wave of anger and emptiness burns its way through every muscle and blood vessel in his body. The ax, slicing its way through the air cuts a black streak of darkness as it chops through the light. Leaving an oily trail behind, there is a flash of shadow and darkness a moment before the head reaches the wailing demon.

Stone end extending, the cracked edge draws to a point, a glistening blade of darkness and blood as it pierces through thin flesh and brittle bone.

The demon stumbles. Ax now embedded between neck and shoulder. Kelly falls away, large streams of green gore fountaining where the ax cuts into ruined flesh turning dark and spidering its way down the man's body.

She trips and Merchant vaults over her like a broken log. The infected holding Kelly jumps in front, a meager attempt to use its body as a shield. A fist to its gut and then a knee to the face, the creature stumbles with half its face caved in and blood and fluid leaking from a crack through the bone.

"Leave… leave me be, brother," the man pleads as he shuffles backward, black soot running down between fingers stained dark between wilting bones.

More green bile pours from the open wound where the ax remains seated. Merchant reaches him, hand firmly griping onto the ax. He heaves and kicks out with a boot across the man's chest.

A wooden fence shatters as the body is thrown through it.

Merchant lets the ax hang heavy in his hand. The fire in his belly returns and he watches as the thing before him, no more man than the creatures still running around this world. The poisoned blood roots its way through his body, leaving a highway visible against the thin pale skin that reddens and pulls tight as his body thins with every ounce of disease that leaks from the open wound.

"I am not your brother," Merchant says.

The wounded man in front of him slides up against a tree, the harsh edges of the bark cutting deep gouges out of the layers of flesh inflamed across its back.

"You'll understand one day," the dying man coughs. A smile returns to his face, a hideous thing against the charred remains where his eyes have burned deep into his skull. "This will not be the end for you and me. We are family. We are meant to be together. Born of one father, we will return—."

The words are cut short as the ax cleaves its way through skull and splits it clear down to the breastbone. A smoking cloud of green gas and bile spews from the opening, burning the tree trunk and the sparsely covered ground as the corpse slides to the side. Small fires ignite and quickly go out as the blades of grass sizzle and turn to ash. Where the tree is scarred, sap spills out and puts out the flames with a sweet smell of burning sugar.

It is over. The scream of hundreds of infected calls into the air with the anguish of the dying and pained. None turn to fight him. Spinning on their heels, they make for the forest edge and disappear back into the shadows.

Merchant takes a deep breath. The stench of blood and gore. A familiar smell. Full of iron and decay. He watches the billowing trails of dark clouds still rising over the ruined town.

Yes, it is over. For him the fight is finished. The tug of the highway and the path west returns, an aching in his heart that nags like an infected cut. He looks where Kelly lays curled onto the ground, her hands cradled against her chest as she sobs and shakes on the ground.

The battle is finished, but there is still one more thing to do.

Chapter 28
Secrets and Promises Hurt All the Same

White blinding pain. Muscle spasms and teeth grinding themselves to little nubs. Kelly has never felt anything like this before.

She can't move her hands. Pressing them against her chest, she rocks and prays for God to take it all away. The memory of her hand, the fingers pushing inside those fires.

Why did she do it?

The heat almost forced her to black out. She wishes it would have. The smell of meat cooking on an open fire. Her own meat, the flesh on her own hand sizzling as her fingers pushed inside that thing's skull.

Her stomach clenches and she needs to vomit, but then she'd have to relax enough to open her mouth. She can't do that. That would bring back the pain of her hand.

Screams are everywhere. Monsters wailing in the distance and she adds her own voice to the mix. Tears burn as they run down her face. The taste of blood fills her mouth and every bone in her body aches and cracks.

"Here, let me see," a man's voice beckons.

Kelly tries to roll away. Squeezing her eyes as tightly as she can, she forces herself onto her back, a meager attempt to reach the other shoulder and distance herself from whoever won't help get rid of the pain.

"Kelly, it's going to be OK. Let me see your hand," the voice says again. Deep and thick, the words contain an odd sense of comfort yet a distance she wants to let grow until the world takes her out of her misery.

"Get the hell away from me," she gets out between sobs.

A flash of pain rocks her body as she is successful in rolling onto the other shoulder. Pulling her ruined hand tighter against her chest, she regrets every life choice she has ever made as the flesh cracks and her closed eyes roll into her head as her mind tries desperately to let go.

"Let me see those hands of yours," the voice returns with a firm grip on her shoulder and back that forces her to sit up.

Vomit spews from her mouth, the acid burning her tongue and choking her as some retraces its steps back into the deep parts of her throat.

"I… said leave me alone unless you are going to kill me, then get it over with," she coughs out.

The stench of sweat and blood is salty and thick as the stranger blocks out the light filtering in through her eyelids. A firm grip tightens around her arms and shoulders, holding her upright and pulling itself closer.

"Open your eyes, Kelly. You are safe now," the voice continues.

Wearily, she complies. The light burns like a torch. The pain of her hands is almost replaced as the scorching sun sears into her vision. Tears leak from her eyes, but the darkness of the figure's shadow lessons the shock as he comes into focus.

Merchant.

Broad shoulders cut to ribbons beneath the slashes of long nails and teeth, the man looks down at her, his dark eyes silent, but the calmness of his voice telling her enough.

"Is, is he?" she starts.

He nods.

"Whatever he was is dead. He won't be hurting you or anyone else any longer," Merchant says. With a gentle pulling, he forces her to let her hands slide away from her body. "It was brave what you did back there. Let me see those hands of yours. Maybe…"

Flesh peels away from the front of her shirt as her hands separate. Cracked and flaking like overcooked steak, three of the fingers on her right hand are charred away to tiny nubs where the knuckles meet her hand and the pinky is dead and lifeless. The left is untouched by flame but a cut slices deep between the two middle fingers and blood streams down her wrists as the wound flaps like an open shirt.

"Oh my," Kelly tries to say and loses the words with another mouth full of vomit.

The world spins and she topples forward. Her vision clouds. This is worse than she thought. Pain ruptures her confusion, refusing to let her pass out and forget it all.

"Maybe the priest can help you. If he can cure the infected," Merchant says.

"Brother George," she begins to correct him. "Brother! Father!"

Kelly tries to rise to her feet, the pain and nausea, the death and destruction, all but forgotten in the sudden realization of what she left behind. Merchant catches her as the muscles in her body, driven by adrenaline, respond with the little strength they have. Gently placing his large hands firmly under her arms, he lifts and steadies her shaking legs.

Bodies lay everywhere. Blood pooling as the corpses cool beneath the mid-day heat. Limbs are torn, bones are broken. She looks up at the man she now uses for support. He looks into the distance. He did this. All of it.

No.

That isn't correct. She swallows hard and coughs up another mouth full of bile but forces herself to swallow it back. She took part in this. These things, these people are dead because of her as well.

She pulled the trigger.

She begged him to come here.

Her hands begin to shake, and the pain is a sharp edge of a knife. This will be the punishment given to her by God. Turn the blade on your fellow man and suffer when it is turned back on you. Taking a deep breath, she moves her legs forward, a weak gesture, but one that the big man is willing to help with.

Slowly and cautiously, they move around and through the rubble of her life. It is a graveyard, but one far older than she remembers. Gray ash, more dust than she can remember, covers everything. The bodies, torn and piled in forgotten eternal slumber look ancient. Skin flakes away where it has pulled tight against the skeleton and clothes flap in the dry heat, a cobweb of sand and weeds caught between gaping teeth and dried mouths.

How can her home be like this?

Kelly takes a deep breath, the stench of rot and the past seeping deep into the crevices hidden within her soul. No, this is not her home. Everything is gone, yet she survives.

There is some strength in that. Like the muscles of the man who holds her steady, there is a resilience in realizing that if God had meant for her to be dead, she would be.

Following the darkened path, littered with scorched earth and a streak of filth that kicks up beneath their feet, Kelly lets Merchant lead her back to the church. It is exactly as she knew it would be. Somehow, deep inside, she could never let herself think it would be any different.

Red lays sprawled on the ground. Her shirt torn and dried the color of the hair no longer sprouting from her head. Wounds cover her body, eyes closed as a wet streak drips from the corner of her mouth, pooling beneath the arm that stretches for the dark figure inches from her longest fingers.

Brother George. His half-naked body lays motionless in the dirt. Gray ash turns the once bright hue of his skin into a burial coat, thin and worn around the edges.

Planting her feet, Merchant is quick to notice and does not push her forward. There will be no saving her hands. No saving Red. There is no saving any of them. Her world begins to swirl in her mind again.

She is alone.

The emptiness swallows her. Grief and anguish flood her with emotions so final it stops her heart, and she drops to her knees. Words escape her lips, harsh and unforgiving, but useless none-the-less.

Merchant lets her rest against his legs as the tears and sobbing rock her body. The loneliness whistles through the dry bones of the town, a sad song and she can feel no darker.

Coughs break the horrific melody.

Wet and shallow, the compressed remnants of life rattle the thick chest of Brother George and the hand closest to Red's corpse begins to twitch.

"Father!" Kelly screams and begins to crawl her way to him.

Gently taking her in his own grip, Merchant lifts her off her knees and carries her like a child the rest of the way. Dark blood greets her as it pools in the corners of George's mouth. The ribs of his chest barely crack the ash layering his skin and his eyes are nothing but slits where dirt and blood has almost succeeded in crusting them shut.

"Father," Kelly sobs.

"Kk.. Kelly," he gets out through a wheezing breath.

"It's OK, father," she whispers back. "The monsters are gone. We are safe now."

His hand twitches and moves its way toward Red.

"Red," he says, his finger stopping as the tip reaches the cold edge of her lifeless hand. "Merchant."

"He is right next to me, father. Red… she didn't make it. She died trying to save us."

The corner of his lip curls creating a new drip of blood rolling down his graying face.

"I cannot help him. He is beyond my reach," Brother George struggles to say.

Kelly looks up and Merchant shrugs back. Waving with her head, the big man squats down near both of them, and gently, he takes one of the hands into his own.

"No," Brother George says. "Give me Red's hand. Kelly, you take the other. Do not let go, no matter what happens."

"Father, she is gone," Kelly says. "Merchant is right beside you."

"Merchant knows there is nothing I can do to help him. What remains of his life is of his making. Only he can save himself from what is to come. Now hurry, Kelly. There is still but one thing I can do for the both of you."

Taking a firm grip on his hand, she waits as Merchant steps away to bring Red over. Laying her body next to his, he places her limp fingers with the unmoving hand that lays crumple next to George's leg.

"Remember, Kelly. I will," Brother George coughs out. "Through the darkness I will always be there with you. Walking beside you."

With his final words, Kelly can feel a heat pushing its way through the hand that holds George's own. She squeezes tighter, biting back the pain, as the feeling is full of comfort and tenderness washes over her.

Suddenly and without warning the world begins to grow brighter. Not like the sun reaching its highest point, but as if the dirt and the grime were to be washed away. Colors become more vibrant, the smells cleaner, and the air is a sweet taste over her tongue as the warm water runs its course through her body.

Looking around, she can no longer see the death and the destruction. The burned buildings and the piles of infected sprawled across the square are all gone. Even the church, the building she has called home for so long is nowhere to be seen. Inside, the warmth turns to a filling. A meal with family that will keep her safe and happy stretches to the ends of her insides. A smile pulls at the corners of her lips.

This is heaven.

It is everything she has ever dreamed it would be. The silky touch of the world around her begins to pull at the lids of her eyes. A heaviness whispers of a rest that will bring back the energy and strength lost from her soul. Turning back time to what feels like an age that no one can remember.

Kelly takes a deep breath. The smell of lilac and jasmine fill her and she lets the sleep take hold. A soft pillow beneath her head. A warm blanket to keep her safe. The rest comes gently, and she does not fight as it takes her away.

***

"Holy shit! Can't you see that!" Snake-Eyes screams.

The ghost is on his knees, white suit and sport coat leaving no marks on the scorched earth. Tears, as translucent as his ethereal skin, run down his cheeks and even the eyes of the snake tattoo on his neck squint.

Merchant staggers back as the light blinds him and forces a hand over his face. The three of them are engulfed in it. A heatless fire. Kelly, Brother George, and Red. The ghost may be blabbering on about what is happening within those flames, but to him it is something he has only seen once in his life and even then, it was too much.

Turning away, he watches as the shadows that fill this world retreat into the depths that spill them forward.

The corpses are everywhere. He can already see the buzzards and other animals circling their way around. Through clouds of ash and smoke, they wait for their chance to come down here and feast on the ruined flesh.

The tug of the interstate pulls at his ribs. A hook that has sank its way between his bones. The call grows more insistent by the minute. He is getting closer. He can feel it.

Snake-Eyes keeps running at the mouth, something about wings and fire, but Merchant does not pay attention. If he spent even another moment listening to everything that asshole had to say, it would be the death of them all. Doing his best to keep the glowing orb behind him, he makes his way over to the truck and the burden that has waited for his return.

Heavy and full, the old army bag sits along the back, the single strap cloth cover pulled tight and the only working shoulder strap worn thin where it sits high upon his shoulder. The faded word ARMY darkens where the light hits it but fades as he hefts the load from the truck.

Axles moan and the shocks bounce as the bag comes free and rests itself onto Merchant's back. He can already feel the new weight that pulls him down.

How many new ones will follow him west. One? A thousand? The voices already echo in his ear, somewhere in there is Snake-Eyes and his insanity that has become as reliable as the wind.

Taking a step away from the truck, the pull of the interstate and the west grips tight onto his chest. A thud behind him hits the ground like a boulder rolling down the mountain. Dust kicks into the air around his feet and blocking his vision from the engulfing flames, he sees the revolver sitting by the back tire.

Empty and useless. He knows the last bullet has been spent. The vision of Barnett's skull exploding as the final shot ended his and Red's deal.

The metal is cold against his finger as he picks it up from the ground. A fine layer of dust finds its way into the tiny grooves and crevices of the weapons molded edges. He rubs a thumb over the cylinder, the familiar sound of it spinning brings back memories. He can still see her handing it to him, the look of desperation in her bright eyes as she demanded he kill Barnett or her. The choice was his.

Of course, it never was. Letting his burden off his shoulder, he opens the strap and holds the revolver between two fingers. None of this is his choice. Every death. All the carnage. All he wants to do is get to where he needs to be. Find that which was taken from him and bring it back. Everything between him and that city is not his choice though he knows the results he will have to carry. Like a conscience he takes it upon himself to carry it where others cannot.

The empty weapon falls into the bag. It makes no sound, and the weight held within his hand grows just that much heavier.

Merchant sighs and closes the strap that conceals the sins he carries.

"Merchant! You aren't leaving, are you?" a familiar voice calls out.

Looking up over the truck, Merchant isn't sure what he sees. It has to be a trick of the light. A reflection created by the fading of the tiny sun as it burns itself out against the front of the church.

"We had a deal back there, and I always keep my promises," Kelly says.

"Don't worry, he's an asshole like that, but he never forgets a deal," Red cuts in.

The two stand there next to each other. Kelly, her skin bright and both hands free of scars and damage. Her clothes remain soaked in the gore they created, but he can see the thin fingers flexing and stretching by her side.

"It's a miracle," Snake-Eyes says as he materializes beside Merchant. "A real fucking miracle. Didn't you see who that was? He was right in front of us the whole time."

"Shut the fuck up," Merchant growls before stepping around the back of the truck.

There she stands. Red and her stubborn self. Scales crack the skin between her freckled shoulders and the hard cut of her jawline. A deep gash of white scar cuts through her scalp, but around it sits the brightest red hair he has ever seen. A few hard-earned scabs pepper the skin of her arms and down where her pants are cut, he can see a few rashes screaming an angry pink and purple, but she still stands.

"How did he?" Merchant asks.

Red shrugs her shoulders.

"It was always him," Kelly says.

She steps forward and takes his hand in hers, the tiny set of her fingers no more than a child's grip within his.

"He was here for us. My hands, he gave them back to me, and Red, he brought her back. There wasn't enough left to cure her again, but she's alive, Merchant. In the flesh and blood, she is alive."

"And fucking hungry. You still have any of those beef sticks?"

Merchant turns an eyebrow up at that. Red lifts her hands up, palms out, a small smile on her lips.

"Look, a woman is hungry here. Don't go getting your panties all up in a wad. I'm back to the old me. All scaly skin and beautiful, but it's just me. No monster in here, an empty stomach, but nothing else."

Even Merchant can't keep the smile off his face. He doesn't say a word. Turning, he goes back around the truck and lifts his bag.

His work is done here. For a moment the burden doesn't feel so heavy as it cuts into his shoulder and pinches the skin around his neck.

"So, where are we going, Merchant?" Kelly asks.

Merchant stops. He lets their steps catch up to him as he looks off into the horizon.

"West," he answers and says no more.

They do not ask. Without a word they follow, and behind them is an army only he can carry.

THE END

About the Author

William J. Seymour is the author of Dark Fantasy which includes the titles Dark Choices, Trail of Darkness, and Merchant. He lives with his family in southern Pennsylvania where he writes into the darkness of the night.

Twitter: @WorldsbyRoh
www.worldsbyroh.com
www.facebook.com/worldsbyroh

Other Book Furnace Titles

Dark Choices

Trail of Darkness

Merchant: Traveling Merchant Book One

www.ingramcontent.com/pod-product-compliance
Lightning Source LLC
Chambersburg PA
CBHW060950190726
48286CB00005B/1512